Hoffman's Hunger

Leon de Winter

HOFFMAN'S HUNGER

TRANSLATED BY

Arnold and Erica Pomerans

The Toby Press

Hoffman's Hunger
Toby Press Edition, 2007

The Toby Press LLC
POB 8531, New Milford, CT 06776-8531, USA
& POB 2455, London WIA 5WY, England
www.tobypress.com

The Publishers gratefully acknowledge the financial support of the
Foundation for the Production and Translation of Dutch Literature.

Originally published in the Netherlands as
Hoffman's Honger by De Bezige Bij, Amsterdam.

First published in 1990 by De Bezige Bij, Amsterdam

Copyright © 1994 by Diogenes Verlag AG, Zurich, Switzerland
Translation copyright © Arnold and Erica Pomerans, 1995

ISBN 978 1 59264 211 3, *paperback*

A CIP catalogue record for this title is
available from the British Library

Typeset in Garamond

Printed and bound in the United States
by Thomson-Shore Inc., Michigan

Translator's note

The quotations from Baruch Spinoza's *Treatise on the Correction of the Understanding* are taken, with very slight modifications to make allowance for the Dutch version used by Leon de Winter, from *Spinoza's Ethics and On the Correction of the Understanding*, translated by Andrew Boyle, published in Everyman's Library by J. M. Dent & Sons in London in 1910, and reprinted with corrections in 1959.

Chapter one

Freddy Mancini had polished off four steaks at the Hungarian restaurant, but he was still hungry as he lumbered down the corridor to his hotel room. It was hot in Europe. Freddy's enormous belly sagged heavily below his sweaty chest, the made-to-measure jeans straining across his fat buttocks. Bobby, his wife, walked lightly beside him. She was giving him a piece of her mind for having ruined his diet.

'You blew it, Freddy. When will you ever learn? You've been so good, sticking to it these last few days—and now look at you! You'll never learn, will you?'

Freddy felt the shame burning in his stomach. But the hunger continued to gnaw away, a hungering after repletion, after perpetual satisfaction. He had read somewhere that there is a special gastric nerve which stimulates the hunger zone in the brain. According to rationalists and optimists, anyway.

The dietician had told him something different a few months ago, back home in San Diego.

'How long have you been coming to see me now, Freddy? Three years?'

'Three-and-a-half. Almost four.'

'That long?'

'What are you getting at, Sandy?'

'From the lips straight onto the hips, you know that perfectly well, but we've also got something in our heads that makes us put on weight. Now in your case, Freddy, in your case it's *all* in the head. In your case hunger is a mental thing.'

At the time it had sounded like a magical incantation and he had nodded foolishly. He had squeezed in behind the wheel of his Chrysler New Yorker, and on the way to the office from which he reigned over twelve Laundromats he had wondered what precisely it was in his head that caused the hunger. The air-conditioning in the car had blown cool air across his sweating cheeks. He was successful and he loved Bobby, they had brought up three decent kids who had married well and produced families of their own, they had a lovely house with a swimming pool, they drove a Chrysler, a Dodge and a Jeep Cherokee, he was a good American, paid his taxes and voted Republican, but he had this one imperfection: he weighed three hundred and fifty pounds. Everything he ate turned to fat. And driving along in the Chrysler, the dietician's words still ringing in his ears, eyes fixed on the road shimmering under the blazing Californian sun, it had suddenly occurred to him that he was not happy. The thought had confused him. He had driven into the parking lot at a K-Mart and had sat staring straight ahead of him for a few minutes. 'I'm not happy,' he had muttered, shaken. He had everything, but he wasn't happy. And suddenly he had felt guilty for not being happy. Bobby! She'd be horrified if he told her just now there was something lacking. He didn't love her any more. No, no, he still loved her of course, just as he loved his children, his Laundromats, his cars, his house and his two cats, yet something was lacking. My God, what could it be?

It had never crossed his mind before that things were complicated. He had no idea what it was he lacked, and that was precisely the reason why he was hungry. It had suddenly struck him with devastating clarity.

His hand had reached automatically for the ignition, but he didn't start the car. Shelves of food glittered through the windows of the supermarket. Hunger pangs stabbed him. He had fought his way out of the car, gone into the supermarket and bought fistfuls of packets, bags, candy bars. Back in the car he had bolted everything down. A mountain of paper wrappers had piled up on the passenger seat.

It had dawned on Freddy Mancini then that from that day onwards nothing would be the same. Although no one could have told from looking at him, a revolution had taken place inside his head, a revolution like Castro's, and for the rest of his life he would have to bear the knowledge in lonely silence: he was a tragic and unhappy figure, someone who had everything yet was a loser. He had shivered in the cool car, buried his face in an open bag and allowed his tears to fall on the salted potato chips.

Bobby opened the door of their room in the Hotel International in Prague. Freddy followed her in. The walls were still giving off the heat of the day. None of her pregnancies had left a mark on Bobby's figure. She had the body of an eighteen-year-old. Of course her skin had seen better days, but when she walked on the beach youths still cast brooding looks at her bikini. She was promising him he'd be sorry for the four steaks tomorrow.

'And it wasn't even as if they were fit to eat!' she cried, exasperated. 'They couldn't have been more horrible, pieces of leather you wouldn't give to a dog! And you wolfed them down as if you hadn't seen meat for years! Hells bells, Freddy, you're just going to have to lose weight. Sandy and Doctor Friedman said you have until the end of next week to lose five pounds. Five pounds, that's all we're talking about! So what do you go and do? You put *on* five pounds. If you dare eat a single thing tomorrow, I'll grab it out of your mouth myself. For your own good.'

'I was hungry,' he said. 'I hadn't had any lunch.'

'Good God! You've been going to Sandy for how long, and still you don't stick to the rules! How many more times do I have to tell you? A million times? A billion? You must eat something for lunch. But something *light.* Then in the evening you can eat normally. Instead of stuffing yourself like a pig. Do you want to die at forty-nine?'

Yes, he said quietly to himself.

She went into the bathroom and Freddy slumped into an armchair. The wood creaked as he squeezed his bottom into the space between the armrests. The tiles in the bathroom lent Bobby's voice a metallic echo. He stopped listening.

She had dragged him along on this trip, four weeks that were costing a fortune. Sandy and Doctor Friedman had advised it. They said he had to break his set patterns of behaviour, it would help him lose weight, and Bobby had booked them both for a group tour.

He'd lost count of how many hotels they'd stayed in. Early that morning they had left Vienna in a bus with air-conditioning, a bar and a toilet and the drive had taken five hours. They had been kept waiting at the border for an hour while grim-looking men with machine guns had gone over the bus inch by inch. In Prague their party had checked in at the Hotel International and had then been taken on a tour of the city, past the castle with its churches and palaces where the government sat, past a river and buildings whose names he had forgotten.

Their hotel was a pretentious pile built in what their Austrian guide had described as 'Stalinist Empire' style. The lobby was enormous, with massive pillars, a vast reception desk, threadbare carpets on the marble floor, sitting areas full of over-stuffed furniture, everything steeped in a penetrating odour of boiled cabbage, and although the building and the broad corridors suggested otherwise, the rooms were like rabbit hutches. This was no Hilton, not even a Ramada Inn or a Howard Johnson. Their bus had been more comfortable.

In the other bed Bobby was breathing calmly and evenly. Hunger stabbed like a bayonet at his stomach, slicing up through his heart and jabbing at his throat. Sleep would not come to release him. He listened to the air whistling through his nostrils. His heavy chest laboured. He changed position, then struggled to sit up, hauling his rolls of fat and flab up with him. The mattress groaned when he dropped back exhausted and gasping for breath. The sheets stuck to his skin.

His nightly turmoil no longer disturbed Bobby's dreams. After long years of growing accustomed to his noises, nothing but the deafening racket of the Bell & Howell alarm clock could summon her back from the distant land she entered the moment she turned off the bedside light. They had dragged that clock with them all the way from San Diego, never stopping to think that those fancy Europeans who had been going on about their single Europe for years had still not been able to agree on something as elementary as a single plug or a single voltage.

Freddy tried to remember how many years it had been since they had last made love. They had as good as stopped after her miscarriage, and when she'd been pregnant with the last baby Bobby had definitely called it a day. After that Freddy had begun to put on weight. He saw the connection between the lack of sex and his girth, but it was too simplistic to suppose he would revert to his normal weight if they began making love again every week. He knew he wasn't up to it any longer, anyway.

Acid saliva flooded his throat and he swallowed. That evening they had been taken to the Hungarian restaurant, close to Wenceslas Square in the centre of the city. Almost everybody had left their limp pieces of greyish meat—described on the menu in English as 'first-class sirloin steak with gypsy sauce'—untouched, but Freddy had helped himself to three from his neighbours' plates. Some of their group who had taken precautions against the quality of communist food had conjured up Hershey bars and Mars bars in family packs from their nylon belt-bags; an automobile dealer from Wisconsin, someone called Browning, had even sworn they'd be able to order hamburgers with ketchup back at the hotel.

Laboriously he heaved himself out of bed. Bobby breathed on undisturbed. She was roaming through lands he would never enter. After this trip he'd stay put in America for good. Of course it was interesting, all these old cities and the history and traditions and the rest of it, but he felt lost here. Czechoslovakia was a Third World country.

He got dressed as quietly as he could. He could hear his heavy breathing in the silence of the hotel. Every movement he made was accompanied by a loud snort, as if he had a steam engine in his lungs. He left the room.

At the end of the corridor an old man sat reading under a dying light bulb. He looked up when he heard Freddy. Freddy saw disbelief in his eyes, and walked on to the elevator without saying a word. Someone in their group had explained that every floor was guarded for twenty-four hours a day, not so much for the safety of the guests as to keep Czechs out. Without a special pass, no Czech could cross the threshold. The hotel lobby was deserted. Freddy shuffled across the threadbare carpet to the reception desk. Then he noticed the two men slumped in armchairs beside the revolving entrance doors. 'Security service' the guide had whispered. He could feel their eyes boring into his body. His clothes offered no protection. He was quite naked.

No one was at the reception desk. Nor was there a bell to make his presence known. He held onto the black marble counter and waited. American hotels always had music and he had often wondered why. Now he could appreciate the overwhelming effect of being alone in a silent building. A few faint sounds could be heard far away in the entrails of the hotel. Other than that there were no noises from the street or creaking doors to drown out his forlorn wheezing.

Back home in San Diego he confined his actions and movements to the bare essentials. He knew he was going to have to lose weight or he wouldn't live another five years, but his hunger was torture, a mad dog in his belly savaging everything within reach. He was unhappy, and that feeling, he realised now, was characterised by the absence of hope. His insatiable longing for a state of repletion bore a veil of inconsolable sorrow.

He grew impatient. Called something out. Was startled by the high-pitched sounds that came bursting from his mouth through the lobby. Behind him he could hear the two men sit up in their armchairs. Then a man his own age, about fifty, appeared in the doorway behind the counter, his suit creased and eyes puffy. He had been taking a nap.

'What do you want?' he asked with no sign of cordiality. He looked Freddy up and down.

'My wife is hungry and I was wondering if she could still get something to eat.'

'Everything's closed,' the man said without hesitation and turned away dismissively.

'Isn't there a sandwich or something? Maybe some cold chicken? My wife's pregnant, she's hungry. I heard you could get hamburgers here.'

The man stopped and stared at him. 'The restaurant closes at nine.'

'And after that?'

'After that there's nothing.'

'What happens if a group of tourists checks in at night? Don't they get anything to eat?'

'Nobody comes at night.'

'But they could.'

'They don't.'

'No?'

'No.' The voice showed irritation.

'She's got to have something to eat, otherwise she'll get sick.'

The man gave a sigh and glanced quickly towards the two men by the door.

'Maybe there's a way. But it won't be easy.'

Freddy nodded. He worked a hand into his trouser pocket, brought out a five-dollar bill and put it on the counter. With the lightning reaction of an experienced receptionist, the man had placed his palm over the banknote.

'Restaurant Slavia,' he said. He slid the note towards him and closed his fist around it. 'It's in a side street off the Francouzska, Ladova Lane, number sixty-three. Ring three times. Private restaurant. Open all night.'

'How do we get there?' asked Freddy helplessly.

'That's not my problem,' said the man.

He disappeared behind the door.

Freddy turned around carefully, afraid of losing his balance—that was to be avoided at all costs, his body could not be returned to the vertical once it had yielded to gravity—and shambled towards the revolving doors.

One of the men got to his feet. Both were in their late twenties, both wore tracksuits. The man stopped Freddy with a wave of his hand.

'Papers,' he said.

Freddy took a gulp of air. 'What for?'

'Police.'

'You don't look like police.'

'Passport,' the man spat. Freddy dug it out of his shirt pocket.

The man pulled the document impatiently out of his hands, then compared the photograph with the original. He studied the visa.

'It's two o'clock. What are you doing up so late?'

'Isn't that my business?'

'What are you up to at this time of night?'

'Look, what's that got to do with any—'

'If you don't give me an answer, I'll run you in for withholding information.'

Freddy swallowed and looked over at the other man, who was impassively lighting an American cigarette, a Marlboro, with apparent unconcern at the threatened arrest.

'My wife's hungry,' Freddy announced.

The first man gave him a sharp look. Then he glanced over his shoulder and said something in Czech that sounded like a question, something that could have been, 'Know what Fatty here is up to?' The man in the armchair shook his head, flicked his lighter. The first one said something else, and the other started to laugh, puffing the smoke out in short bursts.

'Everything's closed,' the man called from the depths of his chair. The smoke continued to puff out of his mouth, like Indian smoke signals. 'You'll have to wait for breakfast.'

'My wife won't last out that long.'

'This isn't New York. People go to bed early here. They have work to do.'

'If you give me back my passport then I'll be able to find out for myself if anyone's still up.'

The man standing in front of him fanned himself with the passport. The other withdrew from the conversation.

'I think you're being impertinent.'

'She has to eat soon, otherwise she'll get sick.'

'All the more reason to watch your tongue.'

'What can you possibly think I'm doing at this hour? What is there to do in this town? What am I suspected of?'

'It's our job to watch over the safety of tourists. I advise you not to go out at this time of night.'

'I'll take a taxi.'

'You know where you want to go, do you?'

'We'll drive around and see.'

'There are people on the streets who have been known at times to behave in an anti-socialist manner.'

'What does that mean?'

'Who are after your money.'

Freddy stared at him, eyes wide. 'A taxi's safe, isn't it?'

'As far as we know, yes.'

'What sort of country is this, anyway? Police all over the place and it's still dangerous to go out!'

'Another insult like that and you'll be locked up.'

'Hey, come on, let me go. What's someone like me going to get up to?'

'You could be in touch with anti-socialist elements.'

'Me?'

'Yes, you. Why else would you be going out at this time of night? Did you really think we'd swallow that story about your wife being hungry? Why don't you tell us the truth? We can arrest you and hold you until you tell us why you really want to go out at two in the morning.'

'Oh, all right, I'm the one who's hungry, if you must know! I admit it, I'm hungry, okay? You can see the size I am! My stomach's rumbling, I couldn't sleep for being hungry, and then I thought to myself, I'll just go downstairs and see if I can still order something, but....'

His eyes filled with tears. The dog in his stomach had taken a firm grip with its teeth. It was trying to tear a hole in his diaphragm and sink its fangs into his fat heart. Pain quivered up his gullet towards his throat. He couldn't stop panting, his lungs weren't big enough to supply his huge body with oxygen.

The man in the armchair said something without looking up, keeping his eyes focused on the clouds of smoke coming out of his mouth. He barked the Czech words out in a monotone, like an order. The other looked round at him submissively.

Freddy lowered his eyes, trying to make the best of a bad job. 'I can't really explain what it feels like when I'm hungry. Most people don't understand.'

His passport appeared in front of his stomach.

'You can go.'

'I can?'

The man made an impatient gesture with the passport. Freddy took it and made a small bow.

'Thank you very much. I'm really not...'

The man had already turned away and was walking back to his armchair.

Freddy looked at the passport between his plump fingers. He had been on the very point of being arrested and incarcerated in a communist jail, all on account of his uncontrollable craving for food. But he had had no choice. All he could ever do was to accept without question every problem his hunt for food put his way. He was weak: a slave to his stomach.

He ignored the revolving doors because he had seen when

he arrived that the individual compartments had not been designed with someone of his size in mind. He caught sight of his reflection in one of the panes of glass, a gigantic baby just learning to toddle. He left the building through the side entrance and stepped out into the mild night.

The air was warm and filled with the smell of oil and dust and grass. The square in front of the hotel lay deserted under the stars, except for one car immediately outside the door, a square model whose back seat he hoped would be large enough. Freddy walked round to the driver's side and saw a grey-haired man sleeping at the open window. He tapped on the door.

The man sat up and blinked his eyes as if Freddy was part of his dream. Freddy asked if he spoke English, then gave him the address of the Restaurant Slavia. The taxi-driver climbed slowly out of his seat and opened the back door, then watched and waited while Freddy worked his bulk into the car. Freddy started by easing his bottom inside. Then, swivelling carefully, head hunched between his shoulders, he squeezed the rest of his body into the space between the front and the back seats, dragging his heavy legs in afterwards. He wasn't sitting comfortably but he was ready.

The driver was middle-aged, and drove his car with care and in silence. The city was poorly lit. Freddy recognised one building which they had photographed on their sightseeing trip, but everything else looked dim and mysterious. The road was paved with smooth round cobblestones that threatened to shake the cab to pieces. His fat quivered at every bump. He and his hunger stared out at the disconcerting city.

Some time ago, before Bobby had put him on a diet, Freddy had sometimes gone out at night in search of relief from his hunger. He would drive his New Yorker up the quiet avenues and boulevards of San Diego, eyeing the junkies and the whores, the cool air from the air-conditioning swirling around his head. During these expeditions he would feel as the crusaders must have felt clad in their armour: he had a mission, was ready to sacrifice his life, cruising through the back streets of downtown San Diego, also known as Hell's Kitchen, in search of a signboard welcoming him with GREAT BURGERS OPEN ALL NITE.

But here there was not a single hamburger joint with chromium-plated counter bathed in light, no rock music from a streamlined jukebox (fifties style, like the menus and the rest of the decor), no boys and girls sinking their teeth into double-deckers, no round-the-clock service. During these lonely hours Prague assumed her natural condition. Haughty facades, black windows, inaccessible monuments. The city was a gloomy museum suffering visitors with bad grace.

The taxi stopped at the entrance to an unlit alleyway. The driver turned round and with a tired gesture laid his arm along the backrest.

'Are we there?' Freddy asked.

The man nodded.

Freddy peered into the darkness but could see no sign or lighted window.

'How much?'

The man shrugged. 'Whatever you like,' he said.

Freddy found a dollar bill among the jumble of Czech crowns which he kept in his breast pocket. The rest of his money was in his back pocket, but when he was sitting down, as he knew from experience, he could not work even the tip of a fingernail down inside it, so tightly did the pants strain over the fat on his belly and hips. The man nodded, clearly satisfied.

Freddy opened the car door and took a grip on the door frame. He hauled himself out, feeling his knees shake as he allowed his legs to take his full weight. Suddenly realising that the taxi did not have a radio, he asked the driver if he would come back in an hour's time.

'You'll have to pay me in advance…'

Freddy pulled the roll of dollar bills out of his back pocket and handed the man another note. He accepted the money impassively. Freddy could see now that the man looked older than he actually was, his hair and eyes tinged with bitterness and capitulation, but his cheeks still smooth and elastic.

The taxi pulled away in a cloud of acrid smoke. Exhaust fumes here smelled differently from those at home. As fast as his legs would allow, Freddy moved out of the smoke and started off in the direction of the narrow street.

He could make out the fronts of houses in the darkness but was unable to find any number beside the doors. Yet there was something tickling his nostrils which told him he was close to his goal. He could smell oil frying, a warm, heavy aroma of French fries and calamari that triggered off a wave of hot saliva—'hunger juice' as he called it to himself, the syrupy fluid that conveyed the mouthfuls of the food he devoured smoothly from his throat to his stomach. He swallowed and tried to work out where the smell of frying was coming from, sniffing hard as he turned around, but the whole alley seemed redolent with it, and the source of the hallucinatory scent remained hidden. He swallowed again, begging the dog in his belly to grant him a few more moments' grace, then moved off along a wall, his senses in a state of high alert.

Even though the darkness seemed to belie the presence in this alley of somewhere to eat, his nose continued to give reassuring signals that he was in the right place, and he hoped that his ears would now confirm the evidence of his nose: if the restaurant was still open then the tinkle of glass and laughter and song, however soft, should be heard.

He supported himself against the wall and shuffled forward, sniffing and listening. His shirt was soaked with perspiration. Could he hear something, the sound of a knife scraping a plate? The pop of a cork shooting out of a bottle? Behind the blank doors and windows of one of these houses people were shamelessly guzzling and swilling, and Freddy had become quite convinced that if he himself didn't taste food and drink in a very few minutes he would never greet the dawn again.

A feeling of faintness and fatigue began to seep down from his neck through his limbs. Perhaps the man in the hotel had given him an old address, or maybe the taxi-driver had pulled a fast one. A crazy thought came over him: this was the spot on which he would die, from an acute gastric acid attack; these black stones would be his grave.

The pain he suddenly felt at the back of his head did not come as a surprise. Not a gastric but a cerebral haemorrhage, he thought resignedly, some little blood vessel that, weakened through famine, had given way. His ankles caved in and he lost his balance. Quickly he clutched at the wall, but that had no more than a delaying effect: irresistibly he toppled over onto the ground. The thud on the cobblestones sounded muffled and did not really hurt.

This was it, then. While out on a hunting expedition for a hamburger or a steak, life had slammed the door on him in a foreign land. And now he wanted to find out everything he could about this experience, what it felt like, even though he would never be able to tell Bobby. Goodbye, Bobby, he said to himself. It wouldn't be long before she found someone else, she was a good-looking woman, and in a few days' time she'd come into his money and be a wealthy widow as well. He lay there waiting for some special sensation, and suddenly he knew what he was expecting: the tunnel with the blinding light he had read about in the *Reader's Digest*, a tunnel filled with celestial song, radiating a peace and quiet unknown to slavish life on earth—a phrase that could be taken literally in his case, he thought wryly. He would meet departed relatives; people he had loved but who had gone before him would be there to clasp him in their arms. He smiled, eagerly anticipating the reunion.

The pain in his head seemed to be fading, and because he assumed that pain belonged to his earthly frame and that only his spirit and soul had access to the long tunnel, he looked on the fading pain as the first proof that his ego was floating away to be admitted to heaven. Then, to his alarm, he remembered that he had never read anything about the near-death experiences of people on their way to hell. Perhaps this was hell, he argued to himself, perhaps the utter nothingness of people who were clinically dead (for there were also, of course, clinically dead people without a tunnel filled with light) was the gate of hell: hell was nothingness. Freddy realised that he was still in control of his intellectual faculties because he was trying to find a logical solution to his present problem, and that meant that there was no other conclusion than that he, complete with spirit and soul, was on the way to THE LIGHT.

And there was light. He could see it, even though he no longer had eyes. It danced diffusely and moved up and down to a rhythm whose music he longed to hear. Next he was aware of two voices speaking a language he could not understand, but whose mysteries, he had no doubt, were about to be revealed. Then he felt something that seemed like a search: hands were groping all over his body. And with a shock he realised that could only mean he was still living in his earthly frame and was not, apparently, properly dead.

He opened his eyes and saw two men bending over him. One of them was shining a flashlight on the fast-moving hands of the other. His trouser pockets were being emptied. And when the man with the flashlight briefly turned his head towards him, Freddy recognised the melancholy face of the taxi-driver. Unknown words fell from the man's lips when he saw Freddy's open eyes, and suddenly the other man lashed out at Freddy with some kind of club.

The blow left a burning sensation inside Freddy's skull. Despite the pain, he felt only one emotion: he grieved for the rapture he had now lost. He had been prepared to die, to take leave of the earth, and to float weightlessly, spirit and soul, through the tunnel. He was sorry that it had all been just the result of a blow to his head from a crooked taxi-driver or his accomplice.

The taxi-driver said something and switched off the flashlight. The men ran away.

He took several minutes to gather together enough strength to sit up with his back against the wall. Then he reached up to grip the bars in front of a window and hauled himself to his feet, feeling his arm muscles bulge. They weren't noticeable under the thick layers of fat, but they had toughened up following the lengthy weight-training they had undergone with his own body. Hunger began to tear savagely inside him, his stomach was being eaten away, he was going to disappear down a hole that was himself.

When he finally stood up he realised he had lost all sense

of direction. No money, no bearings, no words left. Carefully he set his course for the point of light at the end of the alley, hoping to find the street where that son-of-a-bitch of a taxi-driver had set him down. A spasm of pain suddenly ripped through his head. He started off as if on legs of straw. Just how much money had he had on him? Perhaps two hundred dollars. He wouldn't breathe a word about it to anybody.

Freddy reached the end of the alley and discovered that this was not the place where he had got out of the taxi, but another narrow street with tall, lifeless houses, street lamps shedding a grimy light. There was no one he could ask for directions. Hoping for the best he turned to the left.

Two hundred dollars was a fortune in these countries. The guide had told them the dollar fetched eight or nine times the official rate on the black market. In the Hungarian restaurant Freddy had denied himself eight or nine of his companions' steaks. He had only eaten four. They had been swimming in their creamy 'gypsy sauce'—which had meant paprika—and those of his compatriots who had braved the quality of the beef had been driven to a frenzy as the roofs of their mouths flamed. *Cuisine communiste.* They had turned to drinking instead.

Freddy's gamble proved to have been wrong. Another side street. Once again not a soul. He wondered if he might not be dead after all, and have ended up in hell—an empty, silent Prague could only be hell. Suddenly what little light there had been was gone. He was in imminent danger of falling over.

Freddy stood still to allow his giddiness to fade. He was afraid the club had left him concussed and wondered if he could take a plane out to Vienna in the morning so as to be examined in a capitalist hospital. He found a trash can under a large cast-iron staircase in a safe corner of the street, and clung onto it for support while he considered the question. He could not tell Bobby that he had been robbed, or that he intended to have a medical examination. He did not even know whether you could walk into a travel agency in a communist country and buy a ticket. Were there any travel agencies here?

He looked up when he heard something. It all happened very quickly, and a few minutes later he was to dismiss the whole incident as a mental aberration, because what he had witnessed was the kidnapping of one of his travelling companions, the young automobile dealer from Wisconsin, a man in his thirties and the owner of a business called the German Motor Company (he had given Freddy his card), which dealt exclusively in 'used luxury cars'. This automobile dealer had suddenly come running round the corner, followed by two men whom Freddy had never seen before, and then a car had appeared from another street and cut off the dealer's path by driving onto the pavement. The young man had been forced to run round the car, thus losing a few precious seconds, enough time for his two pursuers to catch up with him. They had jumped on him and dragged him into the car, which had made off with squealing tyres and disappeared from Freddy's sight. The whole episode had taken perhaps fifteen seconds.

Freddy had not stirred under his staircase. What he had just seen could not really have happened. And if it had really happened, then it couldn't have been the man from Wisconsin. And there was no question of whether it had been a kidnapping anyway. No, of course it hadn't, it had been an arrest. He rubbed his eyes and felt hunger taking a grip on his body again. The strange incident was driven straight out of his head.

Desperate and disorientated he stumbled upon a taxi half an hour later. He paid with a Czech banknote and asked to be taken back to the Hotel International. His headache continued to pound until morning, when, sick with hunger, he made his way to the breakfast room. He was served soggy bread, some sickly-sweet jam and rancid butter, substandard fare but plenty of it. It was another hot day. He ate and ate, ignoring Bobby's admonitions and increasingly bitter reproaches. At nine o'clock they stepped into the bus for a new excursion. In her seat across the aisle Bobby bit back her anger as Freddy opened negotiations with a lady from Pasadena for the purchase of a bag of M & Ms.

Then the guide, standing in front of the tinted windshield,

asked if anybody had seen Michael Browning from Wisconsin that morning at breakfast, because he was neither on the bus nor in his room.

Chapter two

The night of 22 June 1989

After experience had taught me that all things which frequently take place in ordinary life are vain and futile; when I saw that all the things I feared and which frightened me had nothing good or bad in them save insofar as the mind was affected by them, I determined at last to inquire whether there might be anything which might be truly good and able to communicate its goodness, and by which the mind might be affected to the exclusion of all other things: I determined, I say, to inquire whether I might discover and acquire the faculty of enjoying throughout eternity continual supreme happiness.'

With the delicious salt caviare caressing his palate, Felix Hoffman, a fifty-nine-year-old ambassador who had that evening held a reception for his chancellery staff and the corps diplomatique, tried to make sense of this passage.

They were the opening words of a book he had come across a week earlier in a dusty chest in the attic of his new home. Although he had long ago, as a layman, made attempts to find his way through

21

the jungle of philosophy, he had never before had the courage to tackle the work of the author of this book, Baruch Spinoza.

Hoffman had tried to prop the book up in front of his plate so that he could read it while he polished off the pile of leftovers from the reception, but the book had refused to stand up by itself. He had pulled the champagne bottle closer and leaned the book against it, but that too had not helped because the bottle's contents were inside Hoffman. Elegantly, the empty bottle had slid across the white marble table-top and the book had fallen over backwards. Then he had placed the heavy bucket full of melted ice in front of his plate. The book had stood firm.

He ladled a soup spoon of Russian caviare onto a limp piece of Melba toast, ate it with a smack of his lips, opened the book and read the first paragraph of Baruch Spinoza's philosophical treatise.

The last piece of philosophy he had looked at had been W.F. Hermans' translation into Dutch of Wittgenstein's *Tractatus*, but he had to admit, frankly, that his temperament was not up to the rigorous paragraphs of that book, even though the concluding sentence—'whereof one cannot speak thereof one must be silent'—had greatly appealed to him. In his student days he had naturally pondered his share of Kant, Nietzsche, Sartre and Heidegger, and once he had even, with the help of Bertrand Russell's *A History of Western Philosophy*, attempted to gain greater familiarity with the thoughts of the great philosophers. He knew dozens of obscure poems by Rilke and Morgenstern by heart, had read Hannah Arendt, had flirted with the Frankfurt School and with phenomenology, but none of that had changed his disability: he could not deny that he was a poor intellectual, unschooled in the rules of logic and rhetoric. He felt too insignificant for Leibniz and Bergson; whenever he read anything about the French 'New Philosophers,' he resolved firmly to fill the gaping holes in his knowledge and to find out what Cioran and Levinas had had to say, but nothing ever came of it.

In order not to keep putting his shortcomings needlessly to the test he preferred to read detective stores or spy thrillers. He read because he had to kill time, something he took literally.

The title of Spinoza's book, *Treatise on the Correction of the Understanding and on the Way in Which It May Be Directed Towards a True Knowledge of Things*, had made him smile. Standing under the hot roof he had blown the dust from the book and taken it downstairs.

It was a volume with a fairly large format, a stiff binding and thick, heavy pages. The paper was deckle-edged and yellowed, with stains here and there no doubt because someone had spilled wine over it once upon a time. The print was large and clear. And, having been bound by a master craftsman, the book lay open at its chosen page with ease.

He filled the spoon once again with the splendid blue-black caviare and, not bothering this time with the limp toast, put the whole lot straight in his mouth.

The opening sentence of Spinoza's *Treatise* was the most curious he had ever read. Its tone must have been exceptionally direct and personal for a seventeenth-century writer. Hoffman, unlike his wife Marian, a Vondel specialist, was not a connoisseur of seventeenth-century literature; all he could remember of it was the remnant of an obligatory reading list. Over the years he had of course rummaged about in Marian's learned papers and notes whenever he found them lying about, but he had never felt the urge to immerse himself in her century—her passion for that age remained foreign to him. In their student years he had read her analyses of Vondel's sonnets attentively, but he had stayed a benevolent spectator at a game whose rules remained beyond him.

He and Marian had never shared an intellectual bond. Right from the start she had been his wife and he her husband. They did talk about films and books, but in a primitive, emotional way. Later they were concerned with teething and their twins' childhood illnesses, and the magic of those years had not admitted any discussions of the scholastics' proof of God's existence.

Behind the T in the opening sentence of the book he suddenly saw that strange, elongated, oval head of Spinoza, with its large, gentle eyes, smooth cheeks, straight nose and long, thick hair. The portrait was reproduced at the front of the book; only a sketch, but all the more evocative.

He radiated great peace, this Spinoza, this seventeenth-century Dutch philosopher of Spanish descent, a man who had discovered his destiny and who had a curious eye fixed on a spot to the engraver's right. Hoffman had no way of knowing what there was to be seen there, but the philosopher indisputably had an alert, candid look.

Hoffman's own face was marked with wrinkles and furrows, a complicated delta down which zigzagged the rivulets of sweat he had been producing so profusely during the heat wave of the past few days. His eyes lay hidden beneath the pouches under his eyebrows, but anyone taking the trouble to lift the pouches up would have discovered eyes of undimmed quality: with a bright gleam but startled and sad, like the eyes of a ten-year-old who has just been chastised.

Hoffman had once displayed the same healthy head of hair as Baruch, but over the years his hairline had continued to distance itself from his eyes. Thin grey hair which he kept short, American style, reminded him every day of his approaching end. He had a heavy chin and broad shoulders, was nearly forty-five pounds overweight, had large hands and feet and a voice that could fill a packed hall without the aid of a microphone; he was the last of a family of sturdy, red-haired Jews who in centuries past had been workhorses in Polish and Russian *shtetls* and had looked like Ukrainian peasants.

He leaned over the kitchen table and picked up a bottle. Drinking straight from its neck, he married the strong aftertaste of the caviare with a gulp of tepid Moet.

The table-top scattered the lamplight into all the corners of the kitchen. Hoffman sat wreathed in a silent cocoon of radiance. During the day a tall window above the sink overlooked a long garden; now the dark pane provided a mirror in which the kitchen could look at itself. It was best to keep the windows shut, since it was even hotter out of doors. Mosquitoes crowded outside the glass.

The table was full. Salads, meats and pates, crab and lobster, French and Dutch cheeses, exotic fruits, nuts, bottles of wine and liqueur. No Czech had assembled delicacies such as these since the communists had seized power.

The large house stood in an elegant suburb of Prague and since 1973 had served as the residence of the Ambassador Extraordinary and Plenipotentiary of Her Majesty the Queen of the Netherlands. It was a rectangular building on three floors, designed by a specially appointed department at the Ministry of Foreign Affairs, which had kept a strict watch over the Kingdom's image: solid, stern, modest. Those who crossed the Embassy threshold stepped into the large country house of a gentleman-farmer in the depths of some Calvinist polder.

On the street side nearly half the ground floor was occupied by a drawing room with no fewer than three sitting areas. Two folding doors gave onto a separate dining room with a vast table suitable for official dinners. At the heart of the building was a reception hall, complete with Bechstein and a broad staircase that swept theatrically up to the first floor. On the garden side some prescient spirit had designed a second, smaller dining room for everyday meals, a large kitchen in which elaborate dinners could be prepared, a scullery for the rough work, and an intriguing second staircase hidden behind a cupboard door.

On the first floor were bedrooms and a study with a library, on the second floor further bedrooms, and scattered across the bare boards in the attic under the roof were cast-off pieces of furniture, books and other odds and ends.

Every new set of occupants made the attempt to give the place a personal touch by supplementing Ministry furniture with bits and pieces of their own, and on their departure they always left behind what was surplus to their requirements. That was how Spinoza had finished up in the attic, banished by some departing ambassador or his spouse with an interest in matters existential.

The Moet & Chandon was not bad but Hoffman preferred Taittinger, even though Dom Perignon was considered the best. Dom was merely expensive, Hoffman thought, a champagne for the nouveaux riches. The Moet had been bought for the previous evening by someone from the Embassy—the man's name escaped him, he had not been in Prague long himself after all—who had claimed that Taittinger had been out of stock at the store in nearby Munich which supplied the diplomatic corps in Prague with fine food and drink.

What was Spinoza really trying to say?

'After experience had taught me that all things which frequently take place in ordinary life are vain and futile...' was not an immediately arresting statement. Felix Hoffman could have come to a similar conclusion himself after fifty-nine years of a humdrum existence; he too had learned that all things are vain and futile, but Spinoza was renowned as a great philosopher and would certainly come up with the goods any minute now.

'...when I saw that all the things I feared and which frightened me had nothing good or bad in them save insofar as the mind was affected by them...' was an afterthought that wouldn't set the world on fire either.

All the old philosopher was saying was that one was only afraid of one's own fear. A motor car is an innocent piece of metal, but a murder weapon in the hands of a drunk with the alcohol from a dozen bottles of champagne in his blood—anyone aware of this would (a) not drink another drop, and (b) never sit behind a wheel again.

He read on.

"...I determined at last to inquire whether there might be anything which might be truly good and able to communicate its goodness, and by which the mind might be affected to the exclusion of all other things....'

These were probably the words that had made so great an impact on him during his first reading. Spinoza was going in search of something that could fill the soul, or rather, of something that might bring him happiness, a promise repeated in the last part of the sentence: '...I determined, I say, to inquire whether I might discover and acquire the faculty of enjoying throughout eternity continual supreme happiness.'

Baruch Spinoza was in search of happiness.

Felix Hoffman resolved to read the *Treatise on the Correction of the Understanding and on the Way in Which It May Be Directed Towards a True Knowledge of Things* meticulously from beginning to end.

He got up and opened the refrigerator. The cork of the new bottle of Moet shot from its neck like a rocket. It was difficult to drink straight from the full bottle, and he filled a glass with the fizzing champagne.

That morning he had called on the President at the Hradcany and handed in his credentials.

To the President of the Czechoslovak Socialist Republic,

Your Excellency,

It is my wish to appoint Mr Felix Aaron Hoffman, an esteemed citizen of the Kingdom of the Netherlands, as my Ambassador Extraordinary and Plenipotentiary to your government.

He is acquainted with the mutual interests of our two countries and shares my earnest desire that the long-standing friendship between us be maintained and consolidated.

My faith in his abilities and high principles inspires my complete confidence that you will find the way in which he discharges his duties acceptable.

I beg you to receive him with all due consideration and to give ear when he addresses you in the name of the Kingdom of the Netherlands and conveys my best wishes to the Czechoslovak Socialist Republic.

Beatrix R.

On his fifty-ninth birthday he had received the promotion to which he had been entitled for the past fifteen years. The Ministry had withheld ambassadorial status from him until then, and for years Hoffman had been counting his enemies in The Hague and weighing up his odds. He had become resigned to leaving the Service as a superannuated embassy counsellor. Then suddenly, at the end of his career, they had given him this post, a more positive conclusion to his difficult relationship with the Ministry than his service record had given him reason to hope for.

He had received his first posting in 1960, as Third Secretary in Caracas, followed four years later by his appointment as the 'economic man' in Madrid and, four years later again, by a stint in Lima, Peru. It was pure chance that they had all been in Spanish-speaking countries, because the Service had an arbitrary appointment system and did not believe in training experts who would spend their careers in just one cultural area. In 1971 he had gone to Africa for the first time, to Dar es Salaam in Tanzania, and four years later he was sent back to South America, this time to Rio de Janeiro. By then he was entitled to an ambassadorial appointment, but in 1979 he was sent to Houston as Consul General. In 1983 he went to Khartoum as Temporary Charge d'Affaires, that is, without promotion, and there he had remained until his Prague appointment.

In his Third World posts he had been able to lose himself in the job, for the work had been demanding and never-ending. As far as Czechoslovakia was concerned, diplomatic relations were as good as frozen, and in the economic sphere trade was confined to the odd trainload of Skodas and a few dozen birdcages. Prague was renowned as a dull posting, and he had been afraid that he would be unable to work off his surplus energy here. The appointment had nevertheless filled him with satisfaction.

Wim Scheffers was the man in the Ministry to whom he owed his promotion. Hoffman had met Wim, lean of figure, with grey eyes and sun-ripened cheeks, at the 'nursery', as they called the special training course run by the Ministry. One month after the start of the course, Wim's father, a Jew who had married outside the faith and had therefore managed to survive the war unscathed, had put his neck in a noose and kicked the chair from under his slippers. Low in spirits, Wim had wanted to turn his back on the nursery and on diplomacy, but Hoffman had managed to persuade him to stay in The Hague and Wim had made a career at the Ministry. The two of them referred to themselves as the 'Jewish gang', one Jew and one half-Jew (whatever that might be) who had slipped in through the meshes of the Ministry net.

Scheffers was now Permanent Secretary of State at the Ministry of Foreign Affairs, a bureaucrat who continued to rise in rank as he put on years. He was known as a lady's man.

Hoffman had invited him to Des Indes and ordered a bottle of Chateau Margaux. Wim sniffed at the wine in long and reflective silence.

'A fine wine,' he said. 'Nothing finer than a Margaux.' The waiter filled their glasses.

'I know you're dotty about Margaux. I've sent you a case.'

'You're the dotty one, Felix. You shouldn't have.'

'Without you, I wouldn't have been able to carry on all these years, Wim. Just a mark of my gratitude.'

'You don't owe me any gratitude.'

Hoffman leant across the table and spoke in a confiding tone.

'Let's not mince words. It's thanks to you that I'm off to Prague. None of the rest of that rabble can stand me. Pompous bloody idiots and gutless bastards who can't think further than the little house in the Ardeche they've been scraping and saving to...'

'I've got one of those myself, Felix!'

'I know that, but you're not a bloody idiot, just a Francophile. I don't know what in God's name drives a sane person to become a Francophile, but I pray the Lord will overlook it in your case.'

'The culture, Felix, the culture...'

'Culture, my foot. French whores is what you mean.'

He knew that sort of remark amused Wim Scheffers. Over the years there had been this division of roles: Wim had remained the carefree confirmed bachelor with a secret flame whom he kept hidden away in a renovated farmhouse on the outskirts of a mediaeval village in deepest France, while Hoffman played the hardboiled cynic, trampling on Scheffer's finer feelings like a bull in a china shop and scattering trite remarks. Scheffers had never married.

'No, truly, Wim, I'm most grateful to you, I really am. I've been watching those bungling idiots making fools of themselves for far too long. Now it's my turn to make a fool of myself. I'm happy about that. But it leaves me with a bit of a bad taste all the same—it's happening a little late in life, isn't it?'

'You haven't exactly made it easy for yourself.'

'Oh, so it's my fault?'

'Maybe you'd have done better in publishing or the Elm business.'

'Oh, really?'

'When it comes down to it, you're actually too…too artistic for our lot, you're far too laid back and outspoken. Some people have had a lot of trouble with that, Felix.'

What Scheffers meant was that Felix had a big mouth, especially when he was drunk, something covered by the word 'artistic' in Scheffers's vocabulary.

'And in fact…let me put it to you quite bluntly, Felix, in fact, it's a miracle you're still in the Service. Now and then you really have overstepped the limit.'

'It hasn't been as bad as all that,' said Hoffman.

'Well…take the case of that…young lady in Kenya. That was a bit thick, Felix, much too thick, if you ask me.'

'Let's change the subject, Wim. I've asked you out to celebrate. I should never have started this. Stupid of me.'

He turned the conversation to colleagues, and their gossip banished the Kenyan incident to one of the deepest caverns of his mind, where it rightly belonged.

Hoffman sat down again in the kitchen of his new home in front of the book leaning patiently against the champagne cooler. Without Wim Scheffers's support he'd have been an embittered pen-pusher today. His new job guaranteed him a twenty per cent higher pension on his honourable discharge, and although he was not counting on a long life after his retirement and he really did not need the money, it reassured him to know that he could look forward to a steady income when his working life came to an end.

Hoffman had taxed his body to the limit. He had worked hard, kept long working hours even in hot countries, had eaten and drunk too much and, until a few years ago, had been a chain-smoker. He was afraid of the long afternoons when he left office. He had no hobbies, no passions, no pursuits. Every night since his posting to Houston he had tortured his gullet and stomach with whatever the refrigerator had to offer while reading at the same time, newspapers, magazines and advertising brochures for preference.

Up to now he had come across no such brochures here and wondered if advertising even existed in the Eastern bloc. Aimlessly he tried the novels in vogue at the time, South American authors or English travel writers, but they failed to satisfy him and he reverted to the Russian and French classics and the trusty whodunnits published by the Crime Book Club, of which he was a member.

Every week two of these crime novels were sent to him from Cleveland, Ohio. Two nights and he had finished them. He would sooner have been a member of the Direct Mail Club if he could, able to sample the delights of tons of advertising material every day. That feverish Father Christmas feeling still seized him whenever he had brochures to look through. It made no difference if they were for ladies' underwear or do-it-yourself bathrooms; they saved him from madness simply because they brought his attention to bear on such everyday objects as automatic coffee-makers and supersonic vacuum cleaners. They helped him to collect his thoughts and keep nocturnal insanity at bay.

He had been an insomniac since 6 September 1968. That was the day he had become his own prisoner.

He poured a fresh glass, wiped the sweat from his forehead, and read the next paragraph of the *Treatise*.

I say 'I determined at last', for at the first sight it
seemed ill-advised to lose what was certain in the hope

of attaining what was uncertain. I could see the many advantages acquired from honour and riches, and that I should be debarred from acquiring these things if I wished seriously to investigate a new matter, and if perchance supreme happiness was in one of these I should lose it; if on the other hand, it were not placed in them and I gave them the whole of my attention, then also I should be wanting in it.

Evidently Spinoza, too, had been a man with a career and a family and had, like everyone else, pursued honour and riches, but then he had begun to doubt and had decided to take a gamble: he could either give up what he had and experience supreme happiness, or hang on to what was his and make do.

Hoffman moved a plate of fresh duck livers closer. They had been sent vacuum-packed from Munich, and at the beginning of the evening the cook he had borrowed from the French Embassy had seared them briefly to keep them from spoiling in the heat. He found a knife in the table's cutlery drawer and stuck it into one of the little livers. The tender flesh melted in his mouth.

Hoffman had hung on to what he had. Even though his marriage had come to an end along with his sleep, he had not left Marian. They had decided to live together, as a brother and a sister might go on sharing their lives after their parents' death, using the same kitchen and the same lavatory, but without intimacy.

It was now half-past three, and Marian was fast asleep in her bed upstairs. At night they retired to different rooms, and if it were possible, as it was in this house, they used different bathrooms. He would greet her at breakfast, and if he did not have a dinner engagement he would see her again over supper. She accompanied him on all official occasions, doing her duty as a seasoned diplomat's wife. They remained together because their past precluded a final separation.

Hoffman was a coward.

He was nothing more than a sleepless alcoholic with chronic hunger who had forfeited his right to exist long ago. He knew that he gave in basely to all his weaknesses, which explained why he was forever ready with excuses for remaining with Marian. They were no longer bound by passion. What they shared now was sorrow, an abundance of sorrow.

He looked at the plate and saw that without thinking he had downed three whole duck livers without even tasting them. He filled another glass of champagne. The wine danced on his tongue.

Still a good three hours until morning would deliver him from the darkness. Years ago, in the early seventies, he had tried to utilise the extra life his insomnia provided to write a 'history book in reverse' as he called it at the time, a collection of essays advocating a new form of nihilism, beyond faith and ideology, to the greater glory of sober consumerism. With it, he would out-Popper Popper. He had made piles of notes and stuck them up on huge notice boards. Night after night he had gone in hot pursuit of a structure for the collection, manoeuvring record cards across the board as if he were executing a complicated gambit in a game of chess. But it had eventually dawned on him that all he was doing was trying to find a justification for his own life, that he had nothing to say to anyone else.

During the party he had tried a small piece of Camembert which had had a sharp woody flavour, and he could still see a last runny remnant. He washed the rich cheese down with a gulp of Moet and immediately refilled his glass.

It had happened to him late in life—a moment later and it would have been *too* late; yesterday morning the president of a republic, it hardly mattered which, had received him in his capacity as ambassador. In a cool, lofty room in the Hradcany the two of them had sipped tea and talked of Van Basten and Gullit. At the end Hoffman had mumbled something about the warm friendship between their two peoples.

Then Marian had been allowed to join them and had dazzled in her role as ambassador's wife. They had reached the top of the ladder. But the satisfaction that gave them was something they savoured separately. When they left the Hradcany, sitting back on the leather upholstery of the Mercedes which was at his ambassadorial disposition day and night (the air-conditioning humming, the Dutch flag fluttering over the gleaming black bonnet, the chauffeur wearing a proper cap, Marian experiencing a second youth in a suit she had ordered in Vienna), Hoffman had burned with the longing to take her face in his hands and to tell her, 'We did it together.' But all he said was, 'What did you think of Husak?'

'A creep,' she said. 'He puts on a kindly grandfather act but there's blood under his nails.'

'What's your feeling about all of this now?'

'What do you mean?'

He groped for words. 'Now that the two of us....'

'I'm very happy for you, surely you know that?'

'Yes, but...what do *you* feel about it?'

'I feel the same.'

'I mean, what do you feel about having come so far?'

'*You've* come so far. All I do is to help a little. I have my own interests. As you know.'

And he did not say: Marian, without you I should have died miserably in the gutter long ago. Such words were barred from the protocol of their arid marriage.

He was an economist, Marian an authority on Dutch language and literature. They had first met as students in the refectory of Amsterdam University. During the war he had had to forgo his secondary schooling because he had been in hiding with a pig farmer in Brabant. And after the Liberation the very idea of a secondary-school diploma had seemed like an obscene joke in the harsh light of the reality that had left him an orphan.

Hoffman's father had been a banker, and after the war Felix discovered that he had been left a small monthly allowance. He was able to convince his guardian, the father of his friend Hein Daamen, that he could manage on his own. He did not go to school, did no work, stayed in his bed in a room rented from a landlady in the Plantage Middenlaan, smoked roll-ups, drank tea and idled the time away. He was still very young, but he had money and he met other young people in cafes. His lethargy was foreign to them. They shouted and swore as they strove to convey the shock of the Liberation in paintings and books.

Felix's own contribution to art was confined to buying the garish paintings of his poverty-stricken friends. Prompted by a strange sense of presentiment, he had hung on to all the works by those busily productive painters who were later to call themselves the Cobra Movement. Not until 1952, when he was twenty-two, did he take his school-leaving certificate and enter university.

His Appels and Constants were his life insurance. He kept them stored in a secure heated warehouse in Den Bosch that belonged to Hein Daamen, the elegant but awkward engineer with whom he had been to primary school.

The Daamens were a prominent family in Den Bosch, proudly producing a bishop or mother superior in every generation. In December 1944, three months after the liberation of Den Bosch, Hein had seen his old school friend Felix Hoffman standing in the cold in the Hekellaan, teeth chattering, in front of the ransacked house in which he had grown up. Felix stank of pig manure and his skin was encrusted with dirt. Hein talked him into coming away from there and took him home with him.

They draped paper chains over Father Daamen's high-backed chair as if it were Felix's birthday, and as the house filled with his stench Felix, seated at the head of the table under the conscious-stricken gaze of half the family, ate a bowl of millet porridge, some fried eggs and bacon, a tin of corned beef with five thick slices of Canadian bread, half a German sausage and a bar of chocolate. He wasn't hungry but he cleaned the plates. The paper chains tickled his neck. Then he was given Hein's eldest brother's thick coat (that coat saw him through the winter). Hein observed that turning their guest out would be an un-Christian act and the maid placed a rusty folding bed in Hein's room. They filled a bathtub for him and, before they went to sleep, Mevrouw Daamen selflessly provided instruction in the New Testament. Felix stayed with them until August 1945, cutting into every week with a laborious trip to Boxtel in the midst of military convoys and endless lines of ambulances to visit Eduard van de Pas, the slightly touched pig farmer who had hidden him for two years in the farm's gradually emptying sties alongside God's own untouchables, which the poetic, hydrophobic farmer slaughtered illegally—the only other act of resistance Felix had caught him at—and fed in small portions to the young Jew.

It was from him that Hoffman, whose home had been strictly kosher, learned to appreciate the wonders of home-cured ham.

A whole Parma ham still wrapped in cellophane now lay on the kitchen table, and Hoffman could not resist cutting off a slice. The champagne seemed to him too delicate an accompaniment, however, and he opened a bottle of Brouilly, a fragrant, subtle wine from the loveliest part of Beaujolais. He discovered a few slices of melon in a bowl of salad and placed them neatly on a clean plate from his official dinner service at the side of the ham and under the golden coronet of the House of Orange.

In August 1945 he was sent to a Jewish orphanage, but he ran away and for a few days Hein kept him hidden in his room. The Daamens then agreed to become his guardians and allowed him the freedom to go and rent a room from a landlady in the Plantage Middenlaan, in the old Jewish quarter of Amsterdam. By that time he had learned that his parents had been gassed in a shower and burned in an oven. Hein went to university in 1949, Felix in 1952. For a few years he and Hein saw each other nearly every day. Then Hein married Trudy Overeem, whose father was a director of Philips, and the relationship tailed away, although it never broke off completely. They met just once a year, but would talk with the old familiarity. And once every few years the two couples would dine out together.

Marian kept in regular touch with Trudy. He did not know if they were very close friends, but Trudy was in any case one of the few people with whom Marian kept up a correspondence.

Hoffman brought his attention back to Spinoza, the philosopher prepared to take a gamble, to trade the three illusory goals men blindly pursue—riches, honour and pleasure—for the uncertain pursuit of supreme happiness.

Hoffman read another few paragraphs in which Spinoza went at greater length into his vain attempts to change his life, and was brought up short by the following passage:

> For I saw myself in the midst of a very great peril and obliged to seek a remedy, however uncertain, with all my energy: like a sick man seized with a deadly disease, who sees death straight before him if he does not find some remedy, is forced to seek it, however uncertain, with all his remaining strength, for in that is all his hope placed.

As he cut himself a small strip from the slice of ham and wrapped it carefully round a piece of melon, Hoffman had to concede that he, too, was in very great peril, the peril of irreversible degeneration:

—During urination, it sometimes took half a minute for his jet to gain any strength. When he finally managed to empty his bladder, he had trouble stopping the trickle, which continued even after he had buttoned his flies.

—His anus no longer closed as tightly as it had in the past, and without realising it he would stain his underpants.

—There were mysterious shooting pains in his limbs.

—Once, when in melancholy protest he had gone to hear Leonard Bernstein conducting Mahler, his ears had suddenly begun to ring.

—At night his eyes were pricked by invisible needles.

—Sometimes his stomach had cramps as if he'd taken arsenic.

—Bile rose up in spurts from his gullet into his throat.

—His joints creaked.

—He had ingrowing toenails.

—Hair grew profusely all over his body, except for his head.

—A severe pain would start in the middle of his chest, travel via his neck to his left arm and then shoot down into his fingers. He knew what that meant, had read about it more than once and his doctor, too, had told him: his coronary arteries were clogged, silted up, corroded.

His doctor had advised a strict diet to reduce his cholesterol level.

'If you carry on as you are, you'll have a heart attack for sure. That's been fed into your computer already, so to speak.'

'Is cholesterol always a bad thing?'

'We believe it is, yes.'

'Believe?'

'It's complicated....'

'In that case....'

'My meter doesn't go high enough to measure your cholesterol level, Felix.'

'Really? Well, I'll wait and see. I don't believe in cholesterol, anyway.'

Hoffman was in very great peril, just as Baruch Spinoza had been. His body was heading for total entropy, his mind was shut up with itself inside his head twenty-four hours a day, and in the end his skull would explode.

He washed down the mouthful of ham and melon with a gulp of wine. The Brouilly had a nose reminiscent of rare wood. The wine was not too heavy, with a consistent, unassuming taste.

He read on.

> Finally...these evils seem to have arisen from the fact that the whole of happiness or unhappiness is depen-
> dent on this alone: on the quality of the object to which
> we are bound by love. For the sake of something which
> no one loves, strife never arises, there is no pain if it
> perishes, no envy if it is possessed by someone else, nor
> fear, nor hatred, and, to put it all briefly, no commo-
> tions of the mind at all.

This terrible truth, banal and subtle at the same time, slowed the movement of his hand, and his glass hovered halfway between the table and his mouth. Did the philosopher refer merely to *things* when he spoke of 'the object to which we are bound by love', or did he also include love for *people*?

Hoffman had managed now and then to get the artists' girlfriends into bed (the word 'groupie' would come into use later) in an attempt to practise free love just like Sartre and de Beauvoir, but he had loved Marian from the day he first heard her voice in the refectory. She was the daughter of J. C. Coenen, a professor of Dutch literature whose fame preceded him wherever he went, and she was determined to beat her authoritarian and psoriatic father at his own game, no mean objective for a girl in 1954. Coenen considered Hoffman an upstart, even though Hoffman senior had been a banker. Hoffman, for his part, considered his future father-in-law a frustrated and narrow-minded pedant.

Felix had been sitting in the refectory with Hein Daamen eating a plate of nasi-goreng, a hazardous experiment in Indonesian cooking by the kitchen staff. Without wanting to, he became aware of a row going on between a boy and a girl sitting behind him.

'No, Eddie, I'm not going to go with you.'

'You promised,' the boy said glumly.

'Maybe I did, but I made a mistake.'

'A mistake? A promise is a promise.'

'I'm sorry, but I'm not going to go to that party.'

'What about a film then? There's a new Italian one at the Kriterion.'

'Eddie...when is it going to get through to you? I...I'm not in love with you.'

'Since when? I thought....'

Felix exchanged glances with Hein. Both shrugged their shoulders.

'I'm really sorry, Eddie, but it's better to give it to you straight, isn't it?'

'You don't want me because I'm a Jew,' the boy said suddenly, point-blank.

Felix went pale.

The girl replied in a stifled voice, 'No, it's not like that. It's just that I'm not in love with you.'

'You're a racist.'

'No, that isn't true....'

Felix could hear the sob in her voice. He could not stop himself and turned round.

At the table behind him sat the most beautiful girl he had ever seen. Thick dark hair hung to her shoulders, her slender fingers were twisting together frantically, tears welled up in her brown eyes. A broad-shouldered boy sat with his back to Felix.

'Hey, are you deaf or something?' Felix asked.

The boy turned round to face him. He was solidly built, with an enormous jaw, and Felix saw a powerful hand resting on the back of his chair. Felix knew him; he was one of the seniors in the student corps, Eddie Kohn.

'What's it got to do with you?'

'It's got nothing to do with me. I've been listening to you because you seem unable to talk in a low voice, and I heard you...'—he glanced at the beauty, who gave him a startled look—'...maligning her.'

'Then you didn't hear properly.'

'I heard only too damn well.'

'If I were you, I'd shut my mouth.'

'And if I were you and thought I still had the slightest chance of going dancing with her, I'd shut mine.'

She burst into nervous laughter and, shocked, pressed her hand to her magnificent lips. This made Eddie even angrier.

'Why don't you mind...your...own...business.'

'That's what I am doing....'

Hein laid a hand on Felix's arm. 'Hey, take it easy, Fee, let's eat up and go home.' Hein, then a technical college student, had lost his room because he had given some sort of dubious party for friends Felix did not know. Hein had refused to reveal anything about the party and had now moved in with Felix. But Felix pulled his arm free and looked straight at Eddie.

'She's no racist,' he said to Eddie.

'Oh yes, she is.'

'You're wrong.'

With an iron grip Eddie seized him by the collar.

'You're a racist yourself,' Eddie said in a nasty voice.

Felix looked at the girl, who was watching him anxiously.

'Like to come dancing with me?' he asked.

Eddie looked round at her too, his grip on Felix's throat tightening.

She shrugged her shoulders in confusion, lowered her eyes, then looked up and answered firmly, 'Yes.'

'You see?' said Felix in a strangled voice to Eddie, who was finding it difficult to follow this turn of events. 'She isn't a racist because I'm circumcised the same as you, and if you don't believe me we can go to the toilets and compare our assets, okay?'

Eddie stared at him open-mouthed. Felix saw the girl wavering between amazement and admiration.

Eddie got to his feet. He left his plate of experimental nasi untouched behind him. With an awkward gesture in the girl's direction, Felix conveyed his regrets for his intrusive intervention. She did not respond, staring at him with a glazed expression. He turned back to his food.

'One of these days you're going to get a horrible beating,' Hein promised.

Felix took a mouthful of the new Indonesian hit on the refectory menu. 'Aaah, he was just a pain in the arse,' he said, his mouth full. 'If you give as good as you get they shut up quick enough. They're all the same. All bark and no bite and they run off with their tails between their legs as soon as you snarl back at them. But did you see that girl? My *God*, have you ever seen such a beautiful girl? Do you know who she is?'

He saw Hein looking at something behind him. Felix followed his glance and looked up into the girl's face.

She said, 'When are we going to go dancing, then?'

'Stirrings of the soul,' Spinoza called the pain accompanying such memories. Hoffman gulped down the rest of the ham and the melon and realised too late that this nervous haste had again prevented him from tasting anything. He reached for the herring platter, a regular at all Dutch Embassy parties, and lifted a herring up by its tail.

The platter had been too long in the heat and the herrings were beginning to lose colour, but the taste was still perfect. The man at the herring stall on the sea front at Scheveningen had once told him that for choice he ate herrings that were on the verge of going off. 'Just about to rot,' the man had said as he gutted a herring, 'but before the maggots take over. You don't believe me? Here, have this one on me, on one condition: leave it on the draining board for a day or two. When the stink is almost unbearable, then you eat it, and the next day you come and tell me what it was like. Agreed?'

Hoffman had eaten the herring two days later and the flesh had been tender and appetizing with a strong aftertaste reminiscent of game.

He dropped a second herring into his mouth, sucking the bone clean to just above the tail. Then he stood up and took a bottle of vodka out of the deep freeze. His glass misted over as the cold, viscous liquid poured into it. He downed the vodka in a single gulp. At once the strong liquor took hold of his throat, then moved to his nose and eyes. He shuddered with pleasure. Another glass, and he clenched his teeth as the alcohol stung his gullet. He sat down again.

'But the love towards a thing eternal and infinite alone feeds the mind with pleasure,' Hoffman read, 'and it is free from all pain; so it is much to be desired and to be sought out with all our might.'

What was his own thing eternal and infinite? He had assuaged his sense of honour now that he had become the chief representative here of the kingdom on the North Sea. Once upon a time he might have called serving Marian his own thing eternal and infinite.

Since Miriam's death from an overdose in a junkies' hostel in Warmoesstraat, Marian had withdrawn for good into her research into Vondel's sonnets, 'the definitive study of the subject', as she herself called it mockingly, something she had started a few years after Esther's death. Marian was now fifty-four, and still at loggerheads with her inaccessible father. The world-famous Coenen, silent and bitter, had been a witness throughout to the annihilation of his progeny, and at Miriam's funeral Hoffman had been able to read in his eyes where he thought the blame for it all lay, the original, genetic blame. Three months after Miriam's overdose they had buried him too in the family grave in Zwolle, next to his wife and two granddaughters.

Spinoza wrote about riches, honour and pleasure—false values according to him.

Honour was something Hoffman had also long sought, and now that he had received it in full measure he recalled with some surprise all the times he had in bitterness torn up the Ministry list of promotions. It was, of course, far from disagreeable to be living here in the Embassy, being driven about in a Mercedes by a chauffeur called Boris, but the nights were still long and his hunger still insatiable.

Riches, or rather the absence of poverty, had been taken care of for him by his father. With the small monthly allowance he had enjoyed until his thirtieth birthday he had been able to buy forty-three paintings, which had recently been valued by Christies at some 1.3 million guilders. He had never sought riches, but he recognised that in comparison with the majority of his fellows his lifestyle was conspicuous for being deprived of deprivation.

Pleasure was a more complicated subject. Eating was a pleasure, drinking was a pleasure, fucking was a pleasure—would Spinoza have given all this up, was his idea of 'supreme happiness' a celibate existence and one devoid of all other worldly delights?

A sexual escapade in Kenya six years before had led to a diplomatic row and an embarrassing dressing-down from the head of the department, and had nearly cost him his career. In the insanity of his lubricious state he had made some distressing errors. The affair had been hushed up and he had been sent the bill: a few bribes, damages, and the cost of building a humble little house, just over four thousand dollars in all. That had been before Miriam's death, one year before she had been found in the hostel. It had been his last sexual escapade. He refused to take any more risks.

Honour, riches and pleasure—he could hardly claim that he had been unaffected by them or that he was disposed to renounce them. He could afford whores, mistresses, money enough to quell his erections. In Africa you could get anything you wanted. Sex with a ten-year-old girl, an eight-year-old boy, with three, four or five women, on the back of a giraffe, in the mouth of a hippopotamus, but for getting what he was in search of (Marian's face as it used to look when she came silently to orgasm) money was a futile device.

Everything he owned, his paintings and his rank and status, he would now gladly give for a good night's sleep. In the past he had never realised what a blessing that small death was. For years he had gone to bed and fallen asleep without understanding that waking up was the daily wellspring on which he had freely drawn.

Waking up meant being raised from the dead, and death was there to allow escape from the agonising uncertainties of life. In dreams the worst was weathered and the best revealed, but even dreamless sleep—a banal emptiness, a dull void—lent one the strength to stand up to cruel reality.

He had been unable to sleep now for twenty years. Esther, Miriam's little twin sister, had died on 6 September 1968. Esther was the first daughter he had buried. Sixteen years later, on 12 September 1984, he had lowered Miriam's coffin next to hers.

A few months after Esther's death, when he realised that sleep was threatening to elude him permanently, he had sought professional help, as it is called nowadays. The doctors had tried everything on him, from placebos to the stuff that kills, but sleep refused to come, at least the kind of sleep he had once known.

He had rarely had problems in taking leave of his consciousness, and with Marian in his arms ('Come on, let's have a snuggle,' she would say), he had for years drifted deeply and surely into the morning. During the day his skin would retain the memory of Marian's touch. His belly would hanker after the warmth and security of the next night, his prick pressed to her generous buttocks, his hands round her breasts, his lips on her shoulder. They could calm each other with a caress, with a look. Intellectually, they did not share a great deal. She lived in a remote century, he studied dossiers on trade promotion. In their dreams they had known the innocence of the newly-born.

There was a drug that knocked him out and put him in a state akin to sleep, but the sense of security that marked ordinary sleep—you were there and yet you were not there, a curiously womb-like experience—was completely absent. The sleep induced by that drug was sterile and anxiety-ridden; he felt exposed, even though he was out cold. Later he heard that it had been withdrawn from the market. People had been driven into blind rages, even in their sleep, and had committed murder. The American manufacturers had had to pay millions of dollars in damages.

He had tried injecting morphine, but the sleep he had once known could not be counterfeited. With opium he wafted into a long drawn-out dream full of colour and sound, but the only lasting effect it had was to make him aware of the too many pounds of body weight he was lugging about on this earth. Opium made you lazy.

Natural sleep also freed you from your own identity and character. A basic element stayed with you in your sleep, a vague notion of some animal existence without the impossible paradoxes of the human mind. For twenty years now he had been his own constant guest and he had ended up hating his host.

Vodka and herring are perfect partners and he could not resist the temptation of a third herring. He bit into the tender flesh and took a glance at the book.

Had Spinoza been a healthy sleeper? Something about his sentences suggested that he had been; Spinoza had probably enjoyed healthy, untroubled nights. A man who wrote those sentences was at peace with himself.

He read that by *deliberating* upon his search for the supreme good, Spinoza had been able to reject the false values he had maintained until then. Spinoza had realised that his ability to think and to analyse had brought supreme happiness nearer because the values that had previously held him in their grip had only revealed their illusory character after he had deliberated upon them at length: 'One thing I could see, and that was that as long as the mind was employed with these thoughts, it turned away from its former subjects of thought'—the illusory subjects, Hoffman realised—'and meditated seriously on this new plan: which was a great comfort to me.'

Because he never slept, deliberating was the only thing Hoffman did at night, yet it had never afforded him so much as a glimpse of a new way of life. On the contrary, deliberation had brought him revulsion and bitterness, and he was curious to discover whether Spinoza's claims about the purifying power of deliberation could stand up to the scrutiny of a twentieth-century nihilist (Hoffman's view of himself).

Spinoza contended that 'all things which are made, are made according to the eternal order and the fixed laws of nature', and considered that what really mattered—and therein apparently lay supreme happiness—was an understanding of nature. And in order to understand, man has to be healthy not only in mind but also in body. Yet Spinoza did not lose sight of his main objective:

'But above all things, a method must be thought out of healing the understanding and purifying it at the beginning, that it may with the greatest success understand things correctly.'

Hoffman shook his head admiringly at so much naïve enthusiasm. The philosopher could not in all fairness have meant it. He filled his glass with vodka and read straight on, because Spinoza was now advancing three rules of life that could lead his readers to a better understanding.

First of all, Spinoza argued, we must speak in a manner comprehensible to the masses, so that the objective—improvement and purification of the understanding—might be more surely attained. This rule was for teachers, for those who already enjoyed better understanding, but it was of little avail to a mere beginner like Hoffman.

The second rule was, 'To enjoy only such pleasures as are necessary for the preservation of health.' And the third rule: 'Finally, to seek only enough money or anything else as is necessary for the upkeep of our health and life, and to comply with such customs as are not opposed to what we seek.'

Before insomnia had disrupted his life, Hoffman had had no trouble in keeping his tendency to let himself go under control. Occasionally he would succumb and drink one bottle of wine too many or take a second helping of a dessert, but he had managed to check his innate gluttony because his life with Marian and the twins had been enough to appease every kind of hunger.

He had wanted a daughter, and the birth of two at once had made him deliriously happy. At the time—it was 1960—they had been living in Venezuela, his first post, for just two months, and Marian had given birth in the American Hospital first to Esther and four minutes later to Miriam, their non-identical twins. With the children he had felt that he could laugh at the war, that innocence had been reborn in that collision of sperm and ovum. He kissed the babies in their cradle until their cheeks burned. Day after day he clasped their tiny hands and prayed that there might be a God, and if there was then he begged Him for health and happiness for his children. He changed their nappies and gave them their bottles, and Marian flaunted her modern husband in their conservative diplomatic circles.

Hoffman bought a Super-8 cine camera and recorded the twins dribbling as they crawled across the floor, pulling themselves up by the bars of their playpen, taking their first surprised steps, splashing the water in their inflatable paddling pool with their plastic dolphins, and crying interminably as they cut their first teeth. The love he bore his children was all-consuming.

The twins celebrated their fourth birthday in Madrid, his second posting, and until the end of 1967 Esther never had anything wrong with her other than the usual childhood illnesses. One morning, after having eaten a thick Dutch sandwich of butter sprinkled with chocolate strands, and while standing in the lift beside Miriam ready to be taken to the International School by a neighbour's wife (several diplomats and their families lived in their building and took turns driving the children to school), Esther vomited. The girls returned to the apartment in great excitement.

'Mummy, Mummy!' Miriam shouted. 'Esther's been sick!'

Felix gestured to his wife that it was probably nothing serious.

'Really, sweetheart? Where were you sick?' asked Marian.

'In the lift!' Miriam shrieked.

'Calm down, Mir. Are you feeling ill, Esther?'

She shook her head. 'No.'

'Do you still feel sick? Are you going to do it again?' asked her father.

'No,' she said, and began to laugh.

Hoffman went out with a bucket and cleaned up the small pile of vomit. Later he realised that he should have had it examined, but all he did at the time was to throw away Granny Coenen's chocolate strands, which were perhaps past their best.

One week later, the same thing happened, this time at supper, but Felix and Marian had so often seen their children bringing up their food that they did not worry and only called in the doctor three days later when Esther ran a temperature.

The doctor had been recommended by someone at the Embassy. He was an affable *madrileno* who had grown grey in his profession, but he was unable to find anything out of the ordinary and diagnosed a minor infection. One week later Esther's temperature was still just as high and the doctor prescribed penicillin. Her temperature went back to normal but Esther sank into a so-called 'malaise': she was listless, slept badly and was found to be anaemic. Within three weeks the fever was back, this time alarmingly high. The doctor gave her more penicillin. One morning they found something wrong with her skin. She had had a peaceful night—Hoffman had got out of bed once or twice to look at her—but in the morning when he went in to kiss her goodbye before leaving for work (she now had the room to herself, Miriam having been moved to the guest room when the fever first appeared), he saw that her skin looked dry and wrinkled.

'Have you seen Esther's skin?' he asked Marian.

'No, what's the matter?'

'I don't know. Something's not right.'

Marian went to see for herself and, returning to the kitchen, managed to control herself. He had stood there waiting, briefcase in hand.

'What do you think she's got, Fee?'

'Shall we call Alvarez?'

'He was only here yesterday.'

'Perhaps we ought to ask another doctor, what do you think?' he said.

'I was afraid you might think I was making a fuss, but I've been wondering whether Alvarez is out of his depth. I...I've felt for some time that we should get a second opinion.'

'Why on earth didn't you say so?' he asked angrily. He was chiefly angry with himself.

'You seemed quite keen on him and I thought...'

'My God, how ridiculous. Keen or not, my daughter's health comes first. Marian...'

She flung her arms around him.

'She's going to be all right,' he said. 'She's probably just dehydrated because of the fever. Something like that.'

'It's got to be brought down, Fee.'

'Don't be too upset. I'm sure there's no reason to worry.'

From the Embassy he rang another doctor, who came to look at Esther and could find nothing particularly wrong with her, thought that the penicillin ought to do the job and advised them to give her plenty of fluids. Her temperature went down, her skin recovered and they began to pack for the transfer to Lima.

During the second week of January 1968 strange contusions appeared on Esther's skin. The Peruvian doctors, not knowing what to make of the symptoms, contradicted one another. They were staying in Callao, a suburb of Lima, where they had a barely furnished apartment in a tall block of flats overlooking the Pacific. Their things were in packing cases that had had to make the long journey through the Panama Canal, and meanwhile they were roughing it on a worn parquet floor with garden chairs and a folding table.

Ever since Esther's relapse Miriam had withdrawn into silence. Felix accompanied her to the zoo and to playgrounds, but when she smiled it was only to please her father.

He and Marian took turns keeping watch by Esther's bed. Anxiety kept them from sleeping. During the day Felix would sometimes doze off at his desk in the office and be startled to find that his cigar had burned a hole in some official form. They put up with this for a few weeks, then he flew Esther out to Miami.

Esther had Henoch-Schonlein syndrome, according to the doctors, a complex condition that ran an unpredictable course and could prove fatal. Anxiety exploded into readiness to do battle.

Marian consoled him and he consoled Marian. They decided to fight, not to let the illness get them down and to lend Esther their own optimism.

She was put through two weeks of tests. Marian and Miriam stayed with her, Felix returned to Lima after a week. They rang each other at least twice a day.

'How is she today?'

'She's holding up very well.'

'And Miriam?'

'She wants to become a doctor. She won't budge from Esther's side.'

'Is she still in pain?'

'The doctors say she's being very brave because it must be hurting a lot, but she doesn't complain.'

He said, 'We made two beautiful little girls, Mar, you've given me two wonderful human beings.'

He could hear her weeping through the noise on the line.

Then the doctors diagnosed leukaemia.

It was to be six months or so before Esther died. Chemotherapy aged her, as if her immature little body lived through in a short time what takes the normal person eighty years. Her hair fell out, she had wrinkles and sunken eyes.

Marian and Miriam rented a small flat for an astronomical sum in an unpretentious neighbourhood taken over by Cuban immigrants, where thanks to the influx of Central American refugees the rentals had rocketed sky-high. What he wanted was to make a weekly visit to Miami by air, but The Hague kept him at his desk and despite his appeals granted him only occasional days off. He sent furious telexes and conducted bitter telephone calls with Het Plein, where the Ministry was still housed at the time, but the officials would not give an inch. These were the first shots in the war he would wage with his employers for the rest of his career.

When the family was together in Miami they did what they had always done. They drove about in a hired car and the twins never stopped asking questions, and Felix and Marian saw the world through their children's eyes and lived the childhood they themselves had never had. They walked along the shore, he would carry Esther when she grew tired, and they had endless discussions about the water and the fish and the warm Gulf Stream. Sometimes they would spend a quarter of an hour huddled over a clump of grass, and in their enthusiasm and eagerness for knowledge, time stood still and he could share the whole wide world with his family.

In May that year Esther was flown to Holland in a chartered plane. She was admitted to the Lutheran Deaconesses' hospital in Vondelpark, Amsterdam. She had a room to herself with a view over the park, and listened to records on her record-player. She read Annie Schmidt and cheered up her mother and little sister, who came to visit her every day and when the weather permitted pushed her wheelchair through the park past the hippies sprawling on the lawns beside their rucksacks. She read little stories to the other children. She was brave and beautiful.

Twice Felix was allowed to go to her. He flew to Amsterdam, a flight taking twenty-four hours. He stayed with Esther for four days, then flew back again. Just twice.

While he was working, he had not touched the small capital which his father had left him and which had helped to feed him and a few of his artist acquaintances until he finished his studies, but now he did break into it.

'The best there is,' he had said to the doctors on both his visits, 'the best tests and the best equipment, no skimping on anything.'

And both times he was told, 'We are doing all we can as it is, Mr Hoffman.'

Esther had begun to find it difficult to walk, but her eyes remained those of an eight-year-old child, eager and innocent. Felix discovered a glow in her that he had not noticed before her illness: her eyes had grown wise with the pain and tender with the sorrow she saw all around her day after day.

While long-haired adolescents all over Europe clamoured for free rein to the imagination, Esther turned into a little wizened old crone with gentle eyes. Towards the end of August Felix received an urgent summons and he left for Amsterdam without asking for permission.

The last time he saw her was one hour before she died. A balmy late summer's day held sway outside the window of her room. She was lying still, connected to machines full of little lamps and tubes, and she was smiling and looked well, as if she had not given up and wanted to make it clear to them that she intended to remain with them for a long time yet. They left the room to get a sandwich on Wiliemsparkweg. As they were going downstairs, Felix realised that he had left his briefcase behind. He hurried back to Esther's room.

Cautiously he opened the door and saw her look round at him. He smiled and walked in.

'Hello, sweetheart. I forgot my case.'

She nodded. He picked up the case from a chair and sat down briefly next to her on the bed; he stroked her icy head and cheeks. Hers was a cold illness.

'Miriam and Mummy and I are coming straight back and then we'll read you something, all right?'

She smiled. He held his hand to her ageing cheek and let her feel the warmth of his body. She lifted her skinny little left hand and gripped his wrist, and the sight of her old woman's fingers, those lovely little baby fingers he had once pressed for days on end to his lips, brought an involuntary sob to his throat, and he struggled against the raging sorrow that was slicing through his chest. He did not want her to see him cry.

She shook her head and whispered.

'Daddy, Daddy...it's all right, really, it's all right.'

He sniffed.

'Esther, I love you with all my heart. And I want you to get better so much, so that we can do everything together again.'

'I'm not going to get better, Daddy.'

'Of course you are!'

'Daddy, I'm not going to get better, really I'm not...'

She looked at him with a wisdom in her eyes he would never be able to fathom.

'It's all right, Daddy, it really is all right.'

'It won't be all right until you're better.'

'No. Just let me be as I am. I know.'

'What do you know, darling?'

She smiled, from somewhere beyond the pain.

'I know, Daddy...'

'But what, Esther darling? What do you know?'

She said it once more, barely audible this time, 'I know, Daddy...'

He kissed her forehead.

'We'll be back in an hour, okay? Then we'll read you a beautiful book Miriam's brought you. All right?'

She nodded.

When they came back, Esther was dead.

Her heart had suddenly stopped; the nurses had found her with her eyes closed. Felix saw her lying there, an old woman who had taken her leave in perfect peace.

Marian broke down with grief, yelling and screaming in the tiled hospital corridor. He was unable to calm her, and when she began having cramps and her body became convulsed with muscular contractions, as if she were about to give birth, a doctor gave her an injection. He insisted that she spend the night in hospital under sedation. Felix took Miriam to Grandpa and Granny Coenen in Zwolle.

The last few months he had wept and cursed, and now suddenly his heart was still. He held Miriam close. She clung to him grimly, her little body tense, her nails digging into his clothes.

And in the silence he wondered about just one thing: what was it that Esther had known? What had she meant? Did she know that she was about to die, or had she meant—and that was what her eyes had seemed to be telling him—something else, a truth unknown to him, a certainty given only to a little mite of humanity like Esther, a belief he could never acquire?

It had been wrong to leave Marian in the hospital that first night after Esther's death. At the time it had seemed the best thing for her because she had been out of her mind and he had been terrified. The next day she had flung accusations at him in a shaking voice: her daughter was dead and her husband had allowed her to be locked up, unconscious, in a hospital room.

Later he realised how intensely physical their marriage had been. They had communicated through their children; in the twins their unspoken love had found its natural expression. When sleeping with Marian, when they had touched each other, he had been aware of a way of life that needed no explanation, that transcended words.

They were unable to console each other, for their sorrow was not of the same kind. Hers was physical and raw, his was silent and rational, hidden behind the question that increasingly obsessed him: what had Esther known?

The girls had not had a religious upbringing. The Coenens were not observant, and the only faith that had touched Esther and Miriam in any way was the vague Judaism of their father, who had no family and no Granny or Grandpa.

Esther could not possibly have been referring to some rudimentary form of Christian 'knowledge'. In her world, neither heaven nor the hereafter had yet taken form, although he could not rule out the possibility that a few catechism lessons in Lima or Madrid might have left her with images of heavenly clouds and winged angels. No, her 'knowledge' was of a different kind. Distraught, he heard her words every day in endless repetition, much like the mantra chanted in interminable singsong by those Hare Krishna people who processed through Amsterdam in their exotic robes.

Esther was buried in the Coenen family grave in Zwolle.

He could no longer sleep.

A year ago he had read in the science supplement of the *Nieuwe Rotterdamse Courant* that a large percentage of cases with Esther's form of leukaemia could nowadays be cured: new therapies, new drugs. He had rung his Dutch doctor and the doctor's enquiries had revealed that the report was correct. Had Esther lived too early, had he fathered her too early, had he himself been born too early? If she had come into the world twenty years later, then her illness would not have killed her.

Marian's rage wore itself out in the sorrow following Esther's death: when they realised that Miriam was about to become the chief victim of their tragedy, they turned their attention to the task of protecting her.

A psychologist advised them under no circumstances to deny Esther's death; they should go on talking about it and stop Miriam from feeling anxious or guilty about it. It seemed a surviving twin was more susceptible than other siblings to complicated traumas.

But the continual references to the dead child also kept their pain alive. What had once been unconscious and implicit now became the subject of drawn-out discussion. Spontaneous feelings came to grief against a wall of circumspection. When he looked at Miriam, he saw the girl who was no longer with them. Once, there had been no ulterior motives when they embraced, when the two girls had tugged at his earlobes and climbed onto his shoulders, when he had carried them about, one in each arm; now every touch was a pose. Once the family had been a natural entity; now it succumbed to the forced cheerfulness he and Marian put on for Miriam. The mourning went on, week after week.

Frantic through lack of sleep and blind with sorrow, Felix returned to Lima, and in the absence of his wife and child he went out and got drunk in a series of bars, ending up in a shack full of taciturn Indians on the outskirts of the city and knocking back something that turned the world inside out. A broad-hipped Indian woman kept placing her hand on his crotch until he gave in and went outside with her. He took her in the dark behind the building against a wooden fence. He pounded away at her against the loose slats and she spurred him on with a smile, as if he were a toreador, and when he had come and she had faked her orgasm, he turned round and looked into the glistening faces of a row of drunken Indians.

She was his first prostitute, a fleshy, sweating woman with high cheekbones and smelling of musk. The nights were endless. He had morphine and opium procured for him by disreputable doctors, until finally he decided to attack the night by coming to terms with his sleeplessness and treating each night as an extra day. He went to work at night, and tried somehow or other to get through it in this way.

About ten years before, when he was Consul General in Houston, the snacks he would occasionally help himself to at night had begun to grow into complete meals, compiled from whatever happened to be in his large Whirlpool refrigerator. The gluttony that was king all around him had broken his fragile self-control and once he had started he knew he would never be able to stop again. He would put away entrees and desserts and entire TV-dinners; sitting in front of the television, which went on all through the night, he would demolish plate loads of food with a rapacious hunger. This kind of hunger had been born thousands of years before, when the first human being had walked the earth, when the words 'hunger' and 'fear' were one. In his bloated body he felt like the first man who had stood upright in the African savannah and, rising above the grass, was punished by the absence of God. Afraid of everything that was about to happen. Longing for a fulfilment he could not even conceive of.

Marian gave his hunger a name, along the lines of 'Parkinson's' or 'Alzheimer's'—she called it 'Hoffman's Hunger'.

As he stared unseeingly, without reading, at the page of Spinoza, the recollections fluttered away towards the depths of his memory. He had drunk half the bottle of vodka and he fingered his swollen stomach.

Outside the kitchen window the sky was growing lighter. The garden revealed itself, a magnificent lawn, stately trees, well-tended and well-bred.

He glanced at the marble kitchen table with the wilted left-overs of the night, and felt barely able to get up and go to the lavatory. With a concentrated effort he listened to the grumbling of the early birds, their melodic little songs heralding the sun.

Hands flat on the table, he levered himself out of his chair. Grasping the worktop, he wobbled across the kitchen to the hallway that gave onto the garden. But first he opened the door to the lavatory and sank to his knees.

The mere sight of the lavatory bowl set his stomach heaving. He did not even have to use his finger, his oesophagus began pumping immediately and the first acid wave of vomit shot into his throat, surged over his tongue and splattered onto the white bottom of the bowl.

He looked down at the seething, brownish-grey mash, and the peculiar smell that rose up from it, bitter and sour and disgusting and exciting all at once, set off a new wave. He writhed for a moment, shaken by the violent contortions of his digestive tract, and felt the mash shoot up, and again he vomited a nameless mix of lumps and chunks and bits into the bowl and a scintillating feeling of deliverance came over him. Another two waves exploded from his throat, two mouthfuls of sour mash, and he clung to the bowl as he gasped for breath in exhaustion and took pleasure from the release his stomach now enjoyed.

Struggling, he pulled himself to his feet. He tugged at the roll of toilet paper and wiped his mouth and his chin.

When he stepped into the garden, the sky, already a little brighter, was a lovely, deep, transparent blue. It was warm again, but there was fresh dew on the grass and the birds were joking with one another, and he embraced the trunk of a tree and longed for his children.

Chapter three

The morning of 23 June 1989

John Marks took his Buick out of the garage and reversed the gleaming automobile into the road. As he drove off he zapped the remote, looked in the rear-view mirror and watched the garage door close obediently.

The car glided gently towards the exit road that would take him out of Vienna to his office in Langley. He was not very tall and it seemed to him that this seat was lower than the one in his old car, although he knew that all the models were practically identical.

The Buick was brand new and smelled of fresh plastic. The dashboard had even more control knobs than there were in his old Buick, which he had driven trouble-free for six years and traded in two weeks before, straight after its costly repair job. The dealer had offered him an enormous discount, but that was not the reason for his new purchase. It had been as if the old car had been alienated from him by the repair: he had noticed oily fingerprints on the dashboard, which he could not get rid of even after lengthy polishing, and there was a lingering smell of the garage. The new Skylark, Bordeaux red, complete with fail-safe onboard computer, was less angular, and he now felt securely cocooned in the antiseptic plastic and new leather.

John Marks lived in a duplex in Vienna, Virginia, a small town within easy reach of Washington, D.C. that had been taken over by real estate developers. The extensive new housing developments were home to the legions of government officials that had fled the city, the capital of the most powerful country on earth having proved powerless to solve its drug problems.

Marks had moved to Vienna before the great wave of commuters had come out this way. After his divorce he had first rented a small apartment in Georgetown for a couple of years. Then in 1979 he had bought his present house, in one of the 'old' neighbourhoods of Vienna. His wife had returned to Milwaukee, where she had grown up. He could have stayed on in their old home, but he had preferred to make a fresh start. Lynn's attorney had demanded one half of what their house had fetched, and he had raised no objection, even though his own attorney had advised him not to agree to his ex-wife's ridiculous claims. But lawyers are always looking for something to wrangle over, and he had no appetite for a protracted legal battle about the division of their property.

He did not usually drive to Langley on a Friday. However, they had called him over the hot line, using a code which had made him hurry out to his garage. He was not used to travelling at this hour either, when the roads were jammed with commuters in their Japanese or European compacts.

Although he was employed full-time, his presence in Langley was not required for more than two days a week. On Mondays and Thursdays he left for work late and returned home late. After work he would sit in the canteen eating the sandwich he had brought with him from home, then go and have two or three beers out of his own glass in the company of a few other old hands in his favourite bar, and at about eleven o'clock drive back to Vienna. On the other weekdays he stayed in his attic at home, a large space he had rendered sound-proof and dust-proof. He had had the small round skylight taken out and replaced by an enormous window taking up almost the entire side of the roof. It afforded him a sweeping view over the hills and woods of this part of Virginia.

Three weeks earlier the whole neighbourhood had assembled in the public library after learning that the municipality had sold the nearest wood, one of the last in the district, to the real estate developer who, it turned out, happened to be building the new town hall. John had attended the meeting, the first time in his life he had done such a thing. Despite his aversion to large groups of people, their smells and their excited state, he had even got to his feet and suggested several countermoves.

He was experienced enough to mention his presence at this meeting in Langley, to avoid any misunderstanding about his sudden burst of activism. He was no activist, no Democrat, but he did want to go on enjoying his view.

Traffic had come to a complete halt on Chain Bridge Road as thousands of cars poured from the new housing developments onto roads not designed to take them. The developments and the houses were in place, but the infrastructure was lacking. Every so often he would move forward some thirty yards; there was a good chance he would not make the fifth-floor conference room by half past eight.

It was not the first time in his career that he had received the alarm code, and he sat relaxed now behind the wheel of the Buick with the composure of one who has seen it all before. He had had a telephone installed in the car, and with no other choice but to wait patiently for the traffic in front of him to reach the freeway, he felt safe in the knowledge that he could call them if it took too long.

He had woken up at precisely six o'clock, as always, had showered at length and breakfasted on a glass of pure mineral water and a bowl of natural yoghurt. Then he had gone up to the attic and looked in the first light of day at the latest results of his hobby. He was an electronics freak. He had studied engineering, and had joined the Company as a designer of electronic equipment. At the moment he was working on a noiseless amplifier capable of eliminating the flaws of compact discs, of which, in his view, there was an abundance. He much preferred listening to an ordinary LP than to a CD, which delivered everything with a sterile purity. He was now tinkering, just for his own amusement, with a small device that restored the human touch of the gramophone to the ones and zeros of the digital read-out. In theory his design ought to work—it was not unlike that of the DAT recorder—but it was taking all his spare time to come up with a practical solution to the underlying acoustic problems.

The code had indicated alarm in the SE-PC section, which suggested either that a defector had turned up or that the other side had picked up a member of the Company.

The letters PC meant the problem was in Poland or Czechoslovakia. Poland had been quiet recently, ever since Solidarity had seized de facto power. The elections three weeks before had swept the communists away. The agents in the field over there were only able to report that there was a power vacuum and that at the moment the country was making no significant contribution to the Warsaw Pact. The Polish secret service was in a state of crisis, reassessing whether NATO or the Soviet bloc was the main enemy. People were writing openly now about the murder of thousands of Polish officers at Katyn, and the country's mood was being kept under careful scrutiny because any possible Soviet intervention, as in Hungary in 1956 and Czechoslovakia in 1968—inconceivable at this moment according to Marks, though others in his section did not exclude provocation by hardliners—would lead to an armed clash with the highly motivated Polish military machine, which, after decades of servility, had regained its self-respect.

Marks' guess was that the crisis was in Czechoslovakia. Despite the fresh winds blowing through Poland and Hungary, the authorities in Prague had kept their windows tightly shut against *perestroika*. The old men who had toppled Dubcek in 1968 and had put him to work as a locksmith had grown up under Brezhnev and kept the party running along the old authoritarian lines, which Lenin had once graced with the name of 'democratic centralism'. They and their followers lived in exclusive districts with luxurious supermarkets where there were never any queues of freezing people, and their security services, in close collaboration with the KGB, made short shrift of any show of opposition.

As in every country calling itself communist, official morality was corrupt and pathologically conformist. The public lifestyle it encouraged was not unlike that typical of a small Midwestern town in 1949: austere and sober, with hidden poverty and clear class distinctions.

Marks was better placed than most to form a picture of the way of life of Politburo leaders in East European countries (PC was one of the sections of the SE division, which kept a close watch on the Soviet Union and Eastern Europe; the SE division itself was part of the co-ordinating DO directorate which planned and executed secret operations), and he was regularly presented with evidence of socialist profligacy. He was acquainted with the manner in which some members of his own Congress and Senate led their private lives, but that never—or rarely—happened at the expense of the average taxpayer. Communists had few problems in giving an account of their conduct, for they could always justify it by invoking Marxist ideology—the most accommodating religion invented to date.

Marks led a modest life. The new Buick signified a conspicuous escalation of his normal expenditure pattern (he was aware that he encountered this sort of idiom in official reports and that he had made it his own). Part of his income went to Lynn, as alimony. He invested the remainder in blue chip stock.

Lynn had moved into a new house in Milwaukee with her sister, who was also divorced. Marks was paying off the small mortgage. He did not want Lynn to have any financial worries. Jim, their older son, also slipped her regular sums of money, ensuring she lacked for nothing.

The last time he had seen Lynn had been at dinner the previous Christmas in Jim's brownstone in Georgetown. Jim was a doctor with a wife, Linda, two children, a dog, a Saab and a station wagon, and he took them all on regular excursions to see the wonders of American nature. John Marks' son enjoyed the pleasures of family life. John himself had turned his back on them.

His automobile had made little progress. He sat imprisoned in a sea of throbbing metal and glass. A man in the line next to him was talking heatedly and without stopping into a mobile phone; on the other side, in a little Japanese car, a young woman with a mass of blonde hair sat biting her nails with impatience; through his tinted windshield he could see the heavy figure of the man in front furiously picking his nose.

It had become second nature to him to suspect a covert scheme behind apparently arbitrary events—he himself did nothing else but hatch such schemes all day long—and he examined his neighbours carefully in search of signals that might spell danger.

If the traffic jam were to disperse suddenly right now, he would have just enough time to make the start of the conference. He shifted from side to side, seeking the most comfortable position, and remembered that he could adjust his seat electrically.

He found the switches on the armrest in the door, pulled a small lever towards him, and with a soft hum the seat crept backwards. Another button raised it. Now he was sitting properly. He took a tissue from the cardboard box on the passenger seat and wiped invisible particles of fluff from his fingers.

John Marks was a short man. Even so, women had never ignored him. Lynn was half a head taller, the fertile daughter of a hardy Quaker family from Minnesota. He had met her in the Company. She had been a secretary, working on documents with the lowest security rating.

Lynn had had many admirers in the Company. Later, during their divorce, when she had unburdened herself of all her other objections to him and was left with just this one, she flung at him that she could have had any number of real achievers, men who when they retired still made a million or two in business, or were asked for unspecified but highly-paid advice on security matters by rich Arabs or Japanese. She could have married intelligence agents with 'doctor' in front of their name (the Company certainly had those), or scions of old WASP families (there was a plethora of those as well), but no, she had to go and pick John Peter Marks of all people, and she wondered if she had been out of her mind all these years.

'But you've been happy as well, haven't you?' he said then. 'I have, anyway.'

'Yes,' she whispered, her eyes down, 'I've been happy....'

'That counts for something, doesn't it?' He mumbled the words, hoping she would not hear the catch in his voice.

'But it didn't last long enough,' she protested. 'It'd only just started.'

'Lynn, we've been married for close on twenty-five years, we've brought up two children, that's more than most people can say!'

'But I want more!' she cried. 'It's not all over yet for me. John, look at me, please....'

He looked at her.

'We still have such a long way to go, John, we still have so much to do together....'

He nodded and lowered his head.

'What's got into you?' he heard her say. 'What on earth's got into you?'

He could no longer live with Lynn. He could not tell her the reason, that staying with her would have been a betrayal. For the past five years he had been conducting a secret affair, and the woman whom he had come to love more than Lynn had not had the courage to leave her husband.

It was only when Marian had told him that everything was over between them that he had found himself able to leave Lynn. There was a strange logic to it all, one John could not easily have explained to anyone else, and he did not attempt to do so; he might perhaps have made it clear to Marian, but he never had the chance. In any case, his break with Lynn was inevitable, fated. He was no longer able to sleep at Lynn's side dreaming of another woman now beyond his reach.

It had taken an immense effort to speak to Lynn. She had not understood, which was not surprising, since he had omitted to tell her about the affair with Marian, the main chapter in the story of his life.

At the beginning of the seventies he had been regional controller in Tanzania and had met Marian there in one of the clubs frequented by foreigners. Marian was Dutch, not much younger than he was, and in the full flowering of her prime. At first he had only been interested in finding out if he could recruit her as an informer (her husband was a Dutch diplomat, and for reasons the Americans could never fathom the Dutch had contacts with all sorts of African freedom movements). He had not gone looking for it, nor had she. Yet their relationship had intensified and developed into the kind of friendship he had thought was confined to men. Whenever they could do so without causing a stir, they sought each other's company. And he made the disquieting discovery that they were each other's equal.

At the beginning he was not in love. He had merely found a complement to his life with Lynn. Their marriage had been whittled down to the education of their children, the kitchen and the garden, which would have been perfectly adequate had he wanted to live that sort of life, but he had a deep, unexpressed longing for someone capable of making the subtle moves of the game of chess he was playing for the Company. Lynn had been too down-to-earth for his abstractions.

Once they had started a family and Lynn had left the Company, she aspired after nothing more than safety and security for herself and the children. For years he had been able to provide this. However, in the world in which he daily immersed himself at the Company, safety and security were also so many means to an end. In his work nearly everything a man could devise was considered a justifiable means for obtaining vital information, although it was not possible to say what was vital and what was not. To him, trust, respect, safety and security were means of manipulation. Had he been able to talk all this over with Lynn, they might perhaps have been able to develop their own secrets—and he saw this as his life's destiny: the bonds of confidence he shared with others were only as strong as the secrets he shared with them. But he had not talked about it.

When he first slept with Marian in Tanzania, on the hard mattress in the guest room in his house, they had discovered, with the painful intensity felt only by people over forty, that they were made for each other, and they had cursed the cruelty of life that had kept them apart until then. Too many responsibilities, too full a past. Their love was *secret,* and that added to the strength of his feelings for her.

Even so, the duplicity of his marriage to Lynn began to wear him down. After five years Marian, too, could no longer justify their deception. She was incapable of leaving her husband. Her decision to stay with him had sprung from the same acceptance of fate as his decision to leave Lynn. He had lost Marian as a lover and as an informer, because for her they were one and the same thing. They had said goodbye in Rio de Janeiro one night in February 1977, just before the Carnival. The air in his small apartment had felt sticky to the touch, words had hung sluggishly in the room, their eyes sweated. From that night on he had never again touched a woman. On his return from Brazil he moved into the small apartment in Georgetown. The slow and painful process of divorce from Lynn began. He saw a psychiatrist for a few weeks and tried to explain to him how his life was ruled by fate. The psychiatrist, however, had been principally interested in John's youth in Philadelphia, even though that had been simple and carefree and offered no clue to John's conviction that he had used up life's allocation of love. All John could do was to treat Lynn with respect and to love *the other* in his memory.

He wallowed in memories, steeped himself in them, sometimes immersing himself for days on end in the weeks and months he had spent with Marian. He had not spoken to her since February 1977. He was unable to forget her. One year later the divorce from Lynn came through.

Becoming aware of movement next to him, he returned his attention to his car. Without hanging up, the man who had been shouting down his telephone had suddenly moved forward. Mechanically John accelerated too.

The Buick bounced slightly, then shot forward and John

realised too late that the line he was in was not moving. He slammed on the brakes but the car needed space to stop which was not there. The Buick's nose embedded itself in the back of the old Chevy in front of him.

A violent impact—he was able to cushion the blow easily because of his firm grip on the wheel, the seat belt doing the rest—the tinkling of glass, and it was over.

Adjusting himself to this new situation took only a moment. He and the driver of the Chevy stepped out together, and the two of them met over the dented metal. The man was a good head taller than John and had the broad figure of a bodybuilder in training.

'That wasn't very clever of you, bud,' said the heavyweight.

'You're right,' said John, only too aware of being at a disadvantage. 'I'll see that everything's paid for.' He was wondering if it really had been an accident.

'You bet you will…you better be insured.'

'Yes, of course, don't worry…'

'I got an appointment I can't afford to miss. Wonder what my lawyer will say if I don't make it,' the man observed, the threat of claims for damages hanging in the air.

'Why don't you just get going, then you'll be there on time. Here… ' John produced his papers, and it suddenly occurred to him that the man's fingerprints would be left all over them. 'Make a note of everything and my attorney will be in touch with yours. May I see your papers?'

Grudgingly, the man pulled out a wallet and handed over his driving licence. Marks held the laminated card between thumb and middle finger, touching as little of it as he could. The man's name was Fowles. John would have him investigated.

The damage was worse than he expected. His Buick needed new headlights, a new radiator grille and a new bumper, all smashed by the Chevy's trailer hitch, and the hood appeared to be buckled. He had not had an accident for twenty years, so this one had been coming. Anyhow it just made him a number in the statistics that claimed an average of one accident every so many thousand miles.

But it wasn't the cost he minded. It was the thought of the sleek metal, previously immaculate and unsullied, now abused and violated by a trailer hitch.

Meanwhile the other line of traffic was on the move, and in the distance impatient drivers were beginning to lean on their horns.

The man handed back his papers. John would have to clean them later.

'Maybe we better call the cops,' said the man, afraid of missing out on possible damages.

'I thought you were in a hurry,' said John.

'Yeah. But we still better get the cops,' the man insisted.

John lost patience. 'You're in a hurry, I'm in a hurry, I've shown you my papers and I assure you that I'll accept all the blame and that the damage to your vehicle will be made good.'

'Maybe, huh…maybe there's something wrong with your papers,' the man persevered.

'What?'

'You never can tell,' said the man.

'Mr Fowles, this automobile of yours is worth perhaps a thousand dollars. Even if it were brand new the damage wouldn't amount to more than five hundred, so you really have nothing to worry about.'

He should not have mentioned any figures, for the man shook his head firmly now.

'No, I want the cops.'

'Do me a favour, Mr Fowles, I really am in a hurry….'

'No. I'm not moving till the cops get here.'

People were getting out of the cars behind them.

'C'mon, move it!' someone shouted. 'Go pick a fight some-place else.'

The man turned his huge back on John, obviously intent on waiting.

John went and sat in the car and wiped his hands clean with a handful of tissues. With restrained distaste he anticipated a motor-cycle cop handling his papers with soiled leather gloves; he would not

be able to sterilise them until he was back in his office. Then he rang
the Company to report that he was going to miss the conference.

Chapter four

The night of 25 June 1989

Hoffman had now been sitting on the oak lavatory seat for ten minutes but to no effect. His trousers were round his ankles, revealing pale legs covered with grey hair. When he looked down between his thighs, he could see his tired member drooping into the white bowl, above the empty little pool which was the landing place for the rocks in his guts.

Sometimes it took a quarter of an hour to produce a couple of turds, sometimes he could do nothing at all to relieve the pressure in his bowels. But he knew that he had to sit on the lavatory every day giving his anus a good view of the little pool, because that daily ritual, so his doctor had told him, encouraged the peristalsis of the alimentary canal.

He strained and shut his eyes, but the congestion refused to budge and he slumped forward tiredly over his legs.

He had just fetched Spinoza's book from his study upstairs and had been on his way to the kitchen when a stomach cramp had sent him hurrying to the lavatory. The book now lay half hidden under his trousers.

Constipation was a form of impotence. His intestines had ceased to perform one of the most basic bodily functions—the elimination of toxic matter—and his stone-hard turds scraped and pummelled his gut, begging to be released. He had tried laxatives, as he had sleeping pills, and had forsworn them in the same way. Whenever he had taken the former, as either pills or potions, he had gone around for hours with gurgling insides and shooting pains in his stomach and groin, oppressed by a feeling of being in imminent danger of exploding. In the end he would suddenly lose control of his sphincter and be forced to rush to the nearest lavatory where he would eliminate a huge amount of putrid matter.

He would rather leave his body to its own rhythm, even though that was erratic and exhausting. At the moment of truth, once every four or five weeks, and after he had endured several days of violent cramps, a trail of pain shooting up his spine would signal that his anus was on the point of being torn open. He would then easily and naturally shit the bowl full. The cramps were plainly caused by some sort of turd-grinding process, because this monthly evacuation emptied him as if by diarrhoea. It was his own personal form of menstruation.

Marian had just knocked on the door to say good-night.

'Felix, I'm off to bed....'

'Sleep well,' he said. 'Is Jana going to bed too?'

'She's just gone.'

'Sleep well,' he repeated.

He thought she had left, but after a few seconds he heard her again.

'Are you having trouble?' she asked.

'Oh no, I'm just sitting here for the fun of it.'

She did not respond immediately.

'Good luck,' she said. Her footsteps receded.

'Hey, Marian,' he called, 'I didn't mean it like that...'

She made no reply. That had been five minutes before. From

the pipes he could tell that the lavatory had been flushed and a tap turned on upstairs in her bathroom—the faint sounds of a woman wiping the day from her face.

Jana, the Czech housekeeper who had served the last four ambassadors, lived during the week in two rooms on the second floor. At weekends she stayed with her brother, unless there was an official function at the residence. She was a woman of punctilious habit, about Hoffman's age. At the Embassy there were whispers that she had been working for the secret service for years and could understand Dutch. But the woman was unobtrusive and ran the household with Dutch efficiency, and if she earned a little pocket-money from the secret service, Hoffman had no quarrel with that.

He brought his attention back to the matter in hand, tensed his body and strained. His stomach bulged, he gritted his teeth, and his face contorted. The block in his bowels did not move. He could see stars when he opened his eyes, tiny white spots glittering on the edge of his retina. Panting, he gasped for air.

Jana had quickly grasped that the refrigerator had to be kept full *at all times*, because he ate even at night—especially at night. A woman of few words, she kept a scowling eye on him. He recognised something malignant in her, and from the first day, before they had more than a single verbal skirmish, a state of hostility had existed between them which he found wholly satisfactory.

He had disposed of his predecessor's legacy at his office in the chancellery (a few small paintings of Dutch scenes, a KLM calendar, some delftware, a clock in the form of a windmill), and had moved the furniture around. The Embassy was on Maltezske Namesti, a little square in the Mala Strana quarter, that part of Prague which was squeezed between the Castle on Hradcany Hill and the Vltava river. Mala Strana was a maze of alleys and lanes surrounding squares full of baroque and neo-Gothic churches and palaces, a paradise for painters of the picturesque.

The Embassy offices, the chancellery, were in the wing of the Nostitz Palace, built by Francesco Caratti in 1670 and extensively rebuilt a hundred years later.

The Embassy was on the second floor of the palace and consisted of not much more than a series of rooms off a single long corridor. The corridor stopped at the doors of an authentic private chapel, a small Catholic oratory with a conspicuously muscular figure of Christ, embellishments in gold leaf and lavish frescoes completed by Vaclav Ambroz in 1765.

Hoffman's office was next to the chapel, and had the dimensions of a ballroom. As you walked in, his desk was on the right-hand side, placed halfway down the room on an enormous plain burgundy-coloured carpet. The walls were panelled to a height of about three feet, and above that had been painted a soft greyish-green. The thick walls and high ceilings meant that the temperature inside remained bearable during the long hot summer. His office had more than enough room to spare for a man of his girth, and he had known immediately that he would feel at home in it. But as for work, there was little to do.

Today he had faced his first crisis. Three excitable young men from Dutch television had been filming a demonstration staged by a handful of dissidents on Vadavske Namesti, and the police had smashed their equipment and generally knocked them about.

Hoffman had sent his deputy.

The three worked for a current affairs programme and were well-known faces back home in Holland, or so his secretary had told him. The police had given them a good beating; one of them had even had his arm broken. It was part of Hoffman's job to report such incidents, and he had sent a coded message to The Hague. He expected the draft of an official protest note by the next morning, and would hand it to the Czech Minister of Foreign Affairs. His role was not much more than that of errand boy, sent on his way by invisible masters in a far-off country.

He had had trouble with journalists more than once before. Dutch journalists seemed to have a degree of effrontery that surpassed by far that of other nationalities. They would make a point of attending the funeral of a president dressed in torn jeans and filthy trainers, and seldom had he surprised any of them in full knowledge of their facts. He did not much care whether the police had been right or wrong in beating them up; what annoyed him was the journalists' presumption that they could call on the Embassy whenever it suited them and expect to be baled out.

Three years earlier, when he had been in Khartoum—he had left the place only six months before so that the present heat wave in Europe left him unmoved—the Ministry had appointed him to a commission charged with investigating the death of two Dutch journalists in Namibia. They had been murdered by a South African hit team, of that there was absolutely no doubt, and the commission had sent The Hague a report setting out the circumstances leading up to their death in meticulous detail.

The Ministry had, however, censored the report and had issued a version less critical of the journalists and thus less likely to rub the Dutch press up the wrong way. But the commission and the Ministry and some of the press knew that the two journalists, despite warnings that their lives were in danger, had deliberately set out to provoke a number of right-wing extremists. Hoffman had met one of the journalists once in Cairo, a born adventurer, a heavy drinker and avid womaniser, a young hothead who had spiced his drifter's lifestyle with a sprinkling of leftist thinking. In the event, even the watered-down report was accused of being slapdash and inaccurate and had been savaged by the Dutch press. Hoffman had had a bellyfull of leftist types who carried a Dutch passport and wanted the world re-ordered as they saw fit.

He sat leaning forward, his arms supported on his thighs. Sweat dripped from his chin onto his hands. His shirt hung loosely around his buttocks, and he had flung the tip of his tie over his shoulder to prevent it from falling into the space next to his circumcised member. He stared at his sad little elephant's trunk and at his balls in their shrivelled bags, and thought back glumly to the last time he had made use of an erection.

He had been the Temporary Charge d'Affaires in Khartoum, and the Ministry had organised a week's conference in Kenya for its African development experts. They had met in the Hilton in Nairobi and had ended their labours by going on a serious drinking bout. Their wives had been left behind and the whores had stood waiting in rows, glorious statuesque women with broad mouths and rolling hips.

Most of his colleagues had been drunk, although sober enough to step unescorted into the lifts that took them up to their rooms in the cylindrical building. Hoffman and another old hand, Jef Voeten, the number two in Rabat, had been the last survivors in the large room set aside for their conference, where the diplomatic gathering had dined heavily and at length, leaving behind a sea of empty bottles.

'Felix, old friend,' Jef had said in his Limburg accent, 'if I asked you what I'd like to be doing right now, what d'you think that would be?'

'Having a good fuck,' replied Hoffman, whose body was numbed by alcohol but whose mind was still working.

'My God, Felix,' exclaimed Voeten, 'you can see straight through me! But you got to admit your language is a bit crude.... What I'd say is...making love.... That's what I'd say, making physical love to a woman... '

'But you're drunk, Jef, you can't get it up any more.'

'Course I can get it up all right! Course I can! But you can't any more, Felix. If you ask me, you haven't been able to get it up for a long, long time.'

'I'm afraid I must disappoint you there, sonny-boy. I'm an expert fucker.'

'Bloody hell, Felix, watch your language...fucking's a bloody awful word.... Making love, okay? Come on, Felix, say making love, come on now....'

Jef had sagged forward onto the table and was trying to look at Felix. The drink had made him cross-eyed.

'Making love,' said Hoffman to keep the peace.

'That's right, making love,' Voeten repeated, and slumped back into his chair.

'Felix,' he said, 'I'd really like to know why you can't get it up any more. Because you can't.'

'Of course I can,' said Hoffman, surprising himself by being annoyed at this slur. 'Of course I can get it up,' he said. 'You're the one who can't, Jef Voeten.'

Voeten pushed himself up out of his chair and made a crude gesture with one hand. 'I can bloody well fuck 'em all silly,' he shouted thickly into the empty room. 'I can fuck 'em all out of their tiny minds. So there...'

He fell back into his chair with a satisfied air, as if action had matched his words. Fuddled, the two men sat staring silently in front of them.

'So prove it, why don't you?' Voeten said suddenly. He tried to focus his gaze on Felix.

'Prove it?'

'Yes, go on, go grab yourself a piece...'

Holding tightly onto each other, they made their way to the hotel bar. A dozen women immediately offered themselves for hire. Hoffman pointed to one who looked at him and leered suggestively.

'What do you want, boss?' she asked hoarsely in English.

'You,' he grinned back.

But the attendant stopped the small procession at the lifts.

'This woman is a prostitute,' he said, in a shocked voice that brooked no contradiction. 'The hotel does not allow prostitutes.'

Jef Voeten tried to mediate.

'Listen, sir,' he said, testing his English to the limit, 'we are investigating whether this gentleman' (he waved in the general direction of Hoffman, who was standing ramrod straight, arm in arm with the prostitute; it had not occurred to any of them that they should slip the attendant something) 'is able to raise his masculine organ. You understand?'

The attendant shook his head. 'No, I don't understand. Please take her out. She is not allowed in here....'

She took them home with her. She quoted them thirty dollars, plus twenty more for the use of her house. A rickety taxi carried them out of the town centre over a road full of potholes, and plunged into one of the suburbs.

The three of them sat side by side along the back seat of the

Peugeot 404. The woman had thrown a long dark arm across Hoffman's shoulders. Jef Voeten, talking past Hoffman, searched for the English to explain the purpose of their research to her.

'This gentleman says he's able to…Christ, Felix, d'you think "raise his organ" means hoisting a church organ in English?'

'How should I know?'

He was leaning against her soft and yielding shoulder. She smelled of cheap soap, a sweet scent that pleased him better than Chanel.

'He wants to investigate his ability to do his masculine act, you understand?' said Voeten.

'Yeah,' answered the woman, with a gift of understatement.

'Because, you know, at his age it becomes quite a problem to raise the organ, am I clear?'

'Completely,' she said.

'She thinks I'm talking about a church organ,' said Voeten gloomily.

The taxi stopped in a remote district. There were no more proper houses, they were far out in the countryside.

It was late at night, but people were still sitting about in the open. Lights on tall poles cast an orange glow over the huts. No asphalt or paving stones on the ground, just beaten earth. It smelled of goats and burnt wood.

'Pay the driver,' Hoffman said to Voeten. The woman helped them both out. Their arrival aroused no curiosity. Another European, sweaty-faced, eyes screwed up, stepped out from one of the huts.

'Would you believe it!' said Voeten. 'You know who that is?'

'Who?'

'Hey, Jim!' Jef shouted.

The man stopped. His skull gleamed under the orange light.

'Everything fine, Jim?' Jef called in English.

The man hurried over to the taxi, shoulders hunched.

'Bloody hell, what a coincidence, eh?' said Jef. 'That's Jim Manley. The British number two here.'

'What d'you mean, coincidence?' said Hoffman. 'This is a brothel.'

'Naaah, this isn't a brothel. What would we be doing in a brothel?'

The hut had a straw roof, clay walls, and two small rooms. The woman led Voeten to a chair and helped him into it.

'You, too?' she asked in English.

'What do you mean?'

'Do you want to fuck me too?'

'No.'

Hoffman had fallen onto the bed. Clean sheets.

'Hey, Felix…the English is "elevate". "Elevate the organ".'

She undressed. Hoffman needed no help. She revealed a supple body that shone in the soft light of the oil lamp. Her skin was a light brown and her black nipples were erect.

'Jesus…' he heard Jef Voeten mumble.

She climbed onto the bed and unbuttoned the waistcoat of his tailor-made suit. She ran her hand across his crotch, felt the rod in his trousers. She gave him an enigmatic smile.

'Give it to me, honey,' she said.

'Jesus,' said Voeten again, staring at her buttocks.

'What's your name?' she asked.

'Felix…'

'Feeelixx,' she repeated.

'And you?'

'Tawa…. But you can call me Lindaaa.'

'Tawa is fine,' said Hoffman.

'Jesus,' Voeten moaned again. Sitting astride Hoffman, the woman had bent forward, and Jef was looking straight at her anus.

'How old are you?' she asked.

'How old are you?' he asked.

'I'm twenty-four,' she said. 'Today is my birthday.'

She unbuttoned his jacket. Made by Gieves & Hawkes, 1 Savile Row, London.

Hoffman asked, 'What's the date?'

'The date,' Tawa said with a laugh. 'Who cares?'

'What's the date today, Jef?'

'What the hell's that got to do with anything?'

'The date!' bellowed Hoffman.

'The fifth! Satisfied?'

'The fifth of September is always my lucky day,' said Tawa.

Hoffman felt his erection shrink. Tawa felt it as well.

'Something wrong?' she asked.

'Nothing,' he said.

He sat up, she moved to one side.

'What are you doing?' asked Voeten.

'We're going back,' said Hoffman.

'Back? We're not going back.'

For a moment Hoffman lost his temper.

'Did you really think I'd put on a performance in front of you, Jef?'

He walked to the door of the little hut. 'Pay her....'

He went outside. Thousands of stars stared down at him. He was ashamed: he had almost forgotten the anniversary of Esther's death. It was well past midnight, the sixth of September had already begun. A group of men sitting further up around a fire, big bottles of beer in their hands, glanced across at him expectantly. He raised a hand in salutation. No one responded.

'Bastards,' he muttered.

Behind him, shrieks could be heard. Jef Voeten appeared in the doorway of the hut. Tawa thrust him to one side and turned to Hoffman. She had wrapped herself in a sheet.

'You must pay me,' she said threateningly in English.

'Don't do it, Felix. We haven't had anything.'

'You owe me,' she said.

Felix handed over the sum they had agreed.

'Not enough.'

'It's enough.'

'It's enough,' Voeten echoed.

'Come,' she said, beckoning Hoffman.

'I'd better talk it over with her,' he said to Voeten.

He followed her back into the hut. She closed the door behind him and dropped the sheet.

'Why don't you fuck me?' she asked. She stroked her ravishing body.

'I can't,' he replied.

'Why not? Don't you think I'm beautiful?'

'You're terrific. But I can't.'

'You insult me. Don't you like to fuck black women?'

'I like black women. As much as white women.'

'You despise me. Just like your friend.'

'No, I don't. But I can't fuck you.'

She bent down quickly and took a knife out of a box.

'I want you to pay me more.'

Hoffman shook his head firmly. 'We agreed on fifty.'

She came closer, threatening him with the knife.

'You have to pay me more.'

'Why should I?' he asked.

'Because you insult me.'

She lunged at him with the knife and he fended her off. Suddenly the sleeve of his jacket had a tear, and blood was seeping through it. He knew now she was serious. But he was not the man to give in. He took hold of the oil-lamp.

'Tawa—Linda—calm down and get out of my way.'

'Pay me,' she said. 'It makes no difference to you. You are rich. But for me....'

She was right, of course. But Hoffman could not allow himself to be intimidated.

Again she brandished the knife. Hoffman stepped awkwardly out of the way and the bottles of wine he had drunk sloshed about in his stomach. He stumbled, lost his balance and the oil-lamp slipped out of his hand.

There was a rising sucking sound, like a wind blowing through the hut, and suddenly flames leapt from the bed and licked the walls.

Hoffman, lying on the floor, heard Tawa scream. The bright yellow flames were splendid to behold.

The men dragged him from the hut. The next day, when he was about to leave the Hilton, he was arrested. The local authorities made it clear that in such circumstances money could do a power of good. He paid the chief of police a thousand dollars, two inspectors a hundred dollars each, sixteen police officers ten dollars each, and he gave Tawa three thousand dollars to build a new hut, even though it would cost no more than a few hundred.

Back in Khartoum he found himself at the end of a telephone line, talking to an uncomfortable Minister of Foreign Affairs. Hoffman's arm was in a sling and he had been given tetanus injections.

'I heard about your…er…predicament in Nairobi, Mr Hoffman.'

'Yes….' What could he say? 'We were taking a look at an outer suburb with a view to possible development projects.'

'I see,' said the Minister.

'A lack of communications. Won't happen again, sir,' he said.

'I hope you are entirely persuaded of that, now that you are nearing the end of your career,' said the Minister.

'Absolutely, sir.'

For a moment Hoffman, ensconced on the lavatory, felt his member rise at the memory of Tawa, but a new stab of pain in his guts made the thing shrink back to its normal sad condition.

Wim Scheffers, the Permanent Secretary of State at the Foreign Ministry, had backed him up. His skin saved, Hoffman's automatic promotion had been only a matter of time, thanks to his seniority. He took no more risks, was careful with his drinking in public, kept his distance from women.

Upstairs things had grown quiet. He imagined Marian lying in bed with an obscure anthology of Vondel sonnets, making notes until her eyes fell shut. He had no idea where she found the composure, the sang-froid, to go to sleep. Even while she was still a student she had been able to lose herself in Vondel, years before she had begun to see the elegies on his dead children and his conversion to Catholicism in a different light.

Vondel had been a hosier, the son of an Anabaptist immigrant from Antwerp, and had lived a life beset with personal tragedies. In retrospect, Hoffman could appreciate Marian's passion for him; there was something supernatural about her early obsession, as if she had had some sort of presentiment.

He was in the family lavatory, the one next to the kitchen. There was another lavatory off the entrance hall, an elegant affair with a marble floor. The heat had stirred the stench up from the sewers; the small closet in which he now sat was filled with an acrid smell of putrefaction. The old calendar filled in by Miriam hung on the wall, a batch of well-thumbed sheets. She had bought the calendar when they had made a trip to Italy, in 1976. Miriam had been sixteen. They had been living in Rio de Janeiro at the time, but because Miriam kept out of the sun she never looked healthy.

During the trip she had worn her hair long in a ponytail and walked about in cheap little shoes, purple espadrilles. She had doted on those shoes. He remembered that she had gone on wearing them well into the Brazilian spring. He could see her before him now: a thin girl in a white summer dress, whose pale skin had slowly bronzed during their trip. One evening they had gone to the Circo Grande in Verona, a string of circus and *commedia dell'arte* acts. The clowns had popped up all over the stands, mimicking frenzied scenes from Italian family life which always ended in chaos, and he had watched his daughter's eyes light up with pleasure. After the show they had bought a calendar with reproductions of circus posters and it was that calendar which now hung beside him on the wall.

At first Esther's death had not affected Miriam's school results. She went to the International School in Lima and her marks were the best in her class. She was taught, she read, and she was silent. He made desperate and forced attempts to re-establish their old closeness, but that closeness had been the gift of a blind God, who had turned out to be deaf into the bargain. A child psychiatrist explained that Miriam had shouldered the blame for her little sister's death;

the rivalry between them had led to a repressed death wish, which had now been granted. Miriam felt that she had been responsible for Esther's death and that she was evil.

Sometimes he would call her into the kitchen (he thought that what he had to say would sound less formal in the kitchen), but when she was sitting on a stool in front of him staring at her nails he would forget what he had wanted to say.

They went for walks and made a trip to Ayacucho, but all three of them could only think of the fourth. They went on holiday to Panama by packet boat, but Miriam was as impassive as an autistic child. They visited Surinam, but she refused to leave the circular pool at the Hotel Torarica, swimming thousands of laps.

She became thin as a rake. He found it hard to speak to Marian about it; in whispers they blamed each other for having to bring up a lonely child. He fled from his impotence and took shelter in his office.

The Italian trip had been an idea born of desperation. One day in Rio Miriam failed to come home from school. Marian rang him at about six o'clock: Miriam had still not come back.

For two days Hoffman had criss-crossed the city. Driven by hellish fantasies he had braved the dangerous *favelas,* recruiting informants with dollar bills. The police were not interested in runaway fifteen-year-olds and he finished up with the vice squad. He promised the chief a fortune if he found his daughter. His heart wrung, he searched doorways and building sites at night, children with grimy hands and lost eyes offering him their favours. He searched for her on the steps of the Candelaria church, on the beaches of Leme and Ipanema, under the statue of Christ on the Corcovado. He convinced himself that the worst had happened, but no drowned girl was found on the beaches, and the Rio mortuaries held no body fitting her description.

He was on his feet for two days without a break. Two or three times he returned home to wash off the stink of the streets. Forty-eight hours after her disappearance he came out of the bathroom, hair wet, fighting exhaustion, hastily buttoning a shirt to go down into the city once more, when a silent and filthy Miriam walked into the flat and went to her room without sparing her parents a glance.

She locked her door and refused to open it even though he yelled himself hoarse; he kicked the door out of its frame, splinters flying past his ears, and his mouth exploded in fury at the back of the girl who lay curled up on her bed under posters of pop stars and film stars, her head hidden under a pillow.

When his rage subsided he went to his study and slumped back into a chair with shaking knees, stricken by the realisation that she had already been buried in his mind.

A few days later he had made a suggestion to her.

'Miriam, listen...what would you say if you and I, just the two of us, this summer, the European summer I mean...if you and I went on a trip to Italy?'

She did not bolt, shrugged her shoulders slightly. He had discussed it with Marian and Marian had agreed, even though he could give her no good reason for the plan. The next day he found a note from Miriam on his desk: 'Daddy, I'm glad we're going on holiday together.'

She scarcely spoke in Italy either. She sat beside him in the hire car in silence and climbed the Spanish Steps without a word. But her silence now implied something different. Her hungry gaze took in everything around her. She was wordless because of the impressions overwhelming her; she had no breath to spare for conversation. And then, after the buying of the calendar, she had taken his hand for the first time in years and squeezed it gently.

After the Italian trip she took lessons with a private tutor, Roberto da Silva. Hoffman had been given his name by an agency that supplied au pairs and governesses and similar staff. Miriam brightened. She became more sociable, would offer her opinion and even make jokes. Her vivaciousness communicated itself to her parents, and the mood at home regained some of its old sparkle.

Then one morning she said, 'I'm in love with Mr da Silva. We are having an affair. I am going to marry him.'

Hoffman and Marian exchanged a look and she held him in check with her eyes.

'Do you know how old Mr da Silva is?' asked Hoffman's diplomatic wife.

'What's that got to do with anything?' said Miriam, to avoid answering the question.

'Forty-two,' Hoffman replied.

'Please keep out of it, Fee, okay?' urged Marian.

He left the kitchen and went to his office. For a whole week he kept calm, until he encountered the tutor sitting with Miriam at the dining-room table, the two of them immersed in the French language and the love of Madame Bovary. Hoffman did not normally come home so early, but he had overheard that morning that Miriam would be having a lesson a few hours later.

Da Silva, short and dark, with romantic eyes and greying temples, leapt to his feet when Hoffman walked in.

'M'sieur 'Offman,' he said, '*J'aime Miriam. Elle m'aime. Nous voulons nous marier.*'

'You keep your paws off my daughter,' Hoffman said in his best Portuguese, and gave da Silva the sack.

They sent her to a school in Switzerland, a boarding-school for problem children, under the supervision of psychologists, a last resort for the all but irreclaimable offspring of well-to-do parents.

For days on end she had done nothing there but plait her hair.

He bought her a school-leaving certificate for eighty thousand Swiss francs. That was her admission ticket to a Dutch university. She opted for a degree course in psychology.

The prospect of her imminent independence gave her a new lease of life. She became more talkative and even started to ring them up regularly. Later he discovered that she had started to take heroin the moment she reached Amsterdam. She had smoked it, like the Surinamese, 'chasing the dragon' it was called, but it had not been long before she was injecting. When she was stopped in the Bijenkorf department store with a leather jacket hidden in her bag, she telephoned them from the police station. Once again he flew to Holland laden with a feeling of impending doom. He was the champion at Flying to a Disaster.

When they met, she called him 'Mr Hoffman'. She never called him 'Daddy' again. She stopped going to lectures, did not pay her rent and was thrown out of her rooms. For months at a time sometimes they did not know where she was. She drifted through Amsterdam, sleeping in squats or in doorways. Hoffman owned a solidly-built wooden summer house in the Vught woods, south of Den Bosch, and she took refuge there every time she solemnly swore to kick her habit. Piece by piece she sold the antique furniture from the house to pay for that one last little shot before definitely going cold turkey.

On 8 September 1984 she was found in a hostel on Warmoesstraat, the Pension Brooklyn, dressed in purple trousers and a purple sweater. An overdose, the police report stated, an accident with a cocktail that had overtaxed her exhausted heart. Hoffman knew it was no accident.

Two weeks before her death she had slept in the summer house for a few days. With her parents away in Khartoum, where he was posted at the time, Miriam had systematically cut her likeness out of all the family photographs Hoffman had stuck into albums over the course of the years. She had also burned his films, the films of the twins in the playpen and on the beach, the films of the twins in Marian's arms and with Grandpa and Granny Coenen, the films of them on their first bicycles and at birthday parties with party hats and paper chains and the two cakes saying Happy Whichever-It-Was Birthday and the films of blowing out the candles and the films with the wobbly pictures that Marian had taken, on which he himself could be seen looking grave—grave because of the debt of gratitude he owed life.

He lifted up the calendar pages and looked at September, where Miriam had marked Esther's death with a cross. If they should recall him for consultations—a euphemism to indicate the anger in The Hague about what had been done here in Prague to those good, upright Dutch journalists—he would be able to visit her grave.

For the last two nights he had lacked the heart to plough through Spinoza again. There was little work to do; he would have liked to have felt tired. He had read the papers, the *Herald Tribune,* the *Süddeutsche Zeitung,* and a thin German-language sheet published here in Prague which was full of reports of record harvests and sensational steel output figures. He had been keeping a tight hold on himself when it came to nocturnal snacks, and he now felt clearheaded enough for further improvements to his understanding. The book lay waiting patiently on the lavatory floor for him to perform.

The advantage of this post was its closeness to Munich and Vienna. Except for Budapest, the remaining East European capitals lay far from any frontier with the West, which made it difficult to escape from the petty restrictions of communist life.

He had always loathed communism, while his father the banker, curiously enough, had held communist sympathies. You could do that before the war, it seemed, when the intelligentsia had felt drawn to the Utopian content of the doctrine of Marx and Engels. His parents had secretly helped to finance the Dutch communist party, and had now and then even given a dinner for its leaders, who were smuggled into the house after dark through the back door. When he had applied to join the Foreign Service 'nursery', his fear had been that his parents' communist sympathies might have been put on file by the pre-war Dutch secret service, which would undoubtedly have led to his rejection, but the subject was never raised.

Hoffman suspected that it had been his mother in particular who had championed the socialist ideal. Her father, Jacov Kaplan, had been a Jewish refugee from Russia, a trade unionist who had been arrested but who had managed to escape from a transport.

Jacov Kaplan had roamed all over Europe, becoming a diamond cutter at Asscher's in the end and marrying a poor girl from the Amsterdam Jewish quarter. All their children had been stillborn except Esther, Hoffman's mother.

His father's family had a respectable German background. His paternal grandfather, Aaron Hoffman, had worked his way up in a Jewish department store in Germany and in 1901 was sent to Amsterdam to investigate the prospects of opening a Dutch branch. He had married Hadassah Lopez Diaz, the daughter of a Portuguese-Jewish banker. They had one son, Mozes Hoffman, Felix's father, who after finishing his studies had gone to work in his maternal grandfather's bank.

Mozes Hoffman and Esther Kaplan had met at Heck's in Rembrandtplein, a huge establishment of American-style dimensions where the big bands came to play and where you could spend the whole evening at a *diner dansant*. It was the time of the Charleston and of the first knee-length skirts and of girls with cropped hair.

Mozes was marrying far beneath him, but his parents eventually relented and the marriage under the *chupah* was celebrated in 1928. Two years later a son was born, their only child; they called him Felix, the fortunate, and Aaron after his grandfather.

Mozes, Esther and Felix moved to Den Bosch, where Mozes Hoffman ran the South Netherlands branch of the bank.

Hoffman remembered his grandparents. He and his parents had paid regular visits both to the ultra-modern house overlooking Sarphatipark that belonged to Grandpa and Grandma Hoffman, and to the modest apartment of Grandpa and Grandma Kaplan in Tolstraat. Judaism had long ceased to play any part in his father's parents' life; they were assimilated, they were friends of Mengelberg and Rietveld, they collected art and supported the young painters of the De Stijl group. His socialist maternal grandparents, by contrast, had continued to live as Jews, kept a strictly kosher kitchen and admired Maurits Dekker and Jef Last. Hoffman had no memories of the Depression. He assumed they must have gone through it remarkably unscathed; if anything, he thought, it had rekindled his parents' socialist sympathies. He remembered a heated discussion at home between big men with fat stomachs sitting at a long table with a white cloth. They were communists.

The conservative Catholic circles who governed Brabant would have denounced such gatherings as subversive and Felix knew that he must not speak about them. His parents had faith in the Soviet Union and in Stalin; with tears in their eyes they explained away the Molotov-Von Ribbentrop pact with the lies the party had fed them, and the last time he saw them, just before he was collected to be taken into hiding at a safe house, they were still blindly clinging to the belief that communism would vanquish barbarism within a few months. But barbarism was to sweep everything away to which they had been heir.

Czech communists had beaten up three representatives of the Dutch press and Hoffman had to go and convey his concern, in the name of the Dutch government, at the way their citizens had been treated by the Czechs. It was fortunate indeed that his parents did not have to witness what went on in the Eastern bloc.

How long had he been on the lavatory now? Half an hour? He wiped the sweat from his face with a corner of his shirt.

He bent forward and saw the Spinoza lying on the floor. He had looked up the entry for 'Spinoza' in the Embassy encyclopaedia. Baruch meant 'blessed', and he had been the son of a Spanish Jew who had come to the Netherlands with his parents as a child. Baruch, born in 1634, had been sent to a Jewish school, had learned Hebrew and had later been taught by Franciscus van den Enden, a teacher at the famous Latin School in Amsterdam, run by free thinkers.

Spinoza had quickly gained renown as a philosopher and in 1656 had been excommunicated by the Sephardic Synagogue for refusing to recant—in the eyes of his co-religionists he had committed the twin sins of atheism and pantheism—and to observe the Mosaic Law. He had moved first to Rijnsburg, then in 1663 to Voorburg and six years later to The Hague, earning his living by giving private lessons and by grinding and polishing lenses. Later—and Hoffman thought this a remarkable detail—he was suspected by the 'rabble' of being in league with the French enemy.

In 1672—the famous *annus terribilis*—the French had marched into the Republic with one hundred and twenty thousand men and Holland had taken refuge behind the *Waterlinie*, her artificially flooded defence line. Spinoza had then made a mysterious journey to Utrecht, where the French had set up their headquarters, and when he returned to The Hague his house was besieged by a large crowd accusing him of being a French spy. A year earlier the De Witt brothers had been torn to pieces by the mob, but Spinoza was left unharmed. The object of his journey to Utrecht was never disclosed; it is believed, however, that he had gone as an intermediary on behalf of the 'Great' in The Hague, and that he had discussed a peace treaty with the French. He died of tuberculosis on 21 February 1677 and was buried in the Nieuwe Kerk, on the Spui in The Hague.

Spinoza had lived in Amsterdam during Vondel's century. Vondel was already an adult when Spinoza was born, and an old man when Spinoza died. Hoffman wondered whether the two had ever met.

Spinoza's *Treatise* was the only reading matter he had with him that night, and he reached for the book, which took some doing in view of the size of his stomach, and opened it at the page whose corner he had turned down.

Spinoza had already given him three rules to live by and had now gone on to a section entitled 'On the Four Modes of Perception', a heading that meant nothing to Hoffman.

He leant his elbows on his knees and began to read:

> With these rules laid down, I may now direct my attention to what is the most important of all, namely to the correction of the understanding and the means of rendering it capable of understanding things in such a way as is necessary to the attainment of our end.

This was the kind of language Hoffman could appreciate: going straight for one's goal. He read on and realised that Spinoza was about to explain how one might gain experience and learn from life.

Spinoza began with the understanding or perception one might gain by hearsay, such as one's birthday, or that certain people were one's parents. We learnt that sort of thing by simply listening and looking; it did not take much understanding and every child had that sort of perception.

The second kind of perception was gained by what Spinoza

called 'vague experience'. One witnesses something, for instance, water dousing a flame, and one's conclusion is that water is good for extinguishing fire. Among vague perceptions Spinoza included 'nearly all things that are useful in life'; it followed that the scientific explanation of the phenomenon 'water extinguishes fire' did not fall under this heading. Thirdly: 'Perception is that wherein the essence of one thing is concluded from the essence of another, but not adequately.'

Hoffman's understanding of this was as follows: say you were on a motorway that normally allowed you to travel at speed, but today you were held up in a traffic jam. That meant there had been an accident or that there were roadworks ahead. This third form of perception was based on *reasoning*. What you actually perceived was no more than a long queue of cars, that is, the effect of some incident, and you *guessed* at the cause by reflecting upon the essence of the traffic jam and the incidents that could have given rise to it.

Spinoza was somewhat cryptic about the fourth type of perception: 'Finally, perception is that wherein a thing is perceived through its essence alone or through a knowledge of its proximate cause.'

Spinoza added: 'But the things which I have been able to know by this knowledge so far have been very few.' Fortunately, he gave an illustration, or else Hoffman would have had the greatest difficulty in following him.

The illustration was mathematical: three numbers are given, and one seeks a fourth which is to the third as the second is to the first.

Spinoza pointed out with ill-disguised contempt that 'tradesmen' will say that they had learned the solution of this problem not long before 'without proof from their teachers'. He was plainly referring to the first form of perception, because these 'tradesmen' had learned how to solve the problem by hearsay alone.

The answer to the problem 2:4 = 3:? can be found by multiplying the second term by the third and dividing the product by the first term.

'Others again, from experimenting with small numbers, arrived at the general principle,' Spinoza added. He was probably using this as an additional example of the second form of perception, and he then went on directly to the third, still using the numerical example:

> But mathematicians, by conviction of the proof of Prop. 19, Bk. 7, *Elements* of Euclid, know what numbers are proportionals from the nature and property of proportion, namely, that the first and fourth multiplied together are equal to the product of the second and third.

Mathematicians thus had greater insight into the mathematical problem because they had specialist knowledge, and, unlike tradesmen, did not content themselves with simply parroting the rule providing the solution. Mathematicians had studied the problem in depth and had thus gained true understanding.

Hoffman realised, however, that by the final or fourth form of perception Spinoza was alluding to 'intuitive' understanding, based on training and experience. If someone could 'see' the solution to a mathematical problem without having to work on it, then he was perceiving a thing 'through its essence alone or through a knowledge of its proximate cause'. This was not a simple concept, but Hoffman felt that he now had an inkling of what it meant.

Hoffman saw it coming and Spinoza did not disappoint him: he went on to compare the four modes of perception with one another, and concluded as follows:

> 1. Knowledge based on hearsay was very uncertain.

> 2. The second mode of knowledge, acquired through 'vague perception', is dependent on chance and merely conveys a picture of the outward appearances, for instance the knowledge that water could extinguish fire.

> 3. He went into greater detail with the third mode of

perception. He admitted that it helped us to 'obtain an idea of the thing and conclude it without any danger of error; but nevertheless it is not a means in itself whereby we may acquire our perfection.'

4. 'The fourth mode alone comprehends the adequate essence of the thing, and that without any danger of error.'

Hoffman allowed it all to sink in. By the fourth mode, Spinoza was referring to an *intuitive* form of perception or knowledge, something that was beyond all reasoning, a kind of soul of the understanding, a manner of knowing which was both logical and also inexplicable.

He wondered if he could relate all these ideas to himself, if Esther's last words might not have expressed the fourth mode. 'I know,' she had whispered. Had Spinoza meant something like that or was the understanding he had sought more worldly and more concrete?

His breath caught in his throat. In the eyes of his eight-year-old daughter, suspended between life and death, he had seen the startling lustre of goodness and of perfect peace. With her body, his own sleep had also died, and not only that: he had lost the sense of goodness and wisdom, as if Esther had taken everything with her in the small coffin he had witnessed disappear into the earth.

Doubling up and dropping the book, he bent forward in agony over his legs. He could feel something heavy and solid shifting downwards and forcing his anus open. It was excruciatingly painful, but in an attempt to help his intestines he began to strain, and then the miracle came to pass.

A turd of majestic proportions tore at his arse and suddenly slid smoothly into the lavatory bowl. Hoffman felt a shudder of pain and pleasure. He clenched his fists and gritted his teeth to help him bear the sensation. He clutched at the wall, gasping for breath. Opening his eyes, he stared at the bare light bulb on the ceiling until spots danced across his retina and a sense of deliverance rippled through his body, a physical gratification which numbed his brain for several seconds.

He glanced into the bowl at the long thick turd, massive and fearsome-looking, streaked with blood from the capillary vessels that had burst along its way. A first-class production.

He pulled at the toilet roll and grasped a handful of paper. This was a cause for celebration, he decided. The refrigerator was full to overflowing.

Chapter five

Freddy Mancini was taken somewhere not far from Washington, D.C. in an armoured delivery truck, a Chrysler Voyager. He had been flown into Dulles Airport on an army plane, accompanied by an Embassy official, and now he clambered out of the Chrysler into the grounds of an isolated country house hidden away among tall beeches and pines. Bobby had stayed behind in Rome.

The man from Rome—he had forgotten his name, they had barely exchanged a word all those hours—gave him a helping hand over the gap between the vehicle and the ground. Freddy planted both feet on the gravel, then, watching his step, began walking towards the front of the house. He was back again on American soil and you could keep Europe as far as he was concerned.

The pebbles crunched under his three hundred and fifty pounds. The quiet sounds of the countryside, the sighing of the wind in the leaves, the singing of birds, were balm to his ear.

An older man stood waiting for him in the doorway of the

wooden building, a classic porticoed Southern mansion. The man's face creased into a smile.

'Mr Mancini? Welcome, I'm John Marks.'

With a soft grunt Freddy held out his hand. The man shook it briefly, then quickly put his hands behind his back.

'Good journey?' he asked.

'Fine,' said Freddy.

Marks gestured him inside.

'I'll lead the way.'

The living room contained a large dining table of gleaming dark wood surrounded by chairs with seats in a soft green, as well as a spacious sitting area with two generous sofas and four armchairs. There were lamps all over the room and a colourful abstract painting on every wall. But what really caught Freddy's attention was a piece of electronic equipment bristling with cables, and a tape recorder with big reels.

'Here, take a seat,' said Marks.

He moved a dining chair towards him. As Freddy sat down he noticed that it was wider than the rest of the chairs around the table, and he gratefully acknowledged the other man's attention to detail.

'I expect you're hungry,' said Marks, wiping his hands with some paper tissues.

A woman of Marks' age appeared, well-groomed, with bleached hair and forgiving eyes. She was wearing an apron and carried a tray. She smiled at Freddy as if he were a prodigal son just returned.

'Now, Mr Mancini, I've made something real nice for you, I'm sure you're ready for it.'

She slid the tray in front of his stomach. On a table mat was a plate with a heaped helping of turkey, cranberry sauce, mashed potato and pumpkin. This was Freddy's favourite meal, and he wondered how they had found out that he was crazy about the traditional Thanksgiving dinner. Perhaps they had telephoned Bobby in Rome to ask what he liked.

'That looks just perfect, ma'am,' he said.

'Carolyn,' she said.

'I'm going to enjoy this, Carolyn. And I'm Freddy.'

'There's more where that came from, Freddy,' she said, leaving the room. 'You just let me know!'

Marks, who had sat down opposite him, tapped a cigarette out of a pack. He was short and could almost have been a boy as he sat there on his chair. Marks should have ordered a special chair for himself too, Freddy thought. With a higher seat.

'Carry on,' said Marks. 'Do you mind if I smoke?'

'Not at all.'

Freddy unrolled his napkin and removed the cutlery from it. He began to relax.

'I regret we had to intrude upon your private life so abruptly, Mr Mancini. Unfortunately, the interests of our country have to come before our own. Again, my regrets, but without such measures we should have lost our freedom long ago, paradoxical though that may sound.'

Freddy nodded.

'Don't let me keep you from your lunch,' said Marks. 'I'll talk while you're eating'

Freddy nodded again, this time gratefully. He jabbed his fork into the turkey and could tell immediately that it had been cooked by an expert. A roast turkey is served at least once a year in every American home, and ninety-nine out of a hundred of all those turkeys turn out too dry. Timing was the secret when it came to roasting a turkey, and a minute too long could prove a disaster. But the meat Freddy was eating here was firm and juicy and would bear glowing comparison with any Thanksgiving bird.

'Carolyn is our best cook,' said Marks, noting Freddy's appreciation. 'We wanted you to enjoy yourself.'

'That's real thoughtful of you.'

'You're still on Italian time—six hours' difference, I think—so we won't make this first session too long. There's a room for you upstairs, you should find everything you need, clothes, pyjamas, shaving things. The staff here are at your service, and Carolyn will be in the kitchen twenty-four hours a day in case you need her. Your wish is our command.'

Swallowing a mouthful of turkey, Freddy nodded. He might have landed in clover here, but he could not get rid of the feeling that this house was some sort of prison.

'How long is all this going to take?' he asked, through another bite. He could talk with his mouth full.

'You'll have to allow for a day or two.'

'A day or two…' repeated Freddy. It actually made little difference to him. He couldn't care less about Rome. All that racket and the stench. 'Can I use the telephone and that sort of thing?'

'Of course,' Marks said, as if surprised at Freddy's naïvety. 'But you'll have to ask Robert MacLaughlin first. He works with me, you'll be meeting him soon.'

Freddy went on eating. Marks watched him. Freddy thought he could detect a trace of disapproval in Marks' eyes, a flicker of repressed disgust.

'Our colleagues in Rome have probably done this already, but it goes without saying that I'd like to thank you once again in the name of the government of the United States. We greatly appreciate your readiness to do your duty as a citizen. It will not be forgotten.'

Freddy tried to shrug his shoulders nonchalantly, as if nothing could have been more natural for him than to report to the Embassy in Rome. In fact, it had been a row with Bobby that had driven him to do his patriotic duty. Otherwise he might be somewhere on the Forum right now, standing sweating beside some ruin or other.

'I'm going to have to ask you to sign a declaration in a moment. It's only a formality, but we can't proceed without it. It's to the effect that you will disclose nothing about what is said between us to anyone outside these four walls. Not even to your wife, your best friend, or your children. That goes for your visit to the Embassy in Rome as well. And of course for what happened in Prague.'

'But Bobby, I mean my wife, she knows about my going to the Embassy and she knows I'm here now, doesn't she?'

'Your wife has signed the declaration as well.'

He nodded. Took another bite.

'You are in a safe house here, Mr Mancini. We use them whenever we want to have a quiet chat with someone without being disturbed by all the toing and froing you get in an office, and without all the inconvenience that goes with staying in a hotel. We only do this of course if we're dealing with a valuable contact. We look on you as one of those.'

Smiling, Freddy pulled a face and shook his head. He spoke with his mouth full.

'I told your people in Rome twice over that I still don't understand why you're so interested in what I saw.'

'Did you ask them?'

'They wouldn't talk about it.'

'But you were still prepared to come over here.'

'You paid for the ticket.'

Marks smiled.

'You were a witness to a kidnapping.'

'It looked like one, sure.'

'Everything I am about to tell you, Mr Mancini, is classified information. You will be putting your signature to that in a moment. To be plain: you have no option. You really didn't have one from the moment you stepped over the threshold here.'

'No problem. I'll sign.'

'The man you saw on the night of 21 June was Michael Browning?'

'That's the name he gave us, yes.'

'Michael Browning was working for us. He was there on an assignment. Since that night we have heard nothing more from him. We are concerned for his safety.'

'I worked that out for myself,' said Freddy.

There was an air of sadness about Marks, Freddy now saw, the look of an innocent assailed every morning on awakening by the incorrigibility of the world.

'That was smart of you,' said Marks.

Freddy thought, anyone could have gathered that much, all he's trying to do is butter me up. But why?

'You know what I told them in Rome?' he asked.

'Yes, of course.'

'But you still want to hear me say it again?'

'Exactly.'

Freddy went on eating and tried to work out where all this might lead. He glanced over at the apparatus. Was it some sort of hypnotising machine? Was that why that man was so free with his compliments? He took a large mouthful of turkey and mashed potato and allowed it to melt in his mouth. Suddenly he knew what that thing was: a lie detector.

'We want to know exactly what it was that you saw. And by exactly I mean exactly. But first we must establish to what extent you are capable, without having had any prior warning, of recollecting everything you happened to witness at a particular moment.'

Marks fell silent and looked at Freddy through the cigarette smoke.

'We want to get to know you better. We want to get to know you so as to gain some idea of how you observe things around you. Then we can ask more specific questions and summon up details from your mind that you yourself—we shall push it that far—may have overlooked.'

'I'm pretty sure I haven't overlooked anything.'

'Probably not. But we want to make quite sure. As soon as we have done that, you can go back to Rome. We shall of course compensate you for those days of your vacation that you've lost.'

'There's no need for me to go back to Rome.'

'Oh?'

'I could have done without the whole trip.'

'Is that so? How come?'

'It was an idea my wife and doctor had. To help me diet.'

'Most people look on a trip to Europe as something special.'

'Oh, sure, I know it can be, but...not for me.'

Marks gave him an understanding smile. Freddy was afraid he had said too much.

'Would you care for some more turkey?' Marks asked. 'No obligation!' he added, smiling broadly. Freddy laughed with him.

'Well, if you insist…'

'Carolyn!'

She hurried in immediately, carrying a plate.

'I knew you wouldn't let me down, Freddy. I've been keeping it warm and I said to Robert, he's there in the kitchen with me, I said, Robert, when Freddy's had a taste of this he's going to want another helping for sure.'

'Carolyn, it's out of this world.'

When he had finished eating, they went and sat in the armchairs. They drank coffee and Robert MacLaughlin came in and introduced himself, a faultlessly turned-out young man with a radiant smile and bright blue eyes, an impossibly perfect figure of a kind that Freddy had only seen before in television soaps. Freddy noticed that Marks drank his coffee from a plastic mug. Carolyn had had to go back for it because she had forgotten to put it on the tray with the other cups and the coffee-pot. It was wrapped in cellophane, the sort of disposable mug you find by the washbasin in cheap hotels. After Freddy had signed a couple of forms in which he promised not to disclose any of the proceedings to any third party, Robert rolled the low table with the tape recorder closer and hung a small microphone around Freddy's neck.

Freddy told them about that night in Prague. He had left the hotel to look for somewhere to eat. He had been robbed by a taxi-driver and his accomplice and had gone wandering through the darkened city. At one point he had sat down somewhere and it was then that he had seen it happen.

'We should like to reconstruct exactly where you were at that moment,' said Marks. 'Do you think you can do that?'

'Ladova Lane.'

'That's where the taxi-driver put you down?'

'I'm not sure. I think so.'

'You could smell...food?'

'Yes. There was a restaurant nearby. No question. And it was still open. In the middle of the night! Restaurant Slavia, 63 Ladova Lane. You'll be sure to find it. You show me a picture of the right street and I'll be able to tell you if that's where the taxi put me down.'

'A map is on the way, Mr Marks, and photographs too,' MacLaughlin said.

Marks nodded. 'Good. Please continue.'

'I went and sat down. I was feeling dizzy from being hit on the head and I sat down on a garbage can. It was dark and I didn't know where I was. I felt really lousy. Well...that was when that Browning came along...'

'Did you recognise him straight away?'

'I'm not sure...I don't think so.'

'You were sitting on a garbage can in the street...'

'No, it wasn't in the street. There were some stairs, an iron staircase, and there was an empty space underneath. That's where I sat down.'

'You could see through the stairs?'

'Yes, it was an open staircase.'

'Then what?'

'Well, I was sitting there, and Browning came around the corner. I think...I think I must have recognised him straight away. I'd been sitting talking to him that evening, he told me you could get burgers at our hotel, so I knew who it was straight away. He was coming around the corner, on the other side of the street.'

'It was dark over there?'

'Yes, of course.'

'But you could see him clearly?'

'I've got darned good eyesight.'

'What was he wearing?'

'I don't know...jacket, jeans.'

'Did he have anything with him? Was he carrying something?'

'No. I don't think so.'

'Then what?'

'Then two men turned up behind him.'

'Where did they come from?'

'From the same street as Browning did.'

'Was Browning running?'

'Damn right. Like a bat out of hell.'

'Did he look scared?'

'Couldn't tell. But someone running that fast is sure in a hurry to get away from something.'

'The two men, what did they look like?'

'The same. Jackets. Young. In their twenties. They were running like hell as well. Then they got help from an automobile.'

'Where did that come from?'

'It drove up the street suddenly from out of a side street. It screeched past Browning, then drove onto the sidewalk. He had to go around it and that's how they got him.'

'Do you remember what make the automobile was?'

'No. Something European or Russian, I don't know.'

'How did they grab Browning?'

'One of them dived over the hood, just dived across. He knew what he was doing all right, he was an athletic sort of guy. Then the other one gave him a hand and they slung Browning into the car.'

'Did he put up a fight?'

'Sure, he was trying to get away from them. But it was two against one.'

'Can you show us how they got hold of him?'

'Yes, uh...they were holding his arms and one of them grabbed him by the neck and...I think there was someone else who got out of the car...that's right...'

'There was a third man there as well?'

'I think there was, I'm not sure any more.'

'And Browning went on putting up a fight even after they'd dragged him into the car?'

'Yes, he did.'

'Take your time, Mr Mancini, this is very important.'

'He was struggling all right.'

'Are you certain of that?'

'He was trying to get away.'

'Beyond all possible doubt?'

'Yes.'

'This is extremely important for us, Mr Mancini.'

'I understand.'

'If Michael Browning is still alive, in one of their jails, then God help him, Mr Mancini. He'd be better off dead.'

'You don't say!'

'Browning had a pill on him. We call it an L-pill. I realise this sounds like some sort of boy's adventure story, but that's what it's called, why, I don't know. Browning may have been able to swallow it at the last moment, but then again he may not. You were there, maybe you noticed something.'

'I didn't see anything like that.'

'Was Browning waving his arms about a lot?'

'Yes.'

'He was putting up a fight?'

'Yes.'

'Those pills cause muscle contractions. People go into a coma immediately. You saw nothing like that?'

Freddy could no longer remember what he had seen. He tried to recall those few seconds, but it was as if everything inside his head was shrouded in a thick mist.

'I don't know any more.'

'You just said that Browning was putting up a fight.'

'It looked like it, yes.'

'But you can no longer say for certain?'

'No.'

'Let's get back to the car, Mr Mancini…. Can you remember the colour of the car?'

'No. Sort of grey, I think. I don't know.'

'Did it have its lights on?'

Startled, Freddy looked across at Marks. He remembered suddenly that the car had appeared like a dark shadow.

'No!' he said in surprise. 'As a matter of fact the lights weren't on! Well, I'll be damned.'

'Did it make a lot of noise? Did you hear the engine?'

'No. It didn't sound all that loud. Maybe it wasn't an East European make after all?'

'Maybe not. And it drove up onto the sidewalk?'

'Yes.'

'What was Browning's reaction when that happened?'

'He jumped out of the car's way, squeezed against the wall and tried to run past it, and then that other guy appeared, kind of slid across the hood and grabbed Browning's coat, like this, grabbed the bottom of his coat.'

'You said just now that Browning was wearing a jacket.'

'I did?'

'Yes, that's what you said.'

'Well, it must have been a coat. A long coat, a long dark coat...'

'It's hot in Europe right now, Mr Mancini, a coat or a jacket?'

'A coat...'

He was in two minds about everything he had seen. Perhaps Browning had been wearing a jacket after all.

'Yes, a coat, I'm sure....'

'If it was a jacket, that's fine with us too, Mr Mancini....'

'A coat.'

'Right. A coat.'

Marks gestured to MacLaughlin, who picked up a large envelope, took out five photographs and placed them side by side on the coffee table.

They were of five men's faces. Each one looked very much like all the others.

'Can you pick out Michael Browning?' asked Marks.

Freddy looked from one to the next. Five broad faces with strong necks, thin lips, short fair hair, pale eyes.

He pointed to the one in the middle, giving Marks a questioning look.

'Is that him?' asked Marks.

'Yes...I think so,' said Freddy.

'Do you recognise him or don't you, Mr Mancini?'

'I think so,' Freddy mumbled.

'Mr Mancini, you spent an evening at the same table with Browning, six days ago, and you can no longer recognise him?'

'It's him,' said Freddy uncertainly, staring at the third photograph. 'I'm pretty sure it's him....'

'Turn the photograph over.'

Freddy looked at him blankly.

'The back...,' said Marks.

Freddy turned the photograph over. The name on the other side read 'Joe Kayevski'. He swallowed and gave Marks a guilty look.

'I could have sworn it was him,' he whispered.

'Don't worry about it, Mr Mancini. All we are trying to do is put together a clear impression of what you saw.'

'I saw it all right,' Freddy said, his voice rising. 'I was...I just happened to be there....'

'We're quite satisfied about that, Mr Mancini.'

'The photographs...those men all look so darned well the same....'

'That's why we chose them.'

'Right,' said Freddy. He turned the other photographs over. None of them bore Browning's name. He looked at Marks, his throat dry.

'He's not there.'

'No.'

'Why did you make me look at them, then?'

'To test your memory.'

'That's not fair, Mr. er—'

'Marks. John.'

'John,' said Freddy, 'I don't think that's very funny....'

'May I call you Freddy?'

Freddy nodded.

'Freddy, this isn't some kind of competition, some kind of game. We're concerned with accuracy here, we're concerned with the question, was Michael Browning still alive when they took him away? You're the only key we have to that question, Freddy, and people's lives depend on the answer.'

'What do you mean?'

'Just what I say, Freddy. It's a matter of life or death Understand?'

Freddy broke into a sweat.

'I don't know if I can help you,' he said.

'You've helped us a very great deal already, Freddy.'

'Really? I hope so....'

'You said a moment ago you thought there was a third man.'

'Yes. I think there was.'

'At what point exactly did he turn up?'

'Well...they'd grabbed Browning...then one of the car doors was opened.'

'From the inside?'

'Yes.'

'And then?'

'Well...then...and then he was dragged inside.'

'You never saw a face?'

'No.'

'Just arms?'

'Yes. Arms. No sleeves...what I mean is the arms were uncovered, bare arms....'

'A woman's?'

'Could have been, maybe, I don't know.'

'When the door of the car was opened did the inside light go on?'

Freddy gave him a startled look again. They thought of everything, thought of too much.

'I don't know.'

'You would have noticed it in a dark street like that?'

'Yes, I would…so it couldn't have happened—'

'I'm asking because you might have caught another glimpse of Browning inside the car. Did you?'

'No.'

'When he came to a standstill against the wall…that is what happened, isn't it?'

'Yes, the car had gone up on the sidewalk….'

'When Browning was standing there, did you see him put his hand to his mouth?'

'Yes…no…I don't know.'

In his mind's eye Freddy could see Browning moving his hand up to his mouth, as if he were wiping it, as if he were stroking his mouth like someone thinking feverishly about something—or had he been slipping something into his mouth?

'He did something like this….'

He demonstrated, stroking his lips and chin with an open hand.

Marks and MacLaughlin exchanged glances.

'The car was there in front of him and the men were running towards him?' asked Marks.

'Yes. He'd been running and then he had to stop when the car went on the sidewalk. He stood there and looked at the men. Then he looked at the car again and then he went like this….' He repeated the gesture. 'I didn't think it meant anything special….'

'Was he standing with his back to the wall?'

'Yes.'

'The men were coming towards him?'

'Yes.'

'The car was on the sidewalk?'

'Yes.'

'He didn't have anything in his hands?'

'No.'

'Which hand did he use to make that movement?'

'The one to my right…I think.'

'His left hand, then….'

'Yes. I guess so.'

'The left or the right?'

'The left! That's what you just said!'

Freddy gave Marks an angry look. He was aware his breathing had become laboured.

'Freddy…,' Marks was speaking in a soft, friendly voice, 'all we are trying to do is to find something out from you. That's all. Compared with most people you have an astonishingly good memory. We are very pleased with what you have told us so far. But we want to get every last detail. You witnessed something that is of incredible value to us. And that something is what we are trying to get out of you. I know how frustrated that must make you feel at times.'

Freddy nodded, calming down.

'Sorry, John, but my throat's dry. Could I have something to drink?'

'Coffee, tea, Coke—you name it, Mr Mancini,' said MacLaughlin.

'Coke, thanks.'

MacLaughlin left the room.

Marks took out a cigarette.

'Do you smoke, Freddy?'

'No.'

'Ever have?'

'No.'

Marks flicked an expensive lighter and lit his cigarette with a long flame.

'What was Browning doing over there?' Freddy asked.

Marks gave him a quick glance. He leant to one side so as to slip the lighter back into his pocket and inhaled deeply before answering.

'Freddy…I'd like to tell you, but I'm not allowed to. Not until I know where I stand with you.'

'Where you stand with me?'

'Yes, I have to know whether I can trust you.'

Freddy stared at him open-mouthed.

'Trust me? I…I never did anything over there to…'

His brains refused to come to his aid. He had no idea what Marks was getting at.

'Do you work for them, Freddy?' asked Marks.

'Work?' cried Freddy. 'For them?'

'For the Czechs,' Marks said calmly.

The smoke billowed out of his mouth as he spoke.

Chapter six

The night of 3 July 1989

The Ministry of Foreign Affairs reserved a number of apartments in The Hague for the convenience of the constant stream of diplomats who had been stationed in far-flung parts of the world throughout their working lives, and who no longer possessed homes in the Netherlands. Those diplomats who had become accustomed to the heat of the tropics but still wanted to own a house in Europe tended to buy one in the South of France or in Tuscany.

Felix Hoffman had been recalled for 'consultations'. This was the way in which the Dutch government had made its displeasure known at the abuse of human rights in Czechoslovakia, where without any warning three entirely blameless Dutch journalists had been beaten up. The street disturbance filmed by the young men had been a demonstration by Romanian Germans—so-called ethnic Germans—who were looking for trouble and wanted to be allowed, as the Nazi slogan had it, *heim ins Reich,* 'back to the Reich'.

As far as Hoffman was concerned the fifteen Germans, as well as the three journalists, had got off surprisingly lightly, since to his mind summary execution would have been an appropriate response to this display of Teutonic longing. But he had received word from The Hague that he must come, and he had little choice in the matter: he had packed a suitcase and stepped onto a KLM plane bound for Schiphol.

Marian had stayed at home in Prague, dreaming about Vondel. The decision that Hoffman would go by himself had been reached without discussion, even though he could not tell how long he might be gone. It had been easier that way.

At Schiphol he was met by a stripling from Protocol, a student drop-out with bleached hair, dressed in a fashionably over-sized suit, who accosted Hoffman by the covered gangway and escorted him down to the apron below where a driver with a cap and a Mercedes stood waiting next to the aeroplane. There were journalists in the arrivals hall and the Ministry wanted to prevent him from saying anything that might make things difficult for the Minister.

Summer could be hot in the Netherlands, too.

At the Monkey Rock—the concrete pile that had replaced the elegant premises on Het Plein as the Ministry's home—Hoffman reported to Ruud de Haan, Permanent Under-Secretary of State for Political Affairs. Sitting at a mahogany table that shone like a mirror in a spacious conference room on the fourth floor, De Haan, nicknamed Baldy and flanked by two secretaries, listened to Hoffman's detailed account of the incident. Hoffman sat alone on the other side of the long table, his open file on the polished surface with its disagreeable smell of beeswax. De Haan had gone completely bald, and Hoffman saw him glance across every now and then at his own thinning but still respectable head of hair. In measured tones De Haan voiced his dismay at the incident, then rose. He would be expecting a full written report.

'Have they given me a halfway decent place?' Hoffman asked the driver as they pulled away from the Monkey Rock.

'I've been told to take you to a hotel, sir,' the man said over his shoulder.

'A hotel? Fair enough,' said Hoffman, thinking of Des Indes.

He found himself outside a boarding-house, the Sea View in Scheveningen.

'Here?' he exclaimed when the driver stopped.

The house was on the north side of the promenade, behind the dunes and rows of single-family houses and next to a car breaker's yard that had plainly survived all environmental legislation. Rusting wrecks blighted the horizon.

'That's what it says here,' the driver said.

Hoffman snatched the paper out of his hands. Sea View, Sandy Road, Scheveningen. He handed it back to the man.

'They've made a mistake,' he said with conviction.

'I've never known them do that, sir. They're always sticklers for detail.'

'They've made a mistake,' Hoffman repeated, threateningly.

'If you say so,' said the driver, turning back and glancing across at the scrap yard. 'It's up to you.'

'What do you mean, it's up to me?'

'Well, what do you suggest we do about it?'

'I tell you what, why don't you ring your boss?'

'Okay, okay....'

The man got out and went for help in the boarding-house.

Hoffman, sitting on the right-hand side of the back seat, shifted edgily about on the beige leather. Nervously he slid a finger between his sweating neck and the collar of his shirt. If this was not a mistake—and deep down he knew that it was an unmistakable diplomatic signal—then he'd move into the Kurhaus or Des Indes at his own expense. He'd show them.

Then it occurred to him that the best way to show them was simply to ignore the blatant insult. The boarding-house was the sort German families came to for their summer holidays, working-class types with huge beer bellies who spent their days swilling gallons of beer, downing shiploads of liver sausage and dreaming up new blitzkriegs. Their children built model concentration camps out of Lego, and their wives knitted thick sweaters for the Eastern Front.

The driver emerged, accompanied by a buxom black woman,

an immigrant from one of the overseas territories. He opened the door on Hoffman's side. Heat poured in.

'It seems this is it, sir,' said the driver, mouth pursed. 'Mrs Paardekoper here knows all about it.'

The woman smiled broadly and nodded to him.

'Welcome, Mr Hoffman!' she sang in her rolling Surinamese accent.

Hoffman nodded back. Someone in the department clearly had it in for him.

'We are so happy that you are here, Mr Hoffman!' cried Mrs Paardekoper. 'We shall spoil you like one of our own little boys!'

She laughed loudly. Even the driver saw the humour of the situation.

Hoffman climbed out of the car and shook the landlady's proffered hand.

'Mr Hoffman, you are our first distinguished guest. We are very, very happy to have you.'

'And I am glad to be here,' Hoffman said, meaning it.

'We have given you the Floral Suite,' she said proudly.

He had been assigned two rooms on the first floor hung entirely with flowered wallpaper, including the ceiling, and with a sweeping view over the breaker's yard. There was a lingering smell of new linoleum.

He rang the Ministry on the telephone in his room.

'I'd like to thank you for the charming place you found for me. Who was responsible for that?' he asked Mia Jansen. He had known her voice for years but had never seen her in the flesh, which did not prevent the two of them from pursuing a passionate relationship over the telephone. She always sounded husky, as if she had spent the previous night crying out.

'Jean van Galen.'

'Van Galen? Is he with your lot now?'

'He took over as secretary to the Under-Secretary a month ago.'

'Is he about?'

'He went on holiday yesterday.'

So the bastard had cleared off just in time to stop Hoffman making mincemeat of him.

'Will he be away long, Mia?'

'Three weeks.'

'How on earth do you do that with your voice?'

'I practise at night.'

'When are you going to use your mouth on me, Mia?'

'You're always too far away, Felix.'

'Whenever I hear your voice, I can see your gorgeous lips.'

'I never noticed, but if you say so....'

He had often been on the point of asking her out for dinner, but the potential complications were too great and in any case she probably gave every frustrated diplomat the come-on over the telephone.

'One more question. Do you often put people up at the Sea View in Scheveningen?'

'Uh, to be honest...not very often.'

'Why not?'

'Well...perhaps I oughtn't to say so, but—'

'But what?' he said.

'All right then, in the ordinary course of events we wouldn't put any of our people up in a place like that. But Van Galen felt you should be kept away from the press.'

'Well, I love it here. You can tell Van Galen.'

He had first met Van Galen a few years back in Khartoum. Khartoum was a post in the developing world, suited to the kind of person who had no problem with the odd salamander between their sheets or mud in the tap water. The town, hot and dry, lay in the middle of the desert. If you were young, the years you spent there meant certain promotion to a good European or American post. If you were older, and Hoffman was fifty-three when he was appointed, it meant that they didn't know what to do with you.

Hoffman had been sent out to Africa before, to Tanzania, a terrible posting, but oddly enough he had felt quite happy in Khartoum.

The nights had hummed with life, he had worked very hard raising funds for various irrigation projects and keeping a close eye on them, they had had a Lebanese cook who could perform miracles, and a civil war was raging in the south of the country which provided the necessary excitement and diversion. Marian had worked part-time in a hospital, and she too, he felt, looked back with satisfaction at those demanding years, despite all the trouble with the water and the electricity and the Sudanese inability to keep to arrangements or rules.

It had been the first assignment for Van Galen, a lawyer straight out of the 'nursery'. It was obvious from the very first day, when he turned up dressed in a grey three-piece suit, that he was not cut out for the work. Wearing the suit, he had gone into the desert to inspect the irrigation works financed by the Dutch government, and had returned towards the end of the day dehydrated and half-suffocated. He had flatly refused to exchange his three-piece style of dressing for the customary tropical suit.

Hoffman had been Temporary Charge d'Affaires, a TCA in Ministry jargon. Officially that had been much lower down the ladder than his present position, but in fact he had run Khartoum as his own ambassadorial patch (it was a sort of audit office, Khartoum being a purely economic post for the supervision of development funds).

Having watched the lawyer making a mess of things for a week, Hoffman decided it was time for an exchange of views, the more so as the newcomer had been conducting himself like minor royalty, condescending to the 'natives' in the office, and calling everyone 'Mr' and 'Mrs'.

'Van Galen,' Hoffman said, looking at the young man across his desk, 'why are you dressed like that?'

Van Galen pushed his glasses back up his shining nose. Despite the air-conditioning, the temperature in the building was almost a hundred degrees.

'I don't understand the question, Mr Hoffman,' Van Galen replied.

'I'm not expressing myself clearly enough, is that it? Let me put it this way, you're not dressed for this climate. We're in the middle of a desert here, my lad, it's over a hundred and twenty outside, and you walk around at noon in a nylon and polyester suit as if you think it looks like rain. And that buttoned-up waistcoat! Loose clothes are what you need here, Van Galen. One hundred per cent cotton or one hundred per cent pure wool. I'm only giving you this advice because I've had some experience of countries like this and I'm happy to pass the benefit of it on to you. Oh, and you can drop the "Mr", nobody else uses it, you'll have noticed that.'

Van Galen stared at him coldly through his thick glasses.

'I don't need your advice, Mr Hoffman,' he said.

'You've got it anyway, free, gratis and for nothing,' said Hoffman, with satisfaction.

'Listen,' said Van Galen, standing up and buttoning his jacket over his waistcoat. 'You've got the worst reputation in the Service, although everyone knows that for some obscure reason the top brass have taken you under their wing, and you really think I'd take advice from someone like *you?* I'm afraid you're mistaken, Mr Hoffman.'

The young man enunciated his words with exaggerated care. He was a fast learner, Hoffman had to give him that. When he had finished speaking Van Galen walked towards the door, then turned round.

'I take it that was all?' asked the young diplomat, looking past Hoffman at an invisible spot on the wall.

'My boy,' said Hoffman affably, 'in all the years I've spent in this madhouse you are the most conceited young pup I've ever met, and since I happen to know that your grandfather used to be a minister I don't have to ask how a snotty-nosed little shit like you managed to get a job here, but to avoid any misunderstandings: you'll be gone within the month, and if you don't go of your own accord or if they don't recall you then I'll send you packing myself, and rest assured that'll take some doing because I'll have beaten you to such a pulp first they'll have to scrape you off the ground. But I'm going to give you just one more chance, Van Galen. If you can start behaving like a normal human being from now on, we might still hit it off.'

The young man had turned pale and left the room. Two weeks

later he was found to have a virus infection and his temperature rose so alarmingly that he had to be flown back to the Netherlands. Hoffman felt guilty.

He drove with him in a pre-war ambulance to the airfield. Van Galen had been shot full of penicillin. As they carried him into the plane, Hoffman put a hand on his shoulder.

'Good luck, Van Galen.'

The young man did not react.

'I'm sorry,' Hoffman continued, 'I honestly wouldn't have wished this on you, son. As soon as you're better, come back and we'll go out for a meal. We'll work things out, the two of us. And about that suit...if you're so attached to it, then you'll just have to go on wearing it.'

The young man looked up at him with feverish eyes. He whispered something Hoffman could not catch in the roar of the engines.

'Sorry?' said Hoffman and bent forward.

The young man swallowed and took a deep breath, seeking the strength to speak.

'Jewish scum,' he said faintly.

Hoffman was speechless. Still bereft of words, he stared after the departing plane, an old 707 belonging to Egypt Air, searching in vain for an adequate response.

At the Department of Tropical Diseases in the Harbour Hospital in Rotterdam, the Service's official clinic, they diagnosed allergies that rendered a career in the tropics a risky venture. Van Galen stayed on in The Hague where, suit, spectacles and all, he became the new star in the bureaucratic firmament. Hoffman would have liked to drop in and say hello, but there it was, Van Galen was on holiday.

Supported by Stanley, her husband, a large greying black man with a furrowed face who sat silently in a rocking chair in the lobby, Mrs Paardekoper ruled over her boarding-house as an enlightened monarch might have done. After Hoffman had finished his telephone call he went down to the dining room and was served a lunch of Surinamese delicacies, oily, spicy dishes that were very much to his liking. He was the only guest. Mrs Paardekoper had prepared the food herself, and when he confessed that it was years since he had eaten Surinamese food, she explained everything to him with a broad smile as he polished it off.

He ordered a hired car from Hertz, and when it had been delivered he drove in the boiling heat back to the Monkey Rock, where he went over his report on the events in Prague once again with a couple of dim-witted officials. He also tried to get hold of his friend Wim Scheffers, but Wim was locked away in conference with some Russians and could not be disturbed. Hoffman left a message for him and returned to the Floral Suite.

He made himself comfortable in an armchair near the window, opened his Spinoza and looked out over the breaker's yard. The sun was high overhead. The site covered at least two acres, and several thousand wrecks lay rusting away gently in the salt sea air. He concentrated on the section entitled 'On the Instruments of the Understanding, True Ideas', a title that left him guessing. Still, the first paragraph looked promising.

Having explained which method of acquiring knowledge was best, Spinoza went on to outline the way and method that could lead to the truth.

First the philosopher asked whether, to discover that method, we needed another method, and whether to discover the latter we needed yet another method, and so forth. His answer was as follows:

> It is the same thing as with artificial instruments, of which we might argue in the same manner. For in order to work iron a hammer is needed, and in order to have a hammer it must be made, for which another hammer and other instruments are needed, for the making of which others again are needed, and so on to infinity.

Spinoza went on to say that no more was needed than confidence, the 'native strength' of the understanding, and he compared technical instruments with the instruments of the understanding which had likewise evolved gradually. The method could be discovered by anyone who used his instruments to the fullest extent.

An ear-splitting racket made Hoffman look up. A red Ford Granada in a large cage had crashed to the ground in the breaker's yard, released by an enormous claw suspended from the arm of a crane. Hoffman watched the vehicle bounce up into the air and drop back again.

Once the car had come to a standstill, two sides of the cage began moving towards each other, converting the cage into a gigantic press. Groaning and squealing, the walls compressed the car, and metal tore into metal, accompanied by high shrill screeching. It was like the sound of nails being scraped across a blackboard and Hoffman doubled up and clapped his hands to his ears. The sounds evoked an animal fear, blind panic in a shrieking universe. When a small parcel dropped out of the cage, the whole Ford Granada reduced to the size of a manageable suitcase, the crane had already fastened on the next victim: over the cage there now hung a yellow Beetle, easy prey. The claw opened and the Beetle crashed to the ground and came to rest, suddenly defenceless.

The cage began to close in on it and the Beetle whined. Again Hoffman pressed his ears tight in torment.

He went downstairs and asked Mr Paardekoper how long the process could be expected to continue.

The swarthy-skinned man sat motionless in his rocking chair, chewing, and gave him a long slow look. His skin was almost blue, grey hairs sprouted from his chin, the whites of his eyes looked yellow and muddied. In a corner of the lobby, a small room with bare wooden walls, stood a television set with the sound turned off. You could hear the press even in here.

'The wind's the wrong way,' said the man.

'Oh,' said Hoffman, 'and what if the wind's the right way?'

'If the wind's the right way…,' the man appeared to think about it, 'then it doesn't bother us.'

'Isn't there anything you can do about it?' asked Hoffman, though he knew better.

'Not as easy as that,' the man mumbled. 'I used to know a rainmaker, but a windmaker...not a chance, not here in Holland.'

Hoffman pocketed his Spinoza, fled from the boarding-house and made for the sea front. Crossly he plodded up the dunes, cursing Van Galen under his breath. He was dressed too warmly and was soon sweating heavily, but was soothed at the sight of the sea.

He ran down towards it like an excited child, faster and faster until he was careering almost out of control and had to stop himself from falling.

The long, wide beach was blanketed by a heaving layer of sunburnt seaside trippers, enveloped in a haze of suntan oil. Bared breasts stared up at him proudly. Dogs ran about shaking sea water out of their coats. Joggers passed him, sweat spraying from their faces and with a suicidal look in their eyes. The warm wind tugged at his clothes, his tie danced around his neck, his shoes made tracks in the moist sand. He leaned into the wind for a moment, eyes closed, and listened to the song of the waves. For a few seconds he thought of nothing at all.

He searched for a vacant deckchair by the bathing huts and bought an apple pancake from a wooden stall built on stilts in the sand. He put Spinoza down next to him. He smelt the sea.

He began reading a complicated argument on the difference between the world of things and the world of ideas, eating the pancake as he did so. It melted in his mouth, neither too greasy nor too dry, stuffed with slices of juicy apple. He read to the end of the section and began to see what Spinoza was trying to get at, this time with the help of difficult, almost mathematical, terms.

Hoffman gathered that there was a world of things and a world of the ideas of things, or to put it in Spinoza's own words: there was a circle having a circumference and a centre, and there was the *idea* of a circle. The idea of a circle was as abstract as the circle itself was concrete, but both were part of human experience.

It was possible to think about the *idea* itself, inasmuch as it too could be an object of thought, that is, the *idea of the idea*—and so on ad infinitum. Spinoza had no wish to take his readers on this insane mental peregrination, but merely pointed out further on that, in principle, there was an infinite number of ways of thinking about ideas, or of thinking about thinking:

> Again, the more the mind knows, the better it understands its forces and the order of nature; the more it understands its forces or strength, the better it will be able to direct itself and lay down rules for itself; and the more it understands the order of nature, the more easily it shall be able to liberate itself from useless things: of this, as we have said, consists the whole method.

The question for Hoffman was whether he could liberate himself from useless things, or whether it was in his nature to devote himself to them, and he doubted whether any amount of understanding the order of nature would help him to keep a check on himself (he realised that the utter gluttony to which he had abandoned himself made his early death a strong probability, and yet he continued with it, which must mean either (a) that he was not afraid of death, or (b) that he did not think much of his life).

Hoffman was impressed by the mental leap Spinoza made in the next paragraph: the philosopher contended that in the correct understanding of the order of nature—by means of the right ideas— we were afforded a glimpse of God Himself! Spinoza believed that 'in order that our mind may represent a true example of nature, it must produce all its ideas from the idea which represents the origin and source of all nature.'

Hoffman, having finished the pancake and busy now with a hot waffle sprinkled with icing sugar and swimming in melted butter, found something inherently beautiful in that idea, as if that kind of thinking were a form of artistic activity. True knowledge, true knowing, Hoffman now saw, always had a direct, straightforward tie with reality, for therein lay its tangible and visible form. He realised that there was an essential difference between the idea of the waffle and the waffle he was now eating (a crispy, crunchy concoction that turned as soft as butter on his tongue), but then Spinoza had not been primarily concerned with waffles and pancakes.

The section Hoffman had reached contained many sentences he had to read more than once. Spinoza was juggling with concepts and abstractions that cast no shadows in Hoffman's life and, while enjoying the waffle and a cup of scented tea, he tried to follow the philosopher's summing up at the end of the section.

One thing was quite certain, namely that Spinoza was in search of the truth. In his own circles, Hoffman knew no one who was engaged in such an activity. Marian had gone in pursuit of the truth for a time, but that had been the revealed truth, the truth of the Catholic Church.

Esther's death had driven Marian into the arms of Father Emilio Schuster, the priest of a poverty-stricken parish in Lima. Like Vondel, she had become converted to Rome. She had never before shown the slightest interest in religion, but Esther's grave lay far away in the Netherlands and Marian had found solace in two years of daily prayers for the salvation of her dead child's soul. Hoffman doubted if she had ever really become a true believer; she seemed to him too down-to-earth to swallow the Resurrection or the Immaculate Conception, but he understood her longing to give expression to her sorrow, something for which our secular age had failed to provide. She had masses read and became a benefactress of the parish. Hoffman had often found Schuster in his home immersed in heated discussions with Marian, a man with burning eyes and compelling gestures. Hoffman's arrival had always cut their discussions short.

Schuster's parents had been German immigrants, communists who had fled to South America in the thirties, and their son had embraced liberation theology. Schuster's liturgy had consoled Marian when Hoffman had proved incapable of doing so.

Spinoza had been convinced that the idea of a perfect being (he had actually written the words and obviously believed that it was attainable) was contained in the complete and full knowledge of nature. To that end the understanding had to be improved. But how was that to be done?

All one's prejudices and incomplete ideas had to be dropped, but that was only the beginning; what was of the utmost importance was to trust the intuition, which thanks to nature could be made to flourish in the cultivated person; as a result his mind could then feed on ideas—not just any set of ideas but ideas capable of revealing the origin and source of nature.

Spinoza postulated that all ideas taken together, if that could ever be achieved, would represent the essence of nature. Nature was structured with the help of certain ideas; hence ideas themselves were also part of nature, and if only one succeeded in grasping them, one could attain supreme knowledge. And supreme knowledge, Hoffman thought, could be none other than good old God Himself.

Hoffman's head was spinning. He did not know if he was a cultivated enough person to follow these arguments, but he was certainly enjoying them, so why worry?

He used his index finger to wipe the melted butter and icing sugar from the plate, then licked his finger.

He paid and walked back to the boarding-house. The wind had dropped, the sea was calm, as if nature were holding her breath to gather fresh strength for the evening. Thanks to summertime it was still broad daylight, and Hoffman trudged through the soft sand over the dunes under a blazing sky.

It surprised him to discover that he could still appreciate nature out here, for his love of it had departed with Esther. He was an urban creature, accustomed to exhaust fumes and parking meters. Nature was something you looked for in parks and in zoos. Life behind bars, bred with difficulty—the favourite outing of the twins. For years the glimpse of a sick seal or a duck covered in oil would bring home to him how much he loved his children. But they had vanished just like the Amazon forest being burned by ranchers, as he had read in the paper on the plane that morning, and he could not get the words 'all things shall vanish away' out of his mind. Whatever could not save itself was crushed, whatever was weak was swept away, these were the immutable laws of the universe. A cow, a sheep, a dolphin, almost any creature could melt his heart, but when he had had the chance of tasting whale meat once in Japan he had taken three helpings, and his sake-filled Japanese counterparts had rolled about laughing at the overindulgence of their colleague from Holland.

Apart from food, Hoffman no longer had any great expectations of nature. And yet those dunes and the sun sinking into the filthy sea gave him a strange sort of satisfaction—the thrill of peace.

When he walked into the boarding-house he was soaked in perspiration. He undressed, drew the curtains (large multicoloured flowers) so as not to alarm the workers in the breaker's yard, and placed a standard lamp (with its flower-shaped glass shade) next to his armchair. He looked forward to the next few hours with Spinoza and, stark naked, he started on the next section, 'On Fictitious Ideas'.

> Let us then begin with the first part of our method, which is, as I said, to distinguish and separate the true idea from other perceptions and to restrain the mind lest it confuse false, feigned, and doubtful ideas with true ones.

In this section Spinoza was examining the question of how to deal with hypotheses and assumptions, of how meaningful ideas were to be distinguished from meaningless ones. He offered the following definitions:

> I call a thing *impossible* whose nature implies a contradiction if it exists; *necessary*, whose nature implies a contradiction if it does not exist; *possible*, whose existence, that is, its nature, does not imply a contradiction whether it exists or does not.

Hoffman considered 'Cousin Jan is immortal' to be an example of the first definition. That statement was in conflict with the experiential fact that all human beings are born and later die. Immortality and Jan's humanity contradicted each other, hence the statement referred to an impossible situation (although language allowed us to make it).

'The earth revolves about the sun' was an example of the second definition. This was a necessity because its denial would be in conflict with our experience.

Things were more difficult with the third definition. Hoffman searched for an example. He found it in the statement 'There is intelligent life in outer space'. That statement could neither be proved nor refuted; it depended on factors that were not, or not yet, known.

Hoffman realised that the *Treatise* had to be treated as a child of its time: Spinoza had lived in the seventeenth century, an age abounding with discoveries. Descartes had done his thinking, Newton had seen the apple fall, and Spinoza had tried to develop a system by which an apparently ever more complex reality (complicated in its manifestations but, as was then hoped, clear and comprehensible in its principles) could be described, and hence grasped in its essence.

This splendid section of the *Treatise* was wholly devoted to the attitude to adopt when examining hypotheses. 'The mind', Spinoza wrote, 'when it pays attention to a fictitious thing and one false to its nature, so as to turn it over in its mind and understand it, and to deduce in proper order from it such things as are to be deduced, will easily make manifest its falsity; and if the fictitious thing be true to its nature when the mind pays attention to it in order to understand it and begins to make deductions from it in proper order, it proceeds happily without interruption....' And he went on to calm the anxious by remarking, 'In no wise, therefore, must we fear to feign anything, provided that we only perceive the thing clearly and distinctly.'

He offered three conclusions: (1) if an idea is of a very simple thing, 'it cannot but be clear and distinct'; (2) a thing composed of many parts must be reduced in thought to its simplest parts, and each part must be 'regarded in itself'; and (3) fiction (by which Spinoza seemed to refer not only to hypotheses, but also to such concepts as falsehood, invention and nonsense) proliferates on confused ideas, since 'if it were simple it would be clear and distinct, and consequently true.'

The telephone brought him back to the flowered room.

'Where on earth have they stuck you now?' he heard Wim Scheffers ask.

'Oh, it's not that bad.'

'I promise I'll have you in a decent hotel by tomorrow.'

'Don't worry, Wim, I'm fine here, really.'

'That Van Galen is a little shit.'

'I don't want to move. Truly.'

'Have it your own way. What are you doing for supper?'

'I was thinking of having a bite here. What time is it, anyway?'

'Eight o'clock.'

Someone knocked on the door.

'Hang on a minute, Wim.'

He got up, wrapped a towel round his waist and opened the door a crack. Mrs Paardekoper was standing outside. She looked anxiously at the one eye peering out at her.

'Mr Hoffman, are you all right?'

'Very well indeed, Mrs Paardekoper. I'm just about to take a bath.'

'We thought you were ill. We've been sitting downstairs waiting for you for half an hour.'

'What for?'

'Supper is at half past seven.'

'Oh, I'm sorry, I didn't realise.'

'There.' She tapped on the door. He saw a notice wrapped in cellophane pinned to the inside. 'It says so there.'

'I am sorry, I never saw it…and I have to go out.'

Mrs Paardekoper gave him a woeful look.

'I cooked it specially for you, Mr Hoffman. All Surinamese specialities. Just for you. There's no one else here.'

'I'll be down right away,' he said to preclude any pangs of conscience.

'I'll keep it hot!' she said cheerfully and disappeared.

'Wim?' he asked.

'Yes.'

'Quarter past nine?'

'Fine.'

'Where?'

'Remember the Italian restaurant round the corner from the old Ministry?' Scheffers asked.

'The Pergola? By Het Plein?'

'That's it. Quarter past nine then.'

Downstairs he took a seat between the Paardekopers. She had done him proud with the meal. She told him the names of all the dishes and Hoffman cleared the plates at great speed, rich, highly seasoned dishes of pastry and meat and chicken and fish with full-bodied sauces. Roasted meats, pitjel, rice with black-eyed beans and salted meat, risol, batjauw, little puff pastries, heri heri, moksi metti, tjim tjim chicken, stuffed kopropo.

His cook watched him happily and gave him three helpings. Her husband sat eating in silence, hunched forward with one arm around his plate as if to protect it against a raid from Hoffman.

At eight thirty-five he was able to make his escape. In his bathroom he stuck a finger down his throat and vomited the whole meal up into the lavatory bowl. The finest creations of the rich culinary art of Surinam gushed from the depths of his stomach in a single violent wave. He pulled the chain and wiped his mouth.

Half an hour later he was sitting opposite Wim Scheffers in La Pergola, a busy Italian restaurant that was a favourite with members of the diplomatic corps and officials from the Ministry who continued to frequent the place even after the Ministry had moved. Hoffman had taken off his jacket in the sweltering heat.

'How are things in Prague?'

'Wonderful,' said Hoffman. 'No graffiti on the walls, the streets are clean, no beggars, the ideal country for bourgeois conservatives like you and me.'

Wim smiled. He seemed in fine form. They differed by just three weeks in age, but he looked ten years younger than Hoffman. Wim played squash and golf, wore Italian suits, and had radiantly white teeth that lit up every smile. He went regularly to an expensive barber and was never without a tan. He had kept his jacket on, for he had too much style to be bothered by the heat. He shot his cuffs, displaying his expensive cufflinks, gold buttons inscribed with his initials.

'And here?'

'Nothing ever changes,' replied Wim. 'Fighting for the best jobs, too much paper work, but we keep going.'

Hoffman took a sip of the Barolo '83, not top quality but it had class for an Italian wine.

'And Marian?'

Hoffman shrugged his shoulders. 'She's very busy with her book.'

'Still?'

'Yes.'

Wim knew that Hoffman's marriage had withered years ago, even though Hoffman never made the slightest reference to it (perhaps that was how Wim knew). A waiter appeared and they both ordered melon and Parma ham and pasta alia vongole.

'How's young Sonnema making out with you?' Wim asked.

'He's nobody's fool,' said Hoffman. 'There are no flies on him, he knows how to sell himself. He must be heading straight for the top?'

'He's one of the young stars. One of Van Galen's competitors.'

'Van Galen's a wanker. You should chuck him out.'

'I'll pass it on.' Wim grinned, then said, 'And how are things with you, Felix? Are you managing all right over there?'

'I while away the hours. I've come across a…a piece of philosophical writing…and that helps me through the night.'

'Philosophy, Felix?' Wim said with concern. 'There's nothing the matter with you, is there?'

'Who knows? The strange thing is that I find it very interesting…. Anyway, I'm getting along fine in Prague.'

'Great,' said Wim, just to say something. He took a noticeably deep breath, then embarked on some gossip, and they ate and laughed and two bottles later they were standing outside in the sultry night.

Hoffman had his old Burberry with him, the constant companion which had seen every continent with him, but served no purpose here. It had not rained for weeks. Wim asked if Hoffman had come by car and if he could have a lift.

'I've got something to tell you,' said Wim when they were walking to Hoffman's rented car, a black Nissan. Hoffman had little sympathy for the way in which the Japanese flooded the world with their products, but it was the cheapest car Hertz had on offer. If he couldn't be driven around in a Mercedes, he would settle for the most modest option.

'Yes?'

Hoffman wondered if Wim had come across another of Van Galen's dirty tricks.

Wim walked beside him deep in thought, as if rehearsing his story in his mind, but said nothing more. At the car they climbed in, it started at once and Hoffman drove off.

'Where are we going?'

'I'll show you the way,' Wim said.

He gave Hoffman directions as they went along.

'It's about Miriam,' he said.

Hoffman, suddenly hoarse, said, 'My Miriam?' He shifted on his seat and gripped the wheel.

Wim nodded. 'Yes.'

'Miriam's been dead for five years, Wim.'

'I know, Felix. She's dead, but by chance I came across something that's…that has something to do with her, even though she is dead.'

Hoffman stared at the road through the windscreen, but saw nothing.

'What is it? You know you can tell me anything.'

'Damn it, Felix, I really did give it a lot of thought…whether I should tell you, that is, but I felt….'

'Stop messing about. Let's have it.'

He looked sideways and saw Wim nod. Wim ran a hand over his face, then said abruptly, 'Okay. Listen. Two weeks ago I had a date with a…a woman I had met, and….'

'Where?' blurted Hoffman.

'Where? At the opening of an exhibition. That's got nothing to do with it,' said Wim. 'I took her out for a meal and then…then the two of us…went on somewhere together….'

He fell silent again. He showed Hoffman the next turning to take.

'Well? Where did you go? Don't keep me in suspense.'

'Here we are! Stop!' Hoffman brought the car to a halt in a street bathed in the light of the neon signs on its cafes, bars, restaurants, sex shops.

'The woman I came here with….'

'What was her name?' Hoffman asked.

'Felix, that's got nothing to do with it.'

'I want to know.'

Wim shook his head, sighed. 'Take my word for it, she has nothing to do with any of this.'

'Even so, I want to know what woman you're talking about.'

'Ria Voeten.'

'Jef's wife?'

'Jef's wife….'

'Well, it's up to you, Wim, she looks like hot stuff, an over-ripe melon, mind, but that's your affair…'

'Listen, will you!' exclaimed Wim. 'I'm trying to tell you something!'

'Then bloody well get on with it!'

'Shut up for a moment and listen.'

Hoffman turned towards him and placed his arm along the back of the seat. 'I'm listening....'

'I had a date with Ria Voeten. We went out for supper. For one reason or another our talk got round to porn and she told me that she'd never seen a blue film....'

'A blue film?'

'Right....'

Wim took a breath, then continued. 'So...we went to a...sex cinema, and in the film....'

In a split second Hoffman knew what the upshot of that visit to the sex cinema had been.

He turned away, white. Pain shot from his belly to his chest, as if he were on the lavatory demanding the impossible of himself, and with a sudden din, as if all the amplifiers in all the cafes along the street had been turned up at the same time, his ears were assailed by a deafening cacophony, the well-worn refrain of madness.

He did not want to hear what Wim had to say, he did not want to hear the dirt from his friend's mouth. He was overcome by panic.

'Where?' he shouted.

He turned to Wim and realised that Wim had not heard him. 'Where?' he yelled again.

With a shaking finger, Wim pointed across the street. A small building between two bars. Neon above the entrance: ADULT MOVIES, PRIVATE BOOTHS.

'Stay there!' Hoffman shouted.

He got out and crossed the street.

It was odd that he should have so much trouble walking, as if his knees were jelly and gave him no support. But he managed to reach the entrance, pushed the door open and stepped into a dark foyer.

A red light burned in one corner. A spotty youth sat paging through a magazine at a table. It was as hot as in a Turkish bath.

'How much?' Hoffman asked the girl through the thick glass of the ticket office.

'Ten.'

He put the money down and the girl pulled the ticket out of the slot in the machine.

'When does it start?'

'It's continuous.'

'What's it called?'

With a bored look she pointed to a poster further down the dark foyer that Hoffman had not seen. It read ARDENNES HAM. He heard himself saying it out loud.

'Comedy porn,' the boy behind the table said, sitting up and looking suspiciously at the oddly-behaved customer. 'Made in Holland.'

'How do I get in?'

The boy got up and walked to a wide door. He had the build of a wrestler. There were large patches of sweat under his armpits.

'Please show consideration for other patrons,' he said.

At first Hoffman could see nothing in the blackness of the auditorium. He clung to the door until the film flickered and he was able to make out a large near-empty room with rows of seats and a few scattered spectators. He shuffled to the nearest seat and let himself down into it as a blind man might.

When he came out three minutes later, Scheffers was standing beside the car. Hoffman walked towards him slowly, looking down at his feet as if learning to walk.

Wim said, 'I'm very sorry, Felix. When I realised, I decided… I wouldn't tell you, it was too awful, but…I worried myself sick over it, and then I thought…you *had* to be told. Others know about it, so you should as well.'

Hoffman struck him a heavy blow on the chin with his fist. Scheffers staggered, silent and resigned, and Hoffman seized him by the jacket and drove his big fist into Scheffer's full stomach. Scheffers doubled up and Hoffman let go of him. His friend bent over the bonnet of the car, propping himself up. He groaned and Hoffman saw his open mouth gasping for air.

Hoffman turned and left him when bystanders began approaching, and found an acceptable cafe in a side street. A television set stood on a shelf high up on the wall. A strip light above the bar, a filthy floor, bare Formica tables, the weathered faces of foreign workers. Plaintive, monotonous Arab music could be heard over the sounds of the tv. Greedily, thirstily, he drank Algerian wine. But he stayed clear-headed, thinking and brooding, imprisoned by the nightmare inside his head. He could not stop blaming himself.

When the place closed, Hoffman drove back to the boarding-house. He could feel the alcohol in his blood and knew that he was not in control of the car. He felt like setting fire to the cinema or ripping the film out of the projector. The car lurched along the street, catching in the tramlines several times. He made it back to the lonely building behind the dunes unharmed.

He opened the front door with the key they had given him after the meal. When he locked the door after him, he clung to the wall in exhaustion. He did not think he had the strength to go up to his room.

'Good-night,' he heard.

He turned round. In the dark lobby, Paardekoper sat in his rocking chair.

'Good-night,' he mumbled.

'Chilly outside?'

'So-so.'

'You never know with the weather.'

'No,' Hoffman whispered.

'Wind?'

'Wind?'

'Yes. Windy outside?'

'I don't know. A little, perhaps.'

'Often windy here on the coast,' said the man.

Hoffman nodded profusely, as if delighted to embrace this simple truth.

'Sleep well,' said the man.

In his room Hoffman let himself fall onto the floral bedspread. No voice to drown the storm in his ears, no hand to brush the pain from his face.

A loathsome feeling of hunger seized him. He stood up and tottered downstairs.

'Going out again?' asked the man.

'Yes. Perhaps you can help me. Do you know if there's a cafe or a restaurant still open?'

'At this hour? My wife can get you something if...'

'No, no, I don't want to put her out....'

'There's a hamburger place next to the Kurhaus, on the square. It's open all night....'

Hoffman drove his Nissan to the hamburger stand. A warm wind blew in through the car's open window. Bulky youths in tight T-shirts were standing next to their motorbikes, stiff leather jackets slung over the handlebars. He considered picking a fight with them to get his face bashed in. He ordered chips, croquettes, satay, two kinds of meatballs, cans of beer and Coke. He returned to the board-ing-house with two full plastic bags.

'Get on all right?'

'Fine.'

'Still windy outside?'

'Not that I noticed.'

'Must be, I think.'

'Quite likely.'

'Have a good meal.'

In his sitting room he set out all the small containers on the table. He held his head under the tap and washed off the heat of the night.

He had no cutlery and ate with his fingers, using his little fingers to open Spinoza. He began by wolfing down the double por-tion of chips with 'war sauce', a thick mix of mayonnaise, satay sauce, ketchup and piccalilli (because he knew that the chips would be the fastest to go cold), while he turned to the next section of the *Treatise*, 'On the False Idea'. Hoffman needed all the intellectual capacity at his command to follow the philosopher, yet he knew intuitively that he was saving his sanity by making the effort: Spinoza insulated him from the panic-inducing images of the past evening in the same way as a medicine isolated dangerous bacteria.

As far as Hoffman could make out—force himself to make out—Spinoza made a distinction between a 'fictitious idea' (for instance a hypothesis) and a 'false idea'. The first was no more than an assumption whose 'truth' had still to be established; the second, however, was mistakenly thought to be 'true'. 'Falsity' was easily deduced by anyone who thought clearly and distinctly.

Spinoza contended further that the 'truth' of a thing was an intrinsic 'mark' of that thing.

> For if some workman conceive a building properly, although this building has never existed, nor ever will exist, the thought will be true and will be the same whether the building exists or not.

Putting a meatball in his mouth with trembling fingers, Hoffman wondered whether any mistakes by the workman could be discovered if the building were never completed. If the workman thought that the design was satisfactory, yet no one took the trouble to inspect the building, then his idea could never be proved 'true'.

Who was to judge that? he wondered, while images from the film fought with one another in his head. Because except for the workman no one had given the design any thought. But was a thought only 'true' if it was also true for another? Suppose he had finished the design, say the draft for his collection of essays, could he have earned a Pulitzer Prize for the draft alone?

No, he thought, the prize could only *go* to a collection of essays that actually existed. Yet mental constructions could be 'true', even if they did not exist in reality. Spinoza was right. But what good was that to Hoffman?

> Whence it follows that there is something real in ideas wherewith the true are distinguished from the false.

Hoffman thought, all right, but what is that 'something real'? Spinoza asserted there was a kind of truth that could be directly apprehended as such. Ideas could be tested for their 'truth'. But what about ideas that could not be tested, such as 'God can be deceived'? Could you tell at once that that was a 'false idea'? Spinoza apparently could.

Later in this section Spinoza returned to the crux of his argument: how one could learn to understand the origin of nature, her 'primary elements'. Hoffman, whose child had played the lead in a pornographic film, was quivering with impatience to have the 'source and origin' of nature laid bare. He realised that what Spinoza was trying to do here was to propose a method of scientific investigation, one that would provide perfect knowledge and point the way to supreme wisdom. But what of his own children, Hoffman thought, what could science add to Miriam's role in *Ardennes Ham*? And Esther, what had Esther meant by her words?

Could those words have been 'true' by Spinoza's lights? Might Esther have grasped the 'truth' with her 'knowing'? Might she have known the 'truth' despite the fact that she had died, a gentle little girl who had been lying now in the damp Zwolle earth for nearly twenty-one years, despite her disappearance from the face of the earth simply because she had been born twenty years too soon?

Was that possible for a child?

Did Spinoza's argument not rather presuppose an experienced, mature person capable of developing his analytical and deductive powers—Hoffman had read somewhere that Spinoza tried to argue from the general to the particular—to the utmost? Was it possible for someone to come to know the 'truth' without understanding this *Treatise*? For that, of course, was something Esther could not possibly have done.

Sunk in such thoughts, keeping the images of what Scheffers had shown him at bay, Hoffman passed the night.

Chapter seven

The morning of 4 July 1989

Towards morning Hoffman began belching and letting off explosive farts. Fast food often had that effect on him, as if his alimentary canal were making noisy protest at the oils and other cheap ingredients in the snacks. Salmon, caviare or good pate never produced the same sort of chemical reaction. He felt bloated, and emptied his stomach in his well-accustomed manner. The vomit was more pungent than usual, more acrid and more acidic. His body was in turmoil, but his mind was resigned.

After showering Hoffman left his suite and, having convinced Mrs Paardekoper that he really had no time to breakfast, got into his car and drove back into town.

The sex cinema was still closed. He stayed in the car, waiting for somebody to open up. He had plenty of time; the minutes ticked by painlessly on his watch. The sun had not yet reached the narrow street. Lorries were off-loading supplies for the cafes. The sound of clinking bottles reverberated between the buildings. He had parked outside a sandwich bar, from which drifted the aroma of fresh coffee.

Men with hoses were calling out to one another, the pavements shone wetly. A girl in a short purple skirt crossed the street and his heart missed a beat. But he pulled himself up immediately; the girl didn't even look like her.

At their last meeting she had been wearing a purple mini-skirt which had barely covered her bottom. With her black net stockings, a tight purple top made of cheap nylon, and heavily made-up eyes, she had looked like a whore. She had sworn to him for the umpteenth time that she would kick the habit. She had asked for money, a thousand guilders, so that she could pay off her debts and start a new life. She had quite often telephoned home, reversing the charges, and he had listened to her ravaged voice. As a child she had hidden behind a wall of silence, as an adolescent behind a wall of words.

Two women in improbably thick coats and with scarves round their heads opened the door of the sex cinema, and he got out of the car. When he walked into the lobby the women were taking off their coats. A neon light flickered on the ceiling; the red light was plainly reserved for the evening.

'Is the boss in?' he asked.

Under their coats the women were wearing aprons.

'Boss not here,' one of them said. Immigrant workers, short, dark-skinned women with big hands and thick eyebrows.

'What time does he get here, do you know?'

'Not come here. Shop over there,' said the woman. She pointed towards the street.

'Do you know the name of the shop?'

The woman consulted her colleague, who was taking buckets and mops out of a cupboard.

'Shop bad,' she explained.

'Bad? You mean...like this place?'

She nodded. The other woman, walking away with her equipment, said, 'Venus.'

The shop was fifty yards further down the street. The window was full of dildos, sexy underwear and aids for he knew not what. A buzzer sounded as he crossed the threshold.

On the left, behind the counter, a woman sat drinking coffee next to the till. Under the glass counter-top the dildos had been lined up in battle formation, a whole regiment of artificial pricks. The small shop area was lined with racks stacked with magazines, their covers displaying vast breasts, moist lips, lascivious tongues.

The woman stood up as soon as Hoffman came in.

'Are you the owner of the cinema down the street?' Hoffman asked.

The woman shook her head. She was about forty, with a pair of glasses hanging round her neck by a chain. On the counter, above the dildos, lay a novel by Garcia Marquez. The draught from a fan turned a couple of pages over. The woman placed her hand on the book.

'No. That's Mr Van der Wiel. He's not here.'

She had a cultured voice and he pictured the situation to himself: a lady from a good Hague background who had fallen on hard times and been glad to clutch at this job.

Hoffman took a twenty-five guilder note from his wallet.

'Perhaps you can help me. I saw a film there last night. *Ardennes Ham*. Funny sort of film. I'd like to know…where you got it from.'

The woman looked regretfully at the banknote in his hand. 'I don't know if I….'

He brought out another note and laid both on the counter.

The woman pocketed the notes before the fan could blow them away.

'I think they're called Triple X.'

'And where can they be found?'

'In Amsterdam.'

'Have you got their telephone number?'

'No, I'm sorry. But directory enquiries will have it.'

Hoffman rang directory enquiries from a call box, then dialled Triple X.

He asked to speak to the managing director. Mr Polak was not in, but was expected some time during the morning.

Hoffman drove to Amsterdam, the asphalt scorching hot under his tyres.

The company was on Geldersekade, just behind Zeedijk, and Hoffman parked his car on Nieumarkt, exposed to the full sun. He had not been there for years and found that the square had been turned into a chaotic car park.

The building in which the Triple X office was located was shored up with heavy timbers.

A crumbling passage led him to the company's door, which was covered with stickers advertising films: *Tom Fool and His Big Tool* and *Mary Had a Little Puss.*

Pushing the door open, he found a plump girl sitting in an office crammed with towering piles of papers and square boxes containing cans of film. The girl's round face was encircled by a wreath of thick curly hair. An old-fashioned fan whirled round on the corner of her desk.

'Is this Triple X?'

'Yes. What can I do for you?'

'Mr Polak. Is he in?'

'Have you got an appointment?'

'No. I've come on the off chance.'

'Well you're in luck, because he's usually very busy.'

She pressed a button on her intercom.

'There's a gentleman to see you, Daddy.'

'Who?' Hoffman heard a man's voice ask.

'What's the name?'

'De Vries.'

'De Vries,' she repeated.

'Which De Vries?' asked the man.

'The real one,' said Hoffman.

'The real one, Daddy.'

'The real one? What's he mean, the real one?'

Hoffman leaned across the pile of papers on the desk and spoke at the machine.

'If I could just have a word with you, Mr Polak, I'll explain everything.'

'You can forget any ideas about a part straight away. I've got enough studs.'

'No, it's not about a part.'

'What is it about then?'

'Ardennes Ham!'

'In what connection?'

'Money. Can I see you for a moment?'

'Well…send him in, Judy.'

The girl stood up. He followed her. She was wearing tight jeans that showed off an ample bottom, and a T-shirt that was if anything tighter still and strained over a bust of *Hustler* proportions.

She led Hoffman back along the passage and pointed to a door. A sign read WAILING WALL PRODUCTIONS.

'Triple X does the distribution, the Wall is the production company,' the girl explained.

'Many thanks.'

Hoffman opened the door and peered into a large room. It was furnished in a fashionably minimalist style. A short man with a greying goatee beard rose and came to meet him.

'Are you De Vries?'

'I am,' said Hoffman.

'Never seen you before…Joop Polak.'

They shook hands.

'Sit down, De Vries.'

Hoffman walked across the thick grey carpet towards the black desk. Three leather chairs stood facing it. Polak's was an armchair with a high back in soft leather. Spindly halogen lamps. A designer-made interior.

'I'm right in the middle of a new film. We're shooting round the corner in a lovely little apartment, good crew, classy girl, but

she's new and there can be a little bit of a problem with that sometimes.'

Hoffman sat down.

Polak looked at him, automatic smile in place. He had perfect
teeth, his beard had been trimmed by an accomplished hand. His
hairy wrists bore thick gold bracelets. The air in the room had been
filtered and cooled. Hoffman could hear the soft humming of the
air-conditioning. He was a stranger in this world.

'Well, De Vries, what can I do for you? You don't look to me like
someone wanting a job. But maybe you've got some money to invest? In
that case, you've come to the right place.' The man laughed loudly.

'I'm here to buy,' said Hoffman, his voice shaking.

'A buyer? For the right price I'll sell you my own daughter.
Only kidding. Okay, what do you want to buy?'

Polak was smiling broadly.

'Every print in existence of *Ardennes Ham.*'

Polak shook his head, astonished at such naivety. The smile
vanished.

'You've got no idea how much that would cost you, De
Vries.'

'Five hundred thousand.'

Polak began laughing again.

'Each print cost me ten thousand to make. There are twenty-
five of them. That makes two hundred and fifty thousand. And that
doesn't even begin to include the production costs.…De Vries, you
don't know what you're talking about.'

He looked closely at Hoffman again.

Hoffman made an attempt at a smile.

'Okay, De Vries…you're a Yiddisher boy too, aren't you?'

Hoffman nodded, still smiling. 'Yes.'

'So what does a nice Jewish boy like you want with twenty-
five prints of *Ardennes Ham*? You don't own a cinema, you're not a
pervert, so what are you?'

'A collector,' Hoffman said, as he had rehearsed in the car.

'A collector, my arse. I've had them here, sitting where you're sitting now, and believe me, those boys are something else. You're a respectable gentleman, got all the right clothes. Style, that's what you've got, De Vries, *style!*'

Hoffman smiled politely.

'Seven hundred and fifty thousand,' he said, surprising himself. He had to save Miriam.

Sighing, Polak shook his head. 'What exactly do you want?'

'The film. The prints, the negative.'

'What do you want them for?'

'I want to be the only person who can see them.'

'Is it because of one of the girls?'

Hoffman reddened. 'No. I'm interested in the whole film,' he said.

'Which girl?'

Hoffman shook his head.

'You don't have to be shy with me, you know!' Polak gave a loud laugh. 'Come on, which one are you after? I'll fix it up for you. It'll cost you, but not hundreds of thousands. So, which one of the girls is it?'

He pulled out the bottom drawer of his desk and fished a card out of a filing system.

'I've got all the *Ham* names here. I can't swear the addresses won't have changed, it's a few years ago already, am I right?'

But Hoffman did not want to look at the list of names. He slid forward to the edge of his chair.

'I'm after the film, Polak. I want the negative. Name your price.'

'Two million.'

Hoffman's expression did not change as he heard the figure, and he said, 'One million.'

Polak sighed.

'Listen, De Vries. I'll let you have *Ham* for the right price, okay? But maybe you can get what you want cheaper, right? Because you're no collector. Well?'

'One and a quarter.'

'Which girl, De Vries? Which is the one that turns you on?'

'One and a quarter, I said.'

'No. The price for *Ham* is two million. You know why? Because that joke set *me* back two million. So far I've only been able to recover the cost of the prints. Comedy porn? Forget it. Two million. Otherwise there's no point my getting rid of it. I'm serious. I'd sooner milk it for another few years. And I'm not even counting the interest.'

'I haven't got two million. One point three. That's all I've got.'

'Then go have yourself a nice day with it, friend.'

'Sell me that film, Polak.'

Hoffman heard himself pleading. If he had to, he would kneel down in the dust before the man. A kneeling Jew!

'I *have* to have the film…. I can't tell you why, but it must never be shown again, do you understand? One point three million guilders, that's a lot of money, Polak.'

'Cash?'

'Well…paintings. Assessed value.'

'What paintings?'

'Cobra.'

Polak picked up a pencil from his gleaming desk and tapped with it on a yellow notepad, an American legal pad, whose colour made an interesting contrast with the black desk top. He looked at the file card.

'One of your daughters, De Vries?'

He glanced at Hoffman.

Hoffman turned white. He felt his eyes fill with tears and bit his lip.

'A daughter of yours, right, De Vries?'

Hoffman was unable to respond, but Polak shook his head with annoyance.

'Always the same with these pussy cats…always. Which one was it? You can tell me, you're not the first.'

Hoffman still did not respond.

Polak referred to the card.

'Suzy Jean? No. Linda Hammer? Rosetta Jones? No. Shit. Miss leading lady herself. Esther Kaplan. Bloody hell.'

The tears were suddenly streaming down Hoffman's cheeks. Soundlessly he struggled to keep impassive as the tears continued to flow.

Polak put his elbows on the desk and shook his head.

'Shit, man…couldn't you have kept an eye on her?'

He suddenly changed his tone, tried a different approach. 'So what, anyway? What if she does show off her pussy, does that have to keep you awake at nights?'

'She's dead, Polak. And she destroyed all her own photographs. There's no way that film can ever….'

Polak looked at him appalled. 'Oy, gevalt,' he muttered under his breath.

Hoffman wiped his cheeks.

'Look here, Kaplan—your name's not De Vries, is it?—but her name wasn't Kaplan either. What are you called?'

'Hoffman.'

'Okay, Hoffman, would you like a drink?'

'No, thanks.'

'How much have you got?'

'One million three hundred thousand in paintings.'

'Investments?'

'That's every last thing I've got.'

'Every last thing?'

'It's worth it to me.'

'Give me the one point three in Cobra paintings, Hoffman. But I want to see the valuations, okay? You can have all the prints the day after tomorrow. I'll tell the lab you'll be coming round for the negative. Here, have something to drink.'

Hoffman had the negative and the prints destroyed, except for one which he deposited in a fireproof safe-deposit box at Lentjes & Drossaerts, a bank in Den Bosch. The Cobra canvases had been exchanged for Miriam's film.

Two thousand five hundred metres of film, twenty-four frames per second, ninety minutes of porn.

Polak had also given him a boxful of leaflets. Coloured photographs on glossy paper of Miriam, with strips plastered across her breasts and stomach. The legend explained that *Ardennes Ham* was about the young wife of an elderly Belgian professor who lived with his head in the clouds and neglected his marital duties. His wife sought solace elsewhere, female as well as male. In the end it transpired that the wily professor had engineered the whole thing: he got his kicks from watching, and looked on from a hiding place as his wife performed. The film had been shot at Hoffman's summer house near Vught. The wife was played by Miriam. Hoffman took the box to a paper reprocessing plant and watched as it was shredded.

Chapter eight

The afternoon of 4 July 1989

Freddy Mancini had been in the safe house for a week now. John Marks found it surprising that Mancini had never once asked for the restrictions on his freedom to be lifted. He had made several calls to his wife, who had extended her tour of Europe, and seemed to have completely resigned himself to his role as suspect.

Marks had noticed the phenomenon before: guilt overtaking the witness because he can only manage to come up with inadequate information. Mancini identified himself with the possible victims of the incident he had witnessed, and blamed himself for not having paid better attention.

Marks had twice had him wired up to the polygraph, the lie detector in which whole hordes of members of the Company placed their blind trust (Marks considered it a mediaeval instrument of torture), and increasingly Mancini had contradicted himself. Yet he was the victim of nothing more than his own gluttony

He had had one of the sessions with Mancini recorded on tape and gone over it with his assistants. They had agreed that there was nothing further to be wrung out of Mancini and that he should be put on the plane back to his home in San Diego.

Marks was now on his way to the house, driving his old Buick, which his dealer had let him have back. Marks did not know if he would be able to go on driving an automobile that had been damaged, and wondered if he should look for an assessor who would declare the new Buick a write-off for him, even though that sort of thing went against the grain. He felt at home back in his old Buick, but it had been tainted by the inescapable filth of garage mechanics. He was wearing gloves now.

The front of the new Buick had sustained two-and-a-half thousand dollars' worth of damage. The owner of the Chevy he had run into had had to settle for five hundred. Marks' attorney had assured him that the man had no case against him, but Marks had learned to distrust lawyers.

The house was near Potomac, a small town named after the river, a few miles to the north-west of Langley, which lay on the other side of the river. Just before the town he turned off the metalled highway and took a forest track which led to the secluded house. Trees and dense bushes to left and right, a paradise for squirrels and foxes. After a sharp bend, which he negotiated at walking pace, he was obliged to come to a halt by two men who stepped out from behind a delivery truck. They were wearing sunglasses with mirrored lenses, but they were young and Marks was quick to forgive them.

Though they recognised him, they were required to check his papers.

'Your papers please, Mr Marks.'

John held out his ID from the Company.

They examined the card with great interest, as they had every day during the past week.

'Carry on, sir.'

Outside the house, Robert MacLaughlin stood waiting for him.

'Mancini's suddenly remembered something,' he said when

Marks opened the door of the Buick. His eyes were wide with excitement.

'What does he remember?'

'He says he remembers a bracelet.'

Freddy Mancini was sitting downstairs in the living room in front of the television. His arms lay along the broad arms of the easy chair, his left fist round a can of Diet Coke. He smiled broadly when he saw Marks.

'Hi, John.'

Marks shook hands without taking off his gloves.

'Ready for the trip home, Freddy?'

'Yes….' A shadow flitted across Freddy's eyes.

'You'll be glad to get back,' said Marks.

'Sure, but…last night something suddenly came to me.'

'Oh, that changes the situation,' said Marks without conviction.

He sat down on the sofa facing Mancini and looked at him with as much interest as he could muster. 'Shoot, Freddy, I'm all ears.'

Freddy looked even fatter than he had a week earlier. Carolyn Bachman had made a list of everything she had prepared for him.

'I swear,' she had told Marks, 'I swear there are restaurants that would die for a customer like him. That man is one big guzzling factory.'

'It came to me suddenly last night,' said Freddy, 'in a dream. Usually I forget my dreams straight away, but this time I woke up and then I remembered the whole thing.'

He took a drink, holding the can for a long time over his mouth. When it was empty he put it down next to him on the floor. Two other empty cans were standing there, together with three full ones still in the plastic wrapping of a six-pack. Freddy leant over to one side as far as he could and pulled another can out of the plastic.

Marks lit a cigarette. A long flame shot out of the lighter. He inhaled deeply. Outside nature reigned in silence. He wondered if he should buy the place once it had done its job as a safe house. The Company had been using it for a year now. It had been put up for sale by an elderly couple who had moved to Palm Springs, and the Company had bought it through an agent who had acted as their front. The house would be used for about two years and then put up for sale again through the same agent.

'What I thought to myself was, does that dream mean anything,' Freddy went on, 'because it was only a dream, wasn't it? But suddenly it hit me that it hadn't really been a dream at all but a memory!'

He pulled at the tab, then pushed it back into the can.

'These new cans aren't as good,' he said. 'You used to be able to throw the rings away but now you can't get them off.'

He took a fresh gulp.

'It's about the last part, that part when Browning was being dragged into the automobile. It suddenly came back to me, I'll swear it was as clear and bright as watching a movie, John.'

Marks nodded. Relaxed, he sat back, gazing intently at Freddy.

'Those bare arms were a woman's. I'm sure of that now. You know why? Because now I know there was a bracelet, John, and I remember that bracelet because I saw it in my dream! There was a woman in that automobile! Isn't that the darnedest thing?'

'We've suspected it for some time now, Freddy.'

'But now we know it for sure! A woman! Don't you think it's the darnedest thing they should have sent a woman to arrest Browning? Well, I sure do. There was a woman in that automobile.'

'It's an interesting detail, Freddy.'

'Well, I don't know about that, that's for you to—'

'I shall mention it in the report, Freddy.'

'Fine…I just wondered…what if I should dream some more of that sort of thing, you never can tell…and anyway, maybe you have something I can take which can make a dream deeper…'

Mancini took a drink. Marks looked at him expectantly.

'Well…?'

Freddy put the can down on the wooden arm of his chair.

'I don't know if it makes any sense sending me away now,' he said confidently. 'It's not that I think this place is all that wonderful, but I do want to help you. And I've got a better chance of doing that if I stay here.'

'Let's hear a suggestion, then,' said Marks.

Freddy looked at him in surprise. 'You mean it?'

'What do you want, Freddy?'

'What do I want?' He suddenly sounded dejected.

'Do you really think you can add anything more to our inquiry?'

'I sure do.'

'You dreamed about that bracelet?'

'Yes.'

'You were fast asleep?'

'Yes, I think I was.'

'You think you were?'

'Perhaps I wasn't really *fast* asleep...but I sure was sleeping, yes.'

'Freddy, you know there can be times, don't you, when you are neither asleep nor awake and when everything seems just like a dream? You weren't really dreaming last night, at least I don't think you were.'

'I remembered it, John.'

'I doubt it.'

'Who was there, you or me?'

'That's not something we need argue about.'

'There was a woman there, John. That's got to be a useful piece of information for you, surely?'

'I don't know if I can believe you.'

Mancini blinked his eyes in alarm at the words. He took a drink to cover his loss of composure.

'We appreciate what you've done for us, Freddy, we're grateful to you for having given us so much of your time. You've told us everything as best you could, but I think we'd better forget this story about the bracelet.'

Freddy lowered his eyes, staring at his enormous belly. He was sitting erect, as if the fat acted as a corset.

'I'm sure I can dig out some more,' he said hesitantly. 'If I have enough time, that is.'

'When does your wife get back?'

'Tomorrow.'

'Don't you want to see her?'

He kept his eyes turned away, staring now at the can in his right hand. He ran a finger round the rim.

'Of course I do.'

'Tomorrow she'll be back home. And so will you.'

'I can help you here. Honest I can.'

'Go home, Freddy. It's for the best.'

Mancini held the can over his mouth and emptied it.

Two hours later Marks was sitting in his attic workshop. Outside the big window the old Virginian trees shimmered in the heat. Marks had hung a bulletin board on the wall between the chimney flues and now he was wielding a new felt-tipped pen over a small pile of yellow index cards.

He had no faith in cleaning women and looked after his house himself, spending three hours a day on the job. He had had a water and air purification system installed, every wall was insulated and all the windows soundproofed.

He was working on a report for Chris Moakley, the head of SE-PC, the section within the Company that kept its finger on the pulse of Poland and Czechoslovakia. Moakley, like Marks, had been a regional controller, and his bureaucratic talents (he was a born bookkeeper) had gained him his section. Moakley's office was littered with gadgets for filling and scraping out his pipe. Marks had known him for twenty years and had never seen him succeed in keeping his pipe alight for more than thirty seconds.

Marks wrote on the card: BROWNING ARRESTED. He pinned it to the centre of the board. Employees of the Company working in Czechoslovakia under the protection of a diplomatic passport had tried to clarify what had taken place during the night of 21 June, but had been unable to come up with even the smallest shred of information.

One of the Company's most important sources in Czechoslovakia went by the code name of 'Carla'. She was a Czech intelligence operative who had been recruited as a double agent by an employee of the Company eight years earlier. Carla's identity was known to a small circle only: the local controller in Prague, the heads of SE and the top management of the Company, a total of fourteen people.

The mail Michael Browning had been sent to collect in Prague would have come from Carla.

After Browning's arrest Carla had managed to pass a message to the local controller in Prague, and Marks had a copy of it. Moakley had given him permission to take it home.

Yesterday Moakley had told him that Carla wanted to come over to the West.

'She's had enough. Can't argue with that. She's been useful to us for a long time. She wants to come and pick up her reward.'

Marks had stressed that they did not know whether Carla could still be trusted. If Carla had been picked up before Browning was snatched, then it was probable that it was she who had blown his cover.

'Coincidence,' Moakley had said. 'They haven't got Carla.'

Marks wrote on a card: COINCIDENCE. He pinned it under the first card, to the left. Next he wrote: CARLA HAS BETRAYED BROWNING. He pinned that card to the right of COINCIDENCE, making a triangle with the cards.

If the Czechs, for whatever reason, had arrested Carla, then she would undoubtedly have passed on everything she knew. Carla was a double agent, but he could not rule out the possibility that she might be a triple agent by now, since the local controller in Prague had reported that Carla was still at large.

'What would *we* have done?' he had asked Moakley. 'Suppose we'd caught someone like Carla. We'd have turned her round and let her go. The other side would go on thinking she was a double agent when in fact she'd be working for us again.'

'Browning's cover couldn't have been blown,' said Moakley.

'Coincidence, that's what it was. No one, absolutely no one knew he was coming.'

'Carla knew,' Marks had muttered.

Moakley had devised a system known in the Company as the 'travel agency'.

The difficulties of information-gathering were not resolved when a new source was recruited. Indeed, the recruitment gave rise to a new problem: how was the Company to come safely into possession of the messages the new source wanted to send?

The normal procedure was to put a local employee of the Company in charge of the new source, who knew what codes to use in order to contact his or her controller. For instance, on a prearranged day (these arrangements were made when the source was recruited, usually under difficult circumstances), say the third Tuesday of the month, a potted geranium would be moved from the middle of a window to the left, which meant 'I want a meeting in three days' time'. A variety of codes for messages was agreed in this way with the source.

As a rule the counter-intelligence service of the host country was quick to discover which new diplomats were working secretly for the Company. They were continuously shadowed, their homes were bugged, and everything possible was done to prevent their making contact with the local population. The contact with the source was the moment of greatest danger.

It was rare for a message to be literally handed over, from hand to hand (although it did happen, for instance in a department store). Normally the source would take a message to the drop (perhaps a hollow behind a brick in a wall) and the employee was expected to pick it up, having made sure that he was not being shadowed or was otherwise under observation, and to take it as quickly as possible to the safety of the Embassy. It was a boy scout arrangement, but no better one had yet been devised.

The variant Moakley had come up with was to send someone out who was not active inside the post's diplomatic network, and to use him just once as a courier. The courier had no diplomatic status and his arrest could therefore have grave consequences for him, but his only task was to carry a message from A to B. He knew no names, no secrets, no codes, and if he took the customary precautions his detection could be as good as ruled out.

Mass tourism, which had recently spilled over into the Eastern bloc, had rendered Moakley's variant feasible. The old method continued, but the travel agency had its champions amongst the heads of the Company's departments.

The Company trained employees for this mission on a special base in New Mexico, far from its other training centres. A steady stream of couriers was sent on holiday by the travel agency. For some particularly troublesome spots, such as Czechoslovakia, Albania or Bulgaria, they were given extra preparation, and at their own request issued with a pill that would kill them within five seconds—the notorious L-pill. The pill had been a matter of controversy for several years. Marks had been opposed to the practice of issuing it to couriers—who after all were no more than pawns in a big game—to use at their discretion, but others, including Moakley, took the view that arrest, for whatever reason, could lead to torture, which no one should be compelled to undergo. Moreover, torture resulted in confession and the structure of the travel agency could be blown.... Those for and against had eventually reached a compromise: the courier himself would decide whether or not he would carry an L-pill.

No one working for the travel agency had ever been arrested before. Browning was their first 'industrial accident'. Moakley had asked Marks to help with the investigations.

'Browning was careless. It was a case of routine surveillance of tourists, most likely, and they picked on him by chance. At least I hope that's what it was,' Moakley had said.

'Hope is an uncommon emotion in our job, Chris.'

The point of the thick felt-tipped pen squeaked across the dry card. Marks wrote CARLA WORKS FOR THE CSSR. He pinned the card underneath CARLA HAS BETRAYED BROWNING.

It was all guesswork of course; he had no solid information to bear out his suspicions, but then he had to base everything he did on risk-limitation. He had to take Carla's possible arrest as his starting point, since that was the only way of explaining Browning's disappearance. There was no mileage in relying on coincidence.

CARLA WANTS TO COME OVER TO THE WEST, he wrote. And on another card, CARLA IS A CSSR MOLE.

He looked back at the lonely COINCIDENCE card. If he had been working for the Czechs and had caught a source such as Carla, he would have left Browning severely alone. He would have set Carla to work feeding errand-boys from the other side, like Browning, with 'comic strips' (information that betrayed its concocted nature only after extensive investigation, if then). He took the card down from the wall and added BECAUSE IT IS POINTLESS TO ARREST B IF YOU ALREADY HAVE CARLA.

He gave it some more thought. Suppose someone working for the Czechs had arrested someone like Carla because she had been careless, say had photographed material from the files and been caught at it. He would have interrogated her, and his methods would inevitably have led to her confession that she had been working as a double agent for the Americans for years. He would then have tried to turn her round, to put her to work for his side again, and would have let her go, keeping her under strict surveillance. And to crown it all, he would have issued her with false information that she could pass on to her courier. Disinformation.

The problem with turning agents, however, was that you could never be sure that you had been successful. There were codes by which an agent could warn his controller or courier that the material was tainted and that he was no longer a reliable source. And when the courier returned with the phoney information, American intelligence would believe he was trying to pull the wool over their eyes, while the turned double agent was in fact continuing to work for them.

No, if he had arrested someone like Carla (he would rather not arrest her, preferring to leave her in the dark about having been found out and simply keeping her under observation) then he would also have aimed at rounding up her whole network and causing as much damage as possible in the shortest possible time.

And Carla was still moving about freely in Prague. A coincidence?

Perhaps Browning really had made a mistake. The hotels over there were closely watched and, despite his training, Browning might well have attracted attention when he left his hotel. The environs of the hotels teemed with men in cars with nothing else to do but keep their eye on foreigners. Browning had gone out and they had followed him. He had spotted them and taken to his heels, with the results Freddy Mancini had witnessed.

In this scenario, Carla was still a reliable source and Moakley's travel agency guaranteed strict damage limitation.

Michael Browning had a cover as an auto dealer from Green Bay, Wisconsin, and if the Czechs cared to look into it they would find proof, carefully doctored by the Company, that Browning had been living and working in Green Bay for the past five years. A family introduced a risk factor in such cases, but luckily Browning had just one brother, who had received a visit in the meantime from the Company's condolence team. They anticipated no problems from that quarter.

Marks had taken part in the discussion which had considered the possibility of forcing a diplomatic incident. If the State Department decided to lodge a vehement protest about the kidnapping of an innocent US citizen in Prague, it would be easy to inflame public opinion by feeding material to the press via anonymous 'well-informed sources'. But they had decided in the end to hush the affair up, since the consequences of a diplomatic row were unpredictable.

The party of tourists to which Browning had belonged had readily accepted the story that he had had to return hurriedly to Vienna because of a death in his family. No one had inquired any further.

Presumably Browning was dead by now, had swallowed his pill or succumbed in a Czech cell. It had proved impossible to pick up Browning's scent in the maze of the Czech gulag. The Company had satellites capable of determining the whereabouts of just about every bullet in Eastern Europe, but they could not be used to find a human being.

'Coincidence,' Moakley had maintained. 'It's the only possible explanation. It has to be. Let's hope so anyway, otherwise we've lost Carla as well, John, and I don't think the top floor would like that.'

Marks knew then that the top floor had already come to a decision.

'Carla has to be brought over?' he asked.

'I'm afraid so,' Moakley muttered, sucking at his pipe as flames shot out of the bowl. 'I just hope they didn't ill-treat that boy too badly. The top floor wants to get Carla out. In their view a source making such a request should not be ignored. Carla's been doing her best for us for years. They want to use comic strips. Feed Carla comic strips. The very best. She'll be able to use them to improve her standing. Feed her comic strips which oblige her to leave the country. The Czechs will give her permission. As soon as she crosses the border, we grab her.'

'They could be setting us up, Chris,' Marks had replied. 'If they've turned Carla *and* snatched Browning, which is completely illogical—and that's exactly why they've done it, you follow?—then they've got us just where they want us.'

'And where's that?'

'In total confusion.'

Marks wrote FORGET LOGIC. He pinned it underneath CARLA IS A CSSR MOLE.

They could no longer rely on Carla. Anything was possible. Perhaps Browning had gone to his death by chance, perhaps he had been betrayed by Carla, perhaps Carla had already been working for the other side for a long time. He would have them go through what she had been delivering for genuinely classifiable material. Nothing was impossible.

Except, perhaps, bringing her out to the West.

The British had managed to get a source out of Eastern Europe once. In 1985 Oleg Gordievski, head of the KGB in London, had been recalled to Moscow. His colleagues had suspected him of being a double agent for MI6, which in fact he was, but the British had smuggled him out of Moscow to Finland.

The Eastern bloc had solid borders, fences, electronic alarms, minefields, radar, dogs, infra-red, all under the vigilant eyes of special frontier guards. The KGB alone had two hundred and fifty thousand personnel manning the borders, apart from the military border patrols and surveillance supplied by the satellite states.

The top brass of the Company had decided that Carla was entitled to a reward in the West, and that Marks would have to lure her to Langley with the help of comic strips. They had used the method before: give a double agent good solid material, strengthen his position, hint that he will have access to even more material if he pays a short visit to the West, get him to persuade his bosses that he will come back with really worthwhile material, and ensure that he disappears the moment he arrives. These were protracted, complicated operations. But it was the kind of work at which Marks excelled.

He would have to get Carla out to the West. If she was a turned double agent, then there was no problem, because the Czechs would be keen to get her to Langley (he would make sure that she was denied any insight into the inner workings of the Company), but if she was still reliable then he would have to come up with perfect comic strips and have them placed with great subtlety in Carla's reach. Under no circumstances must the Czech analysts be allowed to discover that the documents—usually a mix of genuine and fictitious information—were a fabrication. Carla's standing with her bosses would have to be consolidated slowly and credibly and her trip to the West promise an enormous breakthrough, a possible jackpot waiting to be won, a jackpot consisting of supercomputers or advanced military hardware.

He wrote LOGIC DICTATES: NEVER TRUST CARLA.

And on the next card, THE COMIC STRIPS MUST BE PERFECT. If Carla was still working for the Company, they were duty bound to help her without causing damage, and to that end they would scatter small secrets throughout the comic strips, so much bait for the Czechs. But if she was a turned double agent, the comic strips must give away nothing of value. Marks decided he had better proceed on the second assumption.

The useless comic strips would have to be insinuated discreetly into Carla's grasp.

For that he had received help. From Carla herself.

He wrote HOFFMAN.

Yesterday Moakley had handed him the copy of Carla's report. 'Our local contact picked it up in the usual place.'

'So it was still there?'

'Yes,' said Moakley.

'Odd,' said Marks. 'What's in it?'

'Nothing of any importance. She names three new diplomats in Prague whom the Czechs consider suitable recruitment material.'

'Three diplomats. Ours?'

'No,' Moakley said, casting a glance at the paper. He shook his head. 'Here.'

He handed Marks the paper. Carla warned them that the Czechs were going to take a closer look at three new foreign diplomats as potential recruits. A Canadian, an Italian and a Dutchman. Marks had given no indication, and Moakley had no idea at all, but he knew the Dutchman.

Marks stood up and went to wash his hands.

When he came back he looked at the cards on the bulletin board and enjoyed the aesthetic pattern they made. His work was in no way inferior to that of a composer or author. He rearranged reality. He invented stories that were more far-fetched than Irving's and more realistic than Updike's. He was the best scriptwriter in the United States, though only the twelve heads of the Company knew it.

He raised the arm of the record-player above the disc and lowered the needle into the grooves of the black vinyl. Brahms' Second. He removed the cards from the wall and began working on his scenario.

Chapter nine

The evening of 4 August 1989

Hoffman took his lightest-weight dinner suit out of the wardrobe. He owned three. Their cost was chargeable to the Ministry because the suits were his working clothes. There were times when he had to attend a reception or party several times a week, and the invitation usually stipulated black-tie.

This evening he was going to a formal reception in honour of the new Italian ambassador. Jana had buffed up his new patent-leather shoes, which stood waiting for him in front of the full-length cheval mirror in the bedroom.

It was rare for him to spend longer than an hour at a time here. He would come to make use of the luxurious adjoining bathroom, or to select his clothes. Once in a while he would lie down on the bed to read a book or watch one of the videos which AUVI, the audiovisual division of the Ministry's information service, sent out all round the world. But he preferred to stay in the kitchen.

The arrest of the three journalists had been front-page news in the Netherlands. The minister had issued statements, expressed the 'concern' of the government and stressed the need for 'dialogue'. Every current affairs programme and every weekly journal had wanted an interview with him, but the Ministry had kept them all at bay. After two weeks Hoffman had been sent back to Prague.

Right now the three journalists were still locked up in a sweltering Prague prison cell, and the return of the Dutch ambassador clearly signalled that a blind eye was being turned to the actions of the communist police. Despite editorials in the *Nieuwe Rotterdamse Courant* and the *Volkskrant*, the cabinet in its wisdom had obviously had second thoughts and was suddenly of the opinion that diplomatic contacts with the Czech government mattered more than the fate of three opinionated Dutch hacks. That was a view with which Hoffman agreed in principle, but his people ought to have appreciated it sooner. Now, thanks to his friend Wim Scheffers, his trip to The Hague had brought the shame of his daughter upon him. Politics were always personal.

Hoffman had invested the Cobras, his personal pension scheme, in the film. He was entitled to a state pension as well as superannuation from the Ministry, towards which he had been contributing for thirty years, but he had lost his nest-egg (a small fortune, in fact). Still, he was convinced that he would never make seventy, perhaps not even sixty-five. So he would never have been able to spend the money anyway.

A few months before her death, five years ago, Miriam had asked for the photograph albums which were kept in the cupboard in Khartoum. She said she wanted to have the photographs copied. He had been reluctant to let them go and found out that the job could be done in Khartoum, but as he was unsure of technical standards there and since he had to go to the Netherlands anyway, he had taken the albums with him. He doubted that she would look after them properly, but he knew that she would be deeply offended if he refused to give her temporary custody of them, and when all was said and done she was now his only child.

He had had a meal with her in Amsterdam, on one of the floors of a large Chinese restaurant on the corner of the Dam and

Damstraat, and there he had handed over to her the two plastic bags with the albums.

Black net stockings, the briefest of mini-skirts, a short tight sweater that displayed the soft curve of her belly with every movement. She seemed to be happy with the albums.

'Fantastic, I've been wanting these photos for such a long time. I've got so few pictures of you both.'

'And we've got so few pictures of *you*. You'll have to send us some more.'

'Come on, you know I'm not photogenic. *You're* going to have to send some more.'

'You look stunning in photographs,' he had replied.

'No I don't, I look hideous.'

'Stunning.'

'Knock it off, Mr Hoffman....'

She fell silent for a moment. Then burst out laughing.

'What would you say to my opening a shop?'

'Sounds fun to me,' he said, not knowing exactly what she had in mind.

'Second-hand clothes. You can see them all over the place these days, shops like that. And they bring in a lot of money, you know!'

'I haven't said they don't.'

'They're real little goldmines.'

'Well, *gold*mines....'

'What do you know, Mr Hoffman? People are really raking it in, you wouldn't believe how much money they make, honestly you wouldn't. And it's always easy to get hold of second-hand clothes, good quality gear, you know? There's plenty over here, but most people go to America, fill a container and bring it back, then have a big sort out and sell the best stuff. I know at least five people who are making a fortune that way.'

'Seems like a good idea to me, darling.'

'Honestly?'

'If you really want to....'

'I do really want to!'

'Well, in that case, you have my blessing.'

'You really mean that, or are you just saying it to keep me quiet?'

'I really mean it, Miriam. I think it's a good idea. If you want to start up a shop like that, then I'll support you. And not just with words, I promise. But first…'

'What *first*…?'

He whispered, not wanting to be overheard. 'You know what I mean, Miriam.'

'What are you whispering for?' she said challengingly.

'Come on now, Miriam, take it easy.'

She said, too loudly for his liking, 'Okay, so I'm a user, so what? I can stop, no problem, because I want out myself. All I have to do is just say to myself one day, all right, today it's over, and it'll be over for good then, but they don't make it easy for you in this country, the way they deal with drugs. Okay, I'm a user and I want to open a shop, end of story….'

'I want to help you, Miriam.'

'Sure, but naturally you won't say *how*.'

'You tell me how….'

'To begin with, I have to find a shop.'

'Well, why don't you look for one? Go see an estate agent.'

'Ah, estate agents are a real hassle….'

'I'll go along with you if you like.'

'Really?'

'Of course.'

'How about tomorrow?'

'I'm in The Hague all day tomorrow, darling. The day after, though, I can give you the whole day.'

'I can't the day after. Are you sure you can't tomorrow?'

He shook his head. 'Can't you put whatever it is off?' he asked.

'Can't you put whatever yours is off tomorrow?' she replied.

'Sweetheart, it's nearly nine o'clock at night. I can't get hold of anybody at this hour.'

'Oh, is that right, Mr Hoffman, and you really want to help me? If I'm important enough to you, then you just ring your people in the morning and tell them you've got something else to do. Like going with your daughter to an estate agent.'

He nodded, sore at heart, and she gave him a telephone number where he could reach her the next morning. When he rang, no one answered. He dialled the number every fifteen minutes as the morning wore on. He waited in his Hague apartment, lamented his helplessness and the day slipped away without his having been able to contact her.

He battled with his anxiety for the rest of the week. Impassively he conferred with the administrators of development funds, drew up reports on the Kassala Flood Protection project and on the Khartoum Central Foundry, dined, met his schedule, worked his way desultorily through detective stories at night and simultaneously grieved over Miriam's fate. The family's failure to keep Esther with them had been punished with lifelong martyrdom. They were no longer the Hoffman family, but Miriam the Guilty and Felix the Guilty. Every 'shift'—he had heard this oddly industrial term used in diplomatic circles for the first time that week—he dialled her number. On the eighth day he was answered by a man's voice.

'Is Miriam there?'

'No.'

It was obvious that Hoffman had just woken the Voice up. It was half past three in the afternoon.

'Could you tell me when she'll be back?'

'Hey, man, I'm not a clairvoyant.'

'Tell her that her father rang. She has my number.'

'Her father, huh?'

'Tell her I want to go to the estate agent with her.'

'Oh, man,' chuckled the Voice, 'you're just about the last person she needs.'

And the Voice hung up.

Two days later, shortly before his departure for Khartoum, she paid him a visit at his Ministry apartment in The Hague.

'Why didn't you get in touch, Miriam?'

'It's always reproaches with you! Why can't you just be glad to see me? I've got other things on my mind than phoning you the whole time, believe it or not. You're not the only one with things to attend to and appointments to keep. I really don't need a father leaning on me to do something or other as well.'

'I'm sorry, Miriam, I can't have understood properly. I'm leaving the day after tomorrow, so why don't we go to the estate agent's tomorrow?'

'Oh, stop going on about estate agents!'

She gave a hoarse laugh. She was wearing cheap rings on each of her fingers, and held a hand to her mouth as she started to cough. She was smoking Gauloises, inhaling the steel-blue smoke as she sat hunched forward on a chair at the dining table. Her slender legs were crossed and she propped herself up with an elbow on her knee.

Her clothing left no question unanswered about her figure; she had what would make a man happy. She got to her feet when her cough refused to stop and made for the kitchen. He heard her drink some water, then call, 'Hey, you haven't got any vanilla cream custard or anything, have you?'

All she would eat was this thick creamy dessert, and every two days he had been buying a fresh carton of the stuff and then throwing it out again, because he wanted to have something for her to eat if she suddenly turned up at the door. But he had given that up and now there was none in the apartment.

'No. I'm afraid I haven't. Shall we go out for something to eat?'

She came back, stopped at the kitchen door, one hand under an armpit, the other holding a cigarette to her mouth.

'Look, tell me honestly... that estate agent, do you really want to take me there?'

'To an estate agent, a lawyer, the bank, you say the word.'

'The bank too?'

'About a shop? Yes.'

'I don't want any shop. People can go stark staring mad in a shop, didn't you know that?'

'What? But I thought—'

'Oh, God, I was just saying any old thing….' She grinned. 'You actually fell for all that, did you?'

'Yes. I actually fell for all that….'

'You don't understand a thing, do you?'

'About what?'

'About me. About the world.'

She laughed again. She stuck the cigarette between her thickly painted lips and inhaled deeply.

'No,' he mumbled.

'Look…I don't want any shop. I want absolutely nothing.'

'Nothing? In the long run I think you're going to want something.'

'No, in the long run, I want absolutely nothing.'

'Darling, you've turned twenty-four!'

'So what? Do you really think I get all uptight about "the long run"? I'll never make thirty, anyway…. Oh, by the way, thanks for the money.'

'Don't talk like that, Miriam….'

She dropped some ash on the floor, looked at it, then brushed it away with the sharp toe of her little boot. She was still leaning against the door-frame.

'Mr Hoffman…could you spare me a little more cash?'

'It's all gone?'

'Hey, come on, how long do you think you can live around here on fifteen hundred guilders?'

He had sent her a cheque for that amount on her birthday, just over a month before, and it must all have been mainlined away already.

'How much do you need?'

'A thousand?'

She was biting a fingernail, did not look him in the eye.

'Miriam, you've just had fifteen hundred from us.'

'For my birthday, yes.'

'What do you need the money for?'

'Nothing special...pay the rent.'

'Why don't you take a job?'

'There aren't any jobs to take.' She was staring at her nails.

'And you don't pay any rent.'

She looked up at him fiercely, and said, 'Do I have to go walk the streets or something? You'd like that better, would you?'

They went out to eat, or rather he ate and she took a few spoonfuls of soup. Next day at Amsterdam Central station he gave her the money. At this last meeting she was flustered, nervous, impatient. She pulled the envelope from his hand, quickly counted the money. She puffed deeply at her cigarette and left him after a quick peck on his cheek. She was wearing her uniform.

Hoffman did up his dress-shirt, its buttons concealed under a fly front. The cuffs had to be folded double, and fastening the gold cufflinks always gave him trouble because of having to thread the links through two holes at once. His fingers were old and clumsy.

He had come across the photograph albums again in his house at Vught. After the funeral he and Marian had gone there together. Their daughter had cut her own picture out of every single photograph. Marian had not wanted to stay in the house and they had taken a room in the Hotel Central in Den Bosch.

He had found pieces of transparent plastic in the gutted house. Not recognising them, he had thought they must be connected with the stuff she injected or smoked, and had thrown the bits of blue and orange plastic away. He now realised that they had been filters, left over from the scenes for *Ardennes Ham* that had been shot in the house. At all costs it had to be kept from Marian.

He had asked Polak to come to Hein Daamen's warehouse in Den Bosch. They had loaded the forty-three canvases into a delivery van, he had sweated like a pig, and Polak had handed over the box with five cans of film.

'Nothing goes in the books, okay, Hoffman?' Polak had said.

Of course not, for how would his accountant in The Hague have entered that kind of transaction? 'Purchase of negatives of pornographic film in which the late daughter of Mr F. Hoffman flaunted her pussy?'

After he had been to Den Bosch and collected the very last print of the film, a box full of shame, he had rung Wim Scheffers at the Department.

'Forgive me, Wim.'

'I forgive you. Please forgive me too.'

'I do.'

'I'm sorry, Felix. I ought never to have told you.'

'The film was there, whether I knew about it or not.'

'I could have kicked myself.'

'Well, now I know. And once you know a thing, you can never not know it again. What are you doing tonight?'

'Taking you out, Felix.'

'You're not trying to make amends, by any chance?'

'Is that what it looks like?'

'Pretty close…. But it's for me to make amends. Did I hurt you that time, Wim?'

'It's okay. I asked for it.'

Hoffman opened the wardrobe in search of a bow tie. He had a whole box of them. A few years back he had bought a dark blue one with yellow polka-dots at Saks in New York, a daring item which had drawn many compliments. Tonight he would wear it again.

This Italian reception was the first big party he had attended here, except for his own of course, but that had been a modest Dutch affair.

It had been a month since he had bought the film, but the few scenes from it he had watched still swam all day long behind his eyes. He had tried drinking himself senseless. Every night during the whole of the first week after his return he had poured vodka down his throat. Every night he had reached the point at which the liquor irritated his guts beyond endurance and the lavatory had been too far away. His stomach had emptied itself on the kitchen floor.

How could you forget without sleeping? You only forgot if you could forget yourself. If he could only stop the machine in his head, that unremitting voice going on ceaselessly inside his head. That stupid voice reminding him of Esther and Miriam and of everything that had made such a tangled mess of his life. It was his own voice, as he knew only too well, and without a voice there was no life; it was only that this voice never let up, never stopped nagging him the whole time about everything he had no wish to hear.

The film he had seen in the sex cinema had had the effect of inflating his self-loathing to unprecedented proportions. For he had not only sat weeping as he looked at Miriam, but during those hundred seconds an abominable wave of excitement had taken over in his lap which had caused him to stare at his daughter like some sick voyeur. He had stood up, had reeled to the exit. Revolted.

His revulsion at what he had seen was not pure. Miriam had revealed herself in her most intimate nakedness, and he had pressed his hands to his eyes and peered out between his fingers.

Forbidden images he had yet wanted to see.

They had unleashed a wave of crude, bestial lust. But then the taboo had reared up savagely and scourged him with lashes that had shaken him to the depths of his soul. A father may not see his daughter thus. He had been overcome with biblical shame.

He must cleanse himself. His mind, his soul, his body. But he knew that he lacked the strength. Simpler to poison himself. If his children had no right to live then he certainly had none. Yet his heart continued to beat and his lungs to suck in oxygen, and he could hear and see and his body continued to function, while the bones of his children crumbled away in the Zwolle earth. He had no right to live, yet neither could he put an end to his life. What his children had been denied was not to be discarded by him as worthless.

He no longer dared face Spinoza. He had been diverted by the *Treatise* and he was still aware of a desire, somewhere at the back of his mind, to come to closer grips with the philosopher's thoughts and to embrace them. But now he had forfeited the right to have a liking for anything.

He sat down on his bed in order to put on his patent-leather shoes with a shoehorn. His feet were swollen and the leather felt tight across his toes. He would have to wear the shoes in, or else he would never be able to walk in them properly. He had bought them, together with a new dinner suit, especially for his posting to Prague. New shoes for a new job. He had ordered them in Waalwijk, from Greve's, where they made the best shoes in the world. He was the Kingdom's representative. He was expected to defend the honour of the shrewd little trading nation on the North Sea, and this evening he felt he could do that best by wearing his new Dutch shoes.

He remembered what his mother had told him: 'Always take care of your hair and your shoes, Felix, that's how to tell a civilised person. Your hair has to be clean and tidy—you know why? Because it shows you keep both your head and your thoughts clean. And you walk about in shoes because you're not an animal, but don't forget, you polish your shoes to show respect for the earth.'

He did have respect for the earth, for in it his children lay. He also had respect for the air, for in it blew the ashes of his gassed parents.

Laboriously he tied up his shoelaces. He was a heavily-built man and the years were beginning to tell.

He had last seen his parents in the spring of 1942, when he had left with the pig-breeder for the farm near Boxtel.

Van de Pas had been a client of the 'Jewish bank'. His family had once been prominent in Brabant, but their wealth had been drunk away and their land sold off. Eduard Van de Pas was the last descendant, an introverted man, an eccentric who spoke to his animals and used modern rearing techniques on them, but killed them without remorse when he needed meat for his table. He read Rilke and distilled his own gin, which he would drink until his eyes crossed.

Hoffman's father had known him for years and had proposed a deal: you hide my son and I will write off your debt. Van de Pas stuck to the bargain. He gave the boy food, a place to sleep and kept him warm.

Felix   remained   hidden   for   two-and-a-half   years.

Uncomprehendingly he read the farmer's books. At night, lying on a straw mattress, he cried.

His parents had cast him out. They had banished him to this farm and had looked for a hiding place for themselves somewhere else. Even though they had explained to him time after time that it was safer for him to lie low somewhere on his own (he imagined a cellar, deep under the ground, dank and dark), he could not understand why he could not go with them. He passed his thirteenth birthday with the farmer, but his bar mitzvah went uncelebrated among the pigs.

It had been his father, not his mother, who had cried when Van de Pas took him away. They had said goodbye at the kitchen door. His mother said, 'It won't be for long, Felix. Perhaps just a few weeks. Then you'll be back home.'

'Where are you both going?' he asked fearfully.

'It's best you don't know,' she said.

'But I'm your child!' he protested.

'Even so, it's safer not to know.'

He gasped with the emotion.

'When will I see you again?' he asked.

'Very soon,' she said. She kissed him.

His father handed him the suitcase. 'Here.'

With both hands, Felix tried to crush the handle.

'Daddy, I don't want—'

'You've got to, my boy, believe me. You're bound to be homesick for a week or so, but later on…I know you'll understand it was all for the best.'

Van de Pas took the suitcase from him. 'Give it to me, that case is too heavy for you.'

Both his parents kissed him at once, one on his right cheek, the other on his left.

'Off you go, then, Felix,' said his mother.

Van de Pas said, 'No matter what happens, I'll bring the boy back, fit and well.'

And then Felix saw his father break down and begin to cry. His mother put her arms protectively round her husband, and said to her son in an anguished voice, 'Go now, Felix, just go. Take him, Mr Van de Pas.'

The pig-breeder pushed Felix out of the door with his dirty hands and the last image he had of his parents was of his mother consoling his father, her arms around him, his head on her shoulder.

At Van de Pas's he had lived among unclean animals. After a few weeks he stopped washing, just like the crazy farmer who fed him. The man swilled his poisonous gin and spoke to his animals. In the evening, behind the blackout paper, he would sit down to read by the yellow light of a paraffin lamp: Rilke, Morgenstern, Holderlin, literature culled from the twilight of madness. He passed the books on to the young Jew, and Felix read, between the black fingerprints left behind by Van de Pas, sombre words he did not understand:

> *Death is great*
> *And we are his*
> *With smiling lips.*
> *When we feel plunged into the midst of life*
> *He dares to weep*
> *In our midst.*

Until the end of 1944 Felix lived in the shadow of this tall, filthy man who was grieving over something or other and was in search of a poem to express it.

Felix was cursed. He did not know where his parents were and he read words that were too big for his eyes. He slept on a mattress filled with straw and during the day helped the farmer, was at his side when he chased a squealing pig into the kitchen and slit its throat. The entrails lay neatly steaming in the abdominal cavity, the skull was split with an axe and everything was eaten, including the trotters.

His parents had cast him out, and even when the Canadians arrived he could not shake off the feeling that he was condemned. Van de Pas insisted that his parents were sure to fetch him, but no one turned up in the yard and the months dragged by. He waited and waited, wondering whether he really deserved to be rescued, forgiven and cared for by his parents, and deep down in his heart he knew that, although he could not tell precisely how, he must have done something wrong for Van de Pas to have carried him off into a world of dying pigs and terrifying poems. When at long last, sick with hope and shame, he had gone back to Den Bosch on an impulse to have a look, he discovered an icy wind blowing through their house on the Hekellaan. Hein Daamen had come to his rescue.

Felix had survived, had returned from his banishment and could recite Stefan George and Hugo von Hofmannsthal by heart, but he knew that it had not been 'all for the best'.

He put on his dinner jacket and looked at himself in the mirror. A somewhat corpulent, arrogant-looking representative of the establishment. The glittering packaging of a black soul.

Sonnema, the young number two at the Embassy, was to attend the reception as well. Sonnema would first look in at the chancellery to find out if The Hague had replied to the last message. The Czechs were keen to buy Tri-zeds from Philips, computers not yet covered by the NATO embargo on equipment of potential military use.

Hoffman went downstairs and as he reached the last step Marian came out of the drawing room, wearing her long black evening dress. Jana stood waiting in the hall.

'I'll do it,' he said to Jana.

Marian turned her back to him and silently he helped her into a gossamer-thin summer jacket.

Her hair still had its original dark-brown colour, apart from a single grey lock, a whitened streak running right across her head, a sign that she was older than she seemed. She had looked after herself, and only from close quarters did her face betray a faint network of wrinkles. She was a little heavier than she had been ten years earlier, the skin under her chin had lost some of its firmness, but her eyes were still large and bright and she moved gracefully and dressed with taste. He had not seen her naked for years and wondered if he would fall asleep if he were to lie in bed in her arms.

He touched her soft shoulder lightly when the jacket was in

place and cast the question from his mind. She gave him a smile, as if briefly greeting some vague acquaintance at a party.

The chauffeur stood waiting in the entrance hall. A gaunt man with sunken cheeks and thin hands, he called himself Boris. Despite the heat he was wearing his peaked cap. He wore it at all times even though, positioned as it was resting on his big ears, it shrouded his dead eyes in permanent darkness. According to Sonnema, Boris was on the pay-roll of the Czech State police, every Czech who answered the telephone at an Embassy or drove a diplomatic car being an employee of the secret police. Hoffman could not pronounce on the matter, but frankly lost no sleep over it.

Sonnema had briefed him on the HSR, the Hlavni Sprava Rozvedsky, or Central Intelligence Directorate, a division of the Ministry of Home Affairs that was deployed on espionage and counterespionage. The HSR kept a watchful eye on the corps diplomatique, and its activities overlapped with those of another division of the Ministry, the Federal Directorate of Intelligence Services, the FSZS, in charge of internal security and of the political police. Sonnema claimed that the chauffeur, a taciturn man with few gestures, was an FSZS agent. Hoffman and Boris kept resolutely silent in each other's company, and there was nothing to indicate that the driver might be on the point of worming the Kingdom's secrets out of its ambassador.

Hoffman was sitting beside Marian in the back of the Mercedes and despite the air-conditioning he could smell her scent.

'What have you got on?' he asked.

'Estee Lauder. Don't you like it?'

'Oh yes. Very much, in fact.'

She smiled. The car tyres rumbled over the cobblestones. It was dusk, but to save electricity the street lighting had not yet been turned on. Skodas, Ladas and Trabants filled the streets, crowded trams swayed along uneven tracks, old Jawa motorcycles groaned under the weight of T-shirted riders.

Hoffman looked at Marian's face, lit up by the headlights of the oncoming traffic, and he felt his guilt constrict his heart like too-tight hessian sacking.

'Your hair looks nice,' he said.

She nodded uncomfortably, not looking at him. It was years since he had said anything like that to her, not since Miriam's death in any case.

'How come I've gone grey and your hair is still its old colour?' he asked.

She shook her head now, gave him a look of surprise.

'That's because you worry all the time and I don't.'

'Really?' he said.

'No, of course not. Do you honestly imagine this is my own colour? At my time of life?'

'It could be.'

'Come on, Felix, don't be silly.'

'So it's dyed then?'

'Of course.'

'How long have you been doing that?'

'Since…I can't remember when.'

'And that white streak?'

'That's my real colour. Just like yours.'

What did he still know about his wife? She would occasionally tell him something about Vondel and mention the many years of study still ahead of her, she would take short trips to the Netherlands to consult the Public Records Office and the Royal Library in The Hague, she had friends in many countries with whom she would sometimes stay or who would come to stay with them, she was part of the circle of diplomats' wives who created a small island of Western civilisation wherever they were sent (playing golf and tennis with one another, swapping recipes, taking part in the national celebrations of scores of foreign countries, committing adultery), but that was just about the sum total of what he knew about her.

Marian and Felix were welded together by their children. The children were dead of course, but that had only strengthened the bonds. Death had condemned them to stay together come what may. He knew nothing about his wife. And he admitted to himself that he did not have the courage to find out more about her than that she dyed her hair.

The Italian Embassy was located in a neo-baroque palace just behind the Dutch Embassy. He shook hands with the ambassador, a pansy with a silky handshake, he shook hands with his wife, an ugly woman whose eyeliner was running, and he lead Marian across gleaming parquet to a crowded salon. The heat was like an oven.

Shoulder to shoulder, glass in hand, sweating men in black dinner jackets and sweating women in long dresses stood making polite conversation under voluptuously curved chandeliers. Stationed stiffly in a corner a small string orchestra played classical music, their offering drowned out by the sound of raised voices.

To the left stood a long table laden with platters and plates. A fork supper, as Hoffman saw at a glance: salads, pates, various braised meats, creamed potatoes, pastas. But he had only just eaten. Dark-skinned men in tight-fitting jackets with brass buttons showed their white teeth as they smiled broadly and made themselves helpful at the table. Diplomats' wives dressed to kill tripped to and fro excitedly on their high heels.

Hoffman handed Marian a glass of champagne, taking a glass of vodka for himself. *Freddo.*

'What do you think of the place?' she asked.

'Well...,' he said. He had no views on the subject. The Italians were doing their best.

The vodka flowed through his mouth, setting everything on fire. This was the strongest vodka he had ever tasted. He immediately took a second glass.

'Take care, Felix,' she said uneasily.

'I always do,' he said. 'And what do *you* think of the place?'

'Very nice. Italians have taste.'

'The ambassador's a pansy.'

'Is he? How do you know?'

'You can just tell,' he said. He emptied his glass.

'You carry on like that, and I'll be going home in five minutes,' Marian threatened,

'Do what you like,' he said, and beckoned the barman for a refill. *'Per favore,'* he pointed.

In protest Marian turned her back on him.

Johan Sonnema, the Embassy's rising star, a beanpole of a young man with a large crop of fair hair and a pair of granny glasses, appeared by his side. Sonnema was an historian and occasionally published an article in the *Nieuwe Rotterdamse Courant* 'in a personal capacity'.

The broad palm of his right hand was clasping the fingers of a girl who seemed to be about eight years old, and was looking about her with glittering eyes at the dinner suits and evening gowns. She had long blonde hair that came down to her waist and was adorned with two red bows just above the ears. Sweat glistened under her eyes.

'Hello, boss,' said Sonnema's deep voice.

'There's some first-class vodka here, my boy.'

'Get me one then, boss. Daring tie.'

'American,' explained Hoffman.

Sonnema saw Marian and patted her tentatively on the shoulder.

'Mrs Hoffman....'

She smiled and noticed the little girl.

'Is this your daughter, Mr Sonnema?'

'Jorinde, shake hands with Mrs Hoffman,' he said. The girl held her hand out demurely.

'Is your name Jorinde?' Marian asked.

Hoffman recognised the look in her eyes and turned back to the bar, his eyes pricking with bitter sorrow. The Italian barman immediately lifted the bottle of Stolichnaya and filled his glass. Hoffman pointed to Sonnema and the Italian produced a second glass. Hoffman took a swallow and glanced back over his shoulder.

'What would your daughter like, Sonnema?'

'Jorinde?'

'Coke, please,' she said, looking away shyly.

'Coke,' Hoffman repeated to the barman.

Behind his back Marian said something to the girl. He heard the child reply. She was visiting Daddy here, she said in a clear young voice; her mother lived in Holland with another man. Sonnema said in his bass voice, 'We were divorced four years ago. Jorinde lives with her mother. But whenever we can we get together, don't we, darling?'

It suddenly occurred to Hoffman that he never spoke to children any more. His work rarely brought him in contact with anyone under the age of thirty-five, and he realised that he was likely to behave like an over-dramatic clown when faced with an eight-year-old girl.

'Here you are,' he said, handing her the glass of Coke. His hand was trembling and he spilled some of the drink.

'Oops, sorry,' he said.

The girl noticed the tremor and clutched the glass with both hands. She looked up at him suspiciously.

Sonnema drew the barman's attention to the drops on the parquet floor, and Hoffman could feel Marian's chilly gaze. He turned round and gave her a questioning look, as if unaware that her silent aggression was in response to his drinking. He handed Sonnema his glass of vodka.

'Anything for you, Mrs Hoffman?' asked Sonnema.

'No, thanks, I'm fine,' she replied distantly.

'Heard anything from the Monkey Rock?' Hoffman asked Sonnema.

His number two raised his glass in a toast and sipped the vodka. He nodded.

Marian took the hint and withdrew. A woman whom Hoffman did not know spoke to her, a stunning-looking woman of about thirty. One of the Italians bustled about wiping the floor clean.

'A message came in two hours ago. Saying "no". Loud and clear. Only to be expected, of course. The equipment apparently contains quite a few components on the list.'

'Do you think the Czechs will retaliate?'

'They get turned down like that all the time, and if they wanted to start doling out reprisals, they'd have their hands full.'

'In that case, why do they keep applying?' Hoffman asked, glancing at Sonnema's daughter, who was looking up at him, eyes wide.

'They just try it on. Every now and then an order slips through the net. They know ours is not a watertight bureaucracy, and once in a while they manage to snap up a computer.'

Sonnema suddenly lifted a finger and bent down to his daughter.

'Can you hear that?' he asked smiling.

The girl nodded, the silk ribbons swaying back and forth above her ears.

'Well, what is it?'

'Mozart,' she said positively.

'Jorinde plays the violin,' said Sonnema. 'She brought it with her so she can practise every day.'

His face shone with love for his daughter. Unable to contain his feelings, he bent down and kissed the girl's forehead adoringly.

Blood beating against his temples, Hoffman averted his gaze and noticed that Marian was still engaged in conversation with the woman. The woman gave him a fleeting look and smiled. He smiled back.

'Who is that woman, Johan?'

'Which one?'

'The one talking to my wife.'

With studied nonchalance, Sonnema turned and swept the room with his gaze. Hoffman followed his eyes and saw that there had been nothing to betray any particular interest on his part in the person speaking to Marian.

'What a beautiful woman,' said Sonnema appreciatively.

'Do you know her?'

'Isn't she the *Rudé právo* lady?'

'A journalist?'

'Yes, I think so. I don't actually know her but I vaguely remember meeting her somewhere or other.'

'A man's come up to them now,' said Hoffman, who had the woman in full view.

Sonnema turned and looked around again.

'Jiri Hladky. Editor of *Rudé právo*. So I was right.'

'What's her name?'

'Can't remember. I must go to the Gents'. Look after Jorinde for me, boss?'

Hoffman nodded. The girl held onto her glass tightly and followed her father with her eyes as his face, red with heat, bobbed away above the guests' heads. Hoffman could not ignore her. The barman gave him another vodka, and he braced himself, wiping the sweat from his forehead. He asked Sonnema's daughter where she lived, avoiding her eyes.

'Deventer,' said the girl.

'What class are you in?'

'I'm going to be in the fourth.'

Hoffman tried to think of something else to ask but failed. Then, though he could see the half-full glass in her hands, he asked, 'Would you like some more Coke?'

'I've still got some,' she said, and held her glass up to show him. He nodded.

'Is it still fizzy enough?' he asked.

'Oh, yes.'

He'd thought of a good question now. 'What sweets do you like, Jorinde?' he asked.

The girl laughed nervously.

'Why are you laughing?'

She shrugged her shoulders. 'It's such a funny question.'

'It is?'

'No one asks things like that. Grown-ups don't, anyway.'

'Well, I do. What sweets do you like best?'

'M & Ms. And liquorice, and chocolate marshmallows. But I like ordinary food too, you know. What about you?'

'Me? I like bear's ears and snake's feet....'

'Snakes don't have feet.'

'They don't? But I always get them at the butcher's. Do you think the butcher's having me on?'

'You know perfectly well that snakes don't have feet.'

She gave him a look laden with irony, adult and knowing.

'I was only joking,' he said. 'I like everything.'

'Everything? Really?'

'Yes, I think so.'

'Even…even crocodile?'

'Yes. I ate some once. In Africa. The meat's very firm and white. Looks a bit like turkey. You've had that, haven't you?'

'For Christmas,' she said. 'What about human flesh?'

'I ate some of that once as well, in…in Timbuktu, if my memory serves me right.'

'Oh, come on,' she said, pulling a face. 'I don't believe that!'

'It was only a joke.'

'Have you got any children?'

Tensely, he shook his head.

The barman came round offering refills. Hoffman wondered how many glasses he had had. He had lost count.

'No, no, I haven't got any children, I haven't, no,' he said.

She looked at him searchingly.

'Why are you acting so strange?' she asked.

'Is that what I'm doing?' he said.

'Yes. You're acting strange,' she repeated with a disapproving air.

'Well, maybe you're right,' he muttered. He put the glass on the table. He realised he was drunk. Sonnema approached, towering two heads taller than the rest of the company. The girl looked relieved as her father laid a hand affectionately on her shoulder.

'Did she behave herself, boss?'

'Right, right,' said Hoffman absently.

'Can we have a look round now, Daddy?' she asked.

'Of course, darling.'

Hoffman's stomach contracted and a sour lump rose from his gullet to his throat. He tensed his neck, keeping his mouth firmly shut.

'Excuse me,' he hissed between his teeth.

He nodded to this person and that, faces he had seen at his own reception. His mouth set, he asked an Italian waiter for the lavatory, then looked for the right door in a well-lit corridor. *Lavabo,* he read.

He entered a room, white from floor to ceiling except for two black leather seats. 'Gentlemen' to the right. Behind the door an area with mirrors and washbasins and three toilet cubicles. He tried the handle of the middle door, but it was locked. The left-hand door yielded. Even before he was able to take off his dinner jacket, the supper spurted out of his mouth.

He sank to the warm marble floor and felt his knees land in something wet. He vomited again and watched yellow flecks splatter onto the silk revers of his jacket. He thought of the tender medallions of veal in Marsala and the creamed potatoes with braised chicory which he had eaten that evening, now half digested and mangled beyond recognition, like his life. He grimaced wryly at the thought of so much metaphor and another load of gastric gruel shot from the wide-open grin of his mouth.

He panted and used a sleeve to wipe the muck off his chin. His jacket had been rendered unpresentable, and he wondered if he could return to the salon in his shirtsleeves. Suddenly he saw himself as a polar bear amidst penguins, and he fought his way upright in the narrow space between the lavatory bowl and the door. He was hoping that socialism did not frown on a proper steam laundry, or else he would have to send his dinner suit to Vienna. He manoeuvred his buttocks so as to give his arse more room and a thundering fart escaped him.

He pushed the door open and was back in the room with the washbasins. A diplomat was standing washing his hands.

The man watched him approach in the mirror, stiffening when Hoffman took the place next to his. He was a tall man with a grey moustache. An Englishman, Hoffman suddenly realised, whom he had met before. Although he was sweating as copiously as Hoffman, he appeared completely unruffled. Hoffman cupped his hands and flung water into his face. The water was tepid. He had drenched his jacket, but Hoffman no longer cared. Startled, the Englishman stepped to one side.

'I beg your pardon,' he said in impeccable Oxford English.

Hoffman looked at him in surprise. 'Sorry,' he said.

The man shook his head disapprovingly and rinsed the soap from his hands.

'Mr Hoffman, why are you doing this to yourself?' he said in his affected British voice.

'And what exactly do you mean by that, Mr uh…?'

'Trevor-Jones. Ambassador Trevor-Jones. We've met before, Mr Hoffman.'

'Ambassador Hoffman-Jansen,' said Hoffman, mimicking his intonation.

'They warned me about you,' said the Englishman.

'Is that so? Who?'

'My sources, Mr Hoffman. You surely don't expect me to reveal my sources?'

Hoffman was soaping his hands at length, the bar slipping creamily between his fingers. In high spirits he cried into the mirror, 'Of course not, Mr Trevor-Jones! Heaven forbid that you reveal your sources!'

The man used an elbow to push the button of the drier and held his hands in the blast of hot air.

'Mr Hoffman…I feel obliged to remind you of your duties.'

'Of course!' exclaimed Hoffman through the mirror. 'Remind away!'

'You are a disgrace to your country,' said the Englishman.

Hoffman saw the contempt blazing in the man's eyes. He walked up to the Englishman, wagging a soapy index finger. The man recoiled.

'Now just you listen to me, you birdbrained nitwit. It so happens that I'm paid to make my country look ridiculous, so don't you run away with the idea that I'm stepping out of line. It so happens that I'm the official buffoon around here, and it's my job to be a disgrace.'

Trevor-Jones shied away and made quickly for the door. There he turned round for a moment.

'I shall be informing the doyen of the diplomatic corps of this incident,' he declared loftily.

'So shall I!' cried Hoffman.

He held his hands under the tap. The door slammed shut. He remembered now that Trevor-Jones had honoured him with a visit at the party he had given on his arrival (it went without saying that the British ambassador should call on the new ambassador of a neighbouring country), and that they had exchanged a few words on that occasion, British understatements that had sounded like heavenly music to Hoffman's ears, refreshing touches of irony that had blown away the dry-as-dust rhetoric of Dutch diplomats. It surprised him now that Trevor-Jones could not take a joke. Then, catching sight of himself in the mirror, he saw himself as Trevor-Jones had seen him.

Vomit was smeared all over his dinner suit and favourite bow tie, and was encrusted around his mouth, his hair was dishevelled, and his eyes pitilessly revealed the colour of his soul. Panic exploded in his chest. He couldn't appear in public like this, he couldn't go back to the reception, he couldn't even go back to the corridor! He staggered into the cubicle again and locked the door.

The mess he had spewed out was still in the bowl, and he pressed the button with which modern designers had replaced the chain. A wave of water swirled the vomit away. He sat down on the lavatory seat and tried calmly to take stock of his situation. If he carried his jacket, he could leave the building more or less unnoticed and tender his apologies later to the Italian pansy. He had suddenly felt sick, he would say, and he did indeed feel sick, his stomach was protesting and he was doubled up under the onslaught of fierce cramps. His limbs trembled with the sudden pain.

It came to him in a flash: he had stomach cancer. He had finally managed to bring his body to its knees. Because he was too scared for a bullet or a rope round his neck, he had chosen this way of putting an end to it all, he understood that now, and the pain wracking his stomach was eased by the sweet balm of this insight.

Even so, he decided to leave the Embassy as quietly as he could. He had caused a scandal that could smash his fragile reputation for good, and his body had entered upon its death throes; that was enough for the time being. What kind of vodka had he been drinking, anyway? Before this evening he had been immune to the stuff, able at times to down whole bottles without any appreciable loss of his faculties, yet here he had suddenly started behaving like a raving lunatic. But was it really vodka he had drunk? He had had a bottle of Julienas at six o'clock with his meal, and was probably not fully accountable for his actions even before he got here. He remembered squeezing laboriously into his dinner jacket, then being diverted by memories and idle musings. That ersatz vodka here had robbed him of what sense he still possessed.

Mescal—why hadn't he noticed it straight away? His hands began to tremble when it occurred to him that the mescal must have been slipped to him by the FSZS. It was a mystery, though, why they should want to trap Felix Hoffman of all people. But since the bottle he had seen in the hands of the Italian barman had obviously contained mescal instead of vodka they had surely wanted to compromise him.

He fingered his burning cheeks nervously. He realised that he had left to go to the lavatory in the nick of time, thus avoiding a situation beyond redemption, at least if Trevor-Jones kept his mouth shut. He would contact him in the morning.

Mescal drove you crazy. In Lima he had seen blind Indians go for one another with knives in the stinking huts where they sold mescal, had seen whores fuddled with mescal taking their pleasure with dogs.

He heard someone come into the washroom, then enter the cubicle next to his. He stood up and opened the door a crack. The washroom was empty and, arms flailing, he took the five steps to one of the basins. He quickly held onto it to steady himself. Then he hung his jacket up on a hook, took one of the face cloths lying next to the basin, held it under the tap and cleaned his lips and chin.

He tried to wipe away the spots on his shirt, but without success, and a wet patch spread across his chest. Using his fingers, he hastily straightened his hair, and decided he could hold the jacket to his chest while making for the exit. But without a jacket he could not possibly wait in the hall for Boris to bring up the Mercedes; he would have to hail a taxi in the street and take it back to the residence.

He opened the door to the ante-room and made for the corridor with his jacket slung over one arm. He wondered why Sonnema had not been bothered by the vodka, and this thought was suddenly followed by a stab in his chest while his ankles were seized by invisible hands dragging him down.

He lost his balance.

He fumbled about for the wall, found nothing to which his hands could cling, and his ankles gave way. His body hit the hard floor. The pain in his chest cut off his breath and he saw the white ceiling disappear behind black spots, balloons released in vast numbers to form a dense layer of cloud between his eyes and the spotlights, and everything went black as if he were about to faint. The razor-sharp sword now slashing away at his wildly pumping heart unleashed in him a panic he remembered from long ago when the farmer, Van de Pas, had heard a car approaching and had yelled at him to run away and he had shoved the pigs out of the way and had fled into the woods barefoot and had run and run. Odd, but suddenly he was running there again, he could feel the branches under his blackened feet and the thorns ripping at his skin, and he hoped he'd find his parents waiting for him somewhere in that wood, and that they'd take him away in Daddy's black Packard and kiss him to sleep and let him listen to fat men at white tables, and he knew that they would surely comfort him and wash the filth from his hands.

He felt fingers under his chin, at his throat, as someone removed his tie and opened the top button of his shirt. He took a deep breath, sucked in the tingling air from an Olivetti air-conditioner —it was an Olivetti, wasn't it, not a Zenith or a Goldstar?—and his lungs filled with a rich blend of aromas. Sweet smells wafted under his nostrils and he breathed in perfume and the heavy fragrance of the old-fashioned powder with which women used to colour their cheeks.

He opened his eyes and saw a feminine silhouette against the glaring ceiling lights.

'Thank you very much,' he said. He moistened his lips and put out a hand looking for something to hold on to. The woman grasped it and he sat up.

She spoke to him in English. 'Can you stand?' she asked.

'Yes, I think so.'

He straightened up, sitting with his back against the wall. Spots still danced in front of his eyes, and the woman was a blur. He shut his eyes tight. It felt as if a smouldering cigarette had burned a small hole in his stomach, there was a scorching pain reaching out for his heart, and he was aware of his body labouring under the weight of its sixty years. He knew then without doubt that he had nothing to look forward to any longer, that he had used up his appointed days, granted by he knew not whom.

'Can you stand? Do you think you can stand?' asked the woman.

He nodded. Of course he hadn't drunk any mescal. He was suffering from a stomach complaint. No stomach could put up with the quantities he had been stuffing into his.

He tried to get to his feet, and the woman supported him under one arm, pulling him up. The exertion made his pain worse. He could feel the blood drain from his face, and he clung giddily to the wall.

'I'll take you to a doctor,' said the woman.

He shook his head. 'No doctor,' he muttered. 'I want to go home.'

'I'll help you,' she said.

She led him out of the cloakroom. He shuffled along at her side, eyes screwed up, head bowed; the light of the white walls was blinding, and he was grateful for her supporting arm. She stopped a waiter and spoke to him in Italian.

They led Hoffman carefully to the depths of the building,

they shepherded him through corridors that grew darker and darker, they took him down stairs, up stairs, and then a door swung open and the mild outside air hit him in the face and he took a deep breath.

The woman asked the waiter to fetch Hoffman's chauffeur and the man let go of him. Hoffman could hear his leather soles smacking against the paving stones as he left them, running.

'You're very kind,' he said to the woman. 'Thank you very much.'

He was still keeping his eyes shut, as if even here, in the semi-darkness, he was afraid of the light. Crickets were chirping in his ears. He did not know who she was, what she looked like, he only knew her gentle voice and her helping hand.

'No need to thank me,' he heard her reply. 'Do you think you can manage by yourself now?'

'Yes, I do, thank you very much,' he said.

'You really must see a doctor, Mr Hoffman,' she said.

'Yes...yes, I'll do that,' he replied. 'Many thanks for the advice.'

'I think this is your car now.'

He heard the Mercedes stop, smelled the exhaust. Boris got out. He hurried towards Hoffman and the woman spoke to him in rapid Czech. Boris took charge of him. Hoffman felt the iron grip of his chauffeur lifting him towards the car, and he raised his head and cautiously opened his eyes. He recognised the woman in the light of the car. She was the journalist to whom Marian had been chatting. The Mercedes' interior light glowed on her face, she looked at Hoffman anxiously with large, grey-blue eyes, her lips glistened, a profusion of blonde hair danced around her head, and she tried to smile when she noticed that he was looking at her at last.

'Are you sure you can manage, Mr Hoffman?'

'Yes, really, thank you. Haven't we met before?'

'I don't think so,' she said.

'You know my name....'

'Yes...,' she replied vaguely. She handed Boris the jacket, quickly said a few words to him and disappeared into the dark passageway leading down into the Embassy building.

Hoffman allowed the chauffeur to help him into the car. Exhausted he sank onto the back seat.

'What's that lady's name, Boris?' he asked in a weak voice.

'I don't know, sir,' said the man.

'I heard she's a journalist.'

'Maybe. Never seen her before. Should I take you to a doctor, sir?'

'No, we're going back to the residence. Turn the air-conditioning up, will you?'

'There's a very good hospital for diplomats near here. If I were you, I'd get them to take a look at me.'

'No,' said Hoffman, whispering because he was at the end of his strength. He had never been ill, never had an operation, but he hadn't enjoyed robust good health either. The diseases he might have caught had been handed down by him to his children, and had left their traces on him through them.

'Go round to the front first, please, and get them to tell my wife that I've gone home. She'll just have to do the honours....'

Boris turned the car in the narrow street. They were at the side of the building and there was no one about. Boris drove back to the imposing main entrance and climbed out.

Footmen in red livery were standing on the front steps under the Italian and Czech flags. Black limousines waited in rows, their chauffeurs hanging about in small groups, cigarette smoke eddying above their heads. Hoffman clutched at the armrest as his stomach threatened to rupture.

Boris reappeared among the footmen, followed by Marian, who was looking searchingly towards the cars. Boris pointed and Marian hurried over to the Mercedes.

She sank onto the back seat by his side.

'What's wrong, Felix?' She ran her hand over his forehead and he saw the sweat on her fingertips.

'Nothing.'

'You look like....' She swallowed the word.

'Death? That's great, thanks very much....

'You must go and see a doctor.'

'I'm not going to any doctor.'

'What happened? I heard you were lying on the floor in the lavatory! What's the matter with you, Felix?'

'Nothing. There's nothing the matter with me. I'm having a bit of trouble with my stomach, that's all.'

'What do you mean, *trouble*?'

'Cramps....'

'Did you fall, or what?'

'I was a bit giddy, that's all. It's all over now, I'm sure. Go back inside and give my apologies to that pansy. I'll send Boris back for you later.'

'Do you want to die, Felix?'

'What do you mean?' he asked as if he did not know.

'Do you want to die?'

'Please stop it, Marian.'

'I can't tie you down,' she said, 'I can't prevent you from carrying on like this.'

In a voice stripped of warmth he said, 'Go back inside, for Heaven's sake, I'm leaving.'

She got out of the car and walked up the steps without a backward glance.

'Home?' Boris asked.

The Mercedes glided back to the residence. Fists tightly clenched, Hoffman sat without moving on the black leather.

Jana opened the door to him. She started visibly at his appearance and rushed forward to help Boris. Slumped between the two of them he staggered into the house.

'Are you ill, sir?' she asked.

'No,' he replied.

She and Boris exchanged a look.

'Shall we help you upstairs?' she urged.

'No, I want to go to the kitchen.'

'You'd do better to go and lie down, sir,' said Boris. 'I'll ring for the doctor and then you can have a good rest.'

'I want to go to the kitchen,' he repeated as insistently as he could, his voice quavering. 'If I can just sit down there, I'll feel better in no time.'

Once seated at the kitchen table he stayed there, exhausted, staring at the empty draining board. His dress shirt was plastered to his back and chest. Jana offered him tea, bouillon, a bath, but nothing could drive out the silent fury in his heart and he asked her to go upstairs.

He could hear Boris and Jana whispering together excitedly in the hall, and shouted at them to leave him in peace.

The front door slammed shut, which meant that Boris was going back to the reception. Hoffman was not sure he wanted to die in Marian's presence. He would sooner remain alone for the night, here at the table, and he stood up and shuffled to the hall in his creaking new patent-leather shoes.

'Jana! Jana!'

Treading heavily, she came down the stairs. He watched her plump hands sliding down the polished wood of the banisters. She stopped on the bottom step and looked at him with undisguised disgust.

'Jana, could you bring me something?' He did not wait for a reply. 'In the medicine chest in my bathroom you'll find a small velvet box. Red velvet. I'd like you to get it for me, all right?'

She nodded and went back upstairs. Her broad hips had never borne children; she had sacrificed her fertile years to Dutch diplomats.

He held on tightly to the turned newel post at the bottom of the banisters. Tonight he had definitely become an old man. Mortality had made itself master of his body and lay waiting impatiently on the threshold of his consciousness. He knew he would die tonight. In the depths of the night, at about five o'clock, he would breathe his last.

Because of Esther's torment he had spent a great many days in hospitals, and had learnt there that five in the morning was the critical hour. Dying was most common at the borderline between night and day. They would discover him tomorrow morning, slumped across the kitchen table, or perhaps he would have slipped off his chair. His bladder would have emptied, but at least his chronic constipation meant they would not find him with shit between his legs. The shame of dying, though, would not be greatly mitigated by that.

Though he could not claim that he was enthusiastic about his impending demise, he was aware of a degree of curiosity about what would happen to his dissolving identity, to his *ego*, if his heart were to stop and his brain be cut off from fresh oxygen. And Esther's words—this memory suddenly lit up like a firework in his head— Esther's *knowing*, he too would come to know in turn. He felt the fury at his stupid death melt away at this expectation, and he sucked air into his lungs, defying the pain in his midriff as he called up to the housekeeper, 'Jana! Bring me the book that's on my desk as well. It says "Spinoza" on the cover.'

Jana had helped him back to the kitchen table, and when he could hear no more sounds from upstairs he had let the black trousers with their perfect creases drop to his ankles, and had opened the little red velvet box. The doctors, anticipating that Esther would die a lingering death, had advised the parents to take a short course in home nursing, and he had sometimes given Esther an injection.

In the little box, on a bed of white silk, lay a silver-plated syringe and an unbroken capsule of morphine. He had bought it in Lima, after Esther's death, and had kept it all these years.

Pain had him in a stranglehold, and although he knew the dangers of administering morphine in the absence of a doctor, he pushed the needle into the aluminium capsule and drew the morphine into the syringe. He pushed the air out, looked for a vein in his thigh, close to the knee, drove the sharp needle through his white skin—he shut his eyes tight at this point because he could not bear to look—and shot the painkiller into his blood. His heart throbbed high in his throat with the tension.

He put the syringe back in its box and it was as if some great hand had lifted the ache and the heat from his body. He knew that what he had done was the act of a lunatic, but the pain had been unbearable. Keeping the syringe for some twenty years had been justified.

He did not want to die in agony. Perhaps that was cowardly and less than manly of him, but he had never been able to appreciate the attraction of heroism. The pain had clouded his mind, and he wanted to devote his last few hours to Spinoza in the hope that the philosopher of pure understanding might show him the way to his daughter. Perhaps I am mad, Hoffman thought, but if I am it has not been by my choice.

The morphine drifted through his veins and it was thirty minutes before he had the strength to pull up his trousers. He turned his attention to the book and with sluggish concentration read the fourteen paragraphs of the next section he had reached.

'I speak of true doubt in the mind,' Spinoza began, 'and not of that which we see to take place when any one says he doubts in so many words, whereas there is no doubt in his mind.'

The section was devoted to doubt and such related subjects as the memory, the imagination and words.

Doubt.

Doubt sprang from several unclear ideas, since, as Spinoza asserted, 'if there be only one idea in the mind, whether it be false or true, there would be no doubt or certainty....'

Hoffman realised that this one idea was a hypothetical construct, that if you had but one idea you would surely know if it was true or false, doubt being impossible in that case. He also understood that the philosopher was saying that doubt arose when one idea stood in the way of another.

> The idea that causes us to doubt is not clear and distinct.
> E.g., if someone has never thought of the deception of
> the senses, either from experience or anything else, he
> will never doubt whether the sun is greater or smaller
> than it appears.

Of course, the sun was only a small disc in the sky, and without any knowledge of the planets and stars and the way in which objects were seen at a distance, it would never occur to one to suspect that the sun was a gigantic sphere, larger than anything one had ever touched or observed.

> Doubt generally arises from thinking of the deception of the senses....

Hoffman knew that from experience. Sometimes you did not know what you were seeing, sometimes you could not tell what you were hearing. 'I know,' his daughter had told him, and with the passing of the years he heard her words more and more clearly and saw her face more and more vividly. Time had brought her closer, a reverse flow as it were, and he feared that his imagination had embellished his threadbare memories.

When he thought about it, slowly and arduously, but in words as light as a feather, he realised that he had confused two subjects: in his mind, he had made a leap from the 'senses' to the 'memory', and the title of the section betrayed that Spinoza was about to do likewise, so that it was best to let his thought follow the philosopher's like a tail-wagging little dog. Hoffman was conscious of his intellectual inferiority; his own reading elicited nothing but personal associations. Nonetheless he would not be put off the *Treatise* now, and he determined to read it to the end this very night.

Feverish with expectation, he tried to recall the preceding sections. Spinoza had outlined a method by which truth could be distinguished from error, and by truth he meant knowledge of nature. Truth was an inherent quality of clear thought, was part of the 'intimate essence' of that thought. Error, by contrast, was caused by confusion and lack of knowledge. With his last sentence, devoted to doubt born of the 'deception of the senses', Spinoza in fact meant this: that our way of looking at things was sustained and guided by our knowledge of true ideas, and that lack of such knowledge gave rise to doubt and illusion.

The next paragraph introduced a comparison which struck Hoffman as brilliant, and which, he felt, demonstrated the salutary path of Spinoza's thinking.

In it, Spinoza contended that knowledge of God was comparable to the knowledge that the three angles of a triangle are equal to two right angles. In other words, the sum of the angles of a triangle was one hundred and eighty degrees, and this was an incontrovertible, irrefutable piece of *knowing*, a form of knowledge in which the logical character of nature was made tangible and in which God's logic revealed itself with majestic force.

The sentences moved in a timeless dance across the page, and Hoffman, relieved of pain and with eyes that were even now able to gauge the thickness of the paper and the depth of the letters, let out a cry of admiration—had the kitchen been able to speak, it would surely have expressed its astonishment at this reader's radiant face. Hoffman could see a luminous triangle over the book, as a special sign 'To Fee from On High'.

Having once more stressed the importance of systematic investigation and of resolving doubt by means of clear and distinct ideas, Spinoza declared that he would go to 'treat briefly of memory and forgetfulness'. Please do, Hoffman thought to himself. The philosopher then observed that 'the more intelligible a thing is, the more easily it is retained in the memory'.

Hoffman nodded in admiration and with fellow feeling, even though he knew from experience that one could also remember things one did not wholly understand. According to Spinoza, the memory was 'nothing else than the sensation of impressions on the brain accompanied with the thought to determine the duration of the sensation'. In other words, when the memory is active one is wandering through a sort of warehouse in which the brain stacks its impressions, impressions that have entered it by way of the senses.

From the choice of words, Hoffman realised that Spinoza mistrusted the memory: people did not know their way about in that warehouse, did not know which impressions were stored where. Only clear, simple items could be stored and retrieved without difficulty, the

philosopher argued, and his next paragraph carried a warning against
the imagination, which he clearly saw as a playground in which the
memory played on swings and built sand-castles to its heart's content.
A man 'may take whatever he likes for the imagination, provided he
admits…that the soul has a passive relation with it' and knows 'at
the same time in what manner, by the aid of the understanding, we
are freed from it.'

The imagination and the memory were indeed Hoffman's
tormentors; he wanted to smash them, destroy them, rid himself of
them. He read on, at his own pace, with somnolent limbs and a wide-
awake gaze, and, moved by the insight granted him by Spinoza, felt
the tears roll down the folds in his face.

The paragraphs guiding Hoffman to the end of the section
illuminated his soul as if a lamp had been turned on in his breast,
which was where, admittedly for no good reason, he located his soul.
Hoffman had never suspected the presence of a lamp there, but its
golden light shone through his eyes onto the pages of the book—a
lantern radiating divine light, he called it to himself.

Spinoza called the understanding a kind of 'spiritual automaton',
by which he meant that it had a unique character and was subject to
laws. Thus if we understand something fully we make use of a power
with which nature has endowed us, *in* the very heart of the mind so
to speak—this was Hoffman's paraphrasing of Spinoza—and we only
come truly alive and attain happiness when the mind's heart begins
to beat, just like the body's.

It was not only the imagination and the memory that could
spawn false ideas and spread doubt, undermining the road to peace
and happiness with pitfalls—everyday speech, too, could be the cause
of great errors, 'unless we take the greatest precautions with them':

> Which is clearly apparent from the fact that on all
> those [things] which are only in the intellect and not
> in the imagination, negative names are often bestowed,
> such as incorporeal, infinite, etc.; and also many things
> which are really affirmative are expressed negatively, and

contrariwise...'

'Yes!' Hoffman thought, while his heart beat faster as if thinking were a kind of race; he could not rule out the possibility that his memory had distorted and magnified his recollection of Esther's words, that she had called out something quite different! He thought he had heard her say the words *I know*, but his senses were misleading, his memory flawed and his emotions kept clouding his understanding. Perhaps she had said, 'I don't know', or 'I think so'.

Could he rely on Esther's having said the words he remembered? And suppose that she had really said them, could he draw any meaningful conclusions from that? Was it possible to develop a *method* to reveal the substance of her *knowing*?

His head was reeling, his body was filling up with liquid lead. It was extraordinarily difficult to put the book down on the table. He watched while his hands descended towards the table as if in slow motion and the book was lowered onto the marble surface. He rubbed his face, exhausted by the effort.

He was afraid he was not going to make it to the end of the evening; if so, he would never know the book's conclusion.

He tried to look at his watch, as though he could read there how many hours he had left, and nearly choked on the great wave of panic welling up inside him and spreading to every part of his body. He raised his arm, felt the dead weight of his muscles and skin and bones, and saw that it was eleven o'clock. Then he felt his heart break. He had heard that hackneyed phrase often enough, but this time he experienced its literal truth, and it was something new and terrifying. The pain in his chest exploded like a grenade, shooting sharp fragments into his neck and shoulders and belly, and he thought: nothing will console me now.

He lost consciousness.

Chapter ten

The afternoon of 7 August 1989

J ohan Sonnema had brought him some work that morning and, propped up on several pillows, he was reading a report compiled by the agricultural attaché. A tray that could be swivelled across the bed served as his reading table.

A large window to the left of the high hospital bed overlooked a rolling landscape of green fields, apparently unspoilt, which now and then disappeared behind thick curtains of rain, to reappear, suddenly illuminated, as the sun's intense rays found a gap in the cloud cover. The first rain for months. The door kept the sounds from the corridor at a distance. He read his files in silence.

When Sonnema had turned up with the pile of folders that morning, Marian had been sitting by his bedside. In high dudgeon she had asked the young man how it could have entered his head to burden her husband with such work three days after he had had a heart attack. Hoffman himself had asked for the files, but that did little to calm her down. 'Then you should have refused to have anything to do with such an insane idea, Mr Sonnema.'

'But Mrs Hoffman, how could I tell my boss that I wasn't going to bring him the papers he asked for?'

'Easily!'

'Marian,' Hoffman said, 'stop this nonsense.'

'You've got to rest,' she said.

'That's what I am doing.'

'Not if you're working.'

'This isn't work,' he said.

'Oh no? What is it then?'

'We diplomats call it *du travail diplomatique*—money for old rope, if you prefer.'

Angrily she got up to smoke a cigarette in the corridor.

When Sonnema had left, she returned.

'Take a rest now, Felix. Do it for my sake.'

'Oh, don't go on about it, it can't do me any harm.'

'The doctor said *rest.*'

'For me, this *is* rest.'

She kissed his cheek and left the room. She would be back at the end of the afternoon. He had read one of the files and had written brief notes to Trevor-Jones and the Italian ambassador (Sonnema had informed them of his heart attack the previous day). At half past twelve a nurse brought him a light lunch. Then someone walked in, a woman.

The first thing he saw at the foot of his bed was the yellow flowers she was holding to her chest. The chrysanthemums had already begun to fade, shabby socialist blooms in the hands of a beautiful creature. He wondered where he had seen her before.

'Mr Hoffman?' she said in English.

He recognised the voice. He smiled.

'Mrs Nová?'

She came closer and with a childlike gesture held out the flowers to him. She was wearing a yellow hood, a kind of sou'wester. A few raindrops lay along the shoulders of her raincoat.

'Thank you very much,' he said. He put the flowers on the bed tray and turned it to one side so that nothing would act as a barrier between them.

'I'll send for a vase in a moment. But really I should be giving *you* a present,' he said. 'Won't you sit down?'

She unbuttoned her raincoat and sat down. Her skirt ended above the knee and he looked down on a superb pair of legs.

'This is a surprise,' he said. 'Would you like something to drink? I can get them to bring something.'

He reached for the small switch hanging on a cord next to his bed, but she shook her head emphatically.

'No, please don't bother. I've just had something.'

'Are you sure?'

She nodded and smiled politely. 'Yes, quite sure.' She took off her hood and shook out her blonde hair, placed the hood on her knees and looked at him, sitting up straight in her chair like a well-brought-up schoolgirl. He saw her glance at the sticking plaster and the tube connecting him to the plastic bag above the bed.

'You're looking well,' she said. 'But then this is our best hospital.'

'The treatment's excellent,' he agreed, looking deep into her eyes. She was tall, with an exuberantly feminine glow, every gesture conjuring up an intimate association for him, as if she were made for erotic encounters. She had full lips, slightly pouted as if in permanent expectation of a kiss, high cheekbones which hinted at something Slav, and grey-green eyes, intelligent and mocking. Her ears were hidden by thick locks of hair, but he suspected elegant curves holding the promise of other secret, more perfumed, folds.

'Did my wife tell you I was here?'

'No. I rang your Embassy this morning.'

'I'm really pleased to see you,' he said.

She gave him a cool smile. 'I was shocked when I heard.'

'Didn't you know?' he asked.

'No.'

'Then you thought I was drunk that night?'

'Oh, well, I wouldn't say that,' she replied uneasily.

'Go ahead, why not? I'll own up to it myself anyway: I *was* drunk that night.'

Another smile. He saw polished teeth, but not set in the rigid kind of battle formation which in the West reflected the height of the dentist's skill. One of her canines was a little askew and lent her smile a suggestion of bloodlust. It made her even more desirable.

'Will they keep you in here for long?'

'Another five or six days. It beats me why I have to stay in bed, but the doctor insists. I feel perfectly fit.'

'Have you ever had anything like this before?'

'A heart attack? No.'

'It must be terrible,' she said.

'I wouldn't recommend it. I was lucky. My wife found me soon after I lost consciousness. They brought me here. This place seems to have all the latest Western paraphernalia.'

'This is the Party hospital,' she said with a conspiratorial smile. 'Are you on any medication?'

'Anti-coagulants, I think they're called.'

She nodded.

At a loss for words for a moment, he swallowed the saliva his fantasies had aroused.

She lowered her eyes.

He had survived his heart attack with mixed feelings. He was breathing, his metabolism was in working order and he was curious about the handful of days apparently still left to him, but at the same time he felt exhausted at the mere thought of the dreary repetition of it all.

Three days ago he ought to have died. Marian had returned home too soon. She had been worried, and that was how she had come to his rescue. Next morning in hospital he had thanked her silently with trembling hands, avid for knowledge about every hour left to him, but on the second day of the rest of his life he had begun to reproach her just as silently for what she had done. He had survived because Marian had wanted him to. His body, an autonomous object that reacted like a machine, had been shifted back into gear and he had to accept that, for better or worse. But he was breathing air to which he was not entitled.

They had knocked him out with something that would not put a strain on his heart. The dreamless vacuity of his artificially induced sleep robbed him of the sense that life and death were simultaneous. In real sleep you were there and yet you were not there at the same time. You could put up with yourself more easily if you could escape for a while every day, but the hole into which these doctors consigned him with their injections brought no relief and hence no liberation: it was nothing but a black void.

'You're a journalist?' he asked.

'Yes.' She nodded, looking up from her thoughts.

'Specialise in anything in particular?'

'General reporting.'

'Have you done it for long?'

'Six years. Before that I was a student. Italian and English.'

'Unusual combination.'

'At the beginning I just did English. But the English Romantics turned me towards Italy. They were all obsessed with Italy.'

'Have you ever been there?'

'No.'

He thought he saw her blush. She was shifting about on her chair. Suddenly she looked up at the ceiling, at the walls. Was she scanning the place for hidden microphones or was she simply avoiding his eyes?

'Have you ever been to Italy?' she asked.

'Yes. Quite often, in fact.'

'Is it...?'

'Beautiful? Yes. Your own beauty would find the perfect setting there.'

It sounded camp, but he had made her feel awkward and was anxious to make amends. Her response to his words came out pat, as if she put up with such comments all day long.

'You are too kind,' she said. 'Presumably everything becomes more beautiful in an Italian setting, doesn't it? May I ask you something?'

'Go ahead.'

'I should like to have a proper talk with you.'

'What are we having now?'

'An interview for my paper. The *Rudé právo*.'

'What about?'

'About the relationship between our two countries.'

'I'd have to get my superiors to agree first.' That was not true, but he trotted the phrase out whenever he wanted to give some more thought to a request.

'Of course.'

'But if it were up to me, I should be more than happy to meet you again,' he said bluntly.

'Then all you have to do is to persuade your superiors.'

'Are you allowed to write whatever you like?'

'What do you mean?'

'Will I be able to speak my mind freely during the interview?'

'You may say whatever you like, of course.'

'But will you print it in your paper?' The answer was obviously no; he just wanted to hear her reply.

'I shall note down everything you say. I don't know if they'll print it all. But that's the same in your country, too.'

'Who has the final say?'

'In the West, it's the editor.'

'And here it's the censor, isn't it?'

'We have our own areas of responsibility, Mr Hoffman.'

'I hope you do,' he replied. 'I must tell you, though…I have little sympathy for your system.'

'That's your privilege,' she said.

'Yes. But not yours,' he said.

She did not react. He could see her magnificent throat moving as she swallowed. He thought of the little folds between her armpits and breasts, where the velvety dome curves away into the shaven hollow.

'I don't have much sympathy for our system either,' he continued. 'Perhaps I'm just an old anarchist—I've yet to come across a decent system.'

'Anarchists and communists don't exactly get on like a house on fire,' she said.

'Officially we can't stand each other, that's true. But I don't think I'm your everyday run-of-the-mill anarchist. I'm a purely emotional anarchist.'

'That's a new one to me,' she said, caught off balance.

'Really? To be honest, it's new to me too.'

They both laughed.

'Your system is based on an old-fashioned, nineteenth-century philosophy, Mrs Nová. Ours in the West is no more up-to-date, not that modernity matters; in fact, it is timeless. Our starting point is man's hunger, the wolf's instinct we try to keep under control. You base your ideology on man's goodness, and the end result is simply that the wickedest wolves prey on the most vulnerable.'

'I don't want to trade arguments with you,' she said coolly.

'Perhaps it's better that way,' he replied with a start, afraid he had forfeited what little chance he might have had of one day pressing his lips to her thighs. 'I didn't want to offend you, but that's the way I see things. Every day there's another report on my desk from one of my colleagues about what's going on in your country.'

'What good would it do you if I applauded your sentiments, Mr Hoffman?' He heard the irritation in her voice.

'I'm not after your applause. I am interested in your opinion.'

'I don't have one. I'm only a go-between.'

'Then you're the first journalist I've ever met without an opinion. But please bear in mind: as far as I'm concerned the system in the West is just as rotten.'

'That sounds more like it,' she said.

'You don't surprise me.'

'So you're the official representative of a rotten system?' she said challengingly.

'Quite so.'

'And will you tell me the same thing at our interview?'

'Certainly not.'

'Pity. Could you tell me what it is you find so rotten about your system?'

'The affluence.'

He realised how ridiculous that sounded, but at this moment, lying in bed, the wilful victim of his own excesses, his throat hoarse with adolescent lust, he could not think of anything better to say.

'The affluence?'

'Yes.'

'Isn't that a…a plus in capitalist eyes?'

'Affluence and guilt,' he said, paling and suddenly serious, and with a certainty that took him by surprise, as if this were the last conversation on which he would ever embark. 'The enjoyment of affluence leads to a gnawing feeling of guilt, Mrs Nová, we don't know what right we have to it, why *we* should have been chosen for the privilege. In the first place, affluence sows doubt and paralysis,' he said, inspired now, 'confronting us with the questions: what to choose, and what to reject? And every day we stare at a box in our living rooms, making the choice between pictures of millions of people starving to death in faraway countries, and light entertainment programmes. We cling to our advantages, unsure of how long we shall continue to enjoy them, and as we consume our over-lavish dinners, we ourselves are consumed by a mythical feeling of guilt….'

What was he getting at? he suddenly wondered. Wasn't he speaking for himself alone? Wasn't he misusing the pronoun 'we'? But he dug deeper, dredging up some grandiose thoughts from the edge of his mind.

'These are monstrous times,' he said, 'the century of mass destruction and affluence and guilt. I nearly died three days ago, and in all honesty I don't know if I wouldn't rather have been left to lie on the kitchen floor.'

He was startled by her look of dismay.

'It all sounds so decadent,' she said indignantly. 'Why can't you just enjoy everything you have?'

'Everything has a price tag,' he said cryptically, although he knew exactly what he meant.

'But you don't have to pay anything!' she said disapprovingly. 'You are privileged and you refuse to enjoy it. That's what I call decadent.'

'But I do want to pay!' he exclaimed, desperate to make her understand. 'Don't you see, Mrs Nová, I do want to pay!'

She shook her head and looked away.

'I'm sorry if I'm unsettling you,' he said.

'You're not unsettling me,' she said with downcast eyes.

'I'm afraid I'm not putting it very well.' He made another attempt. 'I was trying to explain something that can't be explained, I think. I ought to have kept my mouth shut.'

She lifted her eyes and looked at him steadily. 'Aren't you curious about…about the future then?' she asked like a young girl.

'No.'

'The year 2000,' she said, 'don't you want to be there?'

The subject had, in fact, crossed his mind, but he had never discussed it with anyone.

'No. I shall be dead by then.'

'How old are you?'

'Fifty-nine.'

'Then you'll be no more than seventy.'

'I had a heart attack three days ago.'

'If you take it easy, you've got at least another twenty years,' she said as if trying to sell him something.

'I don't need to see the century out.'

'I don't understand you,' she said. 'I really don't.'

He lowered his eyes and wondered if he'd forfeited his last chance. Only adolescents had this sort of conversation, fraught with misunderstandings and woolly thinking.

'Do you have any children?' she asked.

'No.'

'Any other family?'

'Apart from my wife, no.'

'So you…you are, so to speak, the last Hoffman in your father's line?'

'Not just my father's line. I am the last of all the Hoffmans. I am the absolute end.'

'You say that with a certain grim satisfaction.'

'I didn't realise.'

She rose. She was probably taller than he was.

'You are disconcertingly candid,' she said, pushing her hair under the hood. 'I'm looking forward to our appointment.'

'You still want to go ahead with it then?' he asked, taken by surprise.

'I think you'll be a most refreshing subject.'

'Really? I thought…that I must have put you off.'

'On the contrary,' she replied. She buttoned up her coat. He followed the movement of her fingers with as much fascination as if she were opening his flies.

'I always thought people would be glad to be alive after a heart attack. But not you, obviously.'

'You mean, I'm a barbarian because I don't value life highly enough?'

'Yes,' she said frankly.

'No. I value life so highly that I consider myself unworthy of it.'

'I am a communist, Mr Hoffman. I believe in the future. I believe in a world that can be changed.'

'I envy you,' he said.

'If you ask me, you are a victim of your own confusion, not of this century. What is this century? A meaningless abstraction. For you this century is not what it is for a peasant in eastern Slovakia or for a black man in Ghana. We have to view the world against the background of its own dynamism, its own laws. Not against the background of subjective obsessions.'

'I don't understand a word of what you're saying,' he said, gazing spellbound into her face.

'You come from a different world,' she said in a teacher's voice.

'For me, you are that different world.'

She put out a hand and he took it in both of his.

'I'm very grateful to you for coming,' he said. The other night you…let's say…saved my life.'

She withdrew her hand and he felt keenly her escape from the embrace of his fingers.

'I take it I'd have done better to leave you to your fate?'

He fell silent and looked out of the window, as if he might find the answer there. Dark rain clouds skimmed the hills and the landscape had misted over. He felt he had no right to life if his children had had none. Esther and Miriam had not been granted the time to repeat his mistakes, the time to learn how to sneer and deceive and feel contempt (Miriam perhaps, but by then she, though still drawing breath, was already dead), and he wondered if the death of his children was God's way of punishing him.

But a God who meted out such punishment was worse than the devil, and he thought of Spinoza's God, Who was the driving force of nature, Who neither punished nor rewarded, Who was fruitfulness and progress, but Who was yet unable to put an end to suffering and the emptiness of life.

Hoffman was a flawed Jew, circumcised admittedly, but not a card-carrying member. He did not know whether Spinoza had been referring to the God of Moses and Abraham, that God Who was a Person and hence bawled like a Heavenly Market Trader. Spinoza's God was out of his reach, but the God of Moses was an Individual Whom you could address and hold responsible for His actions. If Hoffman was indeed being punished (for his debauchery, which had of course been lying there dormant in his soul even before Esther's illness) then the God of Moses had a lot to answer for, and Spinoza's abstract idea of God must have been mistaken. But if Esther's suffering, and later Miriam's as well, remained pointless and inexplicable and therefore unacceptable—and would remain so to all eternity—then the individuality of the God of Moses became blurred and Hoffman must needs cling to the God of Spinoza. If he wanted to cling to anything, that is.

The God of Moses brought down nothing but rage upon His

head with such punishment as the death of children, the unbounded anger of their fathers; the God of Spinoza, by contrast, begged to be forgiven for not having designed nature without birth and suffering and death.

If Irena Nová—Marian had told him that the Czech journalist had discovered him on the floor next to the lavatories—had left him to his fate, he would probably have died there. He no longer wanted to live. The bestiality of his existence, the fact that his children had died like dogs while his own heart continued to beat stupidly in his breast (just like the heart of any pig or hyena) had made him come to terms with his end.

'Yes,' he said at long last, turning back to Irena Nová, and he wanted to add, yes, you ought to have left me lying there. But he swallowed his words and watched her in silence.

Her hands folded in front of her, tall and graceful and glowing with health, soft and feminine despite the shapeless raincoat and clumsy sou'wester, she stood there looking at him without guile. She had been observing him quietly and her eyes told him that she was afraid of him and that she was keeping her distance—but at the same time they betrayed how fascinating she found him.

He tried not to let it happen, but excitement took possession of his prick and he had to place both hands over the blankets to hide his belly, and it dawned on him that he still had one last aim in life before he gave up the ghost: he wanted to kiss her breasts, he wanted to savour the scent of her loins.

Chapter eleven

The afternoon of 18 August 1989

Hoffman had asked her for lunch at a restaurant on the Namesti Republiky. Normally when he took people out for a meal he would choose one of the big hotels such as the Ambassador or the Europa.

Sonnema had once brought him to this place and it seemed just the right setting for his interview with Irena Nová. The food was just as bad as everywhere else, but the art nouveau decor was original, and the yellowed milk-glass chandeliers radiated a dim homage to pre-war Vienna.

She had dressed for the interview no differently than she had for the hospital: loose-fitting clothes, subdued colours. She had brought a Japanese tape recorder with her, but he asked her not to tape their conversation; he wanted to reserve the right to deny any statements afterwards that seemed to him too outspoken. During the meal—an unexpectedly tasty piece of steak with potatoes boiled until they were falling apart and lukewarm beetroot—she put her questions to him.

She was more distant than she had been at the hospital. She barely looked at him and made notes on a pad on which she had also jotted down her neutral questions. He answered her with the tired phrases of diplomatic small talk.

He had put on an expensive linen suit made in Italy—Europe was again sweating under a tropical sky—and was aware of the glances of the Czechs at other tables. He had made the mistake of overdressing for the occasion, as he would have done had he worn a gold bracelet or a heavy signet ring in his circles. He wore the suit perhaps once a year, since it verged on the unseemly for a Dutch diplomat. It would have been better had he turned up here in his oldest clothes.

Ever since her visit to his sick bed, he had been haunted day and night by erotic fantasies. Feverish images of her body had been an inexhaustible source of speculation and licentious flights of fancy. He had not had sex since Kenya. In the past just visiting a brothel had been enough for him to perform the act with zeal and dispatch, the very thought that a woman might spread her legs for money helping to arouse him. He had been a regular customer of diplomatic brothels in Lima, Dar es Salaam, Rio, Houston, all the posts in fact where he had been stationed after Esther's death. Now he masturbated. A man of fifty-nine who laid hands on himself.

Sex changed over the years, much like the hair on your arms or the shape of a birthmark. But you could not get rid of it. At best you could suppress it.

His suppressing mechanism had broken down in the presence of Irena Nová. Just one of her glances, and he had to find out in the flesh what he had as yet only surmised in his mind, for her glance was erotic, by which he meant that it held the hint of something secret. Her eyes made one want to lay bare the shadowy places in her soul as well as the shadowy places in her body.

He thought of her in his bedroom at night, surrounded by international newspapers and magazines until he was overtaken by the empty sleep provided by Bayer. His heart attack had renewed his acquaintance with his bed. He was not used to spending long hours on his back, but the doctors had prescribed powerful sleeping pills and he swallowed them religiously. He had reflected on Irena's height, her eyes that invited voyages of discovery, and her figure that evoked breathless lust, and found his ambitions focused on these.

Once he had left the hospital and resumed the course of his miserable life, he had just one goal in mind, a heroic assignment that seemed hopeless and involved him in contriving the most farfetched plans. Hoffman did not have much time left, was nearing the end of his journey. She sat there now, untouchable, facing him coolly and unemotionally.

The interview dragged on. When he had dressed in the Italian suit, he had hoped it would make him look younger and boost his chances, but she was showing no interest in his voice, his eyes or his clothes, and was finishing off the interview with practised skill.

As coffee was being served (Turkish, in small glass cups), she thanked him. He could see tiny droplets of sweat on her forehead and her upper lip.

'My pleasure. You'll let me see it?'

'As agreed.'

'What are you doing for the rest of the afternoon?' he asked.

'I still have a few things to finish off,' she said evasively, looking past him at the customers at other tables.

'I have the feeling....' He hesitated and searched for words. 'I have the feeling that your thoughts are elsewhere,' he said.

She gave him a quick glance, withering and hostile, then shook her head tensely.

'No. It'll pass,' she said.

'It'll pass? Then something is the matter?'

She did not reply but stared bleakly at the little cup of coffee standing untouched between her hands.

'If I can help you in any way, Mrs Nová, I'd be only too glad to. Perhaps I could play some small part in your life.'

She gave a scornful laugh, then looked up for a moment and allowed the contempt in her eyes to show. He read in them the cutting message that she was aware of his fantasies and despised him for them.

'I don't need to be helped, Mr Hoffman,' she said. 'I can look after myself.'

'But if you should...' he urged. He could see that he was annoying her.

'I know,' she said brusquely.

He was overcome by a feeling of helplessness. He would never get closer to her than the width of the table between them.

He continued to sit despondently in front of his coffee when she had left. She would be telephoning in a few days to arrange for him to see the full text of the interview, even though it was standard diplomatic practice never to read interviews before publication. The diplomat concerned could then always claim he had been misquoted, that everything had sprung from the journalist's fertile imagination. Yet Hoffman had agreed to break that rule just to meet her again, to allow him to cling to even the slightest hope of making his fantasies come true.

He ordered a bottle of wine and began to empty it steadily. He wanted to think.

There was something hysterical about his desire to sleep with Irena Nová. He wondered if Miriam was any part of this irrational obsession. Miriam would have turned twenty-nine that year and Irena Nová could not be much older, in her early thirties. All at once the magical symbolism of the unconscious did not seem too far-fetched a concept. Perhaps, symbolically, he wanted to be at one with his dead daughter, and had chosen Irena as her surrogate. But on examining this idea more closely, he shook his head in amazement at how his mind could be so off-course, and emptied the bottle glumly and without thirst.

It was still early in the afternoon when he came home. He was slightly tipsy, could feel that his face was flushed, and he hurried to take off his jacket. That so much alcohol in his blood might be putting his life at risk was a matter of supreme indifference to him. As he was uncorking another bottle in the kitchen—his safe haven, his sweet refuge—Marian came in with a silver tray bearing the remains of her lunch. He saw her shock at his appearance. With trembling hands, she put the tray down on the draining board.

'Felix....'

She kept her back to him, staring out into the green garden, and he could hear the emotion in her voice. She too had given in to the heat. She was wearing a short-sleeved dress that revealed the ample flesh of her upper arms. The cork left the neck of the bottle with a polite little pop. The wine gurgled elegantly into the crystal glass.

'Felix....'

He picked up the glass and sniffed. A fine vintage.

'Felix....'

He took a sip and rinsed the wine between his teeth, caressing all the taste buds in his mouth.

'I give up, Felix,' he heard Marian say. He glanced at the hips that had borne his children. They were a reminder of the young woman she had been, and of their version of married sex in a darkened bedroom, torn between embarrassment and lust. He had sought nothing more in those days, he had had Marian and the girls and life was kind to him. He was happy.

'Are you listening? I give up.'

Hoffman pulled out a chair and sat down. Marian was still standing with her back to him, unable to look at him.

'Haven't you got your own life to live?' he asked hoarsely. 'No need to bother about mine.'

She asked, 'Do you want to die so much?'

He could hear that she was holding back her tears. Then she said, 'Do you really want to put an end to it all like this?'

'It's hot. I'm thirsty. I'm allowed to,' he said, untruthfully.

'You're drunk. You were drunk when you came in. Did you go out for lunch somewhere? Oh, I don't really want to know.'

He saw her shake her head, looking out at the newly-watered lawn and the tall trees.

'Why didn't we get divorced that time? It would probably have been better for Miriam as well.'

'Nonsense,' he said.

'Miriam was the one who had the worst of it. It's our fault she's gone.'

'What about Esther? Was it our fault that she got cancer?'

'I don't know.... Sometimes I think there's a supreme being who metes out punishment. Perhaps Esther did die for us.'

He raised his glass and said, 'Ideas like that are leftovers of your Catholic period, darling.' Savouring the bouquet, he took a drink of the wine.

'We made a mess of things, Felix.'

'Oh, really?'

'No sarcasm, please!' Her voice was suddenly loud with anger.

He wagged a pointing finger at her, then realised that drunks in bars used the same gesture when fending off accusations.

'Don't talk to me like that, Marian! You've no right to raise your voice to me like that!'

She stood unmoving at the sink, and made no reply.

Snorting, he sat at the marble table and downed the half-filled glass. He was being unfair, self-centred, vindictive, but he was prey to a rage that could be released only through sour recriminations, only by making her cry.

'You come in here and start ranting about divorce!' he heard himself bluster, a loathsome man. 'My God, I'm sitting here trying to get over a heart attack, a *heart attack*, do you hear me?' He was shouting at her now, eyes starting, hands gripping the edge of the table. 'You're hoping I'll have another heart attack if you talk to me like that, aren't you? That's what you want, isn't it? You'd like me to kick the bucket! You're trying to get me so excited I'll choke on my own blood! You're trying to bump me off, aren't you? You'd like me to drop dead! Well, darling, carry on like that and you won't have long to wait!'

'I don't want you to drop dead!' she screamed. She clapped her hands to her face.

He took a long drink to calm himself, but all the alcohol did was fuel the flames of guilt and shame scorching his soul. He had to break her if he was ever to rid himself of his feelings of guilt. He had to see her tears.

'You know what, my darling?' he said in the most honeyed tones he could muster, given the circumstances. 'It's perfectly possible that what you want is to see everyone dead. Everyone.'

'Bastard!'

She jerked round to face him. 'Bastard,' she repeated. She was holding her clenched fists to her chest, as if he were threatening her physically. But her eyes were pale and dry. She whispered, 'You're a beast. You disgust me.'

She looked at him as if for the last time, then left the kitchen.

At once he poured himself another glass. He had to try to survive until his meeting with Irena. It was the only prospect that gave him reason to draw breath.

If he put a plastic bag over his head, he would suffocate.

If he held his head in a bowl full of water, he would drown.

The air he breathed was more precious than his life.

He grieved for the man he had once been.

The telephone rang and someone in the house answered it. Twenty seconds later Jana opened the kitchen door and stood squarely on the threshold.

'For you,' she said without a trace of warmth.

He pushed himself to his feet and staggered into the hall, holding onto the walls.

With a clammy hand he picked up the heavy black receiver.

'Hello?'

'Irena Nová….'

'Mrs Nová!'

As if she could see him, he tried to stand upright, to conceal his drunkenness, but quickly decided against it.

He said her name once again, more calmly this time, 'Mrs Nová…what can I do for you?'

'About the interview. Can we fix a date for next week? Would Wednesday suit you?'

He had not the slightest idea whether he was free on Wednesday, but refusing her was out of the question. He would put everything else off in order to see her.

'Yes, of course. Wednesday's fine. Where?'

'Same place?'

'Fine.'

'About seven?'

'In the evening?'

'Yes, of course.'

She wanted to meet him in the evening. Boyish delight welled up in his breast, the anticipation of a young lover. 'I look forward to it,' he said.

She rang off.

He clung to the turned oak banister and looked up. Marian was standing on the top step, looking down at him, red-eyed. She was waiting for him to say something and he knew that if he could not find the words a simple gesture with a hand or even a finger would do.

Hoffman staggered back to the kitchen.

Chapter twelve

Hoffman survived the next few days and nights. Every evening an impassable mountain lay in wait for him, which he had to climb with his bare hands. Precipitous and rugged. And every morning he reached the flatlands of the day, with the wonderment of a paralytic who had just been for a walk.

He ordered Boris to drive him to the restaurant on the Namesti Republiky. The sun had slipped behind the hills to the west of the city, and a balmy dusk hung ready to descend over the hundreds of turrets and dormer windows.

The Kingdom's standard fluttered from the bonnet of the car. Earlier that day Hoffman had read a report on human rights in Czechoslovakia, to be sent to The Hague over his signature. The main task that had been assigned to him in Prague was to provide support for dissidents, a gimmick dreamed up by the coterie of 'spokespersons' at the Dutch Foreign Ministry. In fact no one in The Hague, himself included, gave a damn for the dissidents, but the minister knew he could score points in the chamber with exaggerated tributes to muddled humanists and disillusioned communists. The Western press had a soft spot for dissidents, because dissidents were in fact not dissimilar to journalists: confined to the sidelines of politics, convinced at all times that right was on their side, but reduced to silence by a mob of politicians. Journalists, sad creatures who had elevated their rancour into a profession, had no trouble in identifying themselves with these malcontents.

In the Netherlands, too, dissidents abounded, but there they were simply dismissed as troublemakers. In Eastern Europe things were different. With few exceptions (for instance Sakharov, innocence personified) most Eastern bloc dissidents had been looked on as deeply pious heroes, prevented from attending church and dreaming of a Europe under the leadership of the Pope. Hoffman was thinking of the Poles in particular, people who had stopped working, brought their country to the brink of economic ruin, and were now able to spend all day on their bended knees in church imploring the Blessed Virgin for better times.

A troublemaker born in Eastern Europe was a dissident to the West. Thus a semi-literate wretch who could just about write THE CAT SAT ON THE MAT and had the good fortune to be confined in a Gulag labour camp, could find himself published in Munich or Paris as 'a leading dissident author of experimental texts'.

According to one of the directives from the Monkey Rock, Hoffman was expected to keep in touch with local dissidents; his task was to make it plain to the Party and the Czech government that the Dutch nation insisted on the implementation of the Helsinki agreements. Quite apart from the fact that Hoffman was firmly convinced that the Dutch nation did not give two hoots for the Helsinki agreements, he could see no advantage in turning Europe into a battlefield of overblown nationalistic aspirations. In his humble opinion any Sudeten German seeking to revise the post-war frontiers deserved a stringent communist regime.

Hoffman left the contacts with his dissident fellow men to Johan Sonnema, a Catholic intellectual from Franeker who knew all about suppression, and who took pleasure in holding forth about existence, freedom in restraint and the like over a glass of wine.

To Hoffman it seemed as if nothing in Czechoslovakia would ever change. The Poles wanted a Roman Empire with the Pope on the throne, and at the June elections—the first for forty years—they had sent the Party candidates packing. The East Germans were Germans first and foremost and wanted nothing better than to march under a single banner (they had been crowding into the West German embassies not only in Budapest and in East Berlin, but also here in Prague; he had been told they were camping out in the corridors, sleeping under the desks and between the filing cabinets, and blocking up the lavatories). The Hungarians dreamt of some such great and inspiring cause as the Hapsburg Empire (the Party there had opened discussions with the opposition; both of them were tarred with the same brush, in Hoffman's opinion). But what did the Czechs want?

The Czechs' only experience of freedom and democracy had been between 1918 and 1939; and the kind of nationalistic fervour so dear to the Poles and the Hungarians was alien to them. Theirs was the country of the *Good Soldier Schweik* and of Franz Kafka, a nebbich of a little country poised between paranoia and an inferiority complex. It was not even united, but contained Czechs, Slovaks and Germans, each with a language and culture of their own, each ground down by the real Germans, the Austrians and the Russians.

Two days before, there had been an illegal demonstration, and the police had made hundreds of arrests. In countries like this there was never any shortage of people partial to having themselves arrested. On the other hand, in 1968, when the Russians used knuckledusters to work over Dubcek's 'human face', a legion of enthusiastic Czechs had been ready and willing to suppress and torture their own compatriots. In every East European country whole hordes of people could be found capable of rendering a multitude of services to the occupier with even greater dedication, virtuosity and ruthlessness than collaborators used to display during the Nazi occupation of Europe.

People everywhere had dirty hands; every nation provided its own gaolers.

Hoffman was in fact frightened to death of the free Romanians, men who had been able to give the Germans lessons in the best ways of exterminating Jews during the war. The Hungarians, too, could boast of a century of anti-Semitic prime ministers. And what about those Saxons who had christened their country the GDR? He shivered at the thought of Saxons gaining independence and freedom from the Russians or—God forbid—uniting with the West Germans: give a German your little finger and he'll chop off your whole hand.

Fortunately, the little grey men with pinched mouths in Berlin still took their instructions from Moscow. The Moscow brand of communism—nothing but a gigantic oligarchy—managed to keep the lids firmly on the pans throughout Eastern Europe that were on the point of boiling over with nationalism, racism and anti-Semitism. The carve-up of Europe was the least of the evils this century had spawned.

Needless to say he had not mentioned any of this in his interview with Irena Nová, and had been entirely non-committal in all his answers to her questions. Indeed, he had given her nothing of any interest to go on, save that he was capable of talking without saying anything.

For the past few nights he had been giving in to his raging hunger and eating again. Wading through magazines and undemanding detective stories, he would await each morning with resignation and distended guts. He was still taking Sintrom, the drug that thinned his blood, but he had put the sleeping pills away in a drawer upstairs in his bedroom, next to the book by Spinoza which now had confusing and tiring associations for him. It seemed the youthful zest with which he had begun to work on the improvement of his understanding had at last presented its bill, a bill that he knew from bitter experience would always fall due. He now stood revealed as a man of advancing years, nursing a fully-developed strain of self-hatred and driven by a last wish that he could confide to no one.

He often thought in bookkeeping terms. He had had to pay

dearly all along the line. The rough balance sheet he drew up in his mind included the death of his parents in settlement for his survival of the war, and the loss of his children as payment for his career.

More than once he had considered it all, seated on the lavatory or at the kitchen table, wondering if he could not adopt a different system of values. Aware of his limitations and trammelled nature, however, he knew he had no choice in the matter.

He was what he was, he concluded. That meant accepting his own particular form of indolence, which in turn relieved him of any obligation to improve his intellect or his morals. He had become reconciled to this. The heady pursuit of happiness had ended in Esther's coffin; he had now abandoned all hope of peace and understanding as well. Like an escaped balloon, hope had taken flight into the clouds.

As a symptom of his dreamless existence, his subconscious registered every ripple in his state of mind. Death alone could deliver him from himself.

The Mercedes drove across the bridge in front of the Exhibition Pavilion, the Czech contribution to Expo '58. The austere glass and metal building rose up against the steep crest of the hill bordering the left bank of the Vltava. The bridge was asphalted, but once on the right bank the tyres rumbled over cobblestones again. Now they were driving up the street called Revolucni, at the top of which was the restaurant where he had arranged to meet Irena. Boris opened the door for him. It was not that he was too lazy to do it for himself, but Boris had silently made it clear that he considered opening and closing the doors of the Mercedes part of his job.

Summer was not yet over and the evening was mild and close. Hoffman thanked Boris, told him he would be returning by taxi in a few hours, and gave him the rest of the evening off.

The restaurant seemed deserted. When no waiter appeared, Hoffman chose his own table. The place looked as if the foyer of Tuschinski's, the cinema in Amsterdam he had often visited in his student days, had been filled with chairs and tables. His memory took him back to his second or third date with Marian: at an Italian film he had put his arm round her and she had kissed him. He folded his old Burberry over an empty chair and sat down. With the edge of his right hand he could feel breadcrumbs on the white tablecloth; lost in old memories he brushed them into a pile.

Warned by some sixth sense he looked up, rising to his feet automatically as she came in from the passage leading from the dining room to the cloakrooms. The sight of her eased the ache in his soul. She sat down at a different table, then chanced to look in his direction. Without breathing, as if the slightest movement might blur the apparition, he continued to watch her. He stayed on his feet, straight-backed, standing to attention, awaiting the command that would be issued by her smile.

She smiled.

He walked across to her.

She stood up and waited for him in all her glory. Gracefully she held out her hand.

'Mr Hoffman....'

'Mrs Nová....'

He kissed her hand.

'Would you agree this place is a little empty?' she asked as he drowned in her eyes, holding onto her hand.

'Would you rather we went somewhere else?'

'Perhaps we should.'

'Unfortunately, I am a stranger here,' he said.

'But I am not.' Only then did she withdraw her hand from his eager grasp.

She suggested a restaurant with a somewhat ambiguous reputation. Rumour had it that Party bosses were amongst its clients. Irena claimed that it had the best kitchen in town; strangers were not normally admitted. He had heard of it before.

They took a taxi to the Francouzska, a wide street leading out of the centre of the city. She handed him the copies of her article, which ran to just two-and-a-half pages. The street lighting was too poor for him to make out the text.

She looked radiant. She had put on make-up and was wearing an elegant suit, her thick blonde hair falling like a fur collar over the shoulders of the severely-cut jacket. Listening to her telling him about the limited number of all-night restaurants in the city, he wondered if she would accept his offer. He had finally decided he would have to suggest payment, starting with a thousand dollars. If necessary, he was prepared to go up to ten thousand dollars, to hand over to her everything he could still call his own after the purchase of his daughter's debut as a film star. On the local black market a thousand dollars meant a fortune that she could not refuse. What mattered, though, was the right moment to put it to her; after dinner perhaps, as if buying her love were the most natural thing in the world.

He had expected a formal encounter, followed by a quick meal, but she seemed to be in an expansive mood, chatting away, torturing him with her smile.

The taxi stopped and she led him down a dark alleyway, difficult to make out from the street. The narrow lane muffled the noises of the city; their footsteps were all that echoed from the old stones exhaling the heat of the day. All of a sudden he was alone with her. She did not seem afraid of his closeness.

'Do you like game?' she asked.

'I love pheasant, guinea fowl, quail....'

'They say that the estate workers at our president's hunting lodge bring everything they can poach to this place.'

She stopped at a low door in a stone wall that appeared to enclose an inner courtyard. Irena knocked.

'Do they take reservations?' he asked.

'They don't have a telephone, or at least they say they don't.'

A hatch in the door slid open. In the dark, Hoffman could make out the contours of a face. Irena whispered something, but the man behind the hatch shook his head. Hoffman could tell from Irena's voice that they were out of luck.

She turned to him. 'It'll be a good hour,' she said, 'and then they're afraid there won't be anything left.'

'Do you want to wait?' he asked.

'Actually, I'm starving.'

'Then let's go to the Hotel Europa,' he suggested. She said something to the dark face and the hatch shut. They walked back towards the street.

'That's the drawback of these small places,' she said. 'They depend entirely on what they happen to be able to get hold of from one day to the next.'

'I'd be happy to ask you out again next week. Perhaps we can make it a bit earlier.'

'Thank you very much.'

Again they were alone. Dim lighting fifty yards up the wide street cast a yellow glow on her face. Although she was an arm's length away from him, he could sense the heat of her body.

'A thousand dollars.'

He had said it before he had had time to think.

Smiling, she threw him a sidelong glance. It was obvious she had not understood what he said. His heart beat faster as if he were running uphill.

'What did you say?' she asked.

He was getting an erection.

'A thousand dollars,' he repeated in a shaking voice.

She stopped, still smiling, but he could see disquiet flicker through her eyes.

'I don't know what you mean,' she said, like someone failing to get a joke.

He turned his back to the broad main street. The light shone from behind onto his shoulders and she could not see his face. He summoned up the sheer courage of despair, like that of a mountaineer climbing into the unknown.

'A thousand dollars. If you come to a hotel with me.'

'Weren't we on our way to the Hotel Europa?'

'I mean to a room, Mrs Nová.'

She stared at him open-mouthed, blinked.

'I, uh…I don't think I quite understand,' she said slowly.

'A thousand dollars, Mrs Nová, in hard currency, that's a lot of money, and it's yours if you'll come to a hotel room with me.'

She sniffed contemptuously, looked at him with more distaste than even Jana could muster, then turned her head away.

'You don't know what you're saying, Mr Hoffman.'

Then she took to her heels.

He charged after her. Every step hurt. It had been a long time since he had last been forced to run; but he knew that he must not let her get away. He could see her hair dancing about her shoulders. The rod sticking out below his stomach into his trousers made running even more difficult.

He caught her by the arm.

She came to a standstill and gave him the same withering look.

Exhausted, he gasped for air, his heart ready to burst.

'Forgive me,' he said. 'You are….' He swallowed, moistened his lips. 'You are a goddess. I worship you.'

'You don't offer money to a goddess,' she said furiously.

'I couldn't think of any other way to get you to come with me.' Desperation was in his voice; he had played all his cards. But he was on fire.

'That's not the way to do it,' she said, shaking her head.

'I don't know any other,' he said abjectly. 'I want your love, but I know you don't want mine.'

She hid her face in her hands. Hoffman, still panting, stood staring at the shape of her fingers, at her throat.

'Two thousand,' he heard her say behind her hands.

'Two thousand five hundred,' he choked. 'I'll give you two thousand five hundred.'

'Three thousand,' she said in a stifled voice.

'Right,' he said. 'Three thousand dollars it is.'

She made no reply.

He could not see her face and waited for her to steel herself to show the shame in her eyes. He raised a hand and laid it on her arm. She recoiled, her face still buried behind the shell formed by her fingers, and shook off his touch.

'Let's take a taxi,' he said.

'Not the Europa,' she said. She was still hiding her face.

'Why not?'

'They'll want to see your passport there.'

'Another hotel then?'

'I know somebody at the International.'

'I'll leave it to you,' he said. 'I'm grateful to you for thinking of my position.'

Now she dropped her hands, revealing the sadness in her eyes.

'I need the money,' she said.

Chapter thirteen

The early morning of 24 August 1989

He was walking on the beach with Miriam. A howling wind was carrying her words away, and although he could see her lips moving and her panic-stricken look he had no idea why she was gesticulating so frantically. Then he saw Esther, disappearing into the stormy sea.

He fought his way to her through the crests of thickly foaming waves and grabbed her arm. A single wave threw them back onto the beach and he dragged her up the wet sand. Behind him, the water at once filled in their footprints. A shudder of fear ran through him as he pressed his mouth to his child's cold lips, trying desperately to blow life into her lungs. Then she opened her eyes with a smile and embraced him. It had all been a game.

They walked on. Esther was shorter than Miriam and he asked how that had come about. Esther's growth had been stunted, that was all. Marian was sitting on a travelling rug and took little pots of caviare out of an enormous wicker basket, one for each of them.

They sat down and ate.

The sun dried his clothes.

Even before these visions dissolved, Hoffman knew that he was dreaming. He returned from that other world, blessedly released from the nightmare in which his children had died, and when he opened his eyes he saw Irena sitting in the armchair in the corner of the room.

He closed his eyes and lay still for a moment. He had been wandering through a world of miracles and oblivion. He had been holding Esther and listening to Miriam. He had eaten with his family. He had slept. My God.

He sat up and looked at Irena.

She had dressed and was having a cigarette, its thin smoke spiralling up through the light from a standard lamp. The air in the room was stuffy. Despite the open window he felt the lack of oxygen.

'Are you going?' he asked, his mouth dry. He leant on one elbow.

She nodded, blowing out smoke.

'I've been asleep,' he said.

'I didn't want to wake you. But I didn't seem able to write you a note, otherwise I would have been gone by now.'

'I haven't slept for twenty years.'

'What *do* you mean?'

Her voice was soft and tender, like a lover's. He realised that both of them were whispering.

'This is the first time I've been able to sleep for twenty years. Thanks to you.'

'You suffer from insomnia?'

'Chronic insomnia. But tonight I slept. Because of you.'

'Truly?'

'Because of you, Irena, because of you. I truly slept because of you.'

She smiled at him with surprise and satisfaction. Then she stood up.

'I must go.'

'All right,' he said.

'Be careful, won't you? You can leave through the main foyer. Take a taxi.'

She bent down and picked up her handbag.

'Will I see you next week?' he asked.

She slipped her packet of cigarettes and lighter into her bag, looked at him briefly and nodded.

'I'll give you the money then,' he said.

'Small notes, please....'

'I'll see to it.'

He held out his hand. She took his fingers but kept her distance from the bed.

'I slept, Irena. You don't know what that means to me. It's because of you. Your...your love.'

'You don't think you're exaggerating a little?'

He shook his head. 'No, no, I'm not. I fell asleep alongside you. You are my saviour.'

'That sounds almost religious.'

'Because it is.'

She let go of his hand and took two steps towards the door. 'And my article?'

'Splendid,' he said. 'Can be printed just as it is.'

'Are you sure?' She stubbed her cigarette out in a heavy glass ashtray.

'Yes,' he said.

'Look after yourself, Felix.'

He nodded. She opened the door and vanished.

He sank back onto the mattress. The bedclothes were redolent with her intimacy. He pulled a sheet over his head and filled his lungs with her scent.

Lying there inside his small tent, he could feel his limbs begin to glow. A youthful power spread tingling through his belly. He surrendered himself to the memory of her climax and his prick rose again, as if he were twenty. His decrepit body still had the strength to satisfy a woman in her thirties, and he swelled with primordial male pride. Another week and he would fall asleep once more between Irena's breasts. He knew that she might be the death of him, but he would be glad to pay the price.

Suddenly the future seemed full of promise. He would shower Irena with money and presents, bind her to him as she became addicted to luxury and comfort, until he could be pensioned off, destitute and sucked dry, to go and wait for death.

Irena's body was full and firm, he could lose himself in her eyes, he had kissed and caressed her—worshipped her—and when she had seized his head and pushed his hungry mouth away from between her legs he had felt the shudders of her orgasm. She had enticed him to mount her, had led him on. The years had fallen away as in total abandon he had revelled in the desire that radiated through her face.

His prick was throbbing insistently now, and seizing it, he made himself come.

Half an hour later he left the Hotel International tower block. The marble foyer was deserted, except for two men in track suits sitting in large armchairs by the exit. They had filled the ashtray between them with cigarette butts. They had not spared him a glance as he stepped out into the sultry night. Two taxis stood waiting outside and he took one of them back to the residence.

It was a quarter to two. He had slept. His children were dead and his marriage was in tatters, but for the moment he could luxuriate in his rapturous anticipation of the following Wednesday. He still had a good few years ahead of him, years of her to enjoy—for as long as his income allowed.

He had to take his career and Marian into account, of course. He would not be able to help running into Irena now and then—she was a journalist after all—but he was determined to avoid any scandal. The two men at the hotel exit had no doubt been FSZS-men, and he could not afford to take many more risks like that.

But no sooner had he acknowledged these fears than he brushed them aside with the resolve that he would continue to meet her, no matter what the cost. And, however unlikely it might seem, even if she herself was working for the FSZS (you never could tell in these countries) he would do nothing to avoid her. If she was his fate, so be it; in the final analysis, all the rest was not worth a damn.

The taxi stopped outside his house. He had not yet eaten, and the thought of food filled his mouth with saliva. He had tasted her sex; he would now taste the smoked trout which had arrived by diplomatic post that afternoon, part of a consignment of delicatessen from a catering firm in The Hague, sent to him with the collection of brochures and free Hague newspapers for which he had asked.

He could face the rest of the night. He had slept.

Chapter fourteen

The morning of 29 September 1989

After landing at about seven in the evening at Charles de Gaulle in Paris, John Marks caught a connecting flight to Munich, although his ticket was endorsed for a transfer by Air France to Rome.

In Munich he boarded the train to Vienna, with a second-class ticket, and it was well past midnight when he asked a taxi driver to find him a decent hotel for the night. The man took him to the Hotel Alpha in the 9th District, a peaceful area close to the city centre. The hotel was in an unassuming new building in a nineteenth-century street. His room was clean and quiet.

He had memorised the faces of his fellow passengers and knew that he was not being followed. On the trip he had neither papers nor magazines, allowing his mind to wander instead and mull over his memories.

His appointment with Marian Hoffman was at eleven that morning, but he asked to be woken at six. After a shower he drank the coffee the Pakistani waiter had brought up to his room, first pouring it into one of the plastic cups he had brought in his luggage. Early trams rumbled past the hotel. He put on a Brooks Brothers suit which he considered to be his best, a classic and unpretentious affair; those who knew about such things would recognise the quality of the cloth and the cut. He also took with him a light, inconspicuous raincoat, just in case, although the day promised to be warm and dry.

It was a clear, bright morning. He walked for several blocks, then at the approach of a tram embarked upon the obligatory 'dry cleaning': hours of diversionary manoeuvres to shake off any tail. Twenty yards up the street was a tram stop. He sprinted towards it and leapt onto the platform as the tram pulled away. Looking back through the window, he saw a reassuringly empty pavement. He took a single seat close to the automatic doors in the central section, and rode as far as St Stephen's cathedral.

This time he did not allow himself to be distracted by memories of Marian, but concentrated on the possibility that he was being shadowed or was under surveillance.

In the cafe facing the cathedral, Am Stephansplatz, he ordered a cafe au lait, but, not trusting the cup, left the coffee untouched. He paged through a Viennese morning paper stuck in a wooden holder (observing how the fingers of his gloves became blackened by the printer's ink) and watched the door. The cafe began filling up with elderly ladies of a certain gentility, accompanied by their conceited-looking lapdogs. After half an hour he left.

Descending to the subway station under the square, he took the U-Bahn from the spotlessly clean platform to Praterstern, on the other side of the Danube Canal, and waited a few minutes for the gates of the Volksprater to open.

The Ferris wheel had not yet been started up. In front of the main entrance, swarthy men, immigrant workers he presumed, were sweeping the litter into piles with primitive brooms made from bunches of twigs tied to a stick. He hummed the theme from *The Third Man*.

Mingling with the early-rising families now making a rush for the attractions, he strolled across the fairground. He left by another gate, hailed a cab and told the driver to take him to the Südbahnhof. He sat at an angle on the back seat and kept one eye on the traffic behind. He was getting hot in his raincoat. At the station he crossed from platform to platform for twenty-five minutes, as meticulously as if it were wartime. Then he boarded a train, walked through several carriages and got out again. Next—he had taken off his raincoat—he took the U-Bahn to the Südtiroler Platz. There he changed lines for the Karlsplatz. A taxi at the Karlsplatz took him to the Westbahnhof, where he walked up Mariahilfer Strasse towards Linzer Strasse, and turned left towards the Schloss Schönbrunn.

Again he took a taxi (he never ceased to be amazed that Europeans had turned the Mercedes, of all things, that acme of culture and affluence to American eyes, into the continent's taxi of choice) and asked to be taken to Thalia Strasse. At the corner of Watt Gasse, he got out and followed a circuitous route to the Pension Klopstock in Klopstockgasse, a neglected street in the 17th District, a precinct inhabited by immigrant workers and refugees from Eastern Europe who had found themselves stranded in Vienna.

Simon Berenstein sat in the cramped entrance hall behind the shabby secretaire he and Marks had bought at an auction in 1958. He looked up and gave a cursory nod, as if John Marks dropped by every day.

Walking up to him, Marks saw that he was grasping the old-fashioned steel-nibbed pen with which he wrote all his novels in his big hand. Behind him, in the living room, stood the heavy blanket box that contained scores of Berenstein's manuscripts. He had given strict orders that they were not to be published. 'Not until I'm pushing up the daisies.' Berenstein was a Russian Jew who had fled to Austria in the fifties. Marks had never read a single line Berenstein had written, but for simplicity's sake proceeded on the assumption that all his works were masterpieces.

Berenstein continued to write as he talked to Marks.

'Staying long, John?'

'Just today.'

'When are you going to come and visit us for a few weeks again?'

'I don't know, Simon.'

'Never, I suppose?'

'I don't know, Simon.'

'Room 305. She's waiting for you.'

Marks placed the envelope on the top of the secretaire. Berenstein left it there, as if it were of no consequence, and Marks walked across to the ancient lift cage. He shut the door, nothing more than a wire grille, and the lift shook and groaned its way up to the third floor.

It ground to a halt with a jolt. Marks opened the door and looked down the corridor for Room 305. His leather soles betrayed his presence on the dark-coloured parquet floor. He stopped outside the room, knocked with the knuckles of his gloved right hand, did not wait for an answer and opened the door.

Marian was sitting on the arm of a large chair in front of the window. She was dressed for the heat, wearing a dress with a pattern of little flowers and elbow-length sleeves. As he walked in she looked round and smiled nervously. Then she stood up, smoothing down her skirt. Marks stopped in the doorway, still holding the door handle.

The first time he had slept with her had been in the guest room of his flat in Dar es Salaam, in 1972; the last time he had seen her was in Rio de Janeiro, in 1977, just before the Carnival. She was twelve years older now. He could see that she dyed her hair, but had kept a white streak at the front in salute to her age.

He was searching for words. He swallowed, and watched her fingers toying nervously with the clasp of her purse. Both of them were holding back. When she moved towards him, he had to make himself open his arms to her. For years he had dreamt of this moment; now it had arrived he was afraid of her touch. He heard her purse fall and she wrapped her arms around his waist. Outside, cats were fighting.

When her hold around his waist slackened, he let go of her too. She took his hands—his gloves—and they stood there facing each other. She was taller than he was. He could hear himself take a shuddering breath.

'It's wonderful to see you, Marian.' he pronounced the name 'Mary Ann'; he had never got his tongue round the Dutch way of saying it.

She gave a tender nod. Her eyes travelled quickly over his face, examining the lines, the hair on his head. Her fingers caressed the gloves.

'You look well, John.'

'And you don't look a day older,' he said.

She laughed like a young girl. 'Don't exaggerate….'

'No…you look stunning,' he said with a catch in his voice. He blinked to keep the tears back. He did not dare kiss her.

'It feels like yesterday, doesn't it?' she asked.

He nodded. 'Yesterday,' he agreed. 'It's still quite fresh. As if it was only a few hours ago.'

Suddenly tears were running down her cheeks. He led her to the bed and sat down beside her. She wept silently and without restraint, as only those can who have come to terms with their loss.

'Don't pay any attention to me,' she said.

She took a deep breath and pulled a packet of paper handkerchiefs out of her purse. She wiped her cheeks and smiled at him, eyes wide.

'It's so wonderful to see you, John. Tell me everything, where you're living, how you are, and your children and wife, too. I want to know everything.'

He told her that after she had ended their relationship in Rio, he had divorced his wife and had been on his own ever since.

Face grave and listening intently, she clung onto his arm so tightly that the heat of her fingers burned through the material. Then she asked about his house in Vienna, Virginia, and about how he filled his days. She also wanted to know how he had found her, but he kept the truth from her, saying merely that a friend of his stationed in Prague had made a chance remark about the new Dutch ambassador.

She believed him. The truth was that, since Rio, not a week had gone by without her being kept under observation on his orders. He had been authorised to tell her that he received regular reports on her—as with every former agent, routine checks were made on her—but if he did so, she would be bound to feel that her privacy was being invaded, so he said nothing. He asked about her husband and she told him in a whisper, as if Felix could overhear her, that her second child had also died and that being married to Felix was hell.

When someone drummed on the door, she looked at him anxiously. And Marks, who knew what was coming, let Berenstein in. He was carrying a tray with a bottle of whisky and a bowl of sliced pawpaw.

'This crazy combination was not my idea, believe me,' Berenstein said in his Russian accent. 'It was my friend John's.' He placed the tray on the low table by the window.

As he did so Marian kissed John on the cheek, transported unexpectedly back over the years. She had lost count of the times he had embellished their assignations with whisky and pawpaw. It had been all he could find in his house that first time in Dar es Salaam.

'Don't worry if you can't finish it,' said Berenstein, leaving the room. 'Enjoy!'

Marks opened the bottle of Chivas and told her some of the latest gossip from the Company. He would have liked to wash his hands.

Inevitably she was going to ask him the question. She did so after her first sip of whisky. He was not drinking, and did not touch the fruit.

'Why did you want to see me, John? Is something the matter? Or did you...did you just want to see me again?'

'Of course I wanted to see you....'

'But that wasn't all?' she asked despondently.

'No....'

'There's something the matter, isn't there?'

'Yes, there is....'

'Go on, tell me.'

He looked out of the window. A grey courtyard. Overflowing garbage cans down below. Cats scavenging for food.

'It's about your husband.'

'Felix?'

'Yes.'

She straightened her back defensively.

'Well, go on. What is it?'

'He's…he's having an affair with an FSZS agent.'

She gave him a glazed look, without blinking, and remained quite still, as if she needed a few seconds to consider his words. Then she bowed her head.

'Really?' she whispered. 'Has he passed anything on to her?'

'Not yet. Had you noticed anything?'

'No. Who is she?'

'A journalist.'

'Irena Nová,' she said. 'Can you tell me about her?'

'She's thirty-three. College educated. She's a genuine journalist but she also works as an agent. A smart lady.'

She raised her voice. 'Why did I have to be told, John? What do you people want from me?'

'I wanted to warn you.'

'About what, why?'

'I don't want to tempt fate, but things could easily get out of hand.'

'Are you expecting me to warn him?'

'If you have no objection…I've obtained permission for you —you can tell him if you want….'

'No.'

'No?'

'Leave him to it. Let him stew in his own juice.'

'Marian, this whole thing could blow up in his face.'

He emphasised each word with his hands, as if making a plea to a jury.

She said, 'If you mean a scandal, that's what he wants.'

'He has access to sensitive information.'

'Felix? Don't make me laugh. He's just a run-of-the-mill ambassador.' She shook her head. 'He doesn't know anything that could be of the slightest use to them.'

'I assure you that he does.'

She gave him an agonised look, as if begging him to take it all back. He avoided her eyes and looked at the cats below.

'Why couldn't we just have met for old times' sake, John?'

Mumbling, he said, 'Even if we don't bother about the world, the world bothers about us.'

She lowered her eyes, twisting her hands together.

'The whole thing is ridiculous,' she said. 'It's all completely unreal.' She looked up. 'In any case, how is he supposed to get hold of this information?'

'He has a friend, an old friend from his student days, who's in trouble. He's a director of the Physics Laboratory at Philips, Hein Daamen.'

'No.' She shook her head frantically. 'No, John, he wouldn't do that.'

'I'm sorry,' he said.

'Oh, my God.'

Keeping up the momentum, Marks pressed on, staring at the garbage cans below. 'Daamen is a textbook case. Drinks, has extra-marital homosexual relations. Ripe for blackmail.'

'Do the Czechs know this?'

'Of course. They want your husband to get in touch with Daamen.'

'Has he met any other FSZS agents?'

'Yes.'

'You seem to have penetrated them pretty thoroughly, haven't you?'

'We have a particularly useful source, yes.'

'What do you want me to do?'

'You can point out the danger to your husband. You can tell him everything you now know.'

'And you really think that will stop him?'

'Perhaps.'

'No, I won't do it.'

He had expected this response from her, though he had persuaded his boss, Chris Moakley, that they would be able to activate her again after all those years. She took another sip.

'Won't you please help me?' he asked.

'I don't work for the Company any longer,' she said. She picked up the bottle and poured herself another whisky.

'Help me.'

'No. Why? Is there something else, John? Is Felix only part of the story?'

'Yes.'

'Dear God…and there I was thinking that after twelve years I was…I was going to see my old love again.'

'I'm sorry,' he said dryly.

'My God…I don't know if I still have it in me, John. I'm no longer what I was. I want to finish writing my book. That's all I still live for, really….'

'If you say no, we'll accept that without question. But…it would make things much harder for us.'

'You're leaning on me.'

'It's important.'

'To whom?'

'To the Company.'

'But not to me,' she said scornfully.

'To you, too. To all of us.'

'So, tell me about it.'

'You have to sign on the dotted line first, Marian.'

She made a brusque gesture: let's get on with it, then. He removed the form from his inside pocket and unfolded it for her. He handed her a pen.

'Signing this doesn't mean a thing,' she said, and signed.

'Well…?' she asked.

He put the paper away and searched for the best way of beginning.

'Why are you wearing gloves?' she asked.

'Eczema,' he lied. He did not have the courage to confess that he was afraid of contact with the world.

She took a sip of whisky and came over to the window next to him. Together they looked down at the hungry cats below.

Suddenly Simon Berenstein appeared in the courtyard brandishing a broom. Shouting Russian curses, he hobbled about chasing the cats away.

'Have you known him for long?'

'I met him in Riga in '58.'

'Does he work for you?'

'No.'

'What exactly do you want from me? I don't understand,' she said, thinking deeply.

'We have an important source in Prague. Carla. Carla works for the FSZS. But she also works for us. She's a double agent. Carla wants to get out. She wants to cross over. Your husband knows our Carla.'

'Felix? How?'

'This is a state secret, Marian, you've just signed.'

'Who is she?'

'Irena Nová.'

She swung round to look at him.

'She's a double agent,' said Marks in a lowered voice, conscious of the import of the information.

'Nová? But...?'

'But?'

'Then she can surely get the information....' She did not finish her sentence, went and sat down, bent forward and pressed her hands flat together as if she were praying. She shut her eyes tight. 'I don't want to know any more about it, John.'

'You can help us.'

'I can't help you. I honestly can't.... Does Felix know that she's working for you?'

'No. As far as he is concerned she's nothing more than a Czech agent. Your husband....' His voice shook and he swallowed. He was suddenly afraid he might have to do without her help after all. 'Your husband's information can help to get her out of the country. We'll provide Mr Daamen with some comic strips in Eindhoven and then....'

She shook her head.

'I don't want to know any more.' She looked at him imploringly. 'Please don't mix me up in this. I've had enough. No more treachery, no more tricks, no more blundering about in a hall of mirrors. The whole thing is madness. I can't *do* it.'

She rose and picked up her purse.

'You ought to have left me alone, John. We both...we both shared so many memories, the two of us shared something to help us through life.'

'I got divorced because of you.'

'No. You got divorced for your own sake. Not because of me.'

'For you, Mary Ann.'

'You got divorced because of your self-respect. Because of your moral principles. And that was a fine thing. But this is not.'

She walked towards the door. Suddenly she stopped. 'Don't any of you over there in Langley ever get tired of the whole business? What sort of a world are you trying to create?' She gave a laugh of relief. 'You're all just a bunch of sick little boys, John. You included.'

Marks reached for the door handle at the same time as she did, his leather on her skin.

'Please,' he said. 'I'm begging you.'

She gave no response and walked laughing down the corridor.

Chapter fifteen

The night of 28 October 1989

T he Chrysler New Yorker turned into Sunset Boulevard. Freddy Mancini found himself in the traffic jam that built up every Saturday night after the last movie and continued well into the next morning. He had read about it, but this was the first time he had seen the four endless lines of traffic with his own eyes.

Downtown San Diego, too, could sometimes be jammed on a Saturday night. But in San Diego the automobiles were driven by people who had come from somewhere and had somewhere to go, while the traffic on Sunset and on Hollywood Boulevard, where he was due in three quarters of an hour, was created by people who looked on the traffic jam as their evening out. The traffic jam was an end in itself. The traffic jam was the highlight of the week.

He could see fifties automobiles that might have been fresh out of the showroom, their chrome gleaming as if buffed by velvet, jacked-up super trucks on yard-high wheels, and automobiles with adjustable back springs, their rear ends hopping up and down like impatient frogs.

Gorgeous girls waved to him from their car windows, the Miami Sound Machine wafted out of automobiles driven by Mexicans with hairnets and macho moustaches, blacks in big sunglasses with gigantic ghetto-blasters cruised along, spraying their rap over the Boulevard.

His four hundred and thirty pounds drew a great deal of attention. His New Yorker, a two-door sedan, had wide doors (one of the reasons he had bought it) and an adjustable steering column, and he had had a specially adapted seat fitted to support his enormous bulk. He had seen the seat advertised in a magazine someone had recommended to him. It was called *This Is Not Edible*, a monthly for true heavyweights (that is, people weighing at least three hundred pounds), and he had bought the seat straight away. He kept the windows closed, shutting out the hot Sunset air, poisoned with exhaust fumes.

Since Bobby had left him there had been nothing to stop him. He gorged himself day and night. He fell asleep eating and woke up eating. He lived all alone in the house now. His Panamanian maid, Teresa, a downy moustache on her upper lip, spoiled him and talked to him as if he were a three-year-old. Next to his favourite armchair, placed strategically in front of the television, he had installed a refrigerator. Teresa prepared spicy Mexican dishes for him which he supplemented in the course of the evening with TV dinners and fast food, all from the supermarket deep-freeze. His body had gone haywire.

When he looked in the mirror (he would soon have to have the doors of his house widened) he could see no more than a vague resemblance to the skinny adolescent he had once been in the face now larded over by pounds of fat on his cheeks. He had a huge flab of a double chin, pink and round as a fatted pig ready for slaughter. Lying on his bed, he floated on a layer of fat. Sometimes he would try to recall his body's original shape. He had always been trim, and had not even been greatly interested in food until his marriage to Bobby; in his mind's eye he could see the boy he had once been as if inside an astronaut's suit, a scrawny young fellow in a protective outer casing that restricted and hampered every movement. Except that in his case, the space suit was made of fat and muscle.

Bobby had hired an attorney and they were in the process of getting a divorce. She was claiming half of the house (as if you could cut it in two), half of the three automobiles (likewise) and half of his twelve Laundromats. In addition she was demanding a hundred thousand dollars in damages for the years of mental and physical suffering he had inflicted upon her with his insatiable hunger.

Freddy's attorney, David Goldman, took Bobby's claims very seriously.

'A jury could easily find for her, Freddy.'

'She left me, Dave, juries don't like women who walk out on their husbands. She's the one who's been disloyal to me.'

'You'll be there in the courtroom....'

'Meaning?'

'Well, they'll be able to see for themselves why Bobby walked out.'

'Okay, so I'm overweight, but what difference does that make?'

'What difference does that make? Have you any idea what you're saying? It makes one hell of a difference, a gigantic difference, to be precise one half of everything your hard work's ever earned you.'

'Because I'm fat?'

'You're not just fat, Freddy, you're one of the hundred fattest men in the United States, and that means in the whole world. My secretary made enquiries at the offices of that magazine which is your favourite reading these days, and of the hundred fattest men, only four are married, and of those four, three are married to fat women. That makes three happy marriages where the husband and the wife are both stuffing themselves insensible. In only one case therefore was there any question of love, and that case, my dear Freddy, is yours.'

'What are you trying to say?'

'That Bobby's attorney has access to the same statistics and that he will use them to prove that staying married to an exceptionally fat man is almost as unlikely as walking on water.'

'What's your advice then, Dave?' Freddy asked diffidently.

'Lose weight, Freddy, walk into that courtroom like a young god and show them you're not addicted to eating. Because that's what their tactics will be. They'll claim you're hooked, that you're a real food junkie.'

Since that conversation he had lost thirty pounds.

Freddy was due on Hollywood Boulevard at half past twelve, in Room 21 of the Travelodge motel there. The man he had spoken to on the telephone had had no trace of a foreign accent, although he had called himself 'Jan'. A few days ago Freddy had gone to his neighbourhood library and had found that name in books by Czech writers.

Jan was therefore a Czech name. On the phone, Jan had suggested a meeting in San Diego, but that had been too close to home for Freddy. Freddy had suggested Los Angeles instead, and half an hour later Jan had called back to say that L.A. would suit him fine. The Travelodge, at the corner of Hollywood and Vermont, Saturday night at half past twelve. That seemed unusually late, but Freddy realised that such meetings are held at unusual times.

He made slow progress, bashfully acknowledging the raised thumbs and waving hands in the automobiles around him. He kept his windows closed, and the air-conditioner hummed as it blew cool air into the brown-leather interior. He was tuned to a twenty-four-hour news station. The newscaster was talking about a demonstration in Prague that day which had been broken up by the authorities. He'd been to Prague.

On the seat next to him was a box of goodies he had stocked up on before leaving San Diego. He scrabbled in a can of Planter's cashew nuts and felt the bottom of the can. Perhaps he could get a snack at the Travelodge.

The trip to Europe had been a disaster. Bobby had fallen in love with another man, and Freddy himself had witnessed an incident he should never have seen. He had been subjected to interrogation, and felt even more useless now than he had before his visit to Prague. He had been afraid when they sent him back home to San Diego, had

had a presentiment that something was wrong with Bobby, so when she had telephoned to say she would be staying in Miami with Bob Johnson, the greying widower from their group, a well-read man who had said little and spent days studying for the sight-seeing tours promised by the agency, Freddy had put down the receiver resignedly and rushed round to the supermarket. He had felt humiliated and liberated all at once. Bobby had left him for someone else, which could only mean that as far as she was concerned he was piece of dirt, the lowest of the low. But it had also dawned on him that there was no one around any longer to stand between him and his food.

He had begun consuming even greater quantities. And under his fat a terrible rage was born. He could no longer think of Bobby without being tormented by bitter memories. The children refused to take sides; they said 'we understand' and 'we love you as much as we love Mom'. When the letter from her attorney arrived, he felt like killing her.

It was a shocking discovery: whatever the consequences, all he wanted to do was destroy her life. The rage he carried in him had powerful, deep roots. Could he have hated her all those years as bitterly as he did now? Could he have frittered his life away with a woman who had despised and humiliated him from the very start?

After their second child, he had quickly put on weight. It was at that time that his business had taken off; his girth had expanded along with the size of his Laundromat chain. That was also the time when her snide remarks began, as if she begrudged him his success. She would often poke fun at him in company; he had suffered his share of blushes during their marriage. Her behaviour was beyond Freddy's comprehension. She, too, had reaped the benefits from his flourishing business, but she seemed to hate him for the luxuries he provided, as if he had deliberately set out to make her dependent on him.

Bobby had fallen in love. He had spoken to her once more on the telephone, and after that the dialogue had been continued by their lawyers.

'How can you fall in love with someone with the same name?' he had asked.

'His name is Robert,' she had retorted cuttingly.

'Your name's Roberta.'

'Everyone calls me Bobby, or had you forgotten?'

'They probably call him that too.'

'Oh, is that so? They call him Bob. That's more than enough difference. Bob and Bobby.'

'I just think it's funny, anyway,' he said.

'I'm not coming back, Freddy.'

'We're still married.'

'That doesn't prove a thing. I'm staying with Bob.'

'A lot of the time I called you Bob instead of Bobby. You make it sound as if you're staying with yourself.'

'I don't think you're ready to listen to reason.'

'Are you really not coming back, Bobby?'

'No. It's better that way. For you, too, Freddy. The only thing you like to do is eat and I keep stopping you. I hassle you and you hassle me.'

'How do I hassle you?'

'You're fat. And the way you live, you might as well be a sack of potatoes.'

'We always got on well together, Bobby.'

'Listen. I've hired a lawyer and he'll be fixing a date when I can come and pick up my things. I don't want you to be around then, okay?'

'This is my home.'

'If our attorneys come to an arrangement, you're going to have to keep out of the way. Otherwise I'll have you arrested.'

Freddy had stayed around to see what happened anyway, and Bobby had been as good as her word. They had taken him away in a patrol car. She had had him thrown out of his own house in full view of the neighbours. He had refused to budge at first, but in the end he had stopped resisting the patrolmen and they had driven him to the station. Because it was a real arrest they were meant to hand-cuff him, but his arms were so fat they couldn't be brought together behind his back. Two days later her attorney's letter arrived.

It was then that Freddy decided that she had no right to go on living.

But he didn't know anyone who would murder her for money. He wasn't capable of doing it himself and he needed the help of a pro. But where do you find an experienced hit man? Not in the Yellow Pages.

The men he had met in that house by the Potomac were licensed killers. However, he had heard nothing more from Marks or from his assistants, and it wouldn't be a particularly clever move to ask them to murder someone on his behalf. When they had finished interrogating him, they had packed him off home in a plane and abandoned him to his doubts and inadequacies. He would have liked to have stayed on in that house—Carolyn fixed the best turkey dinner in the whole damned world—but after sucking him dry they had unceremoniously cast him aside.

He had kept his mouth shut, and not even Bobby had got a single word out of him. However, the sense of belonging he had felt in that beautiful house had worn off by now, and he thought back tight-lipped to the days he had sacrificed to Marks. No telephone call, no note, no thank you,

The congestion of the Strip had been left behind, and an endless succession of traffic lights and neon signs slid in reflection over the gleaming hood of his New Yorker. He drove to Vermont Avenue, turned left and made for the intersection with Hollywood Boulevard.

You could tell what time it was here—well past midnight— from the street scene. It was busier than San Diego, but without the fairground bustle of the Strip, where thousands of Sunset freaks had been milling about on the sidewalks, punks in front of their punk clubs, Angels around their Harleys, leather boys outside their leather bars.

He found the illuminated Travelodge sign. There was another access from Vermont Avenue, and he parked his car in front of the motel, an L-shaped building two storeys high, simple hotel rooms with a parking place in front of each entrance. The drive from San

Diego had taken him four hours, all of which he had spent inside his vehicle. His special seat, equipped with an electric motor underneath, could be swivelled through ninety degrees, thus saving his body considerable effort when he got out.

Room 21 was at one end of the upper storey. He held onto the banisters with an iron grip and pulled himself up step by step. After five steps he had to stop to catch his breath. It took him a good two minutes to reach the top.

With sweat pouring down his face, he knocked on the door.

A bald man with an egg-shaped head opened it.

'Come in, Mr Mancini.'

'Freddy.'

'I'm Jan,' said the man.

He ushered him inside. The room was narrow, modestly furnished, and the far wall was taken up by a kitchenette. An open door next to it revealed a bedroom. The place was a small suite. A second man was standing in front of the sofa. Like Jan he was about forty, and was wearing an impeccable dark blue suit. Despite the late hour, they both looked wide awake and full of energy, like zealous Mormons.

'Hello, Freddy,' said the second man. 'I'm Peter.'

He pronounced the name the German way. He had a deep, rasping voice.

Freddy sank heavily into the sofa. The wooden frame creaked as it took his full weight. He pulled out a packet of paper handkerchiefs from the small bag he carried strapped to his wrist.

'How was the drive, Freddy?' Jan asked.

'Fine. No problems.'

'Can I get you a drink? Something to eat?' Jan asked.

Thanks. Scotch…and a burger, is that okay?' He extracted a Kleenex from its plastic wrapper and patted his face and the folds of fat under his chin and round his neck.

Jan gestured to Peter, who went over to the kitchenette and rang room service on the wall phone. Jan was obviously the boss.

'It's on its way, Freddy. We're glad you came,' said Jan. He produced a pack of cigarettes from his jacket and held it out to Freddy.

'Cigarette?'

'No thanks,' said Freddy.

The two men were being very attentive. Freddy found he was not afraid of them.

'Notice anything on the way?' asked Jan.

Freddy realised that he wanted to know if he had been followed.

'No, I don't think so,' he said, although he had not been paying attention. As far as he was concerned, this meeting had been arranged in the strictest confidence.

'We were surprised by your letter,' said Jan. He sat down in an armchair facing Freddy. 'To begin with we didn't know what to make of it. That's why we called you.'

Peter poured a glass of Scotch. Jan took a letter from his inside pocket and handed it to Freddy.

'This is your letter, isn't it, Freddy?'

Freddy glanced at the envelope and recognised his handwriting.

'Yes.'

'Take the letter out, please,' said Jan.

'I recognise the envelope. That's my handwriting.'

'Even so, I'd like you to make sure,' Jan insisted. He removed the letter from the envelope and showed it to Freddy.

'That's my letter all right,' said Freddy, detecting in Jan's pedantry, he was sure, the over-fussy bureaucracy of the Eastern bloc.

Jan smiled and put the letter away. Peter handed him the glass. He took a quick gulp, and the ice cubes clattered against his teeth.

'The burger's coming,' said Peter.

Freddy could not detect the slightest trace of a foreign accent in his voice either. These two Czechs had either had perfect training in English or else they were American born.

'You have something of interest to us. At least, that's what you said in your letter,' said Jan.

'That's right.'

'What sort of something?'

'Information.'

'What sort of information?'

'Information about Czechoslovakia.'

'Czechoslovakia?' Jan repeated.

'Yes, I happened to be a witness to something over there, and a certain party in Langley showed an interest in my experiences.'

Jan and Peter exchanged a look. Freddy could see that his words, which he had thought up and rehearsed on the way, had hit their mark.

'That sure is something,' said Jan.

'Sure is,' Freddy agreed. He knocked back the rest of his drink and Jan drew Peter's attention to the empty glass. Peter stood up to refill it.

'Are you doing this…for ideological reasons?' asked Jan.

Freddy shook his head and lowered his eyes.

'No.'

'Can you tell us anything about your motives?'

'No,' answered Freddy.

'I don't know what information you have, Freddy, but naturally I do have to know why you want to help us. Put yourself in our shoes. For all we know you could be stringing us along, you could be an agent provocateur.'

'I want your help,' said Freddy.

'Our help? And that's why you've come to us?'

'Yes.'

'Help with what?'

'I have a problem. If I pass some information on to you then what I want is for you to help me with my problem.'

'Interesting,' said Jan with a broad smile.

Peter gave him his refilled glass. Freddy looked up and nodded his thanks.

'Okay, Freddy, let's get this straight…,' said Jan. 'You write a letter to the Czech Embassy, you say you have something of interest for us, we telephone you and now here you are. So, what exactly are you offering?'

'First I need to know what you can do for me.'

He had prepared this response, too, on the way, and, listening to it, felt he had put it well.

'That depends on you, Freddy,' said Jan.

'What *do* you want?' asked Peter encouragingly.

'If you have important information for us, we are of course prepared to do something in return,' Jan added. At long last he lit the cigarette with which his fingers had been toying.

'First let's hear what you have to say, and then we'll talk about the reward,' Peter said.

'No.' Freddy shook his head. 'Let's talk about the reward first. Otherwise there's no point.'

Again he saw the two men exchange glances. Now Peter took charge of the conversation.

'Don't you think that's a bit unusual, Freddy? Talking about the reward first and only then about the merchandise?' His voice was a deep growl.

'No. Not in this case.'

Peter tried a different tack. 'We're interested, but not at any price,' he said.

'Look,' said Freddy, 'the two of you have come here, which indicates to me that you've done your homework and found something out, or else you wouldn't be here. Am I right? In other words you both know that I've been in that house near Potomac.'

'What house near Potomac?'

'A safe house.'

'Oh, there's a safe house near Potomac, is there?' Jan said coaxingly.

'Yes,' said Freddy. He emphasised the word with a sweep of his left hand, to stop himself giving too much away before he received anything in return.

'Okay,' said Peter. 'Have it your way, Freddy, we'll talk about the reward first.'

'There has to be a deal. In black and white. I want some sort of written contract from you.'

'Okay,' Peter repeated. 'We agree, don't we, Jan?'

'I surrender,' said Jan, and put his hands in the air. The three of them laughed. Freddy was sure then that he had won. Extracting a fresh tissue, he dabbed at the sweat on his forehead.

There was a knock on the door.

Freddy jumped and looked round. But the other two seemed unperturbed by the sudden interruption. Quite relaxed, Peter rose to his feet.

'That'll be room service,' he said.

He opened the door, and there was indeed a black man in a baseball cap standing outside, holding a carton from a fast-food chain.

'Refill?' Jan asked.

Freddy nodded. He watched Peter pay the delivery man and shut the door.

'Here you are, Freddy, your late-night "snack".'

'The first of my late-night snacks,' Freddy corrected. Peter laughed and sat down on the kitchen chair.

'I have back trouble. Can only sit on hard chairs.'

'Everybody has something,' said Freddy.

He sank his teeth into the hamburger, aware immediately of its poor quality: too much sauce, sticky bread, meat flattened like old shoe leather.

Jan put the glass down on the low table between the sofa and his armchair.

'Right. We're in business,' he said, leaning back in his chair. 'What do you want from us, Freddy?'

'A liquidation.' His mouth was full but he had learnt how to make himself understood with food in his mouth.

'A what?' said Jan. He was sitting upright now. Peter slid to the edge of his chair.

'A liquidation,' Freddy repeated.

'A liquidation?' asked Peter. 'What do you mean, a liquidation?'

'That's what it's called.'

'You mean murder?' said Jan.

'That's something quite different,' said Freddy. 'Murder is a crime. What I have in mind is due retribution.'

Jan stared at him in astonishment. Slowly he sank back into his chair again. Freddy took another bite. He could feel the sauce running down his chin and wiped it off with a tissue.

'Who?' asked Peter.

'My wife,' said Freddy. His mouth was full but his words were unmistakable.

'Your wife?' Jan sat bolt upright, looking astounded.

'Your wife. Right.' Peter repeated calmly in his booming voice.

Freddy nodded. He had said all he wanted to say. He had thought about it a lot. He had driven all the way from San Diego for this very purpose, and if necessary he would go to their embassy in Washington, for his body was burning with a righteous hatred and he was prepared to go to any lengths. If the Czechs did away with Bobby, he would tell them what he knew—it wasn't much, but it would be enough to pay the costs of a contract killer (and he knew with no shadow of a doubt that they kept the names of contract killers on file).

'We have to commit a murder and then you tell us everything you know?' Jan summed up Freddy's line of argument.

Freddy nodded.

'And you think it's a little funny of us to want to know in advance exactly *what* we'd be getting?'

Freddy could tell from the question that they were seriously considering his proposal. 'No,' he replied.

Peter suddenly broke into a raucous guffaw, and Freddy looked across at him in surprise.

The man was sitting there, his shoulders shaking with laughter, his head bent low and his face hidden behind a hand. 'Sorry,' Freddy heard him say.

Freddy looked to Jan for support, but Jan seemed to be trying to stifle his own laughter, lighting a cigarette quickly to cover his confusion.

When Peter dropped his hand, his face was composed once more. 'Excuse me,' he said in the impassive tones of a bureaucrat, 'but I suddenly couldn't stop laughing. We'd been expecting you to ask for money, for a car, or a house, or for women, but not this. Your request is a most unusual one, Mr Mancini....'

'Freddy, call me Freddy.'

'Of course, Freddy.... We have never had a request like yours.'

'It's what I want.' Freddy said.

He was offended by their unprofessional behaviour, but he was determined to stick to his guns. With his finger he gathered the remains of the hamburger together in the carton and pushed the pieces of lettuce and slices of tomato into his mouth.

Jan got to his feet and pointed to the mirror above his armchair.

'Do you see this mirror, Freddy?'

Freddy glanced up for a moment and nodded.

'It's a two-way mirror, Freddy.'

Jan put a hand in his pocket and produced an identity card.

'In the room next door is a video camera. This get-together has been recorded. We work for Mr Marks.'

Freddy looked at Peter, who nodded guiltily, as if he was sorry for having taken Freddy for a ride.

'We intercepted your letter. That's part of our job.'

Freddy could make neither head nor tail of what he had just heard. He looked at the mirror and at the ID card in Jan's hand, he searched Peter's face for some explanation, then stared into the empty carton, its grease spots a memento of the hamburger, and suddenly it dawned on him what their game was: these Czechs were trying to put him to the test. He smiled.

'I'm on to you,' he said affably.

'Really?' asked Jan.

'I'm not falling for it,' said Freddy, laughing.

'Not falling for what?' Peter asked in his newsreader's voice.

'For this....' Freddy gestured with his hand. 'Sit down,' he said to Jan, 'and let's get back to business.'

'Would you like to speak to Mr Marks?' asked Jan.

'Of course!' answered Freddy, cheerfully going along with the joke.

Peter stood up and disappeared into the bedroom behind the kitchenette.

Jan sat down again. 'What are you laughing for, Freddy?' he asked.

'Because this is all a big joke,' he said.

'What's a big joke?'

'This so-called set-up of yours. That's an ordinary mirror and you are a Czech.'

'In that case...why would we be behaving like this, do you think?'

'To test me, of course!'

'What for?'

'To make sure I don't slip up the first time I'm cross-examined. You see it in the movies all the time.'

Peter came back and held the mobile phone out to him.

'Mr Marks has been listening to our conversation,' he said. 'He's in Europe. He'd like to speak to you....'

Freddy did not believe a word, but took the phone with good humour.

'Hi, John!' he said breezily.

'Hello, Freddy,' he heard John Marks say.

The line was a poor one and John Marks' voice sounded far away, but the imitation was not at all bad. Freddy had to admit that they were doing their level best to make their act as plausible as possible.

'How are things with you, Freddy?'

'Fine, John. You?' Freddy pulled a face at the two men, but they went on staring fixedly at him.

'Fine. Freddy, I'm worried about you.'

'No need for that, John.'

'I'm afraid there is. That letter of yours is a serious business, Freddy. You gave your country a solemn undertaking to remain silent, you put your signature to that, do you remember?'

'Yes, of course I do….'

A nasty little doubt had begun to creep over him. This man had not only John Marks' voice but his patronising tone as well. Nevertheless, Freddy refused to accept that his letter had fallen into the wrong hands.

'There are heavy penalties for this sort of thing, Freddy. If we decide to press the matter, you'll spend the rest of your life behind bars. I take it you wouldn't like that.'

'Who would?'

'So why did you write that letter?'

'Because you dumped me, that's why.'

'But you wanted to go back to your old life, didn't you?'

'Without Bobby?'

'We cannot accept responsibility for Bobby's actions.'

'Now listen here and listen good, you John Marks clone, you just take care of Bobby and then I'll tell you all I know.'

There was no reply; the line crackled.

'May I speak to Jan for a moment?' John's voice sounded weary.

Freddy held out the telephone. 'Your boss,' he said.

Jan took the receiver and listened attentively, nodding from time to time, keeping his eyes on Freddy.

Freddy was on a high, uplifted by a mood of exaltation and triumph. He had not allowed himself to be fooled by them, and had followed the plan he had worked out the week before to the letter. They had undoubtedly been expecting him to issue denials and disclaimers, then duck and run. But he had stuck to his guns and had stood up for his proposal, as any self-respecting man who believed in his cause would have done. As a thank you to himself, he decided to yield to the delightful hunger pangs now tantalising his stomach, and he turned to Peter.

He could not fail to notice that Peter was suddenly holding a gun, but nothing surprised Freddy any longer.

'Do you think we could order some more food?'

It was Jan who replied. 'Come on, Freddy, we're going to take you to a place where you'll be able to take a good long rest.' He pressed a button on the mobile phone, ending his conversation.

'Suits me,' said Freddy. 'And maybe I'll be able to buy a bottle there as well, because I think we've got something to celebrate.'

'Maybe,' said Jan.

Peter got to his feet and opened the front door. A man was standing outside, his back turned towards them. His jacket said FBI in large fluorescent letters. He turned round and Freddy recognised the black man who had brought the burger. He too was armed now, holding a Beretta riot gun in both hands like a seasoned cop.

'Are you coming?' asked Jan.

'Where are we going?' Freddy asked.

He could not make out why they were all armed, as if he needed defending.

'Why are you walking about with those things?' he asked.

'We have to take you along with us, Freddy,' Jan said.

'Hey, I came here in my own car, I'll drive myself.'

He tried to work his way up from the sofa, to pull himself out of the cushioned depths by the armrest, but it was obvious that he was having serious difficulties. Jan beckoned to Peter and the two of them put their arms under his shoulders and hoisted him out of the valley of the sagging sofa.

'Many thanks,' said Freddy, panting. He picked up his small bag.

'Coming, Freddy?' asked Jan.

'Of course.'

'You do realise where we're going, don't you?'

'To get something to eat and drink, right?'

'No, Freddy. We are taking you to see a doctor. He'll give you a thorough examination. You'll have a sedative, and tomorrow morning we'll continue our chat. Okay?'

'Why?' asked Freddy.

He could make no sense of what Jan was saying. Anxiously he looked at the three men leading him to the door.

'You need a rest, Freddy,' said Peter.

'What for?'

Freddy's voice suddenly sounded high-pitched and young, like that of a child of ten. He stepped out into the night. The air embraced him like the warmth of a woman.

'You're a little bit confused, Freddy.'

They ushered him towards the stairs, but he needed no encouragement.

Freddy let himself fall and gravity did the rest. The iron edges of the stairs cut into his flesh. He remembered how he had fallen in Prague, and although the fall only lasted about a second it was long enough for a silent prayer: I want to get back to the light in that long tunnel, the light that caresses and cherishes, the light that consoles and redeems....

Chapter sixteen

The morning of 24 November 1989

Irena was standing in a queue at the Friedrichstrasse checkpoint.

It had rained during the night; autumn had at last prevailed over the long summer. She was waiting in a crowd of East Germans, allowed now to walk through without hindrance to the Kurfürstendamm. Her little daughter stood patiently beside her, her hands in woollen mittens, a brightly coloured cap on her head, an endearingly small suitcase in her hand, as if she were going to spend a night out.

Vopos, members of the East German People's Police, were in position left and right of the border crossing, in sentry boxes, on watchtowers, everywhere, but they were turning no one away. Tensely, Irena kept an eye on them, but she could see that the passport inspection was no more than cursory. One of the policemen had a wooden board strapped to his belt; he would place the opened passports on it, then stamp a page with the badge of freedom. The control was no more than a formality, but Irena's heart was in her mouth.

She had no Czech exit visa and did not know whether the Vopos had the authority to let anyone other than East Germans through. The queue moved. Just beyond the concrete walls and barbed wire barriers people were falling with cries of joy round one another's necks. Ties and handkerchiefs were being waved from both sides of the open border, yesterday's tears relegated to the past.

'Mummy,' said Vera, 'is there somebody waiting for us too?'

'Yes, there's somebody there for us too.'

Irena stared at the people waiting in the American sector and wondered which of them had come to the checkpoint specially for her. Two camera teams were filming the people as they took their first steps on West Berlin soil. So far, the Americans had always kept their word to her.

The queue moved forward.

She took her child's woollen hand and stopped in front of the Vopo. He looked at her green passport. He had just stamped the scores of passports before hers with a smile, no longer under orders to fire (had he ever fired, she wondered, had he ever murdered anybody trying to cross from one side of his city to the other?), but now he looked confused and she could tell by his face that he had no instructions for dealing with cases like hers. Without rules, without orders, he was as lost as a dog without his master,

'How did you get into the DDR?' he asked.

'I crossed the border,' she said in a controlled voice.

He glanced briefly at Vera. 'How?'

'I came on my own two feet,' Irena said, and now her voice was shaking.

The policeman nodded. A week before her answer would have unleashed a violent outburst. He would have arrested her.

'You have no exit visa,' he told her. 'Officially, you're not here.'

'But I am here.'

'Not officially.'

'If you use your eyes you'll see that I am here, officially.'

She watched him bite down his anger. 'Clear off. Go back where you came from. Get out of here,' he hissed.

She could feel Vera's uncertainty as the child looked up at her, puzzled by the tone of a conversation she could not follow. Irena held her hand firmly; nothing must happen to her child.

The camera crew came closer. Side by side, the Vopo and Irena looked into the thick glass of the lens and the big television camera sent their pictures all over the world. A boom microphone dangled over their heads as, frightened to death, she looked at the Vopo. Under the peak of his policeman's cap she recognised the same fear in his eyes. With the glass eye of the world focused upon them, a forced smile started to break over his panic-stricken face. He stamped her passport.

She pulled Vera along between the concrete walls, avoiding the puddles, and they simply walked into the West. Irena tugged her daughter along, Vera running to keep up in her small red boots. The same grey sky, the same air in their lungs.

They almost ran into him, a man, a young man, standing in front of her.

'Mrs Nová?'

She stopped and looked at him suspiciously. But he was clean-cut, well-dressed and had perfect teeth.

'My name is MacLaughlin. I am here to welcome you on behalf of the government of the United States of America. This must be Vera. Would you care to follow me?'

Chapter seventeen

The morning of 2 December 1989

I n Section XII of his *Treatise,* Spinoza wrote:

> The aim is to have clear and distinct ideas, namely, such
> as arise from the mind alone, and not from fortuitous
> movements of the body.

Unshaven, and dressed in a suit he had been wearing for a week,
Hoffman was sitting at a rickety garden table in the empty living
room of his summer house in Vught. A jar of frankfurters stood
within arm's reach. He was tackling Spinoza again.

The summer house was a solidly built wooden cabin, put up
in 1963 by a company specialising in prefabricated Swedish houses.
Hoffman had bought it in 1971. It had a large open-plan living room
and kitchen, three bedrooms, and a storeroom in which they had
kept pieces of furniture and other odds and ends they had collected
over the years. Miriam had sold the lot.

Hoffman had picked up the basic essentials for refurnishing the place from a cash and carry in Den Bosch. The summer house lay just south of the Iron Man, an idyllic lake in the woods, its shore partly taken over by villas. North of the lake lay the old Vught concentration camp, which since the fifties had served as a kampong for South Moluccan refugees, complete with the old barracks where the screams still resounded. Hoffman's house lay concealed behind bushes and trees, and even now in autumn, when the leaves had fallen, there was no sign of it from the road. A dirt track a hundred yards long joined the property to the road, and its nearest neighbour was a camping site just over a mile further on, now luckily deserted.

Before driving here, Hoffman had bought provisions in Boxtel, a two hours' walk to the south, and had laid in enough to last him at least a week. It hardly mattered to him just then what he put in his mouth. He was simply filling his stomach and keeping alive. At that moment he was emptying the jar of frankfurters. Squeezing two dirty fingers down the neck of the jar, he pulled out one sausage at a time, tapped it dry and sank his teeth into it. Each frankfurter made a cracking noise as the taut skin burst.

The electricity was on, but there was no water. Something must have happened to the supply, because he had checked the mains cock and the pipes in the house and found nothing wrong with them.

A small electric heater was in position under his table, and at night he could watch the revolution in Prague on a portable television set. Behind him, next to the sofa, was the cardboard box with the cans of film. After he had done his shopping in Boxtel, he had removed it from the safe-deposit box at the bank in Den Bosch. He was running a risk, but he counted on the fact that nobody knew about it (not even the Czechs or the Americans).

He was unable to wash. Spinoza set great store by a clean body, but in order to improve the understanding a clean mind mattered far more, and he had been applying himself to the one hundred and ten paragraphs of the *Treatise* to keep from going mad.

Hoffman shut Irena's treachery out of his mind, took a grip on his exhausted body and concentrated his thoughts.

He summed up what he had been reading: Spinoza had gone

in search of happiness. But his path led neither to heaven nor to Bhagwan: it led to understanding. What Hoffman had been reading piecemeal over the past few months was a guide to a *method* by which you could cleanse your understanding.

With a cleansed understanding you could study nature. In so doing, you might be able to comprehend her essential phenomena, and with that comprehension the breath of God brushed your temples. For everything in existence had an interdependence that could be described by laws—and in this Spinoza saw the hand of God.

Hoffman did not know whether it was right to portray Spinoza's God with hand and breath; nature herself was God's hand, and understanding God's breath. But he needed such aids in order to gain some insight into Spinoza's ideas.

The unfolding of Spinoza's method had drawn Hoffman's attention to his own rudimentary notions of perception, the true idea, fiction and similar concepts, and had shown him how ludicrously naïve they were. By contrast, Spinoza had been a learned man, well-versed in science, who had endeavoured to show how a man of science might most profitably pursue his objective (interesting in the same way that an article in a supplement of, say, the *Nieuwe Rotterdamse Courant* might be interesting), but what he himself was more particularly concerned to discover was how the average layman—someone not capable of repairing his car or his TV set, someone who had heard of $E = mc^2$, someone who had bought *Gödel, Escher, Bach* but had remained stuck on the third page, someone who pretended to know his way about when it came to heavy matter in a black hole, someone who was still overcome with wonder at radio waves and frequencies but indulged in talk about photons over a drink, someone who had sold his country—might learn to pray again.

Early that morning, after a long night he had survived by reading the papers, just as the pale sun broke through the clouds of the night, Spinoza's scientific method had suddenly appeared to him as a kind of liturgy. He had on occasion attended synagogue services, but at the moment when the Torah Scrolls were taken out of the ark and read in the presence of the quorum of ten men he had always had to stand aloof, even though he had wanted to join in the chanting and to read the unknown letters.

If Spinoza really considered the pursuit of science a new form of liturgy, was it still possible to pray? Could you ask the God of $E = mc^2$ for forgiveness? Hoffman believed he was interpreting Spinoza's philosophy correctly when he took Einstein's formula for a form of divine nature, but this philosophy left his need for ritual unsatisfied.

That morning, deep in thought about it all, he had gone outside and stood pissing on the black leaves. The warm urine had hit the cold earth with a hissing sound. Holding his cock with both hands, he had thrown his head back as far as he could. The clouds bearing the rain which had lashed the roof all night were receding towards the east, and as Hoffman watched, the sun broke through, its rays spanning the sky and its warmth caressing his face.

Hoffman would have liked to have been Spinoza standing there, gazing at the ball of fire, his head full of questions: how are the sun's rays formed, does their light fall on water particles, what in fact is that light?

These questions were not devoid of aesthetic delight in the mechanism he was observing; on the contrary, they were resonant with religious love and a feeling of affinity, through time and space, with Spinoza and with sun-worshippers (he knew perfectly well that with this he was mixing water and fire, but standing there, on those rotting leaves, he had experienced something that had transfigured him, inspiring him to sweeping analogies).

He wanted to pray.

He had wanted to pray when Esther had died, with that knowing look on her face, and he had wanted to pray when Miriam had died, with a needle in her arm. His final dribbles came to an end, and a few feet further on he lowered himself onto the leaves. He looked down at himself and held his breath at this specimen of human despair and arrogance (despair because he was on the run and no longer expected forgiveness; arrogance because he believed he could reach God). Hoffman asked the Lord in Heaven for insight and understanding, for help in interpreting the *Treatise*.

Liturgy, he thought, perhaps that was the key. It called for a sacred book, fixed rituals, occasionally a few candles and offerings.

He went back inside and warmed himself at the electric fire. Then he sandwiched a few sardines between two slices of dry bread and breakfasted on them as he walked about in the neglected garden. He had not washed, indeed had worn the same clothes since he had arrived, and he knew that he was giving off the musty smell of an old man, but there was no one around to take offence.

During the past three days he had gone back over all the sections of the *Treatise* he had read before, and had now reached the new, unread, part. There were only three sections left.

Section XIII was headed 'On the Conditions of Definition'. In it, Spinoza proposed to describe nature as precisely as possible, which meant analysing its phenomena minutely, peeling off layer after layer to their very essence. In other words, definitions were needed, descriptions of essences. Spinoza distinguished between definitions of 'created' and of 'uncreated' things. By the first he referred to observable reality, by the second to infinite and eternal nature, that is, to God Himself.

The definition of God had to satisfy four requirements:

1. To exclude all cause, that is, to need no object outside its being for its explanation.

2. When its definition is given there must remain no room for doubt as to whether it exists or not.

3. It must contain...no substantives which can be turned into adjectives, that is, it must not be explained through abstractions.

4. It is required that all its properties be concluded
from its definition.

Hoffman was by now dying to discover what this definition actually
was, but Spinoza refrained from giving it here. Hoffman examined
the four requirements again closely.

The first said something about God's origins. God was nothing
but His own beginning. He had not been invented, nor was He the
result of the intervention of some other power; no, He was all.

Hoffman was baffled by the second requirement. He himself
lacked a 'given' definition, and hence could not judge whether or
not it left room for doubt. He was conscious of the wish to see such
a definition laid down in black and white, and though his capacity
for belief remained intact, he also possessed doubt in profusion; if
only his eyes could see a definition, then his heart would believe in
it, he promised himself.

He had brought destruction upon his own head and was searching for some way of atoning—he stared out at the bare grey branches
of the Brabant woods, and remembered driving on the autobahn and
shutting his eyes tight and bracing himself for the first fraction of a
second of the crash, before the metal tore him to shreds. But half a
minute later he was still sitting in the Opel Corsa and had opened
his eyes and postponed the moment of his death to some unspecified future date, a few days or weeks from now. He wanted to know
what had motivated Irena, what had motivated himself. There were
too many questions.

He had to find the answers.

In the meantime, he had to make sacrifices and to cleanse
himself. But he did not know where to start.

Spinoza's third requirement was self-evident: in a definition of
God, there was no need for such words as 'The Highest', 'The Wisest',
'The Mightiest'. Hoffman understood that these were so many empty
phrases along Spinoza's path to God.

The fourth requirement went straight to the heart of Spinoza's
conception of God. The definition of God was the wellspring of every-

thing in existence, and was nothing less than the explanation, the origin and the essence of the world. Perhaps that definition, which was all-embracing, was God Himself, so that Spinoza was incapable of providing it.

If Hoffman understood him correctly, Spinoza meant that by careful and loving investigation it was possible to describe nature in her essential principles, and that through that investigation one could also discover God, even though one was unable to give a comprehensive definition of Him. Hoffman, who was no scholar, recalled Einstein's dictum about the meaningful structure of the world: 'God does not play dice'. Centuries before, Spinoza had said something similar: watch the game carefully, discover the rules, they lead to God.

Hoffman had thought that money would lead to Irena. With no other means at his disposal to win her, he had tried to buy her.

At their fourth encounter, on a broad bed with a stained mattress on the ninth floor of the Hotel International, after the heat of her passion had made him come, she had wrapped herself in a towel, sat down in the armchair under the standard lamp and lit a cigarette.

'Felix,' she said, 'I have something to tell you.'

She looked at him unblinkingly as she spoke: she said that she was being forced to work for the Czech secret service.

He wanted to believe her. She could have told him anything at all, and he would have believed whatever came from her lips. His hunger for her left him with no alternative.

She had made him a present of sleep.

'They have their own ways of breaking you,' she had said. Tensely she dragged at her cigarette. 'They make sure no one in your family is able to hold down a job, you can never get permits for anything, little by little they choke you to death.'

'What did they threaten you with?' he asked.

She told him how they had beaten up her brother, had thrown her mother out onto the street. She was smoking continuously, lighting one cigarette from another.

'Was it really an accident that you were there to help me that time in the Italian Embassy?'

'Of course it was,' she said angrily. 'Do you think that sort of thing can be arranged?'

No, he thought, they could not arrest his heart.

He was, of course, aware that he had become enmeshed in a web of intrigue, but as long as he could continue to refresh himself at her body he remained undaunted. At their next meeting, two days later, she mentioned Hein Daamen. That did give him a fright. He realised that they had done their homework and must have gained access to his personal dossier.

Hein was someone he could not betray. Hein had pulled him through the Liberation, Hein had taken him home with him, he had slept under a black wooden crucifix in Hein's room all through the winter of 1944, exhausted by the waiting, fighting off the choking terror that his parents might have forgotten him.

Hoffman said no to Irena. But she had her arguments ready: Hein had debts; Hein had a boyfriend (something that did not surprise Hoffman, since Hein had been effeminate even as a boy and had looked after him like a big sister); Trudy and her five children knew nothing about the boyfriend or the financial worries; what information Hein could supply had no military importance. She tried to convince Hoffman that it would only be to Hein's advantage if Hoffman could persuade him to photocopy just a few pieces of paper. Forty copies at ten cents each in exchange for 250,000 guilders in a Swiss bank account.

'They wanted to give you something as well,' she had said, 'but I told them you'd be insulted by an offer of money.'

'How much?' he asked.

'One hundred thousand guilders.'

'I'm not insulted,' he said, and they had even laughed out loud.

At their next meeting, this time in a small hotel in the city centre because the International was full of Koreans, she had said nothing about Hein. They had made love, she had showered and left.

She had not pressed him, ready to put up in silence with the consequences of his refusal. He had not actually refused. But he had also stopped short of saying yes.

Oddly enough it was Marian who smoothed his path. She had to go to Holland. And she had fixed up a meeting with Trudy Daamen there.

Hoffman organised a visit to the Netherlands for himself and suggested that they both have a meal out with the Daamens, for old times' sake.

When he told Irena she fell round his neck and dragged him to bed with an all-devouring passion. Two days later he met an officer of the FSZS in the Hotel International.

He flew with Marian to Schiphol. They took separate rooms at the Bel Air in Scheveningen, and on the evening of Saturday, 21 October, they dined with Hein and Trudy at the Blue Lotus in Eindhoven. While the women went off to the cloakroom, Hoffman arranged a meeting with Hein. Two o'clock the following afternoon at the Hotel Central in Den Bosch.

Despite the heater he felt stiff with cold. He had left Prague in a hurry. On the way, in Germany, he had bought underwear, a few shirts and a thick pullover, and he put the pullover on now, over his shirt and tie. A mirror that hung in the moss-covered shower cubicle reflected his tired, unshaven face, the blackened collar of his shirt.

He went outside and walked round the house, filling his lungs with forest air and keeping a sharp lookout for binoculars or the barrel of a gun. Out here they could murder him without fear of witnesses. 'They' might be Dutch, or Czech or American. He was easy prey for any one of them.

Last Sunday he had taken the early train from Prague to Berlin. The day before he had been summoned by a coded message signed by the minister himself to urgent consultations in The Hague. When he had rung the Ministry for further details—the telex was presumably in response to the frantic events of the past week, the eruption of the demonstrations, Dubcek's appearance on the balcony on Friday—he was put through to someone he did not know, one Van der

Voort, who told him that the minister required his presence urgently and requested that he take the 3.30 flight that same afternoon. His seat had been booked.

He had asked this Van der Voort in which department he worked, and the man had answered, 'The minister's private cabinet.' That was new to Hoffman.

Hoffman had rung Wim Scheffers, his voice betraying alarm at impending doom.

'The minister's private cabinet? What's that?' Wim had said.

'And Van der Voort?' Hoffman went on.

'I don't know any Van der Voort. What's going on?'

'Sonnema must have been pulling my leg,' Hoffman had said.

Irena had given him a telephone number, but no one answered. He tried every ten minutes, all through Saturday afternoon. Towards evening he had a taxi take him to a gloomy outer district full of run-down concrete blocks of flats. She lived on the sixth floor on a draughty open walkway with thirty other apartments, behind a door with cracked green paint. The door remained shut.

When he got back home, pale with worry, Marian was waiting for him. She was working downstairs; normally she would have gone to her room upstairs.

'They rang from The Hague. Wanted to know if you'd left.'

'Who rang?'

She looked at a note. 'Van der Voort. Who's he?'

'Some penpusher who's come up in the world,' he said.

He went over to the sideboard, unscrewed the top off the whisky bottle and poured some into a glass.

'You?'

She nodded.

It was one of those rare moments when the two of them were alone together in the drawing room. Marian had taken a corner of the sofa, books and papers all round her like a defensive wall, a cup and a teapot in a cosy on an occasional table. A telephone had been placed within arm's reach on the parquet floor beside the sofa. She took off her glasses, which hung on a short silver chain round her neck, and closed the weighty book on her lap.

'No ice,' he said.

'No.'

He handed her the glass.

With his first large gulp, he almost emptied his own.

She asked, 'Is anything wrong, Fee?'

He tossed down the rest, then walked over to the sideboard to pour himself another.

'It isn't good for you, Fee.'

'I know,' he said.

'I suppose that's why you do it.'

'Maybe.'

'Is something the matter? You know you can tell me. Who is this Van der Voort?'

'A bureaucrat,' he said dryly.

He sat down opposite her, glass in hand. Casually, Marian glanced at a piece of paper.

'Somebody else rang as well. Mrs Nová,' she said.

His expression did not change, and he sipped his drink.

'The journalist,' he explained, showing no particular concern. 'What did she want?'

'She was ringing from Germany. To say the appointment was off. Had you arranged to see her again, then? I thought they'd already published that interview?'

'That was for another paper,' he lied. 'Which Germany? East or West?'

'Is there any difference now?'

He shrugged his shoulders to indicate his lack of interest.

'I think she said she was phoning from Heidelberg.'

Heidelberg had a large US army base. So she had defected. She had taken the train to Berlin and had crossed with the crowds streaming through the ruptured Wall into the West. Her head crammed with secrets, she had taken flight and denounced him. In exchange for protection and political asylum she had given the Americans a list of traitors. And she had named him. Of course she had named him. Her revenge for his doltish attempt to buy her body. The urgent summons from The Hague could only mean that they were waiting to arrest him on Dutch soil. Van der Voort was an agent of the Dutch secret service. Irena had given his name to the Americans and the Americans had passed his name on.

He emptied his glass. Don't crack up now. There's no real problem.

'You look so grim. Won't you tell me what's wrong?'

'Nothing,' he said gruffly. 'There's nothing wrong. Believe me.'

'I don't believe you, darling.'

'Did Mrs Nová say anything else?'

Marian raised her glasses for a moment and peered through the lenses at the note.

'That she hopes you'll forgive her for not keeping the date. That sounds quite personal, doesn't it?'

The telephone rang and his heart missed a beat. Marian leaned to one side and lifted the receiver.

'Yes?'

She listened, nodded. 'Just a moment, please.' She placed her hand over the mouthpiece and whispered, 'Van der Voort again.'

With a groan he got out of his armchair. He picked the telephone up off the floor and took the receiver out of Marian's hand.

'Hoffman,' he said. He moved several steps away from her.

'Van der Voort here,' he heard. 'I gather you didn't make the flight.'

'That's right,' said Hoffman. 'There was still a lot I had to do, and I missed it.'

'That code was initialled by the minister himself,' said Van der Voort. 'You have refused to comply with an order from your chief. That is insubordination, Mr Hoffman, and it could cost you your job.'

'What exactly is *your* job, Mr Van der Voort?'

'You listen to me. You are to take the Malev flight at nine-thirty tomorrow morning. If you are not on it, then I fear for your future prospects.'

'Who are you, Van der Voort?'

'I serve my country, Mr Hoffman. You come to The Hague. We aren't savages. We can be understanding. We know how to let bygones be bygones. *But you must come.* We can't deal with this over the telephone.'

'Right…see you tomorrow.' Hoffman stumbled over the words. He rang off. They were afraid he might defect. But to whom?

Yesterday Dubcek had addressed hundreds of thousands of people. Milos Jakes had resigned and the dissidents had seized power. In Berlin drunken Krauts were sitting on top of the Wall, beer cans in hand, crowing about 'Germany forever'; people had taken to the streets even in Bulgaria. It terrified him. Hoffman was afraid of the masses and the slogans they chanted. He knew that the illusions now sweeping Eastern Europe would all too soon be shattered. Today Bush and that pseudo-communist, Gorbachev, were due to meet in Malta. They failed to realise in the White House and Downing Street that the old communist gang that had ruled over the Eastern bloc had been the best ally they could have wished for.

He put the telephone on the coffee table and sat down again.

'I have to go to The Hague tomorrow,' he said, his eyes lowered.

He took a drink. He was aware of the tension in Marian's face as she looked at him.

'Something's the matter. You won't tell me what, but I know something's wrong. We're not finished, Fee. If we want to we can still have a future together.'

'Listen, Marian, it's nothing. I'll tell you all about it some other time, all right?'

'If it's nothing, then you'll have nothing to tell me, will you?'

'Don't be smart with me, please!'

'Can't you drop your armour for once? Please tell me….'

'Leave me alone!'

He hauled himself out of his chair and made for the door to the hall. But he paused at the threshold.

'Marian….'

She looked up stonily, her eyes bleak.

'How about eating out somewhere tonight?'

She nodded in surprise, a faint smile slipping through her mask.

'Yes, that would be nice.'

They went to dine at the Expo restaurant on the Vltava. She had put on make-up, was wearing an elegant dress, and her eyes were questioning when she looked at him. Beyond the immensely tall windows the city lay at their feet, a maze of dark alleyways and roofs, turrets and chapels. Half a million demonstrators were crowding on the great square in the centre; no sign of them could be seen from where they sat. They talked about nothing in particular, and to his surprise he felt calm and content.

When she went up to her room she gave him a kiss on the cheek. He waited in his study and in the kitchen for the night to pass. He ate and drank and read the Dutch papers, which had arrived by courier on Saturday morning. He left the house at about six o'clock, shutting the door behind him softly. He had decided not to take any clothes. Spinoza and his personal papers were in his attache case. He had walked until he met a taxi. At the station he bought a ticket to Berlin, and departed. His diplomatic passport opened all barriers.

From Bahnhof Zoo in Berlin he had taken the train to Hanover, and because he suspected that the major car rental firms were linked to the police computer, he had hired a car, an Opel, from a small firm in the city.

To start with he had driven south, and after Frankfurt had followed the Rhine, crossing into France at Strasbourg; then, driving through Nancy, Metz and Luxembourg to Maastricht, he had returned to the Netherlands, the country that employed him and was now in hot pursuit of him. He had taken four days over the journey, spending the nights in village inns where they did not ask for papers. His plan was to escape to South America, but first he had to collect his thoughts, to calm his restless mind, here among the trees. For that he needed Spinoza.

It was quiet in the woods. Birds wintering in Brabant were calling to one another; his ears were caressed by the indecipherable rustle of sighing branches. What power ruled over all this, Spinoza had wondered, what laws governed nature? Discover the laws and you discover God, he had taught.

Perhaps, Hoffman thought, the scientist's greatest reward was to make a contribution, however small, to the revelation of God. Hoffman had squandered his life playing the messenger boy. His most immediate contact with science had been the subordination of Hein Daamen. Hein was an engineer and a closet homosexual. Hein was his brother.

He went back into the house and filled a glass with mineral water, spooned in some Nesquik and then drank the cold chocolate. On the way here, he had rung Hein several times. Trudy had told him that Hein had left suddenly on some trip. She had sounded unconcerned.

He went outside again with his glass. He had grown up in these parts. In the village where he had done his shopping a few days ago he had once listened, eyes wide with fear among the pigs, to the bombers overhead. Just as filthy as he was now, yearning just as hard for salvation and the solace of clean sheets, he had waited for his parents. They had no graves. When the Canadians, holding their noses, had occupied the farm, Rilke's *Elegies* had been in his hands. With Auschwitz in full swing, he was reading poetry.

> Every dull orbit of the world knows of such dispossessed
> who own neither the past nor what is yet to come.

Later he learned that his parents had been hidden by a sister of their Hekellaan housekeeper. They had been given refuge under the floorboards in a farmhouse in Berlicum. They had been betrayed.

He was no patriot, he decided, keeping an eye on the dirt track leading to the main road between Vught and Loon, since he had no fatherland. This nation had betrayed his parents and now he had paid them back. He felt no qualms of conscience when he thought of the Kingdom of the Netherlands. It dawned on him that he was a professional outsider, a permanent refugee. He felt ashamed when he thought of Marian, that was all.

He had met Hein at the Hotel Central in Den Bosch.

They had sat in the café on the ground floor, hemmed in by provincial worthies, looking out at the drowsy Sunday market place. They had dined with their wives the night before.

'You're looking well,' Hein had said. 'I noticed yesterday.'

'And you look like death warmed up,' Hoffman had replied.

They had had a few drinks and an hour later they had gone for a meal at De Pettelaer's. By the time Hoffman put him on the last train to Eindhoven, Hein was drunk. He had admitted that he had a boyfriend and that he had run up debts on the stock exchange. He had lost all his money, could not even pay his mortgage. Hoffman said he would help him out.

Two days later he rang Hein. Hein came to the Bel Air in Scheveningen.

'I can help you, Hein, but....'

'But what?'

They were in a corner of the bar, slumped in deep leather seats, drinking whisky although it was only just after noon.

'I've lost all my savings myself, my friend,' Hoffman said.

'What? How come?'

'I'll tell you later. Let's deal with your problem first.'

'You'll never know how grateful I am, Felix. Even if you can't come up with a single cent, just letting me get it all off my chest has done me a power of good—really, I'll never forget it.'

Hoffman, the fraud, said, 'You're my brother, Hein.'

He began his tale about how he knew someone in Prague who would pay for certain information. He mentioned the code name for the radar equipment that the Physics Laboratory was designing for Hollandse Signaal, the armaments company.

'That's industrial espionage, Felix,' Hein said in a shocked whisper, looking round furtively, as if the police were standing by ready to put him in handcuffs.

'I thought so too to begin with, but listen, the information's absolutely useless to them. They'd never be able to make the equipment themselves,' Hoffman said with conviction, as if he knew what he was talking about. 'It's far too complicated for them. They may get the information, but they won't be able to do anything with it.'

Hein nodded, feverishly considering all the implications of Felix's proposal. He seemed to accept without question the slant Hoffman had put on it, and himself mentioned parts of the equipment that could not be manufactured in the East. 'But they might steal those, of course,' he added.

'That's not our responsibility,' Felix had answered.

'My God, Felix, what you're suggesting here is a pretty big step for me to take,' Hein whispered. 'It's a bit much, it really is.'

'I'm a State servant, and I'm telling you it's all right.'

'And what happens if it gets out?'

'It won't.'

'Oh God, Felix, I've made such a mess of my life. I even went to confession the other day for the first time in years, but that smart-ass behind his little curtain told me to say Hail Marys instead of fixing up a loan for me.'

'Getting money this way is a whole lot easier, Hein. It'll never get out. No one will ever know a thing about it. Except you and me. You get those plans copied, which is no problem for you since you run the place, and then give them to me. The money will be waiting for you in a bank in Bern.'

'And there really isn't any other way?'

'Maybe there is. But this is the only one I've been able to come up with.'

Hein cast a suspicious look around the bar again, then leant towards Hoffman. Red-eyed, he whispered, 'It's treason, Felix. It's nothing short of espionage. And you'll be an accessory.'

'If it's going to help you, then I don't care. Anyway, no one will ever know. And it'll get you off the hook. There really is no alternative. You'll gain some breathing space, you'll get the chance to put a bit aside, pay your bills, give your friend a present and send him on his way, and then you'll be able to carry on with your life as normal. No one else is going to help you. And if you don't get yourself out of trouble, you'll be kicked out by Philips anyway. The choice is yours. But make your mind up now....'

Like a wily old performer he had handed Hein all the rationalisation he needed for becoming a traitor. And Hein had gone along with it.

Hoffman went back inside the house, picked up a packet of small sponge cakes filled with almond cream (he noticed that they had already gone dry), and opened the *Treatise* at Section xiv: 'Of the Means by which Eternal Things are Known.'

> It is required with regard to order, and that all our perceptions may be arranged and connected, that as soon as is possible and consonant with reason we should inquire whether there be a certain being, and at the same time of what nature is he, who is the cause of all things: this we should do in order that his objective essence may be the cause of all our ideas....

Or, as Hoffman paraphrased it: does God exist? And if God does exist, what makes Him the cause of all things?

Spinoza's premise was that there was an ordering power which manifested itself in the phenomena of nature. It was essential 'that we should deduce all our ideas from physical things or from real entities'. The study of nature, Hoffman gathered, was to Spinoza the study of God, and the opposite also held: the study of God was the study of nature.

But what exactly was it Spinoza wished us to enquire into? It was 'the series of fixed and eternal things', that is, the series which helps us to grasp the 'intimate essence of things'. The overriding laws of nature, Newton's F = ma and Einstein's E = mc², were vague pointers to a divine presence that sustained all existence.

But where should one begin, and with what knowledge? 'For to conceive all things simultaneously is a thing far beyond the power of human understanding,' Spinoza wrote. Was there any hope for him, then, Hoffman wondered, could he acquire the knowledge needed to discover the divine idea?

In the penultimate paragraph of the same section, Spinoza seemed to hold out a helping hand: once you have one true idea you can deduce other true ideas from it. All you needed therefore was just one truth, just one true idea that allowed of no doubt.

Hoffman had never come across anything that could be called a true idea. He had been a blind consumer, one who had never grasped the 'intimate essence' of the things he had garnered. He knew nothing about natural science, he knew nothing about nature. He had merely devoured, chewed and digested. He was a victim of his circumstances and of his urges.

He emptied the glass of Nesquik to wash the dry cake crumbs down, stood up and, stomach churning, went outside. Pushing the bare branches out of the way, he walked a few yards into the woods, unbuttoned his trousers, stepped out of them and placed them on the ground at his side. Then he took off his foul-smelling underpants. Immediately he could feel the impact on his buttocks of the cold air rising from the ground, and shivered. With cramps shooting up to his kidneys, he let out a groan as he squatted.

Two small, rock-hard turds left his body. The last time he had produced anything respectable had been at least ten days ago. Since leaving Prague he had as good as ceased emptying his bowels, and these were his first stools here. He had been living on packaged bread and tinned meat and vegetables, and was even more constipated than he had been in Prague. He should probably be eating nothing but fresh fruit, for his body too needed to be cleansed.

He had forgotten to take a roll of toilet paper with him, and he seized a handful of leaves and wiped himself clean. When he tried to stand up again, his muscles refused to obey. He reached for a branch, pulled it towards him and drew himself up with both hands. He put on his trousers.

In Berlin he had entered the West through one of the breaches in the Wall, waving his diplomatic passport. The destruction of the Wall marked the beginning of the end. It seemed out of the question that a lasting peace would descend upon Europe. Peace had always been based on fear in the continent.

He had observed the Krauts on both sides of the Wall, and seen their old *Herrenvolk* arrogance radiate from their drink-sodden faces. It would not be long now before they demanded the return of their lost lands in Poland and Czechoslovakia and Russia, and set up a clamour once again for a Greater Germany. What Hoffman had done, had been done not out of patriotic sentiment or the wish to preserve the status quo; he frankly admitted that he had helped Irena in order to get her into bed. A slave to his urges, he preferred such servitude to that of the diplomat—which did not alter the fact that he was beginning to feel ashamed of himself. And yet: if he had the choice all over again between losing her or keeping her with the help of stolen secrets, he knew what he would do. For in fact he had had no choice in the matter.

Or were these musings yet another manifestation of self-pity and self-vindication? Was he not caught between the stupidity of his behaviour and the ability to forgive himself? Egoism alone had driven him to become a traitor, nothing else. He had sacrificed his career, his marriage and his income, and all he had been left with were memories.

He went into the storeroom, opened a cupboard and took out some photograph albums. He carried them to the sofa, intent, he almost felt, on proving to himself that he had a past. Miriam had done her best to avoid mutilating either Esther or her parents. Here and there part of his face might be missing, or an arm. In one of the photographs, however, in which he had been holding Miriam as a toddler on his lap, all that was left of her was her torso, and his own heart had been cut out. She had burned all the films in which she had shone, which was most of them. All he had been left with was one-and-a-half hours of her as a porno star, and when he went to South America he would take the box with him. The thought that Van der Voort or the Americans might find her flooded him with shame.

He was already ashamed because he had survived the war, ashamed because he had been unable to prevent Esther's death, ashamed when he looked at Marian. He picked up a newspaper lying next to the fireplace and read the date: 11 August 1984. One of Miriam's papers. He used it to light the fire. The damp wood crackled and hissed as he sat down in front of it warming his hands. In this house she had allowed them to film her sex. A camera crew had had the run of the place, studio lights had been set up, and Miriam had spread her legs. He had not been able to prevent it.

He reviewed the period of the last few months and its inescapable logic hit him, the inevitability of what he had done. It might have happened later, but it had been unavoidable. That was also what he had said when he had rung Wim Scheffers from Hanover station on Sunday evening.

'Wim? This is Felix.'

'Felix, my God! Where are you?'

'I can't tell you that, Wim.'

'What on earth is going on? I had a visit from Security this afternoon. They're looking for you! Did you know that?'

'Van der Voort?'

'Yes. What's up?'

'Are they going to tell the press?'

'The press? Why? What have you been up to?'

'I passed a few things on to the Czechs.'

'You did what? Why?'

'Why? Just because. For love.'

'A woman?'

'Yes. A woman.'

'Jesus, when they turned up this afternoon I knew it had to be something like that. Why on earth did you do it?'

'I couldn't help myself. Have you heard anything else? When did they raise the alarm?'

'It looks as if Marian did that.'

'When?'

'First thing this morning. You'd gone.'

'So early? Do you think she saw me leave, then?'

'I have no idea. Felix, I've got to say this…you're going to have to turn yourself in. My telephone's probably being tapped anyway, who knows? But come back and give yourself up. They're bound to hush it all up. No one has anything to gain from making a big thing of it. And the Czech secret service doesn't exist any more. Come back here.'

'No. I have things to think about.'

'All right, so what *are* you going to do, Felix?'

'Think. Read Spinoza. Please ring Marian for me. Tell her that I…that I wanted to keep her out of it….'

'Look after yourself, my friend.'

It was safe to say that Irena would be looking after herself. She was in the United States by now, of course. In spy thrillers it was called 'debriefing'. She would be selling herself dear. Right now she would be swapping snippets of information for privileges, and in a few months' time, having satisfied them (and perhaps having taken the head of the interrogation team to bed), she would be given money and a house and a new name.

He had not expected the storm to break in Czechoslovakia, but then who had? In retrospect he realised that the taking of the Wall had been a signal to the entire Eastern bloc to mount its assault. He had read the German papers, had watched German television. The East Germans had gone *shopping*. They had parked their little Trabants and gone looking for things to buy. Freedom had meant the freedom to consume. And had they chosen to queue outside bookshops (queuing, after all, being their metier)? Absolutely not, he thought, they had gone to queue outside the Kaufhaus des Westens, one of the biggest department stores in Berlin. Not exactly proletarian shopping. And it wasn't only the Germans, the Czechs, too, couldn't wait for the day when they'd be able to pay their bills using their American Express Gold Cards. If he'd ever managed to turn out those essays on critical consumerism he'd planned to write, he'd be world famous by now. They were no different from him. He was no better than they.

The realisation pained him.

Spinoza's God offered no way out. He could not ask Him for forgiveness or redemption. He could bang his head against a wall until it bled and no one would heed his supplications. And if he felt in need of a liturgy, his only recourse would be a liturgy in front of a mirror.

Flames danced on the logs and his face and hands glowed. The grief that gripped his body like a straitjacket came even more cheaply than cheap tears. He braced himself and went back to the table. Dismissing his surroundings and his circumstances from his mind, he turned to the last section, 'On the Power of the Understanding and Its Properties'.

The properties of the understanding must be such as to enable us to grasp the laws of nature. But what precisely was understanding? Our understanding had first to provide a definition of understanding; its nature, that is its definition, however, could only be given if we knew that nature beforehand, and that was an impossibility allowing of no escape. For that reason Spinoza had compiled a list of eight properties the understanding was required to possess:

> 1. To begin with, he stated that true knowledge admits of no doubt. If something is known for certain (for instance, that the three angles of a triangle together add up to two right angles) then doubt vanishes and certainty becomes synonymous with knowledge.

> 2. There are concepts that the understanding grasps absolutely (such as 'quantity' or 'extension') and others that need the support of further concepts (such

as 'motion', which has to be defined with the help of other, absolute, concepts).

> 3. Non-absolute concepts are formed from absolute concepts; a concept such as 'motion'—a non-absolute or determinate concept—depends on such absolute concepts as 'space' and 'infinity'. Here Spinoza proffered the geometrical example of the motion of a line, which can be prolonged to form a line of infinite length.

Hoffman inferred two things from this: first, that there was a hierarchy of concepts, headed by absolute concepts; and second, that the understanding comprised such ideas as infinity, ideas we could grasp because nature enabled us to reflect upon them by means of our understanding. Ultimately, therefore, Spinoza was concerned with absolute concepts.

> 4. [The understanding] forms positive ideas rather than negative ones.

To Hoffman, this meant that definitions must not contain negations. Nature, the world, was something that had a positive existence and must be described in such terms.

> 5. It perceives things not so much under the form of duration as under a certain species of eternity, or rather in order to perceive things it regards neither their number nor duration.

As Hoffman saw it, our understanding must therefore be directed primarily at eternity, at the timeless laws characteristic of nature.

This point detained Hoffman for some time. He got up, paced in front of the fireplace and allowed the words to sink in. 'Ideas which we form clear and distinct seem to follow from the mere necessity of our nature in such a manner that they seem to depend absolutely on our power.'

He was struck by the fact that the word 'seem' occurred twice in this long sentence, something quite uncharacteristic of the *Treatise*. Spinoza had plainly not been entirely certain of his argument.

Hoffman defined the clear ideas mentioned in this sentence as the laws governing nature. These *seemed* to follow from 'the mere necessity of our nature'. Or rather, we could not help discovering these laws; we were predestined to do just that because our nature happened to be what it was. But that was not the end of the sentence: '...they seem to depend absolutely on our power.' The argument was a complex one.

Hoffman slumped into a chair and stared at the dying fire. It was all about the *will*, he suddenly thought; what Spinoza meant was, if only we will it we can come to know everything. He picked the book up again and read on.

6. Under this point Spinoza emphasised the scientist's individual freedom: there were various ways of measuring the area of an ellipse, the differences depending on the imagination, on the intuition.

7. The more perfection of any object ideas express, the more perfect they are. For we do not admire the architect who planned a chapel so much as the architect who planned some great temple.

Hoffman wondered whether this list was really a list of the properties of the understanding. What he had read seemed to be a list of possibilities, of all the things that could be done with the understanding and what value to attach to them, as illustrated most clearly of course by the last point. Admiration did not strike him as being characteristic of reason.

Hoffman turned to the last two paragraphs of the book, and then saw that the translator had added seven words at the end of the page: 'The remainder of this Treatise is wanting.' He stared, the blood draining from his face, at the sentence.

The sounds of a car made him catch his breath. Alarmed, he lowered the book and looked outside. The self-assured bonnet of a Mercedes was approaching up the dirt track, the vehicle lumbering over the bumps and potholes, sending water spraying from the puddles. The drone of its cylinders rolled through the woods.

He forgot his old body and like an animal at bay leapt quickly and surely to his feet. He had to flee.

But when he caught sight of the box with the cans of film he found himself unable to move. There lay Miriam's sordid reels, naked and unprotected on the bare floorboards. Removing them from the safe-deposit box had been a disastrous mistake. How could he run away now, leaving Miriam's shame to the Krauts?

He placed the book on the lid and lifted the heavy box. Although his legs seemed to be paralysed by nerves, he managed to drag himself towards the door, his limbs at once soft as clay and heavy as lead, hugging the box as if for support. Using an elbow, he pushed the back door open, and the book slid off the lid; he stepped stiffly through the leaves outside, his knees buckling under the weight of his load.

Branches sprang back at him, lashing his forehead, and he felt abandoned by the ultimate truth. His heart thumping, he was walking under bare trees and a grey sky. He was running away because a car was coming. He was leaving the farm behind to hide in the safety of the woods. The squealing of overwrought pigs was making his head pound and a deadly fatigue was spreading through his arms and legs, but he could not stop now. He was running away because that box held his life and he wanted to give it to his parents. Somewhere under these trees his mother and father were waiting for him at a table covered in white linen and he wanted to bring them this present. He would tell them that they could find $E = mc^2$ inside this box and that a glimmer of the Spirit of the Lord of Heaven and

Earth could be made out in this formula. He was running away and looking for his parents because only his father and mother would be able to scrub the filth from his body. He became aware of the trees looking silently down on him, and suddenly he was shaking with rage because he could no longer bear the wordlessness of the trees who could have told him where his parents were, where their dust was floating and their ashes blowing. And his children, he must not forget his children. The wind swept through the trees and he needed to know which way to run in this forest of bare trunks, and where he would be able to meet the people he had lost on the way.

He stumbled and felt the heavy cardboard box slip from his grasp and he fell down onto a bed of leaves and twigs and fungi. The box split open, and the cans of film rolled over the ground. His heart beating wildly, he sat up and the sight of the torn box dredged up a deep sorrow. Frantically he crawled towards the cans and laid them again in their broken nest.

He was in need of just one true thought, just one idea that admitted of no doubt.

Saliva trickled down his chin; he ran his hand over his head and saw blood on his fingers. Wracked by doubt and impotence and fear he peered through the branches and watched the driver climb out of the Mercedes. He was a short man about his own age and was not in uniform. The man opened the passenger door and a woman stepped out. Hoffman saw it was Marian. She was wrapped in a beige raincoat with the collar turned up, and although the sky was grey and overcast she was wearing sunglasses; shoulders hunched, she hurried into the house.

Hoffman could not move. Gasping for breath, he clung to a can of film and stared at the car, countless questions racing through his mind. The man spotted him behind the leafless bushes. Motionless they stared at each other, separated by a hundred yards of no-man's-land. The wind skimmed over the bare treetops, birds took wing. Marian came out of the back door and paused on the threshold, looking at the book he had dropped. With both hands she took off her sunglasses and came in search of him in the woods.

When she saw him, she held out a hand in forgiveness. Fingers spread, she stroked his arm; when he lay down as if ready for sleep among the cans of film on the cold, wet leaves, he knew with absolute certainty that she would console him.

Chapter eighteen

The evening of 31 December 1989

The Service had been anxious to avoid any fuss. Wim Scheffers knew the ropes and had Hoffman examined by a psychiatrist of his acquaintance. The findings were a foregone conclusion: Hoffman had acted in a state of diminished responsibility. Marian had dug up an unscrupulous lawyer who, together with Scheffers and on the basis of the psychiatric report, had come up with a compromise: Hoffman had tendered his resignation on health grounds and in return was granted an honourable discharge. He turned down the pension, as agreed, and a short report on the early retirement of the Dutch ambassador to Prague was printed in the personal columns of the *Nieuwe Rotterdamse Courant:*

> *His Excellency F. A. Hoffman,* HM Ambassador in Prague, will be relinquishing his office as of 1 January next. The Ministry of Foreign Affairs has announced that Mr Hoffman (59) is standing down for reasons of health. Mr Hoffman served as Temporary Charge d'Affaires

in Khartoum (Sudan) for many years, and has been
ambassador to Czechoslovakia since April this year. He
entered the Foreign Service in 1959.

No word of the affair reached the press.

Marian had made plans. She would buy a house on the Côte
d'Azur or in Tuscany, they would enjoy the rest of their lives together,
they would go on long walks and visit museums and galleries, they
would take each other's arm on crossing the street, they would help
each other to dress when the time came.

Once again he immersed himself in Spinoza, in a new book
he had acquired. Seated by the window with the book on his lap,
he watched as a premature New Year firework did its best to scatter
silver snow over the city, the damp air extinguishing its little stars.
They were in Marian's room on the top floor of the Bel Air. She was
in another chair by the window, studying and making notes. He
realised that she would never finish her work.

Squalls of rain beat against the glass. The television in the
corner showed scenes of incomprehensible gaiety; he had turned off
the sound.

He had bought a biography of the philosopher as well as the
book he was now holding in his hands, the *Ethics*, which seemed to
be Spinoza's main work. It contained such Talmudic sentences as
*'Whatever is, is in God, and nothing can exist or be conceived without
God,'* and: *'Thought is an attribute of God, or God is a thinking thing.'*
Hoffman could now pray, without believing.

When there was a knock, he opened the door. A waiter was
carrying champagne in an ice bucket. Hoffman took the tray from
him at the door, and after Marian had put her books down on the
carpet he set the tray on the small table under the window.

'When does the twentieth century end?' he asked. 'In the year
2000 or 2001? What do you think?'

She took off her glasses and looked at him quizzically. But she
answered, keeping her surprise at the question to herself.

'A hundred means from 1 to 100 inclusive,' she said. 'So I don't think the century is over until after the year 2000.'

'So 2001 is the beginning of the new one?' he said.

He sat down and placed the *Ethics* back on his lap.

'Yet everyone thinks of the year 2000 as a new beginning,' he said.

'It's wrong, of course, but they do, yes. I do it too.'

He said solemnly, 'I want to see the year 2000 in.'

He saw love and concern flicker in her eyes.

'Me, too, Fee,' she said. 'We'll do it together.'

He opened the book and began reading again. She too went back to her work.

A minute later, he looked up and said, 'My point is, I want to see it in because the twentieth century will be over then. Do you understand?'

She took her glasses off. 'No, I don't. What do you mean?'

'We must get this century over and done with. I want to see it die. That's the only way we'll get our own back a little for everything. We shall have survived it, we shall be there to bury it.'

She nodded absently. She pushed her glasses back onto her nose and he looked out over the wet roofs of The Hague. His jaws clenched with rage. It made him feel hungry. He bowed his head and began to pray.

We endeavour to affirm, concerning ourselves or what we love, every-thing that we imagine to affect what we love or ourselves with pleasure; and, on the other hand, we endeavour to deny, concerning ourselves and the object loved, everything that we imagine to affect us or the object loved with pain.

About the Author

Leon de Winter

Leon de Winter is a prize-winning Dutch novelist, born in 1954. He is also an internationally recognized film writer and director. This is his first book to be translated into English.

The fonts used in this book are from the Garamond family